"Care to dance?" The question came out of nowhere.

"No, I—" She swiveled in her chair as she answered and, as their eyes connected, the sentence seemed to stall in her throat. Her tongue peeked out in a nervous sweep of her upper lip, and that was enough to make him decide that he really wanted to dance with this woman.

Gesturing over his shoulder in the direction of the table where the bozos from the other conference were congregated, he said, "There are still a couple of guys over there who've yet to come over and sweet-talk you. I got the impression you might like to avoid another round. Come on, dance with me."

Jade eyed his outstretched hand, considering. She was certainly sick of getting hit on by guys with football-stadium-size egos. But this man, all chiseled hardness, wasn't some puffed-up dolt. It was a pretty sure bet that he knew how to make a woman burn. A quick glance at the heat in his aquamarine gaze was enough for that well-banked spark of wildness inside her to blaze to life.

She did nothing to subdue it. After all, she was going back to Rosewood the next day. The teaching job at Warburg Elementary would begin in a few short weeks. Her life was going to be staid and respectable, and she a veritable paragon.

Tonight she might as well have fun.

※

Trouble Me

A Rosewood Novel

LAURA MOORE

BALLANTINE BOOKS • NEW YORK

A Ballantine Books Mass Market Original

Published in the United States by Ballantine Books, an imprint of The Random House Publishing Group, a division of Random House, Inc., New York.

This book contains an excerpt from the upcoming Book One in Laura Moore's new Silver Creek series. This excerpt has been set for this edition only and may not reflect the final content of the forthcoming book.

ISBN: 978-1-61793-796-5

Cover design: Lynn Andreozzi
Cover illustration: Gregg Gulbronson

Printed in the United States of America

This one is for you, Nick.

Trouble Me

Chapter
ONE

JADE RADCLIFFE had her iPod plugged in and the volume cranked. But while the Black Eyed Peas were doing a fine job of keeping her awake after so many hours on the road, her Porsche's windshield wipers weren't doing squat. Even set to high, they couldn't compete with the rain that was coming down in buckets. Route 95 had become a regular Slip'N Slide. While sliding over water-slicked surfaces was a favorite summer amusement of her nieces and nephews, Jade had been driving too many hours. Her initial "whee"s whenever the Porsche lost traction had turned into tired complaints of "oh, shit."

The traffic had slowed to a crawl, making the driving marginally safer. But at this speed there was no way she was going to reach Warburg tonight. When she left Ocala, Florida, this morning, she was confident that she would reach Rosewood, her family's home in Virginia, by dinnertime. She badly wanted to see them all: Margot and Travis and their kids, Georgiana, four, and Will, nine months old now and thus starting to get interesting. Margot was so besotted she sent Jade daily email updates with photo attachments chronicling Will's achievements, just as she'd done for Georgie. Jade was the only person she knew whose computer kept running out of storage space because she had so many e-photo albums of babies staring up at brightly colored mobiles or giving toothless grins in their high chairs.

The cute munchkins populating Rosewood didn't stop

there. Now there was also Jordan and Owen's baby boy, Edward, nicknamed Neddy, who had been named after Ned Connelly. Having worked his entire life at Rosewood Farm, Ned was like family to Jade and her sisters; Owen and Jordan's gesture had made the old man nearly burst with pride and joy.

And when it came to being completely gaga over their new baby, Jordan and Owen rivaled Travis and Margot.

Earlier in the spring, Jade got a video of Neddy taking his first steps, with Owen filming and narrating the clip. Owen was a pretty cool guy. Suave and sophisticated. But from the excitement in Owen's voice, Neddy could as well have been Neil Armstrong taking that first step on the moon for mankind rather than tottering toward his big half sister Olivia's outstretched arms, while the rest of the Rosewood clan cheered him on.

Neddy would probably be fairly steady on his sneakers by now, and doing his best to keep up with his older half brother, Max. Kate, the oldest of the bunch from Jordan's first marriage, was showing in children's hunter classes and doing a really fine job on Doc Holliday.

Yeah, Jade definitely wanted to be back in the Radcliffe–Maher–Gage fold, insane though her sisters were sometimes. She'd missed everyone this summer while she was down in Ocala, but now, in addition to having a brand-spanking-new degree in education, her training session in Florida had given her the right to boast that she was certified as a hunter/jumper trainer by the United States Hunter Jumper Association. It would come in handy when she began spreading the word about the riding program she was starting at Rosewood Farm.

Through the swish of her windshield wipers, Jade saw the sudden bright flare of brake lights as the cars ahead of her went from a crawl to a stop, turning the highway into a long, thin, rain-drenched parking lot.

She sat, drumming her hands to Phoenix's "1901"

and jiggling her legs against the leather bucket seat so that at least *something* was moving. Damn and double damn. The dashboard clock read nine-thirty P.M. and she hadn't even reached Norfolk yet. There was no way she'd make it to Rosewood tonight. It wouldn't be right to show up on the doorstep at 1:30 A.M. and wake Margot and Travis. Moreover, if Margot heard that Jade wanted to push on through in a storm this bad, she'd freak.

Perhaps she'd show Margot—and Jordan, as Jade knew Margot would get on the horn to their older sister within seconds—how much she'd matured. Leagues removed from the Jade of yesteryear. And it was even all right to pick up her cell and speed-dial Margot's number, since the car hadn't moved an inch since she'd made her decision.

Margot answered on the second ring. "Jade? Where are you? God, it's pouring and the wind is picking up."

"It's pouring here too. I'm stuck on 95 somewhere south of Norfolk—"

"Norfolk! That means you still have a good four hours of driving."

More than that, Jade thought, since every car around her was going nowhere fast. A flash of lights in her rearview mirror alerted her to an ambulance coming up the breakdown lane. "There must be an accident up ahead. An ambulance just drove past. Listen, I'm going to get off at the next exit and find a place for the night. But I'll hit the road first thing, so make sure somebody does a Braverman's run, okay? I've been dreaming of their cinnamon raisin bagels for the past two nights."

"Stopping for the night is a very good idea." Surprisingly, Margot didn't sound stunned speechless by Jade's announcement. "But, Jade, make sure it's a nice place and well lit."

"Got it. No Bates Motel for me."

"Ha. Very funny. You'll call as soon as you've checked in?"

"It might not be for a while yet."

"That's fine. And use the credit card on my account, sweetie. I want you to have a nice night."

"Norfolk Ritz, here I come."

"No need to get carried away," Margot replied with a laugh. "But you'll remember to call, right? I won't be able to sleep until I know you've found a place and are safe and sound."

"I'll call," she promised before hanging up.

As Jade's legal guardian, Margot had probably passed a lot of sleepless nights while Jade was off at college. She'd have passed a lot more of them if she'd known some of the things Jade got up to on the weekends when she wasn't competing with the collegiate equestrian team. A good acre of wild oats had been sown.

That was the Jade of old, the one who sometimes felt the need to step right up to the edge and do something crazy with a wild, fiery lick of danger. But though she'd had her share of parties and experiences, it hadn't prevented her from getting straight A's even with a supercharged course load, being the top scorer on her riding team, and writing a very popular advice column for the school paper.

The four years of parties and serial relationships (she liked the sex just fine, but her life had been way too busy to bother with the guys afterward) while she earned her college degree were over. She was returning to Warburg with a plan she intended to execute with the precision of a military campaign, her ultimate goal being to banish her hometown's less-than-fond memories of her by turning into the most model of model citizens. From now on, her activities would be restricted to teaching at the elementary school, training Rosewood's horses, and concentrating on building a young riders' program. Who could find fault with such a life of utter respectability?

Admittedly, her campaign to present a squeaky-clean image would be easier if she didn't also have hiring a detective on her to-do list. But discovering who was the TM her mother had gushed about in her diary was an absolute imperative. The need had sprung full blown inside Jade the second she'd accidentally stumbled upon her mother's private journal in her half sister Jordan's closet.

Like curious Pandora with her box, Jade had opened the gaudy pink diary and, recognizing her mother's handwriting, started reading. Having entered Jordan's closet simply to borrow a sleeveless ratcatcher for an upcoming horse show, she'd left it with her perception of her mother forever altered. Damningly so.

She'd not only learned that her mother had been having an affair with someone she called TM, she'd also learned in entry after entry the depths of her mother's resentment and dislike for her only child. According to her mother, Jade was endlessly spoiled and obnoxious, a drain that sucked all the energy out of her.

If Jade was the black hole in her life, this TM was her sun, the frigging life-affirming center of her universe.

It must have utterly destroyed Dad to read those words. And he had read them. Her sister Margot had been the one to stumble upon the diary first, finding it in a drawer in their father's office desk. Jade knew her dad well enough to realize that he'd have read the journal as obsessively as she, feeling more and more betrayed with each reading.

Jade despised whoever this TM was for getting involved with her mother. And since she now had access to the money her mother had left her, she saw no reason why she shouldn't use it to hire a private investigator. Dad would approve, even if Margot and Jordan didn't.

So the trick would be to make sure they never found out.

Thank God, she thought, as the traffic ahead began to move. She was actually going to get to shift into first gear and leave these dark thoughts behind.

Jade found a hotel outside Norfolk. The place was ablaze with lights. No Bates Motel–like features about it. It occurred to her as she drove in to the crammed parking lot that it might be a bit *too* busy, and as she grabbed her duffel bag from the Porsche's trunk, she hoped there was a free room.

The rain was still coming down in lashing sheets. In the few minutes it took to shoulder her bag, double-check that her car was locked, and sprint across the parking lot, she was soaked. Stepping into the lobby, she blinked, disoriented by the bright lights and colors after staring into silvery blackness for so long.

Several guests were huddled around the reception desk, asking questions about breakfast and airport shuttles and what might entertain the kids if it was too wet to go to the beach tomorrow and God knew what else, while she shivered slightly in the chill of the air-conditioning and left wet footprints on the plush maroon carpeting. Finally the last guest ambled happily toward the bank of elevators and she stepped up to the desk. Dropping her duffel bag and placing her ultra-sweet Prada hobo bag (a graduation present from Margot) on top of the wooden counter, she smiled at the black-jacketed receptionist.

"May I help you?"

The man was in his mid-thirties and looked as if he'd been on duty for a while—in other words, tired and harassed. He also wore a wedding ring. Deciding that he didn't look the type to hit on her, she gave him a friendly smile. "Yes, please. I'd like a room for the night."

"Do you have a reservation?"

"I'm afraid not."

He expelled a breath. "I'll have to check whether any-thing's available. We've had a crazy week with two con-ferences going on. On top of that, a large wedding party arrived today."

"I really hope you have something. I've been on the road all day, driving up from Florida."

He looked up, his brows raised in surprise. "Florida?"

Jade nodded. "From Ocala. I'm heading to Warburg. The storm started somewhere in North Carolina, and then there was a pretty bad accident about twenty miles south of here. That's when I realized it might be smart to call it a night. I Googled hotels in the area and yours had the best reviews. I'd like to avoid getting back in the car if at all possible." Dragging her soaked hair from her face, she gave him another cheerful smile, as if she had no doubt he'd do everything in his power to help her.

Margot and Jordan would never guess how much she'd picked up from them when it came to the art of sweet-talking. It definitely had its uses. Like now.

"Well, you're in luck," he announced happily. "We do have a room. It has a king-size bed, water views."

She didn't give a fig about the view, since she'd be on her way to Rosewood at first light, but a big bed would be heaven after the lumpy twin bunk bed she'd been as-signed in Ocala.

"That sounds perfect." Jade was already reaching into her bag. "Here's my credit card. Do you need my driv-er's license too?"

"Yes, and the license-plate number of your car, please."

As Jade waited for him to take down her information, the notes of a Rob Thomas song reached her. Turning her head toward the source, she saw couples wandering into a softly lit area.

"The bar looks nice."

His eyes still fixed on the computer, the receptionist nodded. "It's got a dance floor, and Chaz, our DJ, plays good music. On a night like this, the guests really appreciate having a nightspot they don't have to drive to. Plenty of Norfolk residents like to come here for a night of dancing. Here you go, Miss Radcliffe." He handed back her ID and credit card as well as another plastic card. "This is your electronic key. Your room number is 412. Take the elevator to the fourth floor and turn right down the hallway. The room will be on your right. Do you need help with your luggage?"

"No, thanks, I've got it."

He smiled. "Then have a good night."

"After nearly thirteen hours on the road, I'm going to sleep like a baby."

After dumping her duffel bag in the corner, Jade dutifully rang Margot, letting herself fall back onto the king-size mattress as she said, "Hi, sis. I'm here, safe and sound."

"You got a room?"

"Yeah, but the only one they had left was the honeymoon suite. It's a thousand bucks a night, but the champagne's free, so you didn't come out too badly." She grinned up at the ceiling.

"Ha. So in addition to getting your instructor certification, you've been fine-tuning your comedy act."

"Yup. Nice to know motherhood hasn't turned your brain to Swiss cheese."

"If my brain could survive your teen years intact, I should be safe."

"I was prepping you. Now you're ready for anything."

"Thanks," Margot replied drily. "The room's okay?"

"It's got a great bed. Nice and firm." She jounced on it again for good measure.

"Well, get a good rest, sweetie. You must be wiped out after such a long drive."

Strangely enough, now that she'd gotten horizontal, Jade was wide awake, twitchy with adrenaline. But knowing her sister would like to think of her curled up and sleeping as blissfully as Georgie and Will, she replied with a noncommittal "Mmm-hmm."

"We'll all be waiting for you, and so will the cinnamon raisin bagels. Sleep tight, Jade."

"You too, sis." Pressing the OFF button, she sprang up from the bed and began stripping out of her still-damp clothes. A hot shower might do the trick and relax her.

She faced facts after she'd dried her hair with the blow-dryer provided by the hotel. She was more awake than ever, and if she tried to sleep now, she'd drive herself insane tossing and turning.

She was also kind of hungry. There was room service, but then she thought of the bar downstairs. She could go down and have a drink and relax and munch on a few salted peanuts and potato chips. They'd balance out the M&M's and Twizzlers and Reese's Pieces she'd consumed along with her Red Bulls and iced coffees. And it'd be fun to go to a bar in Virginia legally. After getting busted with a fake ID, she'd steered clear of Warburg's bars, convinced that if she made one false step, a particularly scary cop would somehow appear, all wrath and righteousness, to nail her butt. But now that she'd almost reached the ripe old age of twenty-two, she figured she could walk into a bar without glancing over her shoulder. There were definite advantages to growing up.

Dropping her towel, she went over to her duffel bag and dug out a bra, a pair of undies, her white jeans, and a Jean Paul Gaultier chiffon tank, which Margot had been given on one of her modeling shoots but decided looked better on Jade than it did on her. She also grabbed the only semi-dressy shoes she'd packed for Florida: a pair of high-heeled sandals—another hand-me-down from Margot.

Having a fashion model for an older sister, who just happened to wear the same size from head to toe, was pretty darned fantastic. Economical too. Second-grade-teacher pay scales couldn't cover Jean Paul Gaultier or Christian Louboutin sandals.

The steady stream of designer rags and trimmings wasn't likely to run dry either. Even though Margot had two kids and had announced her semiretirement, her agent, Damien Barnes, continued to receive requests for her. That she was still in high demand in the fashion world came as a surprise only to Margot. In Jade's opinion, Margot was more beautiful than ever. Jordan was too, for that matter. Happiness could do that.

Dressed, Jade dragged a brush through her hair and applied some lip gloss. Grabbing her handbag and room key, she headed down to the hotel's bar to have a nice relaxing drink.

Rob Cooper nursed a bourbon on the rocks and cast baleful glances at the bar's rain-streaked windows. The storm hadn't diminished in intensity. And from the looks of it, the front had stalled directly over Virginia, which was damned annoying since the most interesting sessions at the law-enforcement conference he'd been attending had ended earlier, as had his dinner spent catching up with Phil Reynolds, a buddy from their days at the police academy.

There was nothing to do but to wait out the storm in the hotel bar. When it started to move, Rob would too. His weekend bag was packed and already in the trunk of his car. He was itching to get home. But driving through a storm when there was an advisory posted was not a risk he was about to take when he had Hayley to consider.

Strictly speaking, he didn't need to be back in Warburg tonight; his room was booked through tomorrow. His sister, Emma, was babysitting. She and her very-soon-to-be seven-year-old niece had events planned right through Sunday. Hayley had been talking for days about one of the weekend's highlights: an all-things-horsey movie fest. She'd personally compiled the list.

Driving over to Emma's, Hayley had been bouncing in the backseat as she rattled off titles.

"First Aunt Emma and I are going to watch *The Black Stallion* and then *The Black Stallion Returns*. After that, it'll be *National Velvet* and *Into the West* and—"

"*Hidalgo.*"

"Uh-huh. And maybe *My Friend Flicka* too."

He'd glanced at her in the rearview mirror. She was glowing with excitement. "You know, if you get tired of watching movies about horses, there are some great—"

"Daddy!" Hayley's cry was accompanied by a disbelieving roll of her brown eyes. The very notion that Hayley Elizabeth Cooper might ever tire of anything horse-related was beyond absurd.

No sooner had they pulled in front of the doll-size ranch that Emma was renting on Stonewall Lane than Hayley bounded out of the car with her backpack that they'd packed the night before. It was crammed not only with her clothes, toothbrush, hairbrush, and hair elastics but also with Lucky, her stuffed pony, who slept in her arms every night, and with four of her favorite Breyer horses.

As Rob had knelt down, Hayley rushed toward him and, dropping the backpack by his feet, threw her arms about his neck and gave him a loud smooch on the cheek. "Bye, Daddy."

"Bye, Hayley. You be good, okay? And go to sleep when Aunt Emma asks."

The silk of her hair rubbed his face as she nodded.

Then she was cantering off up the walkway like a little girl–centaur, just as Emma came out the front door to greet them.

"Who are you riding today, Hayley?"

Rob watched Hayley rein her imaginary pony to a trot. "Ginger."

"Well, the jumps are still set up in the backyard," Emma told her. The week before, she and Hayley had fashioned jumps using tipped-over lawn chairs and a collection of brooms, mops, and garden rakes. So far, Hayley's horses hadn't shied at any of them. They were that well trained, his daughter had explained proudly. "Once you've finished riding, we can go shopping for dinner."

"Okay. Bye, Daddy. Have a good time at your conference," Hayley called again, and, without further ado, his daughter made a clucking noise and her short, tanned legs picked up a canter, carrying her around the back of the house.

"I thought little girls liked to play with dolls and makeup or do gymnastics all over the lawn," he said, walking up the path with Hayley's bag.

His sister nodded. "Mmm-hmm. And then there are the ones who love horses. You might want to consider signing her up for riding lessons." She took Hayley's backpack from him and slung it over her shoulder. "It'd be a nice birthday present."

"I was thinking I might wait and see if her interest fades." More than half the population of Warburg rode horses, but Rob wasn't sure how he felt about his little daughter getting involved in the sport. He wished he'd looked more carefully into the activities available at the camp Becky's parents had chosen for Hayley when she'd gone to stay with them for three weeks earlier in the summer. He hadn't realized it offered horseback riding as well as swimming and crafts. Not that it would have mattered. He wanted Becky's family to have a say in

Hayley's life too, and it would have hurt their feelings if he'd torpedoed their choice of a summer camp.

"Don't hold your breath, Rob."

To tell the truth, he wasn't all that optimistic about Hayley's love of horses fading anytime soon either. She was a passionate little girl, fiercely loyal and just as stubborn. "You're probably right. I'll ask around about riding lessons."

"Good," Em said simply. "So, you off?"

"Yeah, after I drop by the station. Scott said he had something for me. If the traffic's not bad, I should be in Norfolk around seven. I'll call when I've reached the hotel." He dug his wallet out of his khaki pants and pulled out some bills. Emma was working as an instructor at the fitness studio in town while she finished her college degree. Though she loved the job, the pay wasn't going to make her rich anytime soon. "Here's money for groceries and any extras. I'll be back—"

"Sunday afternoon," she answered for him.

"I was toying with the idea of driving back Saturday night—"

"Don't. We have a ton of stuff planned—Hayley wants to go back-to-school shopping for new sneakers, so I'm really glad you gave me way too much money— and Mom and Dad want some quality time with her."

"But you've got work."

"Scott's around too. He's going to take Hayley out for pancakes after they walk Dexter. You know how she loves that. You'll only be cramping our style if you come back early." Perhaps catching something in his expression, she said, "Rob, you're doing a great job of being a single parent. Hayley's a terrific, well-adjusted kid. But she won't stay well adjusted if you don't start getting a life that encompasses a wee bit more than her and the Warburg police force. Why don't you take advantage of your trip to relax and have a little fun? Because, really, none of

us want to see your ugly mug until Sunday afternoon."
She gave him her sternest look. "Got the message?"

"Yes, ma'am."

On his way out of town, he'd stopped by the police
station and found Scott in the locker room, changing
into his workout clothes. It took about twenty seconds
for him to realize that his little sister and older brother
must have decided on a two-pronged attack. She'd talk
about how there was more to life than raising Hayley;
Scott would focus on his favorite subject—getting laid.
His brother obviously had decided to address the topic
of Rob's sex life—or lack thereof—head-on.

Spotting Rob, Scott turned back to his locker, grabbed
something off the top shelf, and said, "Here, a going-
away present."

Rob stared at the foil packages in his palm. "Gee,
Scott. I'm touched, really touched. But I'm not sure you
want to give up a single one of these. What's the new
one's name? Mandy? Candy? Sandy? Dandy?" He drew
his brows together.

"Randy," Scott supplied with a grin. "As in Miranda
Taylor, who was a year ahead of you in school. And
though Randy is very enthusiastic, I think I can spare
these for a good cause and, man, are you ever in need."

"Thanks. I have condoms of my own." He stretched
out his hand to return the prophylactics.

Scott crossed his arms over his chest. "Yeah, and
they're probably in an unopened box in your medicine
cabinet. You're supposed to use them, not collect them.
Seriously, Rob, the guys and I think—hell, even Uncle
Joe agrees—you need to blow off some steam. And other
bodily fluids."

"You know, I don't often wish I served on a different
police force than my father, uncle, and older brother, as
well as every other meddlesome cop in Warburg."

"Meddlesome?" Scott grinned. "That's harsh, Rob.

We just love you and damned well want you to loosen up. I saw you pull over Mrs. Crawford the other day."

"She was speeding."

"For Christ's sake, Mrs. Crawford is Warburg's head librarian. Mom ran into her at choir practice. She was practically in tears, mortified that she'd broken the law by driving five miles an hour too fast." Scott shook his head. "Nailing nice old biddies with speeding tickets indicates that you are in serious need of an intervention." Grabbing another handful of condoms from his locker, he shoved the packets into the breast pocket of Rob's button-down shirt. "Okay, now you're ready to lock 'n' load."

"Lock 'n' load? No wonder your girlfriends don't stick around for longer than a month."

"And that's just fine by me," he replied, unrepentant. "Variety is the spice of life. Which is exactly what you need. Unbend a bit, little brother, and go find yourself a woman." A rare solemnity came over his features, banishing his teasing grin. "It's been five years since you lost Becky, Rob. We know you loved her—we all did. But it's time to turn the corner. For your sake as well as Hayley's."

Five years that could have been five minutes, so large was the gaping hole in his heart, so fresh the pain. But he really didn't want to talk about Becky with anyone, not even his brother. He stared into Scott's pale-blue eyes and let the silence stretch.

Scott was wise enough to refrain from pursuing the topic. "Drive safe, and remember to unbend a little."

"Don't let Hayley cross the street without holding your hand," he'd said in reply. On the way out of the locker room, he'd stopped to drop the condoms into the trash bin and found a certain grim satisfaction in Scott's pained sigh.

The ice cubes rattled against the glass as Rob took another sip of his bourbon. Thanks to the storm, it looked as if he wouldn't be testing his family's displeasure by defying their edict and returning early. It didn't mean, however, that he was going to start cruising the bar.

Unbend a little. Scott's comment still nettled.

What his brother failed to recognize was that Rob had always been a straight arrow. How could he not be when he had his older brothers' accomplishments to live up to—not just Scott's but Aaron's? Aaron worked for the commonwealth's attorney in Richmond. If their achievements weren't enough of a benchmark, both his father and his uncle had served as Warburg's chief of police. Uncle Joe was on his second term.

Since Becky's death, Rob's world had narrowed to raising his little daughter and working. What else was there? He'd gone out on a few dates in the last year, mainly to get his family off his back. But the women, every one of whom had been pretty, interesting, and accomplished, had left him unmoved. If he couldn't feel a damned thing inside, why bother entering into a relationship?

The fact was that, though he loved his mother and his sister, only two women really mattered: One was the sweetest, funniest six—God, make that nearly seven-year-old in the world. The second had been lying in Warburg's cemetery for five long years. Christ, he missed Becky's laugh, her smile . . . her love.

He knew Emma and the other members of his family had a point. It'd be good for him to start dating and let a woman into his and Hayley's lives. But he couldn't believe he'd ever find one as wonderful, as sweet and kind and loving, as Becky had been. For his daughter's sake he'd try—just not tonight.

With the storm blasting Norfolk, the hotel's bar was doing a brisk business, but Rob wasn't inclined to mingle or approach any of the women sitting at the black lacquered tables, leaning back against the red suede banquettes, or swaying to the music on the dance floor beneath a twinkling mirrored ball. His bourbon was fine company.

He drained his glass. Setting the tumbler on the counter, he glanced over at the bartender to order a second drink. An exercise in futility. The guy's gaze was riveted on the bar's entrance. Whoever had just walked in must be pretty fantastic. Since it was clear Rob wasn't going to be getting another bourbon anytime soon, he decided to take a look himself.

Magnetic was the first word that came to his mind; within seconds she'd drawn every male eye in the bar to her. *Trouble* was the second. A woman who looked like this, slim and yet curvy in all the right places, with sun-streaked hair that fell past her shoulders in thick waves, and with a walk that was bold yet carried sensual promise in each step, could only cause mayhem. White jeans encased legs long enough to put a smile on most men's faces. Thanks to the high-heeled, silver-strapped sandals she sported, those legs were even longer. A corner of Rob's brain registered the fact that it was likely they'd be as long as his—definitely long enough to make a man's mouth go dry.

The top she wore, some sort of printed tank, wasn't terribly revealing. She didn't need to flaunt her charms. Hinting was all that was required. And, yes, underneath the patterned fabric she was deliciously rounded exactly where it mattered, and as lithe as a young cat everywhere else. Every guy in the bar was doubtless thinking how much he'd like to stroke her until she purred.

In the wrong place, a woman this hot could start a riot.

The dynamite package only got more explosive as she neared and Rob took in the lushness of her lips and the high slash of her cheekbones. Passion and drama.

The subdued lighting made it difficult to determine the color of her eyes, but he figured they must be light, probably blue.

Becky's eyes had been brown and as large and innocent as a doe's. The thought had him turning away. But not before he'd noted that the woman was heading toward one of the empty bar stools. The bartender, recovering enough wits to realize that he was about to get caught ogling her, managed to drag his gaze away long enough for Rob to signal for another round.

It was Rob's second nature, as a cop, to listen and observe. And, despite his previous indifference to the women in the bar, he found himself studying this one. Her outfit was sexy but not overtly so; she'd entered the bar alone but didn't appear to be on the prowl. After ordering a Tom Collins with an easy smile for the bartender, she'd begun nibbling on the Japanese rice crackers without sparing so much as a glance at the other patrons. Of course, with looks like hers, she didn't need to check anybody out. The men would come to her, unable to resist.

And not too far from the dance floor, there was a large table of guys. He thought they might be with the other conference—something to do with pharmaceuticals— that was being held at the hotel. One of them had already mustered the courage to approach, while the others around the table monitored his success, their expressions a mix of glee and envy.

This was going to be interesting.

Chapter
TWO

THESE RICE cracker things were addictive, Jade decided. They had a nice little wasabi martial-arts kick. When she got to Rosewood she'd have to get some for Jordan. If she was super-clever, she might even manage to tempt Margot into sampling one or two. Margot's self-discipline when it came to steering clear of any foodstuff that wasn't blue-ribbon health-certified was prodigious. Jade planned to someday exert a little self-discipline in that area too, but until then, gorging on junk food and watching Margot freak out was a lot of fun. Travis wasn't the only one who could get Margot's heart thumping, though obviously his approach was a little more involved.

Content, she popped another cracker into her mouth and then took a sip of her Tom Collins, which was deliciously tart. The bartender had added extra lemon, as she'd requested. Amazing what a good drink and a decent bowl of crackers could do for a body, she thought with a smile of satisfaction, as she raised her glass and took another slow sip of her cocktail.

It was then that she noticed a guy standing about four inches from her elbow. She kept the glass to her lips, hoping he'd place his order and wander off. When he didn't, she realized he wanted to talk. Her first impulse was to sit there and chugalug her drink, because she didn't want to deal with anyone right now. But getting blitzed would be stupid.

With a sigh, she lowered her glass, reaching for more of those crackers as she did—the bartender was doing a great job keeping the bowl full for her. Nice of him to be so useful.

She couldn't say the same about the guy standing next to her. From the corner of her eye, she'd seen that he was staring at her with annoying gob-smacked wonder, as if he was Adam and God had just fashioned her. Sorry to disappoint, but Jade had no intention of being his Eve. She redirected her gaze to the row of brandies lining the wall opposite her and began reading their labels. It was never too early to think of Christmas. Owen might enjoy a really fine brandy as a present.

"Hi, can I buy you a drink?"

The guy was definitely lacking in perception. She held up her glass. It was three-quarters full. "No, thanks."

"How about a dance?"

"I'm kind of tired."

"Well, how about I take this seat here and we can kick back and relax? Get to know each other."

Jade had a sudden wish for her mom's engagement ring, which she'd inherited. It was a big, flashy hunk of rock. Very much an "I'm taken" ring, and so like her dad to have bought it for the woman he loved. And though Jade hated the hypocrisy of what it was supposed to have symbolized, given her mother's infidelity, she sometimes slipped it on her left hand when she didn't want men hitting on her.

Of course, the ring was at Rosewood. She wasn't going to risk having such an expensive bauble lost or ripped off from the dorm in which she'd been lodged down in Florida. She might need to sell it one day.

She couldn't believe it, but the guy was *still* standing by her elbow. Had he no pride? "You know, I'm really not interested in company."

"Really?"

She managed not to roll her eyes. "Really." For good measure, she shoved about four crackers in her mouth at once and chewed busily. If he suggested any more nifty ideas about what they could do together, she'd make sure to give him a cracker-coated toothy smile. A neat trick she'd picked up from her nephew Max. The kid could do a Goldfish-encrusted grin like nobody's business.

Luckily, the guy got the message and left. Unluckily, another one appeared by her side a minute later—and by then she'd already washed the crackers down with a sip of her drink. Bad timing. One gunk-filled smile would have sent him scurrying away from the bar.

The second guy was hardly more imaginative than the last, performing the same song and dance as his predecessor about buying her a drink. Then, as if this might wow her, he told her how pretty her eyes were.

"They're, like, so green."

And so is grass, she replied silently.

Did men who were total strangers actually think she was going to be wowed if they complimented her looks? She wasn't that shallow. What she'd like was for a man who truly knew her to still believe she was beautiful. That would take some doing.

Of course, being attractive to the opposite sex had its uses. Jade wasn't above using her looks to her advantage when she was interested in a guy. After all, a woman had her needs. But if she had to rank abilities, she'd place being able to whistle piercingly through her teeth or being able to do forty really good push-ups in a row far higher than possessing the requisite physical charms to appeal to a man.

Right now her interest in appealing to the male species, especially the ones who seemed to be migrating toward the bar, was in the negative integers.

She managed to rid herself of the second hoverer with

a "Listen, I'm not in the mood to talk tonight. Do you mind?"

His retreat allowed her to take a few sips of her Tom Collins in blessed peace.

By the time number three made his way to her side, any atom of goodwill on Jade's part had evaporated, particularly since she'd realized that all the guys hitting on her came from one central, obnoxious source: a large table packed with alcohol-fueled morons. They must be holding some kind of competition to see who could land her, as though they were contestants on the Fishing Network and she was some juicy bass.

What was worse was that people were starting to notice.

She stiffened on the stool when number four swaggered over. Like his gait, the rest of him was more determined and aggressive than his previous drinking buddies had been. He doubtless believed himself a serious ladies' man; she smelled his cologne before he'd gotten within five feet of her. With a quick sidelong glance, she saw a black shirt that was unbuttoned one too many buttons, revealing a sun-baked chest adorned with gold chains. Nearly blinded by the flash of his toothy smile, she decided she'd seen more than enough. She turned her head to stare at the selection of vodkas lining another section of the wall.

At this rate she was going to be a bona fide expert in liquor brands.

When he didn't leave, she gave an audible sigh. This whole let's-pick-up-the-chick-at-the-bar game had grown old. Maybe it was time to head upstairs. Unfortunately, she had a nasty suspicion that Mr. Blinding Teeth might actually follow her out the bar. No way was she letting him anywhere near her room.

Damn it, she thought; all she'd wanted was to unwind.

"So what's a beautiful woman like you doing in a

place like this? Listen, you sure embarrassed my friend over there." He pointed back to the table at goon number three. "He wanted your phone number so he'll know where to reach me in the morning."

Ugh. When she refused to reply, staring fixedly at a bottle of vodka the color of raspberry syrup instead, he laughed, a braying noise.

"I get it. You're a ballbuster. That's all right. Mine are hard as rocks for you—like the rest of me." With a leer, he grabbed his crotch.

The guy was totally off-the-charts gross. Jade felt dirty just breathing the air next to him. Shifting on the stool, she sent him straight to hell with her eyes. "Get lost, creep," she enunciated clearly before looking away.

This time he didn't laugh. "You know what? Your ass is real tight. I think you need me to loosen it up." He stepped closer, crowding her space in blatant intimidation.

Infuriated, Jade's fingers tightened about her glass. She lifted it and turned a bit so that when she chucked the remains of her drink, they would hit his disgusting face. She was aiming for a bull's-eye.

But her drink-throwing arm stalled, then relaxed, and the glass returned to the bar with a soft *clunk.* Someone had intervened. Laying a hand on the creep's shoulder, he spoke with quiet authority. "That's enough, buddy. The lady's not interested."

"Who the fuck are you to tell me what to do?"

"I'm the guy who's going to make you wish you never pissed me off by making me listen to your bullshit while I was enjoying my drink. Now beat it, and go back to your table. Now."

Jade blinked, and a smile of happy astonishment lifted her lips. How about that, she thought. Chivalry was not dead. And as knights in shining armor went, this one, with his calm confidence, seemed more than capable of slaying any nasty dragons or ugly, conceited trolls who crossed his path.

Meanwhile, El Jerko was doing the macho thing, puffing his chest out as he took the other man's measure, while he debated whether he dared start something. From the fury mottling his face, he must have realized this was not a fight he'd win. Not in a million years.

With a muttered curse that Jade's newfound hero didn't even deign to acknowledge, he slunk off.

Jade immediately forgot about him. She was too busy remembering how to breathe.

Her rescuer had stepped closer. The man was gorgeous. Really, really gorgeous. Electric-blue eyes set in a chiseled face. Ridiculously thick lashes. A wide jaw that ended in a pointed chin with a hint of a cleft. His lips were a tad on the thin side, but that didn't stop Jade from thinking they'd know how to kiss just fine. His arresting face was framed by short black hair. A five o'clock shadow darkened his lean cheeks, making him look slightly raffish.

The heartthrob features she could have handled. It was the weird sense of recognition she had when she stared into the man's face that was making her nerve endings sizzle and her heart bound like a rabbit.

Equally unsettling was that she was certain he felt the same jolt of connection. It was in the quick flare of his eyes, which just as suddenly narrowed, piercing her like twin bright-blue lasers as he tried to place her.

He wouldn't succeed. Because on second thought Jade was sure this man was a stranger. She'd already scanned her memory bank and no guy this hot was in it.

Determined to ignore the disturbing reaction, she managed a nod and a casual "Thanks for the assistance."

"Happy to oblige."

She liked his voice too. Liked its low timbre and the

fact that there was something no-nonsense to it. That added up to a few too many things she found appealing about him. With another nod, she turned resolutely back to the bar.

So she intended to dismiss him as she had everyone else who approached her, Rob thought with one part amusement and three parts curiosity. Had she made any sign of encouragement, any indication that she was looking for a man, he'd have been turned off.

He was far from turned off. Instead, it felt like an electric current was crackling through him, doubtless the effect of seeing how stunningly beautiful she was up close. He couldn't shake the feeling that he'd seen her somewhere before. Probably when he was channel surfing, because she certainly had the looks of a movie star. Those eyes were such an intense green. Must be contacts, he decided.

Intense color aside, her gaze sparkled with intelligence, energy—and awareness. Meaning she'd felt it too: that instant sizzling attraction between them. And, like him, she had no intention of yielding to it. How interesting. He couldn't help wondering what her reasons were.

"Care to dance?" The question came out of nowhere.

"No, I—" She swiveled in her chair as she answered and, as their eyes connected, the sentence seemed to stall in her throat. Her tongue peeked out in a nervous sweep of her upper lip, and that was enough to make him decide that he really wanted to dance with this woman.

Gesturing over his shoulder in the direction of the table where the bozos from the other conference were congregated, he said, "There are still a couple of guys over there who've yet to come over and sweet-talk you. I got the impression you might like to avoid another round. Come on, dance with me."

Jade eyed his outstretched hand, considering. She was certainly sick of getting hit on by guys with football-stadium-size egos. But this man, all chiseled hardness, wasn't some puffed-up dolt. It was a pretty sure bet that he knew how to make a woman burn. A quick glance at the heat in his aquamarine gaze was enough for that well-banked spark of wildness inside her to blaze to life.

She did nothing to subdue it. After all, she was going back to Rosewood the next day. The teaching job at Warburg Elementary would begin in a few short weeks. Her life was going to be staid and respectable, and she a veritable paragon.

Tonight she might as well have fun.

Just tonight.

An annoying little voice piped up, warning her to play it safe. The smart thing to do would be to hightail it up to her hotel room and go to sleep. She ignored the pesky voice; her brain was obviously a little freaked out after such a long day. She could handle a dance with a man—no matter how hot he was.

But when she put her hand in his and felt the zing of energy that coursed through her at this simplest of touches, she wondered whether maybe he was in a whole different league from the college guys she'd fooled around with.

He led her to the dance floor. A slow tune started, one that she recognized instantly from years of listening to the radio in the main barn at Rosewood. It was Phil Collins's "In the Air Tonight." The song rocketed to the top of her list of the world's sexiest songs. Though, come to think of it, "Old MacDonald Had a Farm" might very well strike her as impossibly sexy too, were she listening to it in this man's arms, her body pressed against his, her heart slamming against her ribs as her nerves thrummed.

They moved in sync with the slow rhythm of the bass. His hands began traveling too. Splayed, they moved leisurely from the small of her waist to the curve of her buttocks while the warm breeze of his breath fanned the shell of her ear like a tropical caress. Shuddering, she bit back a moan of pleasure. It escaped her nonetheless as his hands moved again, this time to cup her rear and bring her close.

The hard length of his erection was enough to stop her heart, then make it beat double time. Like the mirrored disco ball hanging above them, her senses spun, glittery bright. Thought and speech were impossible. She could only feel. It was glorious. Crazy and wild and glorious.

She was vaguely aware that Phil Collins had stopped singing, but there was simply no way she could tear her body from his muscular length. Even if she were to manage it, her legs might not support her. A single dance with this stranger had left her weak-kneed and dizzy.

When his head dipped, she instinctively angled hers. Their mouths met in a light graze that left her lips tingling. Her tongue swept over her upper lip, savoring the taste of smoky bourbon and male desire.

His electric gaze tracked the subtle movement and his arms tightened, drawing her closer still, until their bodies were fused. Liquid heat pooled deep in her core. Never before had she reacted so quickly—so combustibly—to a man. But here she was, practically melting on the dance floor, and he hadn't even really kissed her yet.

And, God, she wanted him to. She wanted him to do a lot more besides.

It had been too long, Rob thought, since he'd held a woman in his arms and felt her body yield in unspoken need. He'd missed the smell of scented skin; the soft catch of breath as desire sparked, flared, and caught; the brilliant light of sexual hunger in a woman's eyes.

And this woman responded as if she'd been fashioned just for him, the signs of her arousal as intense as his own.

That was something else he'd forgotten: how red-hot and all-consuming lust could be, so much so that fantasies of the two of them fucking right there on the dance floor crowded his mind. Which was nuts. Public sex wasn't his thing. But while Rob wasn't about to start spouting any crass pickup lines, he couldn't deny the truth any longer: He wanted this woman as badly as did every guy who'd been hitting on her and all the ones who'd been gearing up to do so. He ached for her.

He told himself it was okay. She wasn't like Becky at all; he could lose himself in this blond siren's long-limbed body. Just tonight.

"Do you have a room?"

A room with this man . . . sex with a stranger. Jade swallowed nervously.

She'd be the first to admit that she'd done some pretty reckless stuff in her day, but even her college hookups had been with guys she'd at least *seen* before. So while the huskily murmured question caused her sexual craving to flare into a veritable inferno, she wasn't such a risk-taker that images of her body dismembered and buried in a landfill two states away didn't flash bright red with sirens blaring in her imagination.

But he wasn't drunk, and he wasn't emitting any weird vibes or making any creepy, kinky comments. He wasn't doing anything but making her melt inside and out against his deliciously hard body. She wanted to rub against him all night. Naked and in private.

Her eyes met his and Jade saw the fierce attraction, the hot need she knew was mirrored in her own. Steamy sex on a stormy night. It'd be just for tonight. Then they'd go their separate ways.

She nodded slowly. "I have a room. Do you want to come?" She could hardly believe the sultry whisper was her own. She was pretty sure her double entendre was out of character too. But it was hard to think or care what she sounded like when her brain was feverish with desire.

"I do."

She liked a man of action. Already he was leading her off the dance floor and heading toward the bar's entrance. The dark blues, reds, and blacks of the bar's interior streaked by, then lightened into a swath of beiges as they crossed the lobby. The distance seemed as long as a desert trek. Objects lost their focus; people became a blur. The only thing she could concentrate on was the feel of his hand holding hers. His fingers were strong and, like hers, slightly callused. She wanted them touching her, rubbing her breasts, tweaking her nipples until they ached; she wanted them stroking her inner thighs, lifting her legs, settling them around his shoulders. . . . She stole a glance at his mouth and stumbled.

Dear God, please let him be even a tenth as talented as she was imagining.

"You okay?" he asked, his grip tightening, steadying her.

She nodded, unsure she could trust her voice.

An elevator was waiting. They stepped inside, the door slid shut, and the harsh drag of their breathing filled the small space.

"What floor?"

She stared blankly at the twin column of numbers. Fortunately, the aggravation she felt at knowing he had enough wits about him to think of such pesky details as what floor they should get out on cleared her fevered brain momentarily. She released his hand to step forward and press 4.

"Thank God." His laugh was short. "I don't think I could have stood it if you were on eight. Too long a wait. Even the fifth floor would have been a stretch."

Feeling better to hear him admit that his need was as

raging as her own, she smiled. "Well, then, how about I race you down the hall?"

Rob returned her smile. "You're on." He liked her confident spirit. He liked that she was unbelievably sexy too. He didn't even have her naked yet and the blood was pounding in his veins. He hadn't desired a woman like this in years, not since—then the elevator doors were opening and she was bursting out of them and tearing down the hall, and he was spared having to finish the thought as he sprinted to catch her.

Stumbling into the room, they fell into each other's arms, bodies straining and hands searching. Mouths locked to exchange hungry, devouring kisses. Hearts thundered as hard as the rain beating at the windows.

He raised his head to draw in a much-needed gulp of air, and a thought suddenly occurred to him. "Hey, I haven't asked. What's your name?"

Jade wasn't about to divulge it, not when she was within hours of Warburg. The Radcliffe name was too easily recognized, first because of Rosewood Farm, her family's horse-breeding operation, and second because of Margot's fame as a model. Success had also made Jordan and her interior-decorating company, Rosewood Designs, fairly well known. She didn't want to have to field any questions about her connection to those Radcliffes. Why get bogged down in banal chitchat when she'd never see this man again?

Lifting the hem of her tank top, she pulled it over her head and let it fall to the floor. "Do you really care what my name is?" she whispered.

Rob's gaze locked on the sweetly rounded globes filling the satin bra that was edged with lace. Her nipples, tight as pebbles, strained against the ivory fabric. He pictured closing his mouth over them, drawing them against his tongue as he suckled.

Christ, he thought as everything in him tightened with

need. He raised his eyes, meeting a gaze that reminded him of lying under the canopy of a tree on a lazy summer day. He wanted to lose himself in those sparkling green depths as he sank into her hot, welcoming body. Was it necessary to know her name to do that?

"No, I guess I don't," he murmured, already dipping his head to draw one deliciously rounded breast into his mouth.

Pleasure rocked her as his lips latched on to her nipple and he began to rub his tongue over the wet satin of her bra and tease the distended bud with his teeth. The friction and wet heat against her sensitive flesh made her gasp and sent shivers racing through her. Digging her fingers into his hair, she anchored him there as he continued his sensual onslaught.

His hands were as busy as his mouth. One worked sexual magic on her other breast, pushing her bra back to cup her breast in his callused palm, kneading and fondling it, each tugging caress sending sparks dancing in a hot, thrilling line to her core; the other tugged the zipper of her jeans, peeling the denim down her hips.

Then hands and mouth traveled south, boldly claiming territory, and her eyes closed in anticipation. The reality of him as a lover was more than a match for her finest fantasies.

With a hunger that matched his, she followed his example, eagerly stripping his clothes to taste and stroke the warm flesh that was revealed. Each taste a feast, each stroke a carnal worship.

Oh, yes, he was very, very fine, she thought happily, taking in his naked body, a perfect complement to his striking face. He worked out. That much was obvious from the breadth of his shoulders and the sculpted ridges of his abdomen. His hips were narrow, and his long, straight legs were dusted with dark hair. God, she even liked his feet. Her gaze traveled back up his muscular legs to stare at his cock—right now the most breathtaking part of his anatomy—and she bit her lip, stifling a giggle as all sorts of deliciously raunchy one-liners sprang to mind. She settled on the one about the man with the right kind of tool for the job, and her smile grew.

"Like what you see?"

"Most definitely. You have a very nice d—" She drew out the consonant, finishing with "—imple."

He grinned, and the dimple she'd professed to admire deepened. A sexy, well-hung hunk who had a dimple when he smiled. How utterly sweet.

"Thanks. And you have a very nice . . ."

She felt her body temperature ratchet a few degrees higher as his gaze traveled slowly over her, his eyes caressing her as boldly as his hands and mouth had moments ago. She found herself wondering what he would say—praying he wouldn't spoil the mood—and unconsciously held her breath.

"Tattoo," he pronounced.

She expelled her pent-up breath in a delighted laugh. "Thank you." Yeah, she liked this guy, and now that she'd seen ample evidence that he had a sense of humor as well as an insanely good body, she liked him even more. For a second Jade was tempted to tell him her name—but then she took another look at him and his truly impressive erection and decided she had better things to do with this splendid male specimen than swap biographical info.

Luckily for her, he apparently had other things on his to-do list as well.

"Mind if I take a closer look?" He paused, and a wicked grin lifted the corners of his mouth. "At the tat?"

She swallowed. "Feel free."

Not needing a second invitation, he dropped to his knees in front of her and reached out to trace the outline of the butterfly tattoo that floated between her hip bone and the light-brown hair covering her mound. She sucked in her breath at the electricity generated by his gentle touch. Sizzling and sparking along her skin, it traveled down and center, making her core muscles tighten convulsively, making her wet.

"Excellent detail work. I like the way it looks like the butterfly is in flight. If I were that butterfly, I'd want to land right here."

A moan escaped her as his fingers brushed her curls and found her clitoris. Stroking the nub with the pad of his thumb, he looked up and his smile flashed white. "I wonder, do you taste as good as you look, sweetheart?"

"I—" she began and ended, incapable of speech. Her mind, however, screamed, *God, please touch me now.*

"I bet you do," he whispered, his warm breath fanning her sensitive skin. "But just in case, I better investigate." Then his mouth closed over her, his clever tongue circling and gliding over her pulsing nub, and the sensation was so exquisite that her knees buckled. She laid her hands on his muscled shoulders, bracing herself, as she succumbed to the raw pleasure he was offering. Each leisurely lash of his tongue sent her closer to the edge, left her panting softly with anticipation and desperation. A light graze of his teeth and it was too much. With a broken cry she came, shattering into pieces. Boneless, she sank against him.

Then she was floating as, with effortless ease, he picked her up and carried her to the immense bed.

Still racked by the force of her orgasm, she looked dazedly up at him. Fierce hunger stamped his features. Then her gaze traveled down, past the ridges of his abdomen and the dark arrow of hair below his belly button to his erection, thick and straining, and everything inside her went tight and achy and needy all over again.

Sculpted muscles shifted as he moved, placing a knee onto the mattress and lowering his torso over her. A single word popped out automatically—she'd repeated it so often in her college-newspaper advice column, her editor had kidded her it should be her byline. "Protection."

He jackknifed up. "What? Oh, yeah, of course." A horrified expression crossed his face as he looked over at his pants, lying in a heap on the maroon carpet. "Shit! God damn it! I—"

She didn't think he'd appreciate hearing that he looked really cute when he was embarrassed and frustrated as all get out. But he did. Seeing, too, that he wasn't some slick operator trolling bars for a lay was hugely reassuring.

Relief mixed with amusement filled her voice. "No worries. I got you covered." She rolled off the bed, taking the time to pat his very fine butt cheek before dashing into the bathroom to grab a bunch of Trojans from her toiletries bag. Clutching them tight, she sprinted back and dove onto the bed. As she rolled onto her back, she smiled and let the condoms rain down beside her. Holding the last one flat on her palm, she extended it in offering, just as she would a treat to Nocturne, her favorite stud at Rosewood. With a happy smile she asked, "Now, where were we?"

The sex was amazing—*he* was amazing. She'd never felt like this before with anyone, as if she were a flame burning ever hotter with each stroke, each kiss, each powerful surge of hips driving into her pulsing center, his expression fiercely intense. And when she exploded in a flash of color, he held her in his arms, his body hard and sweat-slicked against hers, his erection still throbbing inside her. Then his touch changed, lingering, learning, exciting her unbearably as it cupped the underside of her breast, kneaded the curve of her ass, or palmed the line of her hip. Desire burst into flame inside her, burning as hot and intense, as uncontrollable, as before.

And with each heart-slamming orgasm he wrung from her through the silvery blackness of the night, he inspired her to give him the same kind of mind-blowing pleasure. Their murmurs filled the room as they moved and shifted, finding new positions. Murmurs turned into moans and helpless gasps as their bodies strained against each other and then together soared into sensual bliss. And if she thought her need seemed uncontrollable, well, his seemed insatiable, a wild passion let loose.

Over and over they came together, each giving as much as demanding, until finally, as the gray of a storm-tossed dawn edged out the night, they fell into a tangled heap of exhaustion.

Rob moved about the half-lit room, silently gathering his clothes, which lay littered on the carpet, but more often simply standing with an unconsciously tender expression on his face as he stole yet another glance at her. She was smiling in her sleep. She looked impossibly fine, her long hair a riotous, gold-streaked tangle about her naked shoulders. He remembered the feel of that hair when he'd dug his fingers into its thick silkiness. It's softness around his fists had been as sensually exotic as the liquid heat of her mouth as she closed her lips around his shaft and took him deep inside. He remembered the lightly flowered scent of it as, nearly blind with pleasure, he'd dragged her up to bring that wonderfully wicked mouth to his. Plunging his tongue past her lips, he'd tasted himself as well as her in that deep, desperate kiss. Fueled by desire, he'd blazed a searing trail of kisses down her neck to the slope of her shoulder, dipping into hollows where her pulse hammered, its beat as wild as the rest of her. As wild as his own.

As he tugged on his shirt, his gaze slid past shoulders that gleamed like gold dust in the soft light. The delicate curves of her body played peekaboo with the white sheet twisted about her, but that was enough. All he needed was a glimpse for his blood to begin pounding in his veins.

She was about the sexiest woman he'd ever seen—satin-skinned, long-limbed, agile as a gymnast, and scorching hot in her unfeigned responses. He might not know her name, but he knew she didn't have a single inhibited bone in that unbelievably fine body. How fucking lucky was he to have stumbled across a woman who could arouse him with a single shimmy of her sleek body?

He should write a goodbye note, thanking her, and lay it on her pillow. It would be a better note, of course, if he knew whom he was addressing.

His gaze strayed to the floral upholstered chair beside the bed as he shoved his feet into his shoes. Her purse, one of those high-end leather jobs, was resting on it. It would be so easy to cross over to the chair, open her bag, fish out her wallet, and check her ID, all without causing so much as one of her thick eyelashes to flutter or a silken limb to stir. But something held him back. He wasn't a cop 24/7.

And why bother anyway? What would knowing her name accomplish? It wasn't as if Rob would ever want to see her again. Even if she lived somewhere in Virginia, he certainly wouldn't want to be in a relationship with her. A sex vixen was hardly the type of woman he envisioned in his life, let alone Hayley's. Better that she remain a delicious, mysterious memory—the woman who'd blown his body and mind alike, as though he were a case of dynamite. A fantasy evening he'd remember with a smile for a long time to come.

As he was smiling now. Rob definitely had to thank her for that, for the excellent frame of mind he found himself in after a night of first-class sex.

He walked over to the head of the bed and crouched

down next to her. For a second he simply cataloged the details of her face: the winged arch of her brows, the dense fan of her long, dark lashes, the straight line of her nose, the tiny flare of her nostrils as she breathed. And that mouth. Jesus, her lips could tempt a saint. And last night had proved beyond all doubt that Rob was not destined for sainthood.

He brought his lips to hers, pressing lightly as his tongue slipped inside. She tasted of sleep and of sex. Delicious.

She stirred, her lips parting in a drowsy smile. Slowly her lids lifted. Against the white of the bed linen, her eyes were even greener. And she didn't wear contacts. Unusual shade, he didn't think he'd ever seen—

"Hi. What time is it?" Her huskily croaked question cut off his thoughts.

"Five o'clock. Time for me to go." Even as he answered, his mind was wavering. He could spare a half hour.

"You're leaving?"

"Yes." He made himself say it and ignored the ridiculous feeling of regret that he wasn't going to climb back into bed with her. The feeling was strong enough to have him reaching out and rubbing the pad of his thumb over the ripe swell of her lower lip, the better to remember her smile. "I enjoyed last night."

"Ditto." She pursed her lips against his thumb and kissed it.

Just like that, he was hard. "I really need to hit the road." Reluctance dragged at his words.

She nodded sleepily. "Mmm-hmm. Me too, but I need a few more minutes' sleep. You have yourself an excellent life." With another sleepy smile, she rolled onto her side and snuggled into the pillow.

Well, that settled that. The lady wasn't interested in a morning tumble. A grin tugged the corners of his mouth as he realized she was once again fast asleep. She was something, all right. And there was no reason to feel any regret that he'd never see her again. This was the perfect parting of ways, easy and trouble-free. Another thing to thank her for—when he next thought of her.

"So long, beautiful," Rob murmured. Straightening, he headed for the door.

JADE TRIED not to show how touched she was by the fact that the entire gang, from Patrick and Ellie Banner, who had tended Rosewood's gardens, grounds, and house for years, right down to Neddy and Will, whose jobs as the youngest of the Radcliffe–Maher–Gage clan were basically to soak up the love showered on them, was waiting for her when she pulled up in front of the old Greek revival house that had been in the family forever. Jordan and Ellie had prepared a brunch, complete with Braverman's bagels—cinnamon raisin included—a zucchini frittata, a mozzarella-and-tomato salad, and fruit-studded yogurts topped with Jordan's homemade granola. The kids ran around on the long expanse of lawn, while the adults sat around the two long tables that Owen and Travis had carried onto the grass and ate and drank coffee. Jade opted for both activities, inhaling food that tasted like ambrosia after the fare offered down in Ocala and the junk she'd been eating on the road, and then springing up from the table to race after Olivia, tackling her niece and launching a full-scale tickle attack while the six-year-old writhed with giggling glee. Or, if Will had taken it into his head to crawl all the way to Warburg and had reached the spot where the lawn met the tall grass of the horse pastures, she'd lope over and scoop him up, trotting back with him under her arm, football style. Will was at the chucklehead stage where he liked that sort of thing.

"You considered attaching a longe line to Will?" she asked Travis, passing him his giggling son and snagging a second bagel. Last night's marathon of sex had entitled her to a few hundred extra calories.

"Only a couple hundred times." Travis plucked the knife Will had grabbed from his plate and gave him a coffee spoon instead, which Will immediately began banging on the picnic table. Jade made a mental note to buy him a set of bongo drums for Christmas. And earplugs for everyone else.

"Actually, Owen and I have a new idea," Travis said. "Once Will begins walking, we're going to put him and Neddy in harnesses and a trace. That way, when they take off, it'll be in one direction."

Jade nodded approvingly. "Good thinking."

Travis smiled, picked up his coffee, and managed to get the cup to his lips for a slow sip in spite of his son's waving arms. "Glad to have you back, Jade, so you can do your share of wind sprints. Georgie's gotten pretty darned quick on her feet."

"That's cool. Riding herd on these munchkins will have me in tip-top shape for September. I can't see how any of those second-graders at the elementary school could be faster on their feet than this lot." She slipped in the news that she'd gotten the substitute-teaching job casually, which made Margot and Jordan's immediate exclamations of delight all the sweeter.

Margot's smile was brilliant. "You've been hired to teach second grade? That is so great!"

"Oh, Jade, congratulations!" Jordan hurried around the table to give her a hug.

After years of being pretty much the quintessential screwup sister, it was nice to feel as if she'd taken a step closer to joining the ranks of her dynamo sisters. "Well, it's only a substitute position, but the salary's decent. And if I do a good job this fall, I think I'll have a fair shot at a permanent position next year. And get this: Full-time teachers in the district get paid to pursue a master's degree. And the benefits include both health *and* dental insurance. Pretty sweet, huh?"

"Supporting the advancement of the teachers is certainly very nice and farsighted of the school district," Ellie said with approval.

"Though it's doubtful you'll ever use the health insurance, Jade. You have the constitution of an ox. And you have to be dragged to the dentist's for anything other than a cleaning," Andy said teasingly. One of Rosewood Farm's trainers, Andy was only six years older than she, but sometimes he forgot that fact.

"That's because dentists are scary people." Jade personally considered dentists right up there on the super-scary meter with cops decked out in uniform and mirrored aviator sunglasses.

"Remember when you had to get that cavity filled?" Miriam grinned across the table at her. She was sitting next to Andy, who was now her fiancé. They'd gotten engaged on this past New Year's and, as they'd found true love at Rosewood, Jordan, Margot, and Jade had offered to hold the wedding celebration for them here, on New Year's Eve. The wedding promised to be a blast—a beautiful blast, if she knew her sisters.

From the proximity of their bodies, Jade had a hunch that Miriam and Andy were indulging in some serious footsie underneath the picnic table.

Ah, true love.

For her part, Jade was happy with true lust. A memory from the night before flashed vividly bright in her mind, of her straddling her dark-haired lover and slowly sinking down his shaft until she was impaled, filled to bursting, and trembling from the exquisite sensation of him thick and pulsing inside her. Mmm-hmm, yes, she was more than happy with true lust.

"It's good to see you're embarrassed by that episode, Jade," Miriam said, catching her eye. "All that carrying on for one teeny cavity. I had to cover Olivia's ears for fear she'd freak when it came time to go to the dentist herself." Miriam had babysat for Jordan's kids while pursuing her graduate degree in physical therapy.

Jade could only be thankful her friend didn't know the actual memory that had caused the heat wave to sweep over her. The conversation would have caused her sisters—and perhaps her brothers-in-law—to have heart failures. So when Jordan returned to the topic of Jade's new substitute-teaching job, she breathed a sigh of relief.

"Well, I'm sure that when they see how great you are with the students, they'll give you a class of your own."

"Thanks for the vote of confidence."

Owen stood, drawing everyone's attention, and raised his mug of coffee in salute. "I propose a toast to Jade, who's brave enough to take on a classroom of seven-year-olds."

When the *hear, hear*s and laughter died down, Jordan asked, "So when did you get the offer, Jade? Did Ted call you?"

Ted . . . It took a second, and then Jade realized that Jordan was referring to Ted Guerra, or *Mr.* Guerra, as Jade called him. But with Kate, Max, and Olivia enrolled at Warburg Elementary, Jordan was on a first-name basis with most of the staff, teachers, and apparently the principal. "Yeah, Ted Guerra contacted me last week. I already knew he'd placed me on the list of substitutes, but then he called to ask whether I'd take over for one of the second-grade teachers who's preggers—"

"That would be Sandy Riley."

Jade nodded. "I think that's her name. Apparently her obstetrician ordered bed rest for her until she delivers.

Guerra asked if I'd take her class for the fall semester. Cool, huh?"

"Fantastic. I hope Sandy's okay," Jordan said. "I'll write her a note."

"Do you know who's going to be in your class? We might know some of the kids," Margot asked.

"No, not yet. But I have a meeting with Guerra tomorrow. I guess he'll give me the roster and the kids' files then. I hope I get some horsey kids, so I can recruit them for my riding program."

Margot paused in the midst of stacking the now-empty plates. "You sure it won't be too much, teaching school and giving riding lessons in addition to your own training and riding? You won't have a moment to yourself."

"This from the woman who's juggling two demanding careers, raising two kids, and evidently still has enough energy to keep her husband looking real happy?"

"But, Jade—"

"And don't you start in on me either, Jordan," Jade warned. "You're as much of an overachiever as Margot. Your interior-design company is going gangbusters, you help out at Gage and Associates, you've got four—count 'em—four kids, serve on countless committees, and you're still at the barns every day, helping Ned with the foals and riding whoever needs exercising."

"But—" Jordan tried again.

"But what? I'm supposed to be a slacker-girl and sit around playing video games and updating my Facebook status or maxing out my credit card at the mall after I've finished working with the horses Travis and Ned assign me?"

"No, but teaching school is exhausting, and then there's all the prep work that goes into it—"

"Reality check, sis. It's second grade I'm teaching. I think I can handle the rigors of the curriculum."

"You can't expect modesty from the girl who's never met a test she didn't ace," Miriam said, laughing.

Jade grinned at her friend. "I'm trying not to make you all feel bad. I know how tricky those multiplication tables can be."

"It's the sevens that always stumped me," Andy said.

"I'll lend Miriam some flash cards you can practice with," Jade replied with a wink. "As for lesson planning and grading, I figure I'll do them at night. Might have to sacrifice watching *American Idol,* but that's getting old anyway. And I'm only going to offer riding lessons three days a week in the beginning—think I'll be able to fill the classes, Ned?"

"Write up a flyer and I'll drop it off at Steadman's tomorrow—I need to pick up some bell boots for Night Watch. They stick it in their binder. Adam and Sara Steadman think the world of you. You can be sure they'll spread the word that you're offering lessons."

"Thanks, Ned, I'll write one up tonight." Returning her attention to her sisters, she said, "It'll be fun teaching riding. It's important to instill good riding fundamentals early on."

"Ain't that the truth," Ned chimed in. "Some of the kids entering horse shows have no business sitting in the saddle. Sloppy riding at such a young age becomes a real hard habit to break. Who better to teach what hunt seat equitation's about than Miss Jade? After all, she has plenty of experience. I still remember her coaching Kate over her first crossbar jump."

"And have you guys considered that when these kids get older, their parents are going to be buying them horses? Where do you suppose they'll shop for that first gorgeous hunter?" Jade asked with an arch of her brows.

"Are you thinking Rosewood Farm?" Andy asked with a grin.

"Excellent deduction, Andy."

Travis laughed. "I gotta say, Jade's plan is scarily brilliant. Kind of like the kid herself."

Jade blew him a kiss. "Have I told you lately how much you rock as a bro-in-law?"

"Hold it right there," Owen said. "I refuse to be cast as the bro-in-law who does not rock. It's time we show Jade her graduation present."

"You mean you've finished the pony barn?" she asked. "I was so hungry—I decided I needed my sleep more than breakfast at the hotel—that I drove straight up to the house. This I gotta check out." Brimming with excitement, she jumped up from the table.

Ned, who was carrying his namesake, stood up and shifted the toddler to his chino-covered hip. "It's awful good to have you back, Miss Jade." His pale-blue eyes twinkled beneath his shaggy silver brows.

"Isn't it, though?"

As the other adults hastily downed the last dregs of coffee and rose to their feet, Jade cupped her hands and gave a shout to her four older nieces and nephew gamboling on the lawn. "Come on, kids. We're going to inspect the new barn. Here, Georgie, you can ride piggyback and tell me everything Mommy's been teaching you on Doc Holliday."

Owen had pulled off the new construction beautifully, Jade thought. Nestled between the main barn and the broodmares's barn, and painted the same soft weathered white with a matching gray roof and squared cupola, the pony barn blended seamlessly.

While she drank in the details of the barn, her heart did funny things inside her chest. Seeing the first part of her idea for a riding program at Rosewood Farm become a physical reality meant so much, not simply because her dream was being realized but because it represented the wholehearted support of her family. When she'd proposed the idea of opening the farm to teach the local kids to ride, she hadn't expected their enthusiastic response. As one, they'd urged her to go for it. And now they'd done even more.

They'd gone and built a *barn* for her. Her very own barn.

She swallowed to make sure her voice sounded normal. "It looks perfect, Owen. Even better, it looks like it's always been here. Dad would be happy."

"Yup. RJ would be real pleased. Your mom too," Ned added. "She was always proud of your riding, Miss Jade."

Bless Ned for saying that. Most likely Ned would have choked on the words if he'd ever read a page from her mother's diary. Thank God Margot and Jordan had never shown it to him, for then he'd know what her mom had really thought about her—*Stop it. Do not go there,* she counseled herself. *Don't let her spoil this moment for you.*

With a bright smile, she turned to Owen. "You most definitely rock with the best of all brothers-in-law. The barn's great, just fantastic. Thank you."

"You're welcome, kid." Owen smiled. He had a killer smile. It was the thing she'd first liked about him. That he was perceptive enough to recognize that Jordan was an amazing woman was the second.

"Don't rush your fences, Jade," Travis warned. "You can't pronounce Owen's latest equine accommodation fantastic until you've inspected it from bottom to top— though it is," he added with a grin.

"Well, then," she said, hitching Georgie higher up on her back. "I want the deluxe tour."

"We put in six box stalls, as requested."

"So now there'll be room for Doc and Archer to come live here with the other ponies, right, Aunt Jade?" Max, her eldest nephew, was marching alongside her like an army soldier. She was pretty sure his footsteps were ringing louder than anyone else's.

"Right, Max, because you and Kate and Olivia are being really terrific about letting me use Doc and Archer when I teach the other kids."

"And we're gonna get to ride the other ponies too," Olivia piped up.

"That's a fact. I'll need a lot of help exercising them, and you guys are already good riders."

"Fortunately we have a steady supply of child labor here," Margot said wryly.

The group had come to a stop in the center of the immaculate barn, and Jade looked about her. "Nice. Very nice."

Owen smiled. "Travis, Ned, and I decided on standard-size box stalls in case you ever want to put horses in here. But I went for the same sliding-door design that we have at Hawk Hill." Owen and Jordan used their barn and fields to house Rosewood's retired broodmares. "I figured sliding doors would be easier to negotiate when the kids are leading the ponies in and out of the stalls. I realize it's a different design than Rosewood's other barns—"

"But it works better with a barn this size." She glanced around, taking in the pristine concrete floor, the pine-wood box stalls gleaming gold in the daylight. It looked wonderful and was going to look even more wonderful when she bought four barn mates for Doc Holliday and Archer. She could already imagine the space filled with kids learning how to pick hooves and pull manes and use a currycomb. She nodded happily. "This is perfect. Really. Thanks, guys."

"The tack room's down here, opposite the club room."

She turned to stare at Margot. "Club room?" she asked blankly.

"That's Jordan's and my contribution to the barn. We thought the kids would need a place to sit and stow their school stuff without it cluttering up the aisles."

Margot and Jordan led the way down the wide aisle. Pushing open a door, Margot waved Jade inside a room that was roughly the size of two box stalls. A pair of windows gave the room a bright, airy feel. On the far wall stood a line of cubbies with hooks for coats and backpacks, and in the center of the room two sofas faced each other, with armchairs at either end.

"Swank" was all she could say as she looked about her. Her brows came together in a slight frown. The club room was great, but it bothered her to think of her sisters spending extra money when they'd done so much for her already. After giving them each a fierce hug of thanks, she said, "I'll reimburse you for the furniture."

Jordan shot that idea down quickly. "Don't be silly. Everything you see here is from the third floor of the big house. Remember my telling you that I was redecorating this spring? Margot and Travis wanted to make the third floor over for guests—you know how much Damien Barnes and Charlie Ayer like to come and stay. It needed a whole new look."

"Those sofas were the ones you had when you were living with the kids up there?" Jade asked.

Jordan nodded. "I simply got new slipcovers for them and the chairs. On sale. The fabric's washable, by the way. The rug's price was slashed too."

"And Doug and Jesse put up the cubbies and the tack-room equipment gratis. Their graduation present to you," Owen added.

Doug and Jesse were two of the builders who worked for Owen and his architectural firm, Gage & Associates. They'd helped Owen restore Hawk Hill, the house next door, where he and Jordan and the kids now lived. With Owen's attention to the architectural details, Jordan's

eye for design, and Jesse and Doug's exquisite crafts-
manship, Hawk Hill was now as stunning as Rosewood.
Its renovation had given Owen a ton of business in the
area.

"That's so sweet of them," she said. "I'll drop by
whatever site they're working at tomorrow and thank
them."

"Well, that's easily done, as tomorrow they'll be about
a couple thousand feet away." Owen smiled.

"Doing repairs on the house, huh? I'll make a Braverman's run for them. Pastrami with the works still Doug
and Jesse's favorite?"

"Yes, but, Jade?" Jordan said.

Jade wondered why Owen's smile seemed to be conta-
gious. Everyone was grinning. "Uh-huh?"

"Owen's present? There's more."

"More?" she repeated blankly.

"Yeah, more! It's a big surprise, Aunt Jade!" Olivia
hollered, with Georgie and Kate chiming in gleefully,
grins stretching their little faces. All of a sudden Jade
realized that all the kids—the ones who were verbal,
that is—had been unusually quiet throughout the tour
of the pony barn. Their tongues probably all bore teeth
marks from biting back whatever thrilling surprise lay
in wait for her.

"Personally, I don't know how you could top a six-
stall pony barn, but I guess I'm gonna find out."

JADE GOT her answer. They'd built her a house—or re-built it, to be precise. She hardly recognized Bramble Cottage. Originally, the cottage had been used to house Rosewood Farm's workers, but for years it had sat vacant, as Tito and Felix, Rosewood's grooms, both had families too large for the two-bedroom house. Ned had his own cottage, Thistle Cottage, and before Travis and Margot married, Travis had lived in the apartment over the main barn—where Andy and Miriam now lived.

"This is for me?"

"Yes," Jordan answered her. "Isn't it cute?"

Jordan was right. The cottage *was* cute. Just by looking at its exterior, Jade could tell that Owen must have had fun with the project. He'd altered the façade, creating a porch screened by columns, just like at the main house, and enlarged the windows to create an airier look.

"Wait until you step inside. Owen had a blast going through John Butler's pattern book when he updated the interior," Jordan said, her voice filled with pride and love.

"And guess what, Aunt Jade?" Kate said. "Mommy and I picked out the colors for the walls."

"Me too! I helped." Unable to contain her excitement, Olivia was jumping up and down as though on an invisible pogo stick.

"Then they'll be the colors I like best, won't they?

This is amazing, guys. Thank you." Though Jade was usually able to crack wise with the best of them, right now all she could think of was how incredibly lucky she was to have a family like this. They'd done so much for her, supporting her every minute of the day since Mom and Dad died, and for far too long she'd returned the favor by being hell on wheels.

Owen's gaze scanned the little white house. "It's not quite finished yet," he warned. "Doug and Jesse still have to sand and finish the floors and perform a few final tweaks and touch-ups. But everything should be move-in ready by the end of the week. Do you want to see the inside now, or wait?"

"Most definitely now."

The lot of them filed in and gave Jade the tour of the cottage. Walking through the rooms, she reveled in the collective chatter as they discussed what she would need to put where: a sofa, some chairs, a TV, a pretty round table where she could eat and do her grading work, some patterned curtains—but not ones that were too girlie—and a really comfortable bed. They knew her so well. . . .

Damn, she loved these guys. Telling herself to get a grip before she embarrassed them all by blubbering, Jade directed an accusing finger at her sisters and brothers-in-law. "I detect a nefarious plot here. You remodeled Bramble Cottage because you want to get rid of me. At the very least make me learn how to cook."

Margot gave a dramatic roll of her eyes. "You, Jade, are suffering from paranoid delusions. Travis, please tell her how many tears I wept at the prospect of giving up 24/7 entertainment for Georgie and Will."

"Oceans. Margot was practically in mourning," Travis said.

"You've got Owen and Travis to thank for your new digs. They thought you might like to have a place where you could enjoy some privacy when you wanted it, rather than having your bedroom door busted down by the likes of Neddy or Will."

A graphic image of what she'd been up to last night flashed in Jade's mind. The last thing she wanted was for a G-rated audience to walk in on that kind of show. Although neither one-night stands nor sexual encounters of any kind were on her agenda, she did intend to line up a private investigator to find out who her mother's lover had been. That particular activity had to remain just as private, hidden not only from the little nippers scampering in and out of her quarters but from her sisters as well. They wouldn't understand her need to dig up old painful memories, and she wasn't sure she could explain it to them convincingly. So, yeah, it would be good to research investigators here at the cottage, where awkward interruptions could be kept to a minimum.

Jordan's voice brought Jade back to the immediate conversation. "Naturally I'm all for you learning how to boil water, Jade, but I'm hoping you'll also be coming to Hawk Hill for dinner several times a week. You could come tonight. I baked brownies." Her smile was accompanied by a mischievous wink as Margot gave a cry of outrage.

"That is so sneaky and underhanded of you, Jordan!"

Unfazed, Jordan merely shrugged. "Jade's a free agent; she's going to go where the deal is sweeter."

"*Sweet* being the operative word," Margot huffed. "Well, I'll just have to ask Ellie to make her fried chicken for tomorrow night, won't I?"

Jordan's eyes narrowed at Margot's upping of the ante.

"Wow. Ellie's fried chicken. I've forgotten what that tastes like. I think I dream of it sometimes though," Travis said, his mouth lifting in a crooked smile.

"So now do you see how hard it was to get your sisters to agree to renovating the cottage?" Owen asked.

Jade grinned. "Yeah. So, to be clear: What are you two expecting in return for this shameless and blatant bribery?"

"Babysitting," Margot and Jordan pronounced in unison.

"For these monsters?" She summoned her darkest scowl at the kids, who'd decided to hold a one-legged race across the empty living space. Neddy and Will had joined in, tottering and crawling energetically across the drop cloth and, when that grew old, rolling about and laughing like the goofballs they were. As for the others, it was looking as if Georgie might win the race over her older cousins. While Georgie had Travis's dramatic dark looks, she took after Margot in a big way: She liked to win. "You guys drive a hard bargain."

"Think of it in terms of doing a good deed for bros-in-law who rock, kid," Owen suggested.

Jade pretended to consider. "Okay, if you put it that way. I guess I can give up a couple of nights now and again."

From the four matching grins, one would think she'd just handed her sisters and their husbands the moon.

Ned cleared his throat. "Now that we've got that question settled, how about Miss Jade grabbing her breeches from her bag so we can get a spot of work done before the day is over?"

"An excellent idea, especially since I want to do Jordan's brownies justice. Who do you have lined up for me to ride?" She had a moment of nostalgia for her beloved gelding, Aspen, the first horse she'd trained, the first horse she'd had to sell.

It had taken saying goodbye to Aspen to understand why Margot broke down whenever it came time to load a horse they'd sold into the van.

But Ellen, the girl in Chicago who'd bought Aspen, was really nice, with soft hands, a good seat, and a heart as big as the dark-bay Thoroughbred gelding. Watching Ellen fall in love with Aspen the second he nuzzled her outstretched palm made parting with him somewhat easier. Knowing the two would be good equestrian partners helped too. Aspen was a horse with enough talent and scope to carry Ellen for years to come.

This wasn't an easy business—raising, training, and selling horses. It demanded time, care, and love, and really good judgment, the last especially important when the day came to sell the horse you'd raised from a wobbly-legged foal. Luckily, no one at Rosewood would ever part with a horse simply to make money. Rosewood Farm's horses went to the very best owners they could find, which made laying that last goodbye kiss against the velvety muzzle of a horse you loved a tiny bit easier to bear.

"Ned and I were thinking you might like to work with Cosmo and Valentine," Travis told her. "We'd also like you to take over Carmen's training."

"You've begun entering her in some three-day events, haven't you?" Like Valentine and Cosmo, Carmen was a five-year-old.

Ned nodded. "That's right. We think she's got the talent and scope to be a top competitor. She's a real firecracker. Just your speed."

"Sounds good." She turned to Owen. "You sure you're willing to trust me with Cosmo's training?" When Owen and Jordan got engaged, Ned had somehow convinced Owen that, in addition to three young stepchildren, he needed the beautiful young colt in his life. To everyone's delight, Owen had agreed.

Owen grinned and lifted his shoulder in an easy shrug. "Jade, I can use all the help with Cosmo I can get."

"Don't believe a word he says, Jade," Margot said.

"Owen's doing great with him. Travis has him riding Cosmo at least twice a week so they get to know each other. And yesterday Owen jumped a pretty tricky course on Mystique."

"Yeah, he did super-well," Kate added. She always paid attention when it came to how the horses were ridden.

Owen mouthed a "Thanks, Kate," to his eldest step-child. "Mystique is very forgiving."

Margot nodded. "She is, isn't she? And in a year or two it'll be Cosmo taking you over the same jump course."

"Both Cosmo and I need a lot of work before that happens. I've seen you train the youngsters, Jade. I'd be really grateful if you could help bring Cosmo along."

"Nothing would make me happier. And, Owen, I love the cottage."

They'd managed to herd the kids back outside and direct them up the drive toward the barns and the house. The day had turned hot, but the humidity was still relatively low, so it wasn't too unpleasant. The birds were singing and the kids were chattering excitedly, debating who would ride Archer and who'd get Doc.

The combined effects of driving a good eighteen hours in the last twenty-four and passing a near-sleepless night should have left Jade feeling ragged around the edges. Instead, there was a spring in her step and, if they hadn't been marching up the graveled drive, she might have been tempted to do a cartwheel simply because she could.

Life was very good.

Extending her arms wide, she smiled up at a sky as dazzling a blue as the stranger's eyes had been. She sent a silent thanks to him, whoever he was and wherever he was, for providing a most excellent night of restorative sex.

"That's some happy face," Miriam observed. "Care to share?"

Jade lowered her face but didn't bother to erase her goofy smile. Nothing wrong with feeling good. "Thinking about a guy."

"A Florida guy? They can be hot."

"Nope." She shook her head. "Not a Florida guy. I met him last night. We danced and stuff . . ." Her smile stretched like taffy. She had a feeling the memories he'd given her would be making her smile for a long time to come.

"And stuff? As in good hot stuff?" She elbowed Jade in the ribs playfully.

"Shh! Pipe down!" Jade stole a glance at her sisters. Luckily, they were fielding questions from Max and Georgie about whether an ice cream trip to the Shake Shack was in the foreseeable future. "This wasn't just good. It was superlative hot stuff."

"Nice. Did you get his number?"

"No, why should I? I've got way better things to do with my time than call guys up—unless they happen to be balding, adorable men of the cloth."

Miriam gave a laugh. "I guess the Rev will do in a pinch."

"Stuart's been bragging he can match my four-bagger."

"Wait. What's that one mean again?"

It was Jade's turn to elbow her friend. "Miriam, please, you've got to keep bowling terms straight. A four-bagger—aka a clover, and sometimes referred to as a hambone—is when you bowl four strikes in a row. A strike is when your bowling ball hits all the pins. Don't you dare ask what a pin is or I'll break down and cry."

"And Stuart thinks he can throw a four-bagger-clover-hambone whatever?"

"So he claims. I know he's God's BF, Miriam, but I'm going to have to take the good Reverend Stuart Wilde down a couple pegs."

"A girl's gotta do what a girl's gotta do. But, Jade, I'm

worried that bowling is a poor substitute for getting superlative hot stuff. You sure you don't want to check out
what some of the available men in Warburg have to
offer?" Miriam teased.

"Thanks, but no, thanks."

Chapter ❧
FIVE

ON MONDAY afternoon Jade was seated in the office of Ted Guerra, the Warburg Elementary School principal. She'd been in her fair share of principals' offices before—usually for disciplinary reasons—and Guerra's office was a nice departure from the usual ho-hum decorating scheme. It had lots of books, puzzles, and student art. Paintings and drawings covered the walls, and there were even some clay sculptures adorning the book-shelves. On his desk were photographs of his wife and children, the youngest of which looked to be in his late teens.

"Here you go, Jade." Ted Guerra handed her a stapled sheaf of papers. "Just sign the last page of the contract and we'll be set." He lifted a ceramic coffee mug that read *Teachers are heroes* and offered her one of the ball-point pens that filled it.

Taking the contract and pen, she flipped to the last page, signed her name where he'd indicated, wrote in the date, and capped the pen. "It's that easy? Nothing more to it?"

"Not a thing," he replied with a shake of his head. "As soon as Sandy Riley called me with the news that she wouldn't be able to teach this fall, I made immediate arrangements to offer you the temporary appointment. Nothing is more confusing to students than opening the school year without a head teacher. Luckily, we had all your relevant documentation, since you'd applied for a teaching position. In addition, I'd already run a criminal background check on you. Happily, you don't have a record."

Jade answered his smile with a weak one, while inside, her stomach knotted in anxiety. Ted Guerra had moved to Warburg only recently; he wouldn't have necessarily learned about her delinquent past and that the reason she didn't have a rap sheet was because her brushes with the law had all occurred when she was a minor.

But Warburg had more than its fair share of tongue-waggers, so she was more resigned than surprised when he cleared his throat. "I have, however, heard some stories about your high school years. Is there anything you'd like to clarify?"

She liked Ted Guerra. Liked his open, freckled face and the intelligent hazel eyes, liked that his receding hairline made him seem boyish rather than old. Above all, she liked that his expression hadn't gone sour with self-righteous disapproval simply because he'd heard about her unhappy and out-of-control teenage past. The fact that he was giving her a chance to explain told her a lot about his sense of fairness, an important quality in a principal.

Still, this was hardly her favorite topic of conversation. Taking heart that he'd broached the topic of her previous misdemeanors *after* she'd signed the contract—a pretty sure indication that whatever he'd heard wasn't bad enough to prevent him from hiring her—she said, "When my parents died, I went through a dark period. I was really angry and scared and made a lot of stupid and reckless decisions."

He'd probably heard the rumors surrounding her mother's infidelity too, but there was no way she was going to address them. Instead, she said, "Luckily, my sisters, Margot and Jordan, were there for me, and with their help I was able to straighten myself out. Getting in trouble with the Warburg police was a darned good wake-up call too," she added wryly. "Mr. Guerra, I promise that since my last run-in with them at age seventeen, I haven't had so much as a parking ticket."

Ted Guerra nodded. "When the stories about you came to my attention, I looked again at your file. Your academic record and your letters of recommendation are outstanding." Noting the blush that warmed her face, he said, "Really, *outstanding* is the only way to describe someone with a double major in anthropology and education whose thesis received highest honors and who graduated at the top of her class. I'm impressed by the fact that you overcame your difficult adolescence. Not everyone manages to do so—or to do it as successfully. Moreover, I think your past experiences will serve you well as a teacher."

It was a good thing he didn't appear to expect a response, as she would have contradicted all the glowing things he'd said about her by sounding like a total twit, babbling her gratitude.

Instead, he continued, all brisk and businesslike, "Now, I've drafted a letter to the second-grade parents, explaining that you'll be taking over for Sandy until she can come back after winter break. I'll of course highlight your credentials and experience as a student teacher, but I thought it might be nice if, along with my letter, you could write one to the children telling them a little bit about yourself. Nothing too involved, just enough to make them know how pleased you are to be teaching them."

"Sure. That's no problem."

"I called Sandy Riley to let her know you'll be subbing for her. She's delighted—she knows your sister Jordan. She said she'd be happy to lend you her lesson plans from last year if you think they'd be helpful."

"I'd love to look them over, perhaps use them as a springboard for my own plans," she replied.

"Good," he said with a nod. "I'm going to drop by and see how she's doing. I'll collect the materials then. Let's see, what else do we need to cover?" He paused to consult a handwritten list. "Oh, yes, your classroom. I'll take you to see it so that you can figure out what you want on the walls. We've got some visuals in the supply room you can use. There are also some math manipulatives, puzzles, and flash cards. Most everything else you'll have to buy on your own. You've got a three-hundred-dollar budget. After that, expenses and supplies come out of your pocket. A lot of the teachers write a letter to the parents to send in basic supplies like Kleenex. You can draw up a list and put it in your letter or save it until parents' night—that's scheduled two weeks after school opens."

"Okay. And what's your policy on animals in the classroom? Can I buy some fish for the class? It's a good way to get the kids observing nature."

"Sure. Tricia Creighton, who's teaching the other second-grade class, has a terrarium with turtles and lizards. Your room has a southern exposure, so you can have plants in there too."

"Sounds good." Great, in fact. Anything that could turn a blah, ho-hum institutional space into one that excited the imagination was a huge plus. If none of the kids had allergies, perhaps she'd buy some gerbils too and devote a whole corner of the classroom to nature. But no birds. She couldn't bear the sight of a caged bird.

When a phone call for Ted momentarily interrupted their meeting, Jade took the opportunity to compile a mental list of the things she'd be buying in the coming weeks. As shopping lists went, it was a great one. Topping it were the four new ponies she needed to buy for her riding classes. Just below the search for suitable school ponies was a trip to buy a colorful school of fish. She was pretty sure that tetras and cyprinids could live in a tank together. She'd check and then drive to the pet store located on Route 50 and see what fish they stocked. The pet store was next to Screamin' Susie's—a punk hair salon and an old haunt. God, she'd have to pop in to Susie's and say hi to the gang. The trick would be walking out of the shop without having her hair dyed lime green and chopped à la Sid Vicious. It was going to break Susie and co.'s hearts to hear that those rocker days were long gone.

Also on her list was a pilgrimage to Steadman's Saddle Shop to pick up pony tack. Then somewhere, sometime, before the first day of school, she had to squeeze in an outing to buy clothes that weren't jeans, breeches, or didn't come off a fashion designer's rack. She'd ask Margot and Jordan to accompany her as wardrobe advisers; they'd get a major bang out of dressing her like a schoolmarm.

Ted Guerra hung up the phone. "Sorry about that, Jade. I'm trying to get a company to donate microscopes to the school. So, let me give you your class list and then we'll head down to the classroom and take a quick tour of the school so you get a sense of the layout." He picked up a folder that was sitting on top of a pile of papers. "Here," he said, passing it to her. "This has your class roster and your students' evaluations for kindergarten and first grade. Being a local, you might already know some of your kids."

Curious, Jade flipped open the manila folder to see whether she indeed recognized any names. Warburg was a small town, and the children were close in age to Max and Olivia. The list was in alphabetical order. She scanned it, past Chris Alden, Rosie Baxter, Jay Blount, Deirdre Cerra, Hayley Cooper, Patrick Faherty . . . Her gaze stalled, then jumped back to Hayley Cooper.

A choking panic seized her. She coughed to clear her throat. "Um, Ted, this Hayley Cooper . . ." She swallowed. And coughed again. Violently. "Which Cooper is she related to?"

"Do you want some water for that?"

She waved a hand and shook her head, so Ted continued. "Her dad's Rob. He's on the police force here. Do you know the Coopers?"

She must be cursed. Really. Wasn't it only the day before that she'd been crowing to herself about how great her life was, how smoothly things were falling into place, and now this had to happen. She had RoboCop's kid in her class.

Why, oh, why, was her luck so lousy? And she'd just signed the contract; she couldn't bail now. Wouldn't either. She wasn't some wimp to be intimidated by the fact that she'd be teaching the child of the guy who had busted her ass not only once but *twice*. She wasn't a juvie anymore. But still, *damn it all to hell,* she thought. This promised to be a truly awkward situation.

Jade swallowed the thick lump of dismay that was threatening to choke her and tried for a fairly normal, nonhysterical voice.

"Yeah, I kind of know Rob Cooper." The Coopers were a bit like the Radcliffes in that both families had their specialty. The Radcliffes bred and trained horses; the Coopers raised cops. Practically every male in that family had served or was serving on Warburg's police force. But she'd dealt only with Rob—aka RoboCop— and she would have been happy if she never had to lay eyes on him again.

"Oh, good," Ted replied with a satisfied nod. "As you'll soon discover, Hayley's a sweet kid. Bright and eager. Rob's doing a marvelous job parenting."

She tried to smile at the enthusiastic endorsement, but it was hard to reconcile her memory of him—the quintessential hard-assed cop—with Ted Guerra's description of Rob Cooper as a first-rate father.

"Actually, Jade, Hayley was one of the reasons I thought you'd be the perfect hire. You can relate to what she's going through, having lost a mother yourself."

Ted Guerra's comment caused Jade's brow to furrow. She was fairly certain she'd never heard anything about Rob Cooper's wife dying. If she had, she must have stored the memory in some far recess of her mind. Avoidance was key in dealing with anything pertaining to Officer Rob Cooper. Heck, she even made elaborate detours whenever she was in town so she wouldn't pass the police station and perhaps catch sight of him in his scary mirrored aviators and unsmiling face. She had this unshakable fear that if she so much as jaywalked, he'd catch her at it. It was absurd, but, hey, wasn't that the definition of superstitions, that they defied the rational?

But the news that he'd lost his wife made Jade feel a pang of sympathy for him and his motherless daughter. How rough for both of them. "Uh, I don't think I'd heard about his wife. . . ." Her sentence dangled as she tried to remember if she knew the wife's name. Nope, a total blank.

"Rebecca," Ted supplied.

"When did she die?"

"It was several years back. As I said, Hayley's a great kid, extremely well adjusted. But at this stage of development, issues can arise unexpectedly. I think you'd be the right person to help her handle any emotional problems that might occur."

"I appreciate your faith in me."

And, really, wasn't this why she wanted to teach in the first place? She wanted to help kids, share with them the things she knew and had experienced. That Ted Guerra believed she had the potential to help a child made her more determined than ever not to freak just because the little girl's dad had been as frightening as any bogeyman to Jade's teenage self.

But she was no longer that unhappy teen. When she saw Rob Cooper again, she'd probably laugh herself silly over how utterly non-intimidating he was. Heck, he'd probably developed a gut from a steady police-officer diet of donuts. . . .

Rob finished his last set of chin-ups, the veins bulging in his arms as he pulled his body up and held it, releasing slowly as he dropped to the ground. He walked over to the sit-up bench and switched places with Eric Drogan, his workout partner. Forty crunches followed by three minutes of jumping rope and the set was complete. Next they grabbed medicine balls for wood chops, side throws and slams, squat presses, and push-ups. They ended the last part of the workout with a set of plyometrics: lateral hurdle-jumping and tuck jumps.

"Damn, that was brutal," Eric said, toweling the sweat off his face and neck and plucking his soaked shirt from his shoulders after he and Rob had stretched their hamstrings and quads.

"Yeah, it felt good, didn't it?" Rob grinned as he brought his water bottle to his lips and chugged.

"That's because you're five years younger than me and don't spend your day sitting in front of a computer. We've got to get Scott in here. I want to see him cry." Scott and Eric had been on the football team in high school together, Scott playing quarterback, Eric wide receiver. They'd remained best friends.

"He's got Emma designing workouts for him."

"Forget it, then," Eric said. "He'd kick my ass and then offer to write a freelance article describing it in detail for the *Courier*. And in spite of Scott having slept through Mr. Jawolski's Honors English class, it'd be a damned good piece. That lazy SOB writes better than most of my staff reporters." Eric was the news editor for the local paper, the *Warburg Courier,* and though he pretended to complain about his junior staff, it was the excellence of their reporting that kept the *Courier* alive when so many other small papers were closing their doors. "You got time for a brew? After this workout I won't even have to drink one of those damned light beers."

"Sorry, I can't today. Hayley's birthday is on Wednesday. I still have a couple presents on my list."

"What does she want?"

"A pony. Correction. She wants a herd of ponies."

"A herd of ponies, huh? That's what I like about Hayley. She thinks big. So, are you going to spend the rest of the afternoon building a corral in your backyard?"

"Nope. I'm going to swing by Steadman's Saddle Shop and see if they can recommend a good riding teacher for youngsters."

Eric slung his gym towel over his shoulder. "They'd know better than anyone. Every horse person in Loudoun County shops there. You planning a birthday party for Hayley?"

Rob nodded. "A family party on Wednesday and tomorrow, as a warm-up to the big event; seven of her friends are coming over for pizza, cake, and a sleepover."

"A sleepover?" Eric, whose face was still flushed from the workout, shook his head. "Man, you've got guts. You going to wear your uniform to keep the peace?"

"Not necessary. I think I can keep eight little girls in line."

Showered and changed into his street clothes, Rob drove through the quiet Warburg streets and pulled his Mustang into Steadman's parking lot. It was funny: He'd lived in Warburg his entire life but had never entered the saddle shop, though he knew its owners, the

Steadmans. Like the Coopers, they were Warburg natives and the kids had all gone to the same schools, though not at the same time as Rob. Sara and Adam Steadman's children were older, though he seemed to recall one Steadman—a nephew—being in high school a few years ahead of his sister, Emma.

The bell attached to the store's door chimed as he entered. Immediately, the rich scent of leather filled his nostrils, and his eyes picked out the gleam of stainless steel—bits and whatnot—among the tack on display. While he stood taking stock, Sara Steadman, dressed in lime-green trousers and a yellow top, her silver hair cut in a short bob, came up to him. "Hi, may I help you—oh, it's Rob Cooper, isn't it?"

He nodded and smiled. "Yes. Hello, Mrs. Steadman. I came here to ask whether you might have the name of a good riding instructor."

"Lots of names," she informed him with a nod. "We keep a binder listing the local barns that offer services such as boarding, training, lessons—private and group, what ages and levels and discipline." She walked toward the counter in the back of the store, leading him past displays of saddles and bridles and halters and circular racks filled with white, pale blue, yellow, and pink shirts, dark-colored breeches, and that other kind of riding pants whose name Rob didn't know, just as he didn't know squat about what Sara Steadman was happily rattling on about.

"I'm afraid you've lost me, Mrs. Steadman. Discipline?"

"The type of riding the barn teaches," she explained. "Around here, English dominates, but there are some Western riders too."

"Oh. I think I'm looking for an English instructor."

"Well, then, you'll want to look in the first section of the book." She opened a three-ring binder nearly as thick as the Bible to the first page and tapped it with her finger. "We have a key here to help explain each barn's specialty, equitation, hunter, cross-country, dressage . . ." As she ran her finger down the typed page, that totally lost feeling came over Rob once again. Too bad Hayley wasn't crazy about basketball. There was a sport he knew.

Adam Steadman had just finished ringing up a customer. Seeing them, he came over. "Well, if it isn't Officer Cooper. My wife break the law again?"

"Adam!"

"Happily, no, Mr. Steadman. And it's Rob. I'm off duty."

"And looking for riding lessons, not arrests," Sara said, shaking her head as if despairing of her husband.

"And who's going to be taking the lessons? You?"

Rob laughed. "No. Riding's not exactly my cup of tea. I want to find an instructor for my daughter, Hayley. She took a few lessons earlier this summer and has become horse mad."

"Bitten by the horse bug, huh? Well, that's a great thing, especially in this day and age. Far too many kids are sitting on their fannies staring at some computer or idiotic video game. So you're looking for lessons for your little girl. She's what, six?"

"Seven, the day after tomorrow," Rob said.

Sara Steadman beamed with pleasure. "Isn't that wonderful."

"What you need is a really good children's riding instructor, and it so happens that you're in luck, Rob. Ned Connelly was in here earlier today. Sara, did we already file the announcement?"

"Yes, I didn't want to mislay it. Just a sec." She began flipping through the pages.

"Ned Connelly. He works for the Radcliffes, doesn't he?" Rob asked.

"Yes, at Rosewood Farm. Beautiful place. And they breed fantastic horses. Our nephew, Brian, bought a mare from them, an event prospect," Adam told Rob, as if that meant something. "Gypsy Queen's a terrific goer."

"Travis Maher runs the horse farm for them." Rob knew Travis. A good man, who had made something of himself in spite of his father being in and out of custody for public intoxication and disruption of the peace more times than any kid should have to witness. "Is he offering the riding lessons?"

Adam shook his head. "Travis only works with a handful of adults who've bought horses from Rosewood. It's a good way to make sure the green horses get the proper training. No, the children's program at Rosewood is being run by the youngest of the girls—Jade."

"Here's the flyer," Sara announced happily. "I'll write down the information and the days and times Jade will be teaching. Kids' lessons don't start until the third week in September, so everyone can get settled into the school year, but you'll want to give Jade a ring ASAP."

"Sara's right about that," her husband said. "Once people hear about Jade offering lessons, her classes will fill up fast. She's an outstanding rider and she's already proven herself as a teacher. She taught her nieces and nephew, and now those kids are winning their equitation classes. . . ."

But Rob had stopped listening to Sara and Adam Steadman. He was busy remembering what the teenage Jade Radcliffe had excelled at: seeking out trouble and finding it in spades. Out of respect for the Steadmans, he managed to keep his face expressionless, even as mentally he drew a big fat line through the idea of Jade teaching Hayley.

Jade Radcliffe. Christ, he'd blocked her from his mind for so long, the bitterness he felt at hearing her name took him by surprise. Though it shouldn't. Not when losing Becky was an ache in his heart he felt every single day.

Because if not for Jade Radcliffe, Becky might still be alive.

Rob hated thinking of that late-spring night. He'd been on duty when a call came through to the station that minors were drinking at the Den. The Den was known as the hookup bar in town, and the joint's owner had been skirting the underage-drinking law with increasing frequency. From Rob's earliest days on the force, underage drinking had been a hot-button issue for him, as too many young lives were lost to drunk driving.

The anonymous tip had been on the money. And one of the minors nabbed had been none other than Jade Radcliffe, who'd gotten into the bar with an ID as fake as AstroTurf. Not only had she been in possession of a fake ID—a Class 1 misdemeanor—she'd been the cause of a fight that had broken out when a friend of the Radcliffe family tried to hustle her out of the Den over the objections of one piss-drunk, lousy excuse for humanity.

While Rob had been busy hauling Jade Radcliffe's scrawny underage butt down to the station, Becky had been sick at home, dosing herself with chamomile tea, applesauce, and dry toast as she battled the stomach bug that had hit her earlier in the week.

Only as it turned out it hadn't been a bug or the flu, or even the vicious menstrual cramps that often plagued Becky. It had been acute appendicitis, and when Becky's appendix ruptured, the bacteria flooded her system and laid waste to it. Sepsis had attacked her body with devastating efficiency, shutting down her organs one by one.

Instead of sleeping, Becky had stopped breathing.

And while his sweet, beautiful wife lay dying, Rob had been down at the station dealing with Jade Radcliffe; Owen Gage, the Radcliffe family friend; and Howie Driscoll, the drunken slob who'd done his best to beat the crap out of Gage when he'd tried to stop Jade from shaking her booty in one of the Den's notorious "dance" contests.

Rob had booked Howie first, since he'd already starred in one too many bar fights, then slapped Gage with a healthy fine for disorderly conduct. By the time he'd gotten around to testing Jade Radcliffe for alcohol, she was shaking with fear, from the top of her platinum-spiked head to her feet.

That she'd told the truth about not having consumed any alcohol meant squat—he'd already busted her before for underage drinking. He figured it was just a matter of timing. By the end of the dance contest she'd entered, she'd have probably worked up a decent thirst. With the fake ID tucked into her jeans' pocket, she'd have had no trouble sauntering up to the bar and ordering whatever concoction tickled her teenage taste buds. A couple of drinks later, any iota of common sense would have deserted her, leaving her ripe for a truly stupid and dangerous stunt. Consumed as he was with figuring out how to make Jade Radcliffe sorry she'd ever waltzed into a bar with a fake ID, he hadn't spared a thought for Becky.

But then his cell rang and his life changed forever.

His mother's voice was almost unrecognizable from the effort to remain calm, and her story so strange as to be almost unbelievable. She'd dropped by the house with a quart of homemade chicken soup and some orange Jell-O, because she'd been worried Becky might have skipped dinner, and found her in bed—not asleep, but utterly unresponsive. She hadn't been able to find a pulse. The paramedics were on the way.

Rob had raced to the hospital but arrived too late. The infection had spread too far and too fast, the ER doctors told him. They hadn't been able to do anything to save her.

His Becky, his wonderful, loving wife and the mother of his child, was gone.

It was so quick, so terrifyingly quick.

She had been alive and then she was dead.

Rob closed his eyes against the pain that assaulted him. Opening them, his gaze landed on Jade Radcliffe's name. *No*, he thought. *No damned way.*

He knew it wasn't right to blame Jade Radcliffe for Becky's death. He knew it. But knowing and doing didn't always go hand in hand. The Steadmans were obviously fond of Jade. Considering the Radcliffes' involvement in all things equine-related, Rob didn't doubt that Jade was a very good rider, but that didn't change the fact that he didn't want Hayley anywhere near her. There were riding barns all around the county. He'd ask some other horsey people and find a suitable instructor for Hayley.

MARGOT HAD made good on her promise to ask Ellie to prepare her fried chicken. Jade had already helped herself to seconds, which was fine since she'd ridden Cosmo, Valentine, and Carmen during the afternoon—in addition to working with a young mare named Blanche. The session with Blanche had focused on getting the brown Thoroughbred mare to stand still when Jade mounted her, then having her walk calmly toward the rail, the first baby steps in the under-saddle training process. If all that activity hadn't justified an extra few hundred calories, well, Jade figured she'd burn them off after dinner when she sweated over the letter she had to compose to her new students.

To go with the fried chicken, Ellie had made a salad of spinach and paper-thin sliced mushrooms, a mini-mountain of which Margot had on her plate. They lingered over the meal, enjoying the summer evening with its deep-lavender sky and the blue-green of the lawn and gardens. The perfume of the roses growing near the porch where the family was dining mixed with the scent of citronella candles burning brightly in the lanterns Margot had placed on the long wooden table.

The sound of the car wending its way up the drive and then stopping in front of the house was easy to detect in the quiet of the evening. A door opened, then another one, and Jade heard Jordan's voice, answered by Owen's deeper one, and then a shared laugh.

"Dessert's arrived," she remarked to no one in particular. Jordan, Owen, and Neddy were joining them for dessert. Kate, Max, and Olivia had left earlier to visit their father and stepmother, who lived in D.C. Like his older siblings, Neddy was also having a sleepover. He was going to be staying here at the big house so that Jordan and Owen could have a night to themselves—which was probably why Owen and Jordan had been looking pretty darn giddy.

Next week, after Margot made one of her whirlwind trips to New York where she'd be posing for a shoot for *W*, it would be her and Travis's turn to have a free night. Jade had seen the date on the kitchen calendar marked with stars and hearts, so it was an easy guess that, come the day, Margot and Travis would be seriously jazzed too.

Jordan climbed the porch steps, a large ceramic bowl in her arms. Out of compassion for Margot and her upcoming shoot, she'd made a peach and raspberry fruit salad for dessert. Jade didn't mind the lack of Jordan's killer brownies; she'd eaten one for breakfast.

Setting the bowl onto the side table where the dessert plates were stacked, Jordan sat down beside Jade, snagging a mushroom off her plate as she did. "Yum. I love Ellie's lemon vinaigrette. She knows just how much pepper and cayenne to add. So how did your meeting with Ted go, Jade?"

"Good, he's a nice guy."

Jordan nodded, filching another mushroom. "I like how supportive he is of his teachers. It's made such a difference in the energy level and enthusiasm in the school. Did he give you your class list?"

"Yeah, Jade. What about the class list? You haven't mentioned anything about it," Margot said.

Probably because Margot and Jordan were both going to freak when she read off a certain name, Jade thought, squirming inwardly. Oh, well, they were going to find out sooner or later. "The list is on the kitchen counter. I'll go—"

"No, I'll get it," Jordan said, rising. "Owen and I brought a nice white wine to go with dessert. We think it might be perfect for Miriam and Andy's wedding, but we wanted your opinion first before we have a wine tasting with them. Shall I bring everyone a glass?"

"Most definitely," Jade said. Her nerves were getting jumpy thinking about what her sisters were going to say when they saw Hayley Cooper's name.

"It is so weird, your being legal, Jade." Margot shook her head.

"Yup. In all fifty states." Jade grinned.

"Do you need help with the glasses?" Travis asked.

"No, thanks. Owen should be downstairs now—Neddy was out like a light the second the car started. Owen's probably opening the bottle."

They'd cleared the dishes to the side table and replaced them with five dessert plates when Jordan and Owen returned, armed with a bottle of Sancerre and glasses—and, in Jordan's hand, the manila folder Ted Guerra had given Jade.

"Neddy settled?" Jade asked as she eyed the folder and then her sister's face. Jordan hadn't peeked inside. Otherwise, she wouldn't be nearly so calm.

"Sleeping like a lamb. Didn't even stir when I put him in the crib," Owen answered. "That long ride he took with Ned on Lena must have done the trick."

"So let's drink a toast to Ned. And may the Orioles not lose too badly tonight," Jade said. Ned was as dedicated an Orioles fan as they came. Instead of joining them tonight, he was parked in his favorite recliner in Thistle Cottage, his dinner on a tray propped on his knees and a beer resting by his feet, watching the Orioles against the Blue Jays.

After they'd all drunk to Ned's health and commented on the inability of the Orioles to defeat anyone this season, Owen said, "So, Jade, your meeting with Ted Guerra went smoothly?"

"Yeah—"

"And this is Jade's class list." Jordan picked up the file she'd set by her glass. "Can I look at it?"

Jade took a fortifying sip of wine. "Go ahead." Jordan was bound to be mellower than Margot.

It took a while, which was strange as Jordan was very detail-oriented, but finally her half sister gave the expected soft cry of dismay. "Oh, no, Jade, I am so sorry! What rotten luck. Eugene Harrison—I did wonder whether you'd get him."

"What?" Jade said. God, *she* was the one with the poor attention skills. Obsessed with having Hayley Cooper in her class, she'd missed Eugene Harrison's name completely.

"Eugene Harrison? Is that who I think it is?" Owen asked.

"Can I see that?" Margot stretched her arm across the table so Jordan could pass her the list. "And in answer to your question, Owen, if you're thinking, *Holy crap, that must be Eugene and Nonie Harrison's grandson,* you'd be on the money."

"Their son, who's also Eugene, and his wife, Christy, moved back to Warburg last spring," Jordan explained to Owen, who'd been in Warburg for only five years and thus was still a relative newbie when it came to knowing the genealogy of its families. "Eugene and Christy told everyone they decided to relocate for the schools, but Marla heard a different story, about something happening down in Charlotte that suddenly made Eugene a less-than-perfect bank VP. According to Marla, he was let go *without* a severance package."

"Ouch. That had to hurt," Travis said.

"Ouch, indeed. Too bad I can't feel a whole lot of sympathy for them. Christy and Eugene have only been back for a few months, but they've already made it clear that all of Warburg should be kowtowing to them," Jordan said.

"A Harrison trait." Owen picked up the wine and refilled their glasses. "So I gather this means there are now three Eugene Harrisons in Warburg? Isn't that terribly redundant?"

"Yeah, but it's better than having three Nonies. That wouldn't just be redundant, it'd be downright ugly," Travis said. "By the way, this is a nice wine, Owen. I think Andy and Miriam are going to like it."

"Thanks. Let's have another toast: to the one and only Nonie." He grinned. "If there were ever a definitive argument against cloning, Nonie would be it."

Travis laughed. "Very true."

"Poor Nonie," Jordan said with a decided lack of sympathy. There was no love lost between the Radcliffes and the Harrisons.

Margot had remained silent during the exchange, as she studied Jade's class list. Jade counted the seconds and got to *three,* then Margot's cry of "Oh my God!" and her sharp blue gaze zeroed in on Jade. "I cannot believe you didn't mention this." Passing the folder to Travis, she said, "Take a look under the C's."

"What, are you talking about Hayley Cooper? She's a sweet little girl, Margot," Jordan said. "Remember how cute she was in the winter pageant dressed up as a snowflake? She and Olivia stole the show."

"Uh-oh, I have a sinking feeling that Hayley Cooper's dad is going to be none other than Rob Cooper—your favorite police officer. And mine," Owen added with a quick scowl. "I'm still annoyed at his sticking me with a two-hundred-dollar fine after I put my face on the line for you, Jade."

"Rob Cooper's probably forgotten all about Jade," Jordan said.

Margot cocked an eyebrow in disbelief. "No way. After the stunts she pulled?"

"Rob Cooper doesn't strike me as the type to hold grudges."

Margot shook her head. "Sweetie, you're too forgiving—"

"Hon, I'm gonna have to side with Jordan on this," Travis said. "Rob's not likely to give Jade grief. It's been years since she crossed paths with Rob in his official capacity. And he'll be seeing her as a teacher—not a delinquent. And parents appreciate good teachers."

Jade decided it was time to put in her two cents' worth. "I hope you're right, Travis. But I've got to admit that if I'd had my crystal ball and seen I was going to be teaching his daughter one day, I probably wouldn't have signed RoboCop up for the donut-of-the-month club."

"You know, I seem to recall mentioning that that particular idea might come back to bite you," Margot said drily.

"You did indeed, O Prissy One."

While Margot shot Jade a narrowed-eyed glare, Jordan swiveled in the chair to face her youngest sister. "Did you just call Margot prissy? I thought that was my title."

"Nope, Owen saved you. Since getting hitched you've grown increasingly un-prissy."

"Thanks for noticing," Jordan said, beaming.

Owen graced Jade with a wink.

Across the table, Margot raised her hand and wagged her fingers. "For the record, I would like it noted that I am *not* prissy. And as for Rob Cooper, he showed a great deal of restraint in his dealings with you. I will always like him for that."

"Personally, I've never thought of the word *prissy* in

association with any Radcliffe female—certainly not you three," Travis said gallantly. "As for the matter of having both a Cooper *and* a Harrison in the first class you ever teach, well, it could be a whole heck of a lot worse."

"Yes." Owen nodded in agreement. "Jade could have half the parents in her class wanting her tarred and feathered."

Jade barely managed to avoid spitting out her wine. "Gee, thanks for pointing that out, guys. Listen, I'll be fine, truly. I'm taking the Doris Day approach." At the four blank looks she received, she huffed impatiently, "Come on, as in, 'Que Sera Sera'? You all seriously have to get up to speed with your pop references."

Across the table, Travis's shoulders were shaking with laughter as he brought his wine to his lips. Good, she thought. One family member distracted, three to go. "So, Owen, do you think Jimmy Stewart was in agony every time Doris started singing?"

Owen cocked a dark brow at her obvious ploy to change the subject but obliged her nonetheless, saying, "I wouldn't dare speak for Jimmy Stewart, but *The Man Who Knew Too Much* was definitely not my favorite Hitchcock. Give me *Rear Window* any day."

"Grace Kelly was divine in *Rear Window*," Jordan said, rising from the table and beginning to clear the dessert plates.

"A goddess," Margot said solemnly as she stood to help, placing the empty glasses on a wooden tray. "Do you remember the actress who gave Jimmy his massages and who helped Grace sneak into Raymond Burr's apartment? What was her name again?" she asked.

While they searched their collective memory banks for Thelma Ritter's name, Jade breathed a sigh of relief at no longer having to worry about Rob Cooper. She wouldn't have to think about him again for another twenty minutes, until she began composing her letter to her new students. A reprieve that could last even longer if she volunteered to do the dishes. Dishwashing had never looked so good.

It was 8:30 P.M. on Tuesday night, exactly two and a half hours since Hayley's birthday cake—decorated by Rob's mom with a prancing chocolate-and-vanilla-frosted pony and *Happy 7th Birthday, Hayley*—had been consumed, along with tubs of ice cream and bagfuls of Gummi worms, and a shell-shocked Rob was wondering if this horde of girls was ever going to calm down or if the house was ever going to look the same.

Every piece of furniture in the living room had been pushed against the wall—eight girls were as strong as an army of ants—in order to clear a space for a dance floor so the girls could practice dance moves to Taylor Swift, Miley Cyrus, and Justin Bieber.

How in hell had they memorized all these inane lyrics? More puzzling still, when had Hayley learned them? And which one of these future *American Idol* contestants had had the bright idea to raid the kitchen for spoons to serve as mikes, the better to belt out the tunes? Was all this stuff programmed into their DNA?

Upstairs, his bedroom had undergone a similar transformation. Before they'd decided to turn into musical divas, the girls had been going at it like WWE stars. His bed had been turned into a trampoline and then a wrestling arena, his pillows used as assault weapons.

Not even the second-floor bathroom was left inviolate. He'd already had to take the plunger to the bathroom toilet—to shrieks of high-drama disgust and exaggerated gagging noises.

"They looked so cute and harmless when they arrived," he said, trying not to check his watch again. He realized he might start whimpering if the watch hands didn't start inching closer to nine o'clock, the hour when he could send the little demons—oops, darlings—to the family room with their sleeping bags and backpacks. He no longer held out much hope that they'd sleep, but at least they'd be contained.

"Little girls, cute and harmless? Ha, that's a good one." Emma had come by to lend a hand after teaching her aerobics class. "They're much more terrifying than boys. And this is just the beginning, Rob. Wait until high school. You'll be missing the days of watching them gyrate to Miley and Company. Oh, and speaking of high school, guess who I spotted this morning?"

"Who?" he asked, jumping back from his post by the door to avoid being run over as two girls streaked by. He caught the words *costume change* before they thundered up the stairs.

"Jade Radcliffe. She was at Braverman's picking up an order. I don't think she saw me—not sure she would have recognized me anyway, as I was a year behind her in school—but she looked great."

The two or three memories Rob had of Jade Radcliffe didn't mesh with "looking great." In one of his mental snapshots, she was passed out in the back of his patrol car and reeking of vomit and Jägermeister after he'd broken up an underage party. In another, she was shrouded in an overlarge hoodie and had just dumped a bucket of filthy water—a putrid mix of day-old vomit and soap—over his boots and police uniform. He'd spent minutes yelling at the pointy tip of her hood as her bony shoulders shook—whether from terror or mirth he'd never ascertained. The last time he'd seen her was at the Den, when he'd busted her with her fake college ID. Her hair had been chopped to an inch from her skull and bleached yellow-white. He remembered her face, how fear had leeched it of color until it was almost as pale as her hair. Her lips had been pressed into a thin, quivery line and heavy mascara had lined her vivid green eyes. No, looking great was not how he ever remembered Jade Radcliffe.

He frowned, annoyed at the realization that Jade had the same exotic eye color as the woman with whom he'd spent the night in Norfolk. His brow cleared as he recalled how very different the woman's eyes had been, sparkling with intelligence, shining with pleasure.

Emma was still talking. "I guess Jade's back working at Rosewood Farm."

"Yeah, she's teaching kids how to ride."

"How'd you know that?" In the next breath, Emma used the I-don't-take-anybody's-crap tone she'd learned from growing up with three older brothers. "Katie. That side table is *not* a dance stage. Get down now. *Now,* Katie."

And Katie Girard, who'd previously played deaf to all adult admonishment, dropped to the floor.

"Good job, Em. Thanks." Had Katie broken that table, Rob would have been tempted to handcuff her. Becky had bought the table the first year of their marriage.

"You're welcome. So when did you hear about Jade teaching riding?"

"I went to Steadman's Saddle Shop to ask whether they knew of any good riding instructors. Adam Steadman told me she's giving lessons."

"Wow. So are you going to sign Hayley up?"

"With her? No."

She raised her dark brow inquiringly. "No?"

"There are other riding teachers in Warburg."

Emma shrugged. "Sure there are. But I bet Hayley would really like Jade. I always thought she was the coolest girl in high school."

"Popular, you mean."

"Hardly," Emma scoffed. "Blair Hood, Courtney

Joseph, and Amanda Coles made it their personal mission to treat Jade like a pariah. And they tried to get everyone else in school to as well. The rumors they spread about her, the nasty tricks they pulled on her, were really shitty, Rob. And still Jade managed to be cooler than any of them. God, there was this period where she changed her hair color about every other week. It was wild."

The admiration in Emma's voice had him glancing at her in surprise. He supposed he'd been too absorbed in his life with Becky and their baby girl to pay attention to the goings-on in his kid sister's high school—unless one of the students happened to cross his path while he was in uniform, as Jade Radcliffe had. He was about to question her further when an earsplitting shriek rent the air, followed by a crash that had them both glancing up at the ceiling.

"My turn." He sighed, already moving toward the stairs.

It was going to be a long night. But Hayley had a huge grin on her face as she and Jenny Ferris did the bump while they warbled along with Miley, singing "Hoedown Throwdown."

He'd do almost anything to see that smile on his daughter's face, even allow his house to be wrecked by a band of female imps.

Chapter ❧
SEVEN

IF A person wanted to shop for a horse, the man to turn to was Ned Connelly. Not that Jade's brother-in-law Travis or even Margot or Jordan weren't excellent judges of horseflesh, but looking over a horse from teeth to tail, making sure the animal was 100 percent sound and would suit the job for which it was being bought, put a twinkle in Ned's eyes like nothing else could. It didn't even matter to him that they were shopping for ponies rather than broodmares or studs to improve Rosewood Farm's bloodlines. Ned was as happy as the kids buckled in the backseat of the Rover.

Jade had drafted Kate, Max, and Olivia to come and help pick out the ponies. She'd been watching them ride since they could walk; seeing how they did on unknown ponies would give her a good sense of whether the ponies would be proper school ponies. A school pony had certain requirements. It had to be kind and patient, willing to let a novice learn on its back with good grace. While most ponies had their quirks, Jade intended to vet the four she was buying as carefully as possible to avoid bringing home any ponies from hell. She'd seen the like plenty of times: the ponies that intentionally brushed up against jump standards in order to knock a kid off the saddle, the ones that bolted into the middle of the riding ring for an impromptu roll in the dirt, never mind that a saddle and child were still attached to their backs, or the others that engaged in a constant tug-of-war with the reins. She'd even once seen a kid literally slide down a pony's neck, doing a slow-motion face dive into the dirt.

Of course, an argument could be made for learning how to ride the tough cases—both horses and ponies—but Jade believed that for young riders it was better to have them first develop the skills and coordination necessary to good riding. Then they could tackle the more temperamental mounts.

Dressed in jodhpurs and paddock boots, Kate and Max, with Olivia sandwiched between them, squirmed with excitement at the prospect of trying out the ponies Jade had made appointments to see.

Jade was feeling pretty excited too. She felt lucky to have three young riders of different abilities and size to test the ponies—though even six-year-old Olivia was no novice. Fearless and determined to ride as well as her older brother and sister, she'd begun cantering at age five.

Jade knew that by the end of this day the kids would have learned a ton about riding and ponies. What better way to keep the traditions her family embraced alive in the youngest generation? And how great that the three kids who'd shown her how much fun it was to teach were helping her pick out the school ponies! Having Ned Connelly join them today was the proverbial icing on the cake. Ned had been her and Jordan and Margot's first teacher and would be sharing his decades of knowledge with all four of them today.

The very day Jade had returned to Rosewood, Ned started calling around to breeders and owners. They'd picked Windy Hill Ponies for their first visit; this was the farm where Jordan and he had found Archer, the pony the kids rode along with Doc Holliday, who at age twenty-four still won ribbons in children's hunter classes.

Located about thirty minutes north of Warburg, Windy Hill bred its own ponies but also acted as selling agents for owners who'd outgrown their mounts—a sad eventuality for most pony owners. The farm's manager, Ralph Whittaker, had told Jade and Ned that he had a number of sound, seasoned campaigners that could be ridden as school ponies, taken out on the hunt field for a morning's ride, and also do a competitive turn in the show ring—reasons enough for Ned to be nearly as excited as Kate, Max, Olivia, and Jade herself.

From the backseat, Max piped up. "Aunt Jade, are we bringing the ponies home today?"

"No, Max, today we're going to try to find some we really like. If that happens, I'll come back for another visit to see whether they're just as nice the second time, because some ponies can be nice one day and then super-cranky another. We want ponies that are as fun to be around as Doc and Archer." Noting the three disappointed faces reflected in the rearview mirror, she added, "Don't worry, guys, Doc and Archer will have new barn mates very soon."

"And as soon as they do, we get to start riding them, so they'll be super-good for the kids who are going to be taking lessons with you." At eight, Max liked to plan in a big way. He'd probably be ready to run a company by age twelve.

"That's right. You all are going to be very busy."

"I hope Carly Ferris and her sister, Jenny, sign up for lessons with you, Aunt Jade. Carly and Jenny are nice," Kate said.

Jenny Ferris. She was one of Jade's future second-grade students. What a relief to know that there was one kid in her class who was non-headache material; if Kate liked her, that was recommendation enough.

"We'll have to see. Mr. and Mrs. Ferris may have other after-school activities lined up for them."

"No, Jenny really wants to ride." Olivia's voice rang

with conviction. "She and Hayley are always asking me stuff about riding."

And that would be Hayley Cooper. It occurred to Jade that she could get a full report from her nieces and nephew on a number of the kids in her class, a report that would reveal far more than anything she'd read in the first-grade teacher's evaluations.

She flicked the indicator, taking the exit off Route 15 and heading west. "So what do you guys think of Hayley Cooper? You were in the winter pageant with her, right, Liv?"

Olivia nodded her bright blond head. "Hayley and I were snowflakes. She was really good. But I felt kinda bad for her, 'cause at the dress rehearsal lots of mommies were helping with the sets and costumes and makeup and stuff and Bobbi Neese asked Hayley where *her* mommy was and Hayley said she was dead and then she left quickly. Then I had to pee and, when I went into the girls' bathroom, she was there. She was crying. It was so sad."

Jade swallowed. She didn't like to think of a little girl crying for her dead mother. It brought back too many memories. "I hope you did your best to make her feel better, Liv."

"I asked her if she wanted to play jacks until it was our turn to snow. Hayley can go all the way up to fivesies. I can too now, but I could only do threesies back then. I don't like Bobbi Neese. She's mean. I think she knew Hayley's mommy was up in heaven, but she asked Hayley anyway."

"That's crummy," Max said. "Don't you think so, Ned?"

"I sure do."

Jade felt Ned give her a sidelong glance, and consciously she relaxed her fingers on the steering wheel.

"You'll want to turn right at Overhill Road, Miss

Jade. Then it's about a quarter of a mile farther on the left."

"Thanks, Ned," she said, pleased her voice was steady. Lots of kids lost their parents and had to deal with the hurt. There was no reason to get choked up over it, she told herself.

From the middle of the backseat, Olivia leaned forward and tapped Jade's shoulder. "Hayley Cooper really likes horses. Maybe she'll want to take lessons at our farm too. She and Jenny Ferris play together lots."

It was unlikely that Rob Cooper's daughter would ever take riding lessons with her, but there was no point in explaining the whys and wherefores to Olivia. "I guess we'll have to see whether she signs up, won't we?"

"How about we concentrate on finding some good ponies today so that there *are* lessons to give," Ned suggested. "Because I'm pretty confident the rest will work itself out just fine after that."

"Yeah, let's do what Ned says." Max bumped the back of his reddish-brown head against the leather upholstery in an enthusiastic nod. "Let's find some good ponies for Aunt Jade."

"And Rosewood," Kate added.

"And me," Olivia giggled.

"Why for you too, Liv?" Max asked.

" 'Cause I need more ponies to love."

No ponies had ever been as thoroughly inspected as the ones at Windy Hill, Jade decided. Ned and she had gone over them from the tips of their pointy ears to their swishy tails and then down to their tiny hooves. Legs were checked for swelling, heat, or stiffness; hooves for cracks, abscesses, or any sensitivity. Eyes and noses had to be clear. And, as it was high summer, the ponies' coats needed to be gleaming with health.

Of course, this was only the beginning of the inspection. She and Ned closely watched the ponies Ralph Whittaker showed them, noting how their ears worked around the children—if they remained cocked forward or pinned back with their tails swishing in warning. Did any of the ponies shift restlessly as the kids moved around them, perhaps picking up a rear hoof? Did any appear head-shy, making it next to impossible for a child to learn how to slip on a bridle or attach a halter? Any pony that showed even the slightest annoyance around Kate, Max, and Olivia was immediately scratched from Jade's list.

Once in the exercise ring, the ponies were scrutinized just as carefully. It was great that she had three different riders to watch, in addition to Ralph's thirteen-year-old daughter, Jessica, who hopped on each pony as well. For today's visit, Jade decided that she'd let the kids do the riding. If any were fine enough to warrant a second visit, then she'd get in the saddle herself, never mind that her booted feet would be hanging well below the barrels of the ponies' bellies.

Luckily, the ponies Ned and she were most interested in were large, the biggest measuring 14.1 hands, for not only would that allow her to ride them should they require some fine-tuning, but as a financial investment they would offer a greater return. Larger ponies wouldn't be outgrown too quickly by her young students.

"This lot looks very fine," Ned said quietly.

Jade gave a little nod, watching the four young riders circle them on the rail of the exercise ring. Olivia was posting to the trot of an all-white pony named Dickens; Kate, astride a flashy bay named Maggie Mae, had just picked up the canter; and Max was circling in a two-point position on a chestnut named Hopscotch. Jessica was on another chestnut, this one a mare called Sweet Virginia, who had four matching socks and a stripe down her face, and was taking a three-foot double-oxer jump like a dream.

Ralph had been in the horse-dealing business for years and had known Ned for almost as many, so he was pretty mellow about the somewhat unorthodox method of showing the ponies to them. Nor did he mind when Jade called the kids into the center of the ring to have them switch mounts so that she could see whether with the change of riders the ponies performed any differently.

Jade asked the kids to ride in single file, as they would in a lesson. Then she had them pass one another, switching the order of the ponies to test whether any got antsy being in the middle or having to bring up the rear of the line.

They'd walked, trotted, and cantered in both directions, taking the ponies over a variety of jumps. Olivia stuck to cavalettis—rails laid on the ground—and a low crossbar; Kate and Max took them over an in-and-out, a coop, and a brick-wall jump; and the highest fences were reserved for Jessica. By the end of an hour, they'd thoroughly sampled the ponies' abilities.

Sweet Virginia—her barn name was Ginny—was clearly the star of the afternoon, and Ralph had priced her accordingly. Three thousand dollars was a hefty price for a school pony. Jade's first instinct was to cross the chestnut mare off her list. But then Ned—his gaze trained on Sweet Virginia cantering up to the in-and-out, with Kate sitting slightly forward as she followed the pony's takeoff over jump—adjusted the brim of his straw fedora and said quietly, "That little mare looks awfully neat and correct. The kids could take her to shows along with Doc and Archer." The observation made investing in the mare a different proposition altogether. Jade would be buying her for the family.

Ned had also liked the white pony, Dickens, right off the bat. "I could see Neddy and Will riding him in the short-stirrup classes." Jade wasn't surprised that Ned was already considering what his namesake and Margot and Travis's son would be needing in terms of a pony before Will, at least, could even walk. Ned was the sort of person who took the long view. "And Georgiana would look as pretty as a picture on Maggie."

And, that quickly, they had three ponies tagged as worthy of Rosewood Farm.

Olivia provided the fourth. Hopscotch was her favorite. After taking the chestnut over some cavalettis, she trotted over to the center of the ring with her eyes shining. "Hopscotch is a good pony, Aunt Jade; we should get him."

"What do you like best about him, Liv? Was he smooth over the rails for you?"

Olivia's black helmet bobbed as she nodded. "Yeah, but that's not the only reason. Hopscotch acts like he's having fun when you're riding him."

"Good to know. Why don't you see how he does a figure eight before you cool him down?"

Olivia was too young to realize the importance of her observation, but, along with a general soundness and barn manners, a pony's attitude was one of the top criteria. As Jade watched Hopscotch cut through the middle of the ring with his ears pricked forward, his trot chipper and perky, she, too, saw that he'd be great for a child to learn on—easygoing and forgiving. In that respect he was like Doc Holliday, her old pony that Kate, Max, and Olivia had inherited. Jade could still remember jumping her first crossbar with Doc, digging her fingers into his thick black mane as he hopped over it. That jump had seemed so big, yet Ned had explained that she could trust Doc to carry her over anything, because he just loved to jump; she had, and he'd been a wonderful pony, even helping her win the Warburg Hunt Cup in their last competition together.

Waiting until Ralph Whittaker had moved out of earshot to help Olivia dismount from Hopscotch's back, Jade said, "So, Ned, it seems like I have four potential prospects to come back and try out this week."

"Give Joe Bromley a call and ask him to drive up here and check them out to make sure we haven't missed anything. If you like the way they go for you, and Joe gives them a clean bill of health, I don't see any problem with buying all four of them. There's an advantage to the ponies knowing one another. The hierarchy's already been established."

"Good point. And I'd like to get the ponies settled at Rosewood as soon as possible." Especially since she had a couple of other things on her to-do list, such as setting up her second-grade classroom and planning lessons and activities for the first week of school.

Finding a private eye might take a wee bit of time too. It was good that Jesse and Doug were done putting the finishing touches on Bramble Cottage and that Jordan had given her the green light to move her things into it. Being in her own place and not worrying about anyone overhearing her conversations when she began calling private investigators would make the process a whole lot easier.

And she was going to be so busy over these next couple of weeks, it was a good thing she didn't have the telephone number of the man from the Norfolk hotel. She should stop thinking about him and wondering what it would be like to be with him again and whether he could really be as sexy and as deliciously talented as her memories of the stormy night she'd spent in his arms. It was pointless to regret not having exchanged numbers—let alone names—with him. Even if he lived within a forty-mile radius of Warburg, she didn't have time to think about a guy. Or burn up the sheets with one. So what if he was the only man she'd met who made her want to test the faithfulness of her memories.

Sleep deprivation, Rob learned, could have different side effects. The morning after Hayley's party, Rob could only be grateful that birthdays happened once a year. The way he felt now, he would need every single one of the 364 days before Hayley's next one to recover from the shrieks, squeals, tears, and all-around high drama produced by eight little girls over the course of an interminable night.

During the night he'd spent with the woman in Norfolk, he'd hardly closed his eyes either, caught up in the wild craving for the green-eyed vixen with the enchantress's body lying beneath him or rocking above him. Why succumb to sleep when he could taste and touch and stroke her inside and out? The next day he'd been wrung out—in every sense of the word—but he'd also been energized. And happy. He'd found himself smiling at memories he hadn't even realized he'd hoarded: of her slim body arching like a finely drawn bow in wordless offering; of the soft shudders of pleasure falling from her lush parted lips; of the sleek welcome of her body tightening around him, cream and satin. Memories that could make a man feel like a million bucks.

This morning, neither the sympathetic looks from the moms and dads who picked up their daughters with tacit apologies for the fact that upon the stroke of midnight their little princesses had transformed into unholy melodrama queens, nor the ingestion of a full pot of wickedly strong black coffee improved Rob's sleep-deprived grouchiness.

As a result, within four hours of his shift, his tally of parking violations reached a record high. But the tickets he wrote and stuck under windshield wipers were justified. It was the end of summer, with tourists flocking to Warburg to stroll down its leafy streets and brick-laid sidewalks, shop at its pretty boutiques, and enjoy its restaurants and coffee bars. The drivers who operated under the assumption that parking rules and meter limits applied only to others were, thanks to Rob, being given a little reality check.

So, too, were the drivers who didn't bother to ease off the gas pedal where the local highway became Main Street and the speed limit reflected the population density. That's the spot where Rob elected to set up his speed trap.

His tolerance for the bullshit stories drivers concocted and that he'd already heard dozens of times—"Gosh, I never saw the twenty-five-miles-an-hour sign," or "My aunt's in the hospital," or "It's that time of the month, Officer, and I really needed to get home," or "Your radar gun must be broken, I never speed"—was, in direct proportion to his parking-ticket quota, at an all-time low. But it was Nonie Harrison, one of Warburg's leading snobs, who took the day's prize for most obnoxious, unrepentant speeder.

She hadn't even bothered to *touch* the brakes as she flew past him, his radar gun blipping at a red-hot forty-three mph, eighteen miles above the posted limit. When he pulled her over with a flash of his lights and squawk of his siren, she'd actually looked affronted and then infuriated when he asked for her license and registration.

"This is too silly, Officer Cooper. I'm on my way to town on official business."

Even if Edmund Schantz, Warburg's mayor, were not taking his annual vacation on North Carolina's Outer Banks as he did every August, Nonie Harrison's story wouldn't have flown. No "official business" warranted breaking the law and speeding in a residential area.

He ignored her comment, silently waiting for her to comply.

Nonie Harrison narrowed her eyes. Then, with an impatient "hmmph," she leaned over and opened the glove compartment, drawing out the registration card. From her purse she pulled out a wallet and handed her Virginia driver's license and the registration to him.

"Thank you." He took his sweet time walking back to the patrol car to run a check on her license and car. Standard operating procedure with self-important speeders: make them cool their tires.

According to the computer records, Mrs. Harrison's tires were in sore need of some cooling down. She must have had some "official business" last March too. Craig Lewis, another officer on the force, had clocked her doing fifty in a thirty-five-miles-an-hour zone.

Conceivably, Rob might have let her off with a stern warning, but the fact that she'd gotten caught speeding twice in six months changed things. The existence of a previous ticket indicated her disregard for these particular rules of the road. Her lack of concern was somewhat surprising, as Virginia now had some of the highest penalties for speeding in the nation. Well, he thought, since the first ticket hadn't made an adequate impression, perhaps the second, heftier fine and the additional points tacked onto her license would make her think about easing her leaden foot off the accelerator.

He walked back to the late-model silver Mercedes. Waiting had put Mrs. Harrison in a visible snit. She didn't bother to conceal her anger as she took back her registration and license. "As I told you, Officer Cooper, the only reason I was driving a little fast was because I had official business in town—*important* business."

"Most people would consider going eighteen miles above the speed limit more than a little." Interesting. She didn't even have the sense to look embarrassed. Curiosity compelled him. "What kind of official business do you believe could justify speeding in a twenty-five-miles-an-hour area, Mrs. Harrison?" Maybe, just maybe, she'd intercepted a death threat against the president.

She smiled as she launched into her explanation, as if it were all she needed to go on her merry, self-absorbed way. "I'm going to see Ted Guerra at Warburg Elementary—who clearly doesn't know the first thing about being a school principal."

He frowned. Rob knew Ted Guerra. Liked him too. Guerra was the kind of principal who tried to foster a sense of community in the school and among the kids, the kind who went to pains to know every student by name and spend time in the classrooms as well. Last year, Ted had eaten lunch in Hayley's class a number of times. Rob remembered how excited she'd been when Ted had come and read aloud *I Just Forgot* to her class; for weeks afterward, it had been one of her favorite bedtime stories.

So whatever Nonie Harrison's reason for frothing at the mouth, it had nothing to do with Ted Guerra's qualities as a principal. It had to do with what Mrs. Nonie Harrison, of Warburg and Palm Beach, wanted. Something Ted must have failed to deliver. Whatever it was, Rob knew she was the type of person who would make sure Ted paid for it.

He decided to do Ted a favor. By the time Nonie Harrison drove away (and if she knew what was good for her, it wouldn't be an inch over the speed limit), she'd have found a brand-new person to dislike. Rob was more than happy to take on the role.

At the moment, though, Nonie Harrison was nodding, obviously interpreting his frown as a sign that he shared her outrage that Ted Guerra didn't run his school exactly as she liked. "If I'd been in town for the school-board-meeting vote, I'd have made Ted Guerra understand what an insult it was to hire Jade Radcliffe—even as a substitute. You can be sure hell will freeze over before I allow my grandson to be placed under her supervision."

Jade Radcliffe? Christ, suddenly her name was popping up all over the place. He didn't know where she fit into all of this, but he knew enough not to trust Nonie Harrison's version.

He watched her right hand move to the ignition.

His voice stopped her. "Mrs. Harrison, you were driving at forty-three miles an hour in a twenty-five-miles-per-hour zone. Moreover, our computer records show you were issued a speeding ticket last spring."

"But—"

He ignored her interruption, filling out the speeding ticket as he continued, "Driving twenty miles an hour over the posted speed constitutes reckless driving in the Commonwealth of Virginia and is punishable by a fine and four points on your license." Carefully, he tore off the ticket and passed it to her.

The amount of the fine had her gasping in shock. "A *thousand* dollars—why, this is outrageous!"

"No, ma'am. It's the law. For your sake, as well as the community's, I hope you'll drive a little more responsibly now. If you don't, your third ticket will be even more costly and could also result in the suspension of your driver's license. So, if I were you, I'd pay real close attention to speed limits from now on. You have a good day."

His shift over, Rob went home and showered, standing under first steaming hot and then frigid cold water in the hopes that he'd emerge revived before he headed over to his parents' place, where Hayley had spent the day. To celebrate Hayley's big day, his folks had taken her to buy some new school sneakers, play a round of miniature golf, and eat a burger at the Shake Shack.

This evening there'd be a family gathering—his oldest brother, Aaron, was driving up from Richmond—for a dinner of fried chicken, grilled corn, and garlic bread, Hayley's favorites, and then an ice-cream birthday cake and a small mountain of family presents.

After grabbing his wallet, car keys, and cellphone, Rob stopped on the way out of the house to fish the mail from the black metal box that was screwed into the clapboard siding to the right of the front door. Quickly, he shuffled through the pile of letters and flyers, tucking under his arm the large envelope with Warburg Elementary School's address inked in the upper left-hand corner. It must contain the class list Hayley had been asking about every day for the past two weeks. She'd get a kick out of opening it and discovering who was in her class. He wondered whether she'd get Mrs. Riley or Mrs. Creighton as her teacher. Not that it mattered. He'd heard excellent things about both of them.

Another letter from the elementary school caught his attention, as this one was addressed to him only. He turned the envelope over and tore it open, assuming it must be yet another school form or the announcement of a special event to add to the calendar. If it contained anything exciting, he'd be able to share the news with Hayley.

He read the first three sentences and by the fourth was cursing under his breath. He scanned the remainder of Ted Guerra's letter quickly, his anger mounting.

Damn it all to hell, he thought, retrieving his cellphone from his pocket. He didn't care where she graduated in her class or how much student teaching she'd done, Jade Radcliffe wasn't going to be teaching his kid.

From memory, he punched in the number to Warburg Elementary, intending to tell Ted he'd better find another replacement for Sandy Riley, and fast. The school's answering machine brought him up short. Of course no one was there. It was a quarter to six on an August evening.

Well, he'd leave a blistering message that made his feelings plain. At the prompt, he punched in Guerra's extension number. But when the beep sounded for him to begin speaking, an image of a ranting Nonie Harrison flashed in his mind. His thumb hit the END CALL button.

"Damn it all." What in hell should he do now?

"You do nothing" was his mother's answer after he'd shown her Ted Guerra's letter informing them of Sandy Riley's early maternity leave and that Jade Radcliffe would be taking over her class for the fall semester.

Upon arriving at his parents', Rob had first stopped to give Hayley a kiss and remind her not to get Dexter too excited as she raced him around the perimeter of the backyard. At the last family gathering, Scott's Lab mix had vomited his dinner and then gobbled it back up—a sight Rob preferred not to revisit.

He'd then offered a "Hi, smells good" to his dad, who was roasting ears of corn on the grill, and a "Hey" to Emma and Scott, who were keeping their father company and laughing at Dexter's joyful leaps and ecstatic barks. After that he'd headed to the kitchen, where he knew his mom would be putting the finishing touches on the celebratory dinner. Not only had his mom raised four kids in Warburg, she'd also worked as a reading specialist at the elementary school before taking an early retirement after Becky's death to help him with Hayley when he was on duty. Who better than she to advise him on how to get Hayley transferred out of Jade Radcliffe's class?

When he'd handed the letter to her, he half-expected he would need to grab the pad and pencil near the telephone to jot down notes so he wouldn't miss a single one of her instructions. But his mother read the letter without any sign of alarm. Then she simply passed it to Aaron, who'd been filling her in on life in Richmond as he nursed a Stella, and turned back to the stove to transfer the remaining pieces of crispy golden fried chicken to the large blue-and-white ceramic platter Rob had given her on her fifty-seventh birthday. She was acting as if Ted Guerra's letter contained nothing more interesting than an announcement that the school's hallways had been painted over the summer.

"So, Mom, what should I do?" he'd finally asked, only to feel his jaw drop at her calm reply of "You do nothing."

"I do nothing?" Rather than watch his mom wield the tongs with a Zen-like serenity, Rob began to pace the bright-yellow kitchen.

"That's right," she replied in the same irritatingly calm tone as before. "Ted Guerra doesn't strike me as someone who's easily impressed. It's clear from his letter that he thinks highly of Jade Radcliffe—who wouldn't? The girl has obviously worked hard, taking extra courses to get her teaching certification in addition to her degree. Personally, I think there's a lot to be said for the energy a young person brings to the classroom. I like Tricia Creighton a lot, but she's been teaching second grade since before Aaron started school."

"If memory serves, Mrs. Creighton was old even then," Aaron said. "Hayley would exhaust her. Heck, look at poor Dexter." He pointed toward the kitchen window.

Rob glanced out the window. Dexter had flopped onto his stomach, his long tongue hanging out while he watched Hayley circle the yard at a brisk canter. "That's not what I'm concerned about. Jade Radcliffe is hardly the person I want—"

His mother didn't seem to be listening. Laying the tongs on the platter, she addressed his brother. "Aaron, will you carry the chicken out? And ask Dad if he's finished grilling the corn. And tell Scott that he should make sure everyone has something to drink. Hayley already put in a request for pink lemonade."

But the second her oldest son was out of the kitchen, she turned and folded her arms across her middle, just above where her apron was tied. "Rob, what's this really about?"

"Mom, you do remember who Jade Radcliffe is?"

"Of course. I remember that she was a terribly unhappy girl who lost both parents—"

"Do you remember that she was also the girl who I was busy booking down at the station on the night Becky died? If Jade Radcliffe hadn't been at the Den looking for a wild time—"

"And if I hadn't waited until ten o'clock before calling your house that night, I might have gone over to check on Becky earlier, and maybe she'd still be alive."

"Surely you can't believe that—" He couldn't finish the thought aloud.

"That maybe I'm to blame for Becky's death? It makes as much sense as blaming Jade Radcliffe. So do you blame me too, Rob?" she asked, looking him straight in the eye.

"No, of course I don't." He shook his head, appalled by the notion.

"Why not? I knew Becky was feeling poorly, so I'm much guiltier than Jade Radcliffe, who was just being a reckless teenager. If you can forgive me, then you have to forgive her." Her tone gentled. "Don't do this to yourself. Don't become a bitter and angry man. Becky wouldn't have wanted that."

His voice was raw with despair. "I miss her, Mom. I miss her so damned much."

She stepped forward and wrapped her arms around him, as if he were ten years old rather than twenty-nine.

"We all do. But she's not really gone, Rob. There's so much of her in Hayley. I see it every day."

He swallowed. "I know," he said quietly. "She's got Becky's smile."

"Then let's go out and celebrate the beautiful girl you and Becky made together." She rose on the toes of her sandals to kiss his brow. "Okay?"

Expelling a ragged breath, Rob nodded and repeated, "Okay." He wouldn't spoil Hayley's birthday dinner for anything. "So I let the classroom situation be?"

"That's right. Of course, if you have any concerns, you should take them up with Jade Radcliffe. But take my advice and wait until after she's had a chance to get a sense of the kids and the class dynamics—and after parents' night too. That's the worst night of the year for a new teacher."

"I bow to your superior wisdom."

His mother's bright-blue eyes twinkled as she gave him a bowl of purple coleslaw to carry outside. "You should make a habit of that. Now, let's go give that little girl of yours her dinner and presents. Seven years old. It seems only yesterday that you were seven, bound and determined to do whatever Scott and Aaron were up to. I can still remember when you jumped off that high-platform diving board. . . ."

The birthday presents were unwrapped with the ice cream cake. Hayley was ecstatic over the Hula-Hoop and bead kit Emma gave her; the enormous box of col-ored pencils and markers and the book of horse stickers from Aaron; the pretty necklace with a horse pendant, along with several outfits for school, that Rob's mom and dad gave her; the boxed set of the *Pony Club Secrets*, along with a purple backpack for school, from Scott; and, from Rob, a pair of jodhpurs, paddock boots, and a riding hat. Sara Steadman had assured him he could return or exchange anything that didn't fit. Inside the big glittery pink-and-gold birthday card with a 7 emblazoned on it, he'd written that she was also getting riding lessons once the school year began. When she read the message, she whooped in delight. Flinging her arms about his neck, she gave him a loud smooch on his cheek. "Thank you, Daddy! You're the best dad ever!"

"You're welcome, sweetheart. I'm still investigating which barn is the best for lessons."

Then, Hayley being Hayley, she skipped around the table, showing everyone the birthday card so that they could read about her upcoming riding lessons. Then she raced inside the house to pull on her new jodhpurs and had her grandpa fasten her new necklace. She would have probably started Hula-Hooping while wearing her riding helmet if Rob hadn't called her over and presented her with the envelope from the school.

"Is it my class list?" she asked breathlessly.

"Why don't you open it and see?"

Emma was sitting next to him. She leaned close, peering over Hayley's shoulder. "Yeah, Hayley, open it up. I want to know who's in your class. Aren't you dying to know too, Scott?"

"The suspense is killing me. Hayley's only been talking about it nonstop for the past two weeks."

Accustomed to Scott's teasing, Hayley wrinkled her nose at him and then turned to Emma. "Will you help me with the envelope, Aunt Emma? I don't want to rip it."

"Sure thing." Emma took the envelope, peeled back the gummed end, and pulled out a sheath of papers. Glancing at the topmost one, she said, "Looks like you got a letter from your teacher. . . . Oh!" she exclaimed in surprise, and her gaze met Rob's.

A lift of his brows signaled to her that he was quite aware of who'd written it, and her face cleared.

"Hayley, guess what? You have a new teacher this year," he said.

"You mean I don't have Mrs. Riley?" He caught the note of anxiety that had crept into her voice.

"No, your new teacher's name is Miss Radcliffe." He wasn't going to broach the topic of what a substitute teacher was, as it might cause Hayley even more anxiety.

"I think you're going to like her," Emma said, adding her support. "Shall I read her letter to you?"

Hayley nodded and leaned in toward Emma's chair.

"Okay, here goes." Emma raised her index finger to the sheet of paper so that Hayley could follow along as she read. *"Dear Hayley, Hi, my name is Jade Radcliffe, and I'm going to be your second-grade teacher while Mrs. Riley is having her baby. As I'm new at Warburg Elementary School, I thought I would tell you a little bit about myself. I grew up in Warburg and live with my sisters on a horse farm that's been in our family for a long time. I spend a lot of time riding and working with our horses. When I'm not doing that, I like to read books, listen to music, and spend time with my family. I have two older sisters who are married, and they both have kids. I have three nephews and three nieces, so things get pretty busy around my home. I'm really looking forward to meeting you and all of the students in the class and learning more about your lives in the weeks ahead. It's going to be a fun year! In the packet, you'll find our class list as well as a list of school supplies. Don't worry if you can't get them all by the first day though! See you on the morning of the twenty-third! Sincerely, Miss Radcliffe."* Emma paused, then said, "And she wrote a P.S. at the bottom. That's what you put when you want to add something after you've finished the letter."

"What'd she say?"

"Hayley, I saw that your birthday is this Wednesday! Have a very happy day!" Emma lowered the letter. "Well, that was nice of her, wasn't it?"

Seated across the teak table, Rob's mother caught his gaze. He answered her silent inquiry with a tiny nod. Yes, Jade Radcliffe had passed her first test. Her letter had not only dispelled any of Hayley's anxiety over having an unknown teacher, it had also lit a spark of excitement in her brown eyes. Jade received a gold star for having included birthday wishes. Smart. Then again, he'd never doubted her intelligence.

"Your new teacher sounds great, Hayley. You lucked out, kiddo," Aaron said.

"Yeah. And she has horses." Hayley's expression was as awestruck as her voice.

"That's right," Emma said. When she looked about to say more, Rob gave a quick shake of his head. He didn't want her mentioning that Jade Radcliffe was also giving riding lessons. Knowing Hayley, her mind would take flight. Soon he'd be explaining why it wasn't an absolutely perfect idea for her to take riding lessons at Rosewood Farm.

Shooting him an exasperated look, Emma took another tack. "Say, Hayley, do you know Olivia and Kate Stevens?"

Hayley nodded. "Uh-huh."

"Miss Radcliffe is their aunt."

"Their aunt?"

"Yes, her older sister is Mrs. Gage," Rob's mother informed her. "Such a nice woman."

"I like Olivia—she's funny. And Kate's really nice."

"So, Hayley, you ready to see who's in your class?" Rob asked. He didn't want Hayley to get too excited about all the wonderful things she was discovering about her new teacher. Especially when he wasn't sure she'd remain Hayley's teacher.

"Yeah!"

"All right, then. Emma, you want to do the honors?"

Emma shuffled the sheaf of papers in her hands. "Ah, here it is, the long-awaited class list," she intoned dramatically, while Scott and Aaron drummed their fingers on the table and Hayley giggled. "Now, shall I begin with the A's or the N's?"

"The A's. Because I don't want to miss anybody, but, oh, I hope Jenny's in Miss Radcliffe's class with me!"

Okay, Rob thought as he listened to Hayley's squeal of excitement when Em got to the F's and read off Jenny Ferris's name; it was pretty clear that Hayley was in seventh heaven. She was going to be counting the minutes until she could shoulder her new purple backpack; walk into the elementary school with her best friend, Jenny; and meet her new teacher, a woman who actually lived on a horse farm.

The least he could do was to hold off judging Jade Radcliffe's abilities until he'd gathered more evidence. But if he didn't like what he saw, nothing was going to stop him from calling Ted Guerra.

Chapter
EIGHT

DRESSED IN oversize dark glasses, a baseball hat worn with the brim pulled low, and a baggy windbreaker, Jade knew she wasn't going to win any style awards, but the outfit wasn't intended to flatter so much as to serve as a disguise. It would be pretty difficult for anyone from Warburg who might be eating lunch in the Upperville diner to recognize her.

She'd even driven to the Plains Drifter in Travis's SUV, since her fire-engine-red Porsche was too eye-catching. Luckily, she'd had the perfect excuse when she'd asked Travis to loan her his wheels: She needed to go to the pet store to pick up an aquarium and all the necessary fish supplies for her classroom and then swing by Steadman's to buy tack for the new ponies. No way could she fit all that stuff in a Porsche 911.

She hopped out of the SUV, the windbreaker ballooning like a garbage bag about her, and walked toward the diner's entrance. By the time she was halfway across the parking lot, she was sweating beneath the nylon shell. As sweat trickled down her spine, she scanned the other parked cars, distracting herself from the heat by wondering whether the private investigator she was meeting was already inside the restaurant. If so, what kind of car would a PI named Greg Hammond drive? A Ford or an import? Dark green or flashy silver?

And what would Hammond look like? She hadn't been able to form much of an impression from his voice.

All she knew was that he was male and that his office was located in Fairfax, Virginia.

Wrapping her hand around the hot metal handle of the diner's glass door, she pulled it open and stepped inside to the frigid blast of the air-conditioning and the thick smell of grease. It wasn't yet noon, but the place was nonetheless fairly crowded. Hammond had told her to sit wherever she wanted; he'd find her. She slid into a booth by the window and glanced around, half-expecting some guy in a fedora and a wide-lapeled suit to slide onto the blue vinyl bench opposite her. Or maybe he'd be wearing a badass black leather jacket, never mind that it was broiling outside.

Jeez, she was becoming ridiculous in her old age.

Determined to act normal, as if she met with detectives daily, she picked up the laminated menu and studied it, for once not even tempted by any of the calorie bombs being offered. She doubted, though, that Margot would be mollified to learn that she was too nervous to inhale her usual quantity of sugar and carbs. She'd be too busy having a conniption fit that her little sister was meeting a private eye. Was intending to hire one . . .

"Jade Radcliffe?"

Startled, she dropped the menu onto the retro Formica. "Um, yes, I'm Jade."

"Greg Hammond." He stuck out a hand, and she shook it, staring up at him dumbly. It surprised her that he looked so *normal,* not like someone who spent his life tracking down white-collar criminals, blackmailers, missing persons, and adulterers, poking and prying into everyone's past. She placed him in his late forties, maybe even early fifties, because there was more salt than pepper in his short-cropped hair. His eyes were brown. Rather than sporting a fedora and trench coat, he was dressed in a white shirt beneath a slightly creased slate-blue linen jacket and light-beige trousers. He had a healthy tan and looked like he might play golf on Sunday mornings. But his erect bearing hinted at more than just swinging an iron. She bet he had a military background. And from the solid body beneath his linen jacket, she figured he could probably bench-press twice her weight without breaking a sweat.

Okay, maybe he didn't look quite so normal after all, Jade thought. What Greg Hammond looked like was tough, capable, and as if he had zero tolerance for BS.

"Mind if I sit down?" he asked, waiting for her to say, "Please," before sliding into the space opposite her.

She glanced around so he wouldn't catch her staring and realized the restaurant was now crowded. "How'd you know who I was?"

The corner of his mouth lifted. "Not too difficult. You're the only person here who's trying to look inconspicuous. By the way, it's okay to take off the cap and shades—the jacket too. The people who come to the Plains Drifter are typically on their lunch hour. They're focused on getting their order and eating and then, if they have enough time before their break ends, dashing in to one of the stores on Route 50 to do some shopping or run an errand. Even if someone was inclined to eavesdrop, it's too noisy at this hour to hear much."

Jade decided she was just as happy to shrug out of the windbreaker, because even with the air-conditioning cranked high she was roasting. She removed her dark glasses too. The cap remained, however. She didn't want Hammond to think she was a pushover.

A waitress came over to the booth. "Can I get you started with something while you look over the menu? Or are you ready to order?"

"I know what I'd like," Hammond replied.

Did he have the diner's menu memorized, or was he trying to make it so that the waitress wouldn't have to come back and interrupt them? The latter, Jade decided.

"I do too," she said. "I'll have the Caesar salad and an iced tea, please."

Nodding, the waitress scribbled the order on her pad, then plucked the menu from Jade's hand. "And for you?" she asked Hammond.

"The Cobb salad and an iced coffee."

"Cream? Sugar?"

"Black, unsweetened."

"One Caesar, one Cobb, coming right up. Ya'll want water?"

"Please."

When the waitress left, Hammond placed a slim black briefcase on the tabletop, unzipped it, and pulled out a legal pad, a pen, and a business card. "Here you go," he said, passing it to her. "This has all my contact information."

While she looked at the card, running her thumb over the heavy stock's edge and trying to imagine what other cases Gregory J. Hammond, licensed private investigator in the Commonwealth of Virginia, who also happened to be bonded and insured, had worked on, Hammond clicked his silver pen and wrote something in the upper right-hand margin. He was a lefty. She didn't know why, but the sight of the thick gold band on his wedding-ring finger made her feel better. She wondered whether he had kids.

He glanced up and met her gaze. "With your permission, I'll be taking notes of our conversation."

"Sure—I guess that's okay." Oh, God, she was actually going to have to talk about her mother's infidelity, a topic she avoided at all costs.

"Over the phone you mentioned that you wanted me to investigate a case of infidelity."

She cast a grateful smile at the waitress, who appeared just then with two glasses of water. Taking hers, she gulped down a mouthful. "That's right. I saw on your website that's one of the things you handle." She'd also liked the fact that Hammond Investigations had been in business for twenty years. If his had been a fly-by-night operation, it would have folded by now. And, unlike some of the investigative-agency sites, Hammond's hadn't given her a weird feeling, and when she'd screwed up the nerve to dial the office's number, an intelligent-sounding receptionist had answered the phone before connecting her to him.

"It is," he replied. "Divorce and infidelity investigations are the most common requests we receive, though recently there's been a rise in dating and premarital background checks too."

So much for true love. Then she thought of Margot and Travis and Jordan and Owen and Miriam and Andy. They were the lucky ones. She, however, was too like her mother to hope for the same.

Hammond continued speaking. "Over the phone you mentioned that the person you'd like to have investigated is your mother." His lack of surprise that she wanted to investigate her own mother meant either that he'd had people request far weirder stuff, which if one went by today's reality TV shows with dysfunctional families on parade seemed more than plausible, or it meant that Hammond was an expert at hiding his thoughts. "Could I have her full name?" he asked.

She took another gulp of water. "Nicole Warren Radcliffe."

"And do you suspect she's still cheating on your father?"

"Not anymore. She's dead."

At this Hammond looked up, his brown gaze assessing. She was glad she'd opted to keep the baseball cap on her head, knowing it shadowed her eyes. The noise in the diner rose around them, as if someone had cranked the volume knob. Hammond didn't seem to notice as he studied her silently and she tried not to squirm. Finally he asked, "And your father's name?"

"Robert James Radcliffe—the fifth."

She watched as he wrote a *V* after her father's name.

"And when do you believe your mother was unfaithful to your father?"

"It would have been about six and a half years ago."

"Is your father aware that you're investigating the possibility your mother was unfaithful?"

"No, because he's dead too. He and Mom died when their plane crashed into the Chesapeake. It'll be seven years this October."

Not even someone as clearly practiced in guarding his responses as Greg Hammond could mask his surprise and confusion. "I'm not sure I understand. Why are you—"

"Why am I contacting you if both my parents have been dead and buried for all these years? You're going to tell me that it's better to let them rest in peace, right?" When his lips flattened in a stiff line, she gave a tight smile. "Yes, I've heard that line a couple of times before. Well, the whole resting-in-peace thing isn't giving *me* much peace. I need to know what kind of woman my mother was. I've come back to live in Warburg and make it my home. I can't handle having to wonder each time I cross paths with a man who has the initials TM if he could have been Mom's lover. I have to learn once and for all who he was, and when I do, I want to . . ." Her voice stalled and died.

Hammond laid his pen down on the legal pad and placed his hands flat on the table. "You'd like to do what precisely, Miss Radcliffe?" he prompted evenly.

Although she'd only just met Hammond, she recognized instinctively that the wrong answer would have him returning his notepad to his briefcase and walking out of the diner without a backward glance.

She gave a shrug. "Spit in his face, probably." It was true; she wasn't about to commit murder or anything. But that didn't lessen her need to know the guy's identity one bit.

"Nothing more?"

"Nothing that would run afoul of the law. I have a healthy respect for the Warburg police." Actually, *fear* was the better word.

He looked at her for a moment. "Just remember, I track down information and sometimes criminals. I don't work for them. And I don't commit crimes."

His statement only made her trust him more. "I'll remember."

He gave her another long look. "Okay," he said with a nod. "Now, you mentioned that you believe the man your mother was seeing had the initials TM. How do you know this?"

God, here came the awful part, she thought, shifting restlessly on the vinyl seat. "Mom kept a diary."

"I see. Does the diary still exist?"

"Yes."

"And am I right to assume the diary is in your possession?"

She gave a short nod.

"I'll need to look at it to glean whatever clues your mother left about this person TM."

Yeah, like what a transcendent experience her mom's being with TM had been, Jade thought, recalling those passages in the diary. He must have been some kind of lover for Mom to be so blissed out whenever she wrote about him. She certainly hadn't been feeling the love when she described her own daughter.

It had been bad enough knowing that Jordan and Margot had read her mom's diary. Now a stranger was going to be studying every single entry with the equivalent of a magnifying glass. By the time Hammond closed the cover, he'd realize just how little Jade's mother had cared for her.

Hammond must have noticed something in her expression—not a terribly difficult feat when her jaw was clenched so tightly it ached. "Are you all right with my reading your mother's diary?"

Damn it, she thought. It was time she fished or cut bait. She either wanted to find out who the bastard TM was or she didn't. Silently, she pulled her leather bag closer to her lap, opened it, and withdrew the hideously ugly pink leather journal. As she handed it to him, she had to fight the temptation to say something along the lines of, *Mom wasn't always like this. She loved Dad. And she didn't hate my guts.* What was the point? Anything she said would only make her look pathetic.

Hammond didn't open the journal to glance at its creased pages, which were testimony to the countless times she'd pored over it, trying to understand the words and thoughts within it, only to be racked by hurt and confusion with every attempt.

He stowed the journal out of sight in his briefcase as the waitress arrived with the two salads, then sat back against the vinyl bench while she fetched their drinks. Depositing them on the table, she asked, "Can I get you anything else?"

"No, thanks. This looks great," Hammond answered.

Jade just shook her head. The waitress gone, she stared at her salad. How could she possibly eat this thing? Her appetite had vanished.

Hammond didn't seem interested in eating either. He took a long sip of his iced coffee, pushed his own plate to the side, and picked up his pen. "Did your mother have an address book?"

"Sure, but we didn't keep it. Besides, she'd never have put him in it anyway."

"Did she use a cellphone?"

"It went down with the plane." Somehow this was even harder for her to say than her bald statement that her parents had died. Maybe it was because she couldn't shake the image of her mom trapped in that small plane as it careened downward and then crashed into the choppy waters of the bay.

The ER doctor had assured Jade that her mother had died on impact. What were her last thoughts?

As terrible as it had been to see her dad lying critically injured in the ICU, at least Jade had been able to touch him and look into his face one last time before his body gave out. She had nothing like that with her mom. No last wrenching goodbye. No closure. No peace. She grabbed a napkin and twisted it in her hands.

He reached across the table and briefly laid his hand over hers, a simple gesture of comfort. "Sorry. I should have guessed that. I doubt the cellphone would have done any good. As your mother's been deceased for some years, the phone company would have deleted her records by now."

The sympathy in his voice made it worse. She nodded tightly. Picking up her iced tea, she kept drinking until she'd drained the glass. And still she couldn't speak.

"Are there people I can talk to who might have any ideas about the identity of your mother's lover? Family members?"

"No!" The objection came out far too loud. Lowering her voice, she repeated no less emphatically, "No. I don't want you to talk to my sisters or anyone at Rosewood about Mom and her lover. They don't know I've contacted you, and I don't want them to find out either. They'd just worry."

"Anyone else?"

"Nope."

"You're not giving me a whole lot to work with, Miss Radcliffe."

Hammond couldn't refuse to take the case, she thought. Although she hardly knew him, she already sensed she could trust him. And Lord knew she didn't want to go through the hell of explaining to another private eye what her mom had done. "I'll tell you what I know and what I've figured out from reading her diary. Whoever TM was, he must have lived close to Warburg, because Mom was able to see him fairly often without raising Dad's suspicion. If this guy had lived farther away and she was gone for hours at a time, Dad would have definitely begun asking questions. And she was terrified of him finding out that she was seeing someone."

"This TM didn't have to live near Warburg. He could have met your mother at a rendezvous point."

Again Jade shook her head. "I don't think so. Mom wouldn't have risked being spotted entering a hotel unaccompanied by Dad. It would have caused too many tongues to wag. And cheesy motels were definitely not her style."

Hammond picked up his pen again and jotted something on the pad of paper. Jade breathed a silent sigh of relief. If he was writing information down, it must mean he was going to take the case.

"Did your father ever find out about your mother's affair?"

"Yeah. He must have found her diary somewhere in the house. He went and fired Travis—his last name's Maher," she added for clarification. "Travis was Rosewood Farm's trainer and barn manager and Dad's right-hand man. And friend. The only reason Dad would have done something so freakin' nutty was because—"

"Of Travis Maher's initials," he finished for her. "What makes you think your father wasn't right, that he isn't your man? If Maher worked on the premises, he'd have been nearby. Easy to make assignations."

"Travis wouldn't have done that to Dad. Never in a

million years. He has principles. And Mom was pretty awful to Travis, constantly bringing up the number of times his dad had been arrested for public intoxication. Let's just say Travis didn't find it nearly as amusing a topic of conversation as she did. Then there's the fact that Travis was totally in love with my older half sister Margot. They're married now, with two kids."

Her explanation seemed to convince him. "Okay, we'll keep Travis Maher off the list of possible candidates. What else can you tell me about TM and your mother?"

"Other than that TM must have lived somewhere near Warburg?" Her brow furrowed. "The field's fairly wide open. You're going to need to look for wealthy men between the ages of twenty-five and sixty-five."

"Why wealthy?"

"Because Mom was an ultra-snob. Like I said, no cheesy motels, no guys from the wrong side of the tracks—even if, like Travis, they were really good-looking."

He cocked an eyebrow. "Okay, then, after I go through the diary, I'll start checking for names in the social register."

Her lips curved in a smile. Greg Hammond was all right.

"Well, it's not much, but you've provided enough background to get me started." Laying down his pen, he continued. "Let's go over the nuts and bolts of how I work: I charge a hundred dollars an hour, plus expenses like gas. I'll draft a proposal detailing the parameters of the investigation along with an estimate of the hours involved, so you'll have an idea of how much this is going to cost and whether finding out TM's identity is worth it to you. Once you've agreed to the terms, I'll provide you with status reports as well as detailed invoices. Is that acceptable to you, Miss Radcliffe?"

"Yes it is, Mr. Hammond." The inheritance she'd received was enough to afford those rates for a while, not that she believed the investigation would take too long; Hammond struck her as an efficient type of person.

And, thanks to Margot and Travis's expert bargaining advice, not even buying four ponies had depleted her resources too much. She'd negotiated a great deal for the four schooling ponies she'd picked at Ralph Whittaker's barn. With the economy in the tank right now, people were eager to sell—even Sweet Virginia's owners had come down in their asking price. So if Hammond's investigation took longer than expected, the rest of her inheritance should cover the cost. She couldn't think of a better way to spend every last penny of it than in discovering the identity of her mother's lover.

Hammond's voice interrupted her thoughts. "One last question for today."

"Sure. Go ahead." She straightened on her seat, bringing her gaze level with his.

"How old were you when your parents died?"

"Fifteen." The word came out sounding flat, and she wished she hadn't straightened her spine, but slumping would reveal too much, as would ducking her head.

"That's a tough thing to go through that young."

"Losing your parents is tough at any age."

For a second he studied her face, what he could see of it beneath the curved brim of her cap—making her grateful she'd had the sense to keep it on—before giving her a short nod, as if to signal that he'd gotten the message: She didn't want pity or sympathy.

Putting his legal pad and pen back in his briefcase, he glanced at her untouched Caesar salad. "So, you feel up to eating that?"

She checked her watch. She still had to go to the pet store and swing by Steadman's. "Hate to spill the family secrets and run, but I think this lunch is going to have to wait for dinner. I've got a long list of errands to run—"

"I understand." He raised his hand and signaled the waitress.

"I'm afraid we lost track of time," he offered with an apologetic smile when she approached their table. "Can we get these salads to go?"

"Sure thing. You want the check too?"

"Please," Jade said.

The waitress tallied the bill and ripped the check off her pad, then laid it on the table. Jade stretched out her hand, but Hammond got there first. "This one's on me," he said.

"That's not necessary. I—"

"Relax. You'll be paying my expenses from here on out."

"Good point. Okay, then, thanks."

"You're welcome." He gave her an easy smile. "I'll be in touch soon, Miss Radcliffe."

AFTER LEAVING the diner, Jade had picked up the supplies for the aquarium at the pet store. All that was missing were the fish, but she'd decided to hold off buying them until the day before school opened, so she could bring them directly to their new home. Moving them twice, from the store to her cottage and then to the classroom, would stress them unnecessarily. She didn't want to deal with the horror of dead fish floating on the surface of the tank during the first week of school.

Steadman's Saddle Shop was her next stop. Known as the best tack shop in Loudoun County for the quality of its merchandise and the attention the Steadmans gave their customers in choosing the right saddle, martingale, or riding helmet, the store tended to be busiest in the morning or during the lunch hour. Thus Jade wasn't surprised to find the parking lot nearly empty in the middle of the afternoon. While it would have been nice to see some of the local horse people and have a chance to spread the word about her riding program, she was just as happy to inspect the selection of tack without interruption. And she'd be able to catch up with Adam and Sara Steadman in the process.

Entering Steadman's was like walking into a vault of memories. When Jade was a kid, her dad brought her with him when he needed to pick up a new bit or halter or protective boots for one of the horses. He and Adam had been good friends, and, while they were talking horses and local competitions, Sara would slip Jade a lollipop, and a carrot treat to give to Doc when she got back to Rosewood.

She occasionally came here with her mom too. In hindsight, not all of those memories were pleasant. For instance, there was the day her mom brought her to buy a show coat; Jade was five years old and entering her very first walk-trot class at the local horse show. A beaming Sara Steadman had led them to the children's section, where miniature hunt coats hung from a circular rack.

"From here to here, Jade, are the coats in your size," she'd said, spreading her arms around a section of the rack. "Tell me which ones you like and we'll try them on you."

Jade hadn't hesitated, marching up to the dark-gray pinstripe jacket. "I want this one, because it's the same as Margot's and I want to ride as good as she does."

No sooner had she finished her sentence than her mom grabbed her by the elbow, pulling her back. "We'll take a navy coat, Sara."

Even at that age, Jade had felt the awkwardness of the moment. After a short silence, Sara said, "It might look nice to have your daughters in matching coats—"

Before Sara could finish, Jade's mom cut her off. "I have only one daughter."

Which Jade had realized was true. As Mom had said so many times, Jordan and Margot were her *stepdaughters,* so that must mean they didn't really count.

But Jade also knew that interrupting people was rude, which was probably why Mrs. Steadman had that strange expression on her face.

Then Mom had turned to her, and even now Jade could hear the edge in her voice when she said, "You'll wear a blue jacket to the Crestview show, Jade, and that's final. The jacket will go well with all the blue ribbons you're going to win. And soon you'll be winning more classes than either of them." She'd made it sound like a promise.

No need to ask who "them" was. Jade didn't understand why Mom disliked her not-real daughters and seemed to actually *hate* Margot, but it must be because Margot was always trying to get Dad to pay attention to her. It made him angry. And it made her mom's eyes narrow until they were green slits.

But on that afternoon, Jade was her little darling, her adorable angel. And Jade was getting a blue riding coat and was going to win blue ribbons on the best pony in the whole world.

Never once did it cross Jade's mind, then or even in the nine years that followed, that her mom would ever think of her as anything but her darling, her beautiful green-eyed princess.

But at fourteen she'd gone from beloved to reviled practically overnight. Despised almost as much as Margot—and, boy, that was saying something.

Her earlier meeting with Greg Hammond must be causing these long-buried memories to assail her. She needed to shake them off and remind herself that she was at Steadman's because of the *future,* a future she was building with the sisters she loved despite her mother's poisonous attitude, so that together they could keep alive their family's tradition of raising and working with horses.

When the tack shop's door shut with a tinkling chime of the brass bell, Adam Steadman looked up from behind the cash register, where he was ringing up a customer's purchase. His face split into a wide smile of welcome. "Is that you, Jade Radcliffe? Sara! Look who's here."

"Jade! We were hoping you'd be dropping by soon!" Neat in her pleated beige trousers and floral-printed cotton shirt, Sara hurried over to enfold Jade in a grand-motherly hug. Stepping back, she said, "Don't you look wonderful!"

Jade grinned, thinking Sara wouldn't have been able to say that if Jade were still wearing the getup she'd cho-sen for the Plains Drifter Diner. "You look great too. The summer's been a good one?"

"Oh, yes. Busy as can be, but that's a good thing. Adam would drive me nuts otherwise. We were so ex-cited when Ned came in with your flyer. We've been tell-ing everyone about your riding program."

"I know, and thanks so much. I've been getting a lot of inquiries. One of my classes is almost filled. I've got the Reed boy, Jamie and Jane Donovan, and Mary Car-dillo." All were children of horse enthusiasts and loyal customers at the saddle shop.

Sara beamed. "I'm sure they'll all be filled very soon. Gosh, it's good to see you, Jade. I'd forgotten what lovely hair you have."

She was referring to Jade's penchant for outrageous dye jobs, which had lasted into college. "I'd almost for-gotten what it looked like too," Jade confessed in a con-spiratorial whisper. "But don't let Margot know I said that."

Finished with his customer, Adam joined them. "So, Jade, did you buy those ponies Ned was telling us about? Ralph Whittaker has some fine stock."

"Yeah, we really lucked out. Joe Bromley's checked them out and given us the green light. Tito and I are picking them up this week."

"How exciting. Such a big change for Rosewood Farm, having ponies there and offering riding lessons," Sara said. "I think it's a great idea."

Adam nodded in agreement. "It's a smart expansion plan. Even in these difficult economic times, you've got to grow the business."

"I hope you're right. You should come by and see the barn Owen built for the ponies. It's great."

"We'd be delighted to. We need to make a full report to Brian. He'll be pleased to hear what you're doing for the young riders in the area." Brian Steadman was Adam and Sara's nephew and an excellent three-day-event rider.

"How are his clinics going?" Brian had begun offering clinics up and down the East Coast.

"He's having a terrific time. But I think he's ready to take a break and focus on his own riding," Sara said.

Jade nodded in understanding. Being a clinic instructor was intense work; one always had to be "on." Personally, she preferred the tinkering and fine-tuning that came with teaching students over the long haul. She also enjoyed being able to see the results of the hard work the horse and rider put in.

"Knowing you're back to stay in Warburg might be the thing to make him come home himself."

Adam's comment made Jade grateful for the store's soft lighting. Neither Steadman could see her blush of embarrassment.

Really, Adam should know better than to play matchmaker. Brian was a great guy and a terrific rider. He didn't need his uncle lining up dates for him, nor had he ever. Back in high school, the girls had been crazy for him, Jade among them. Luckily, she'd had just enough smarts not to act on her crush. Because the thing about Brian was that he was almost *too* nice, and back then she'd had a whole lot of dark stuff inside her. Had she and Brian dated, she'd have messed things up between them for sure—that, or Blair Hood would have started gunning for her again.

Blair Hood, who'd targeted Jade as her archenemy in school, had memorized the mean-girl handbook. It was probably the only book Blair bothered to read. Thank

God Jade didn't have to deal with the likes of Blair and her nasty, catty friends anymore.

But even though high school was over and Jade wasn't nearly as screwed up as she had been following the death of her parents, she sensed that perhaps Brian was still too nice a guy for her. She'd bet her four brand-new ponies that he wasn't the type to indulge in a wildly steamy hotel hookup with a stranger.

"It would be great to have Brian back in the neighborhood," she answered politely.

"I'll be sure to tell him you said so," Adam said with a wink.

Oh, Lord. "Above all, tell him not to cash his clinic checks, because when he comes back to Warburg he's going to want to come out to the farm and see the new crop of youngsters Ned and Travis are starting. A couple of them look like they'll make nice eventing prospects." Then, before either Steadman could wax eloquent on what a stupendous, good-looking, talented sweetheart of a dude their nephew was—all of which she knew perfectly well—she made a show of whipping the shopping list from the side pocket of her hobo bag. "So, Adam, I'm in the market for some pony tack. I was thinking we'd do saddles first. What have you got in sizes fourteen and fifteen inches? If you have any used saddles in good condition, that would be stupendous."

The days before school opened were filled from morning to night. Jade would have preferred it, however, if they'd been crammed to bursting. It was how she operated best. Too much downtime and little niggling worries started to creep into her brain. Jade knew she was good with kids. She enjoyed their curiosity, their openness and hunger to learn, their incredible sense of wonder. But what if the kids Ted Guerra had assigned to her class hated her? What if there wasn't that all-important

sense of connection? What if she couldn't reach in and
flick on the switches that lit their minds and made them
eager to learn about ecosystems, multiplication tables,
the fifty states, and to tackle their first chapter books?
What if she was a flop as a teacher? What if, when Sandy
Riley returned, she found a class of second-graders who
hadn't learned a thing and hated school? The thought
made her sick with dread.

Picking up the ponies at Windy Hill with Tito and
Ned helped. As did the fact that everyone—from Owen
to Patrick and Ellie Banner—was waiting to greet the
four new equine additions when the van rumbled back
up Rosewood's long drive.

"Oh, Jade, this one's so cute," Margot said, walking
up to stroke Dickens's velvety gray muzzle after Jade
had led him down the ramp. "I adore white ponies."

"Can you take him for me so I can go grab Sweet Virginia?"

"Sure." Margot grasped the nylon lead from Jade and
walked the gelding into the middle of the courtyard.
"What's his name?"

"That's Dickens," Olivia informed her. "And Tito's
bringing down Hopscotch. He's my favorite."

"I can see why, Olivia. He's really nice. A happy, relaxed fellow. Notice how he's looking around with his
ears pricked forward? Not worried at all. You all did
some great pony shopping."

"Yeah, we were the ones who picked them out. Aunt
Jade and Ned just watched us," Max said proudly.

"And take a look at this last one, babe," Travis said to
Margot as Jade brought Sweet Virginia down the ramp.

"Wow. Congrats, sis." Margot's voice was solemn.
"She's something." The four of them—Ned, Tito, Margot, and Jade—paraded the ponies around the courtyard
between the four barns with everyone else looking on.

"So, y'all approve?" Jade asked. She knew her own

face was split in a grin of happiness, but it was so very
fine to see the frank appreciation stamped on Margot
and Jordan's faces.

"They're adorable, Jade. And we're so glad they're
here," Jordan said.

"I'm glad you got ponies worthy of your new barn,
Jade," Owen teased.

"And we get to help ride them for Aunt Jade," Olivia
said.

"Don't say that too loudly, or Doc and Archer are
going to feel like you don't love them anymore," Kate
said.

Olivia shook her head so vehemently, her pigtails
slapped her tanned cheeks. "No, they won't. They know
we love them, and now they have new friends to play
with. Ponies are herd animals," the six-year-old told
them, with unshakable authority. One of her birthday
presents had been an encyclopedia of ponies. Jordan and
Owen had been taking turns reading it to her before bed.

"That's right, Olivia. So let's bring these guys into the
barn and get them settled in their digs. That'll give Doc
and Archer a chance to catch a first whiff of their new
pals."

"And then can we ride them?" Max asked eagerly.

"You've lucked out, Jade. Not everyone has a live-in
troupe of riders to exercise their mounts," Travis said,
grinning.

"And I've got Georgie, Will, and Neddy waiting in the
wings. The lot of them will be semipros by age twelve."

"Sounds like Jade's got it all figured out," Owen said.

"You bet." Wouldn't it be nice if that were true of the
rest of her life, Jade thought.

The distraction of working with the new ponies at
Rosewood and familiarizing herself with their habits
and dispositions, along with the hours she spent training

the horses Travis and Ned had assigned her, helped Jade stop worrying about what awaited her when the school bell rang come Tuesday morning.

She spent her evenings holed up in her little cottage, trying to prepare for her new job as thoroughly as possible. Lesson plans were drafted, charts constructed, name tags for cubbies and desks copied, the week's first homework assignment considered. Jade opted for a short questionnaire, so that the students could tell her a bit about themselves and she could see what their spelling and handwriting were like. A few math problems would also ease them back into the habit of adding and subtracting on paper.

Jordan had created a lovely working environment for her. The cottage was cozy but not fussy. The living room was dominated by a large off-white twill sectional (Jade had had to promise not to sit on it with her boots) decorated with green and blue throw pillows. Candlestick floor lamps framed the sofa, and a square coffee table rested before it.

Although there was a second bedroom, which held a large desk for her laptop and printer, Jade often found herself working at the antique benchwright table that served as her dining table. Jordan and Owen had come across it at an estate sale, and Jade found it the perfect length for laying out sheets of poster board when she was making job charts and writing out the rules for the classroom.

At the far end of the table sat the stack of four-by-twelve-inch desk tags she'd made. Next to it were the ones for the kids' cubbies. Every time she'd written Hayley Cooper's name, she had to quash the nervous flutters that made her Sharpie pen waver.

She knew she had no reason to be so nervous. Her classroom was taking shape, the space above the chalkboard decorated with the alphabet in both print and cursive, the walls covered with a map of the world, a birthday chart, the job chart she'd made, an oversize calendar, and, as a visual aid for the first unit the class would be studying on ancient civilizations, an array of posters depicting Egyptian pyramids, artifacts, and hieroglyphs. She was doing everything she could to create a learning environment that was both inviting and stimulating.

On the day before school opened, Jade was at the elementary school, putting the finishing touches on the classroom, fish for her sparkling new aquarium included. She'd placed the aquarium on top of a wide freestanding bookshelf, the perfect height for seven-year-olds to view the fish darting about inside the tank. She spent minutes inserting the aquatic plants and positioning a sunken ship, some different types of coral, and a perforated rock on the graveled bottom. Then, after checking the filter and double-checking the water temperature, she began to introduce the fish.

"Be well, be happy," she whispered as she carefully transferred six fish into the tank, more nervous about the lives of these vibrantly colored and patterned little fish—who immediately began darting this way and that in the clear water—than she was about her four new ponies.

But she *knew* horses; tetras, not so much. And though the ponies had been at Rosewood for only a few days, they were adapting just fine. The kids had ridden them in both the outdoor and indoor rings, and Jade herself had taken them out cross-country, through the wooded trails and over the late-summer fields. They'd been as well mannered hacking around Rosewood as they had been when she'd taken them on a test ride at Windy Hill.

Indeed, the ponies had been so good out in the field that she was already thinking that, as Kate and Max would be riding Doc and Archer in the children's division of the Warburg Hunt Cup, Olivia could enter the hunter trial competition on one of the new ponies—perhaps even ride her fave, Hopscotch. And if Jade convinced Owen to enter the Warburg Cup on Mystique, a seasoned field hunter, it would mean that more of her family than ever before would be riding in the hunt club's most prestigious event. Wouldn't that be cool?

She sprinkled some food into the tank, relieved when the fish darted to the surface to feed. They swam, they ate—so far, so good. She wondered what names the students would give them.

A knock on her open door had her spinning around. It was Tricia Creighton, the other second-grade teacher, whose classroom was across the hall.

"Hi. Oh! The room looks really great. You've pulled everything together nicely. I love the reading corner." Tricia nodded her head at the spot across the room where Jade had set up a low circular table for group reading and three bright beanbag chairs for the kids to curl up in with a book.

"Thanks." Jade considered Tricia's approval the equivalent of a gold star, since the older woman was a veteran of the trenches. Jade had been bowled over to learn that Tricia had been teaching second grade for *thirty* years. "And thanks for the tip about contacting publishing houses for the posters." Jade had followed Tricia's suggestion and called some New York publishers. A few had been generous enough to send her posters of books she hoped the kids would read this fall: *Building with Dad, Traction Man Is Here, Dogku,* and *Roger, the Jolly Pirate*.

"And let me take a look at the fish," Tricia said, crossing the room to peer into the tank. "The kids are going to love them."

"I hope so."

Something in Jade's voice, perhaps its fervency, had Tricia glancing up. "Are you nervous about tomorrow?"

"Between you and me and the chalkboard? My stomach's in knots," she confessed.

"Don't be. This is a great age to teach. The kids want to learn and they want to like you. A pretty terrific combination, if you ask me, and why I've always loved teaching this grade."

"Still, any last-minute advice would be greatly appreciated."

Tricia smiled. "The best advice I can give is don't try to do everything at once—you'll only overwhelm yourself as well as the kids. Oh, here's another pearl of wisdom to share: save your nerves for parents' night. That's a much tougher audience, ten times worse than your most disruptive, bratty kid."

Jade swallowed. "Really?"

"Without a doubt. So save your worrying until . . ." She glanced over at the calendar Jade had pinned to the right of the chalkboard. "Ten days from now."

"And here I was getting all worked up, fretting over whether I could talk about the Egyptian gods in a way to get the entire class excited."

"Piece of cake. I have a bunch of great Egyptian projects I've done over the years that I'd be happy to share with you. And though parents' night is the pits, it nevertheless serves a purpose. Spending an evening presenting your curriculum to parents and then having one couple ask why their little Johnny isn't being taught Fermat's last theorem, since his IQ is off the charts, or demand that you take such and such morally offensive title off your reading list makes you want to drop down on your knees and thank your lucky stars you're teaching their kids instead of them."

Jade couldn't help but laugh. "Wow, none of this was

mentioned in my education classes. Nor by any of the teachers I student-taught for—not a peep."

"One of many fun secrets that life is waiting to hammer you with. But I'm a firm believer in 'forewarned is forearmed.' In that spirit, come talk to me when you start menopause." She grinned at Jade's horrified expression. "Have I succeeded in distracting you from worrying about tomorrow and what's going to happen when you're standing in front of all those little faces?"

"Absolutely. I'm going to sleep like a baby tonight."

"Glad to hear it. I'd be lying if I didn't say your first day will be tiring and that, by Friday, you'll realize the term *TGIF* was invented by teachers. Speaking of which, a bunch of us—Kerri Kroeger in fourth grade, Andrea Hess in phys ed, Lena Rodriguez in Spanish—go out on the last Friday of every month to munch on nachos at Pepito's on Route 50 and vent. Feel free to join us whenever you can."

Jade felt an odd rush of pleasure at Tricia's casual invitation. High school had been such a brutal experience socially and emotionally that, apart from her sisters, Miriam Banner, Stuart Wilde, the guys at Rosewood, and a few other horse people, she didn't have that many friends in Warburg. It was strange—strange but very good—to realize that might change. "Thanks," she said. "If I manage to survive parents' night, I may take you up on that."

"You're tough, you'll be able to handle anything that walks in here—but remember to use PowerPoint."

Chapter ❧
TEN

"WHAT ARE you gonna wear tonight, Daddy?" Hayley asked as she speared a meatball on her fork and then twirled the spaghetti around it.

"Wear? What's wrong with what I have on?" Rob made a show of inspecting the front of his blue-and-white plaid shirt, which he wore with stonewashed khakis. "I didn't spill any sauce on it, did I?"

She wrinkled her nose at him as she chewed. Swallowing, she said, "No, but you have to look really nice. *It's go-to-school night,* and I want Miss Radcliffe to like you, because—"

"She's so neat," he finished.

Miss Radcliffe's general coolness had become Hayley's refrain since the first day of school. Her heart-shaped face would shine with happiness as she recounted what they'd done and how wonderful Miss Radcliffe was: "She's really pretty and funny and she had this fun game to help us learn everyone's name—though I already knew Jenny, Lucy, Colleen, Jay, and Arthur from last year. *And* we got to name the fish, and one of my names was picked!"

Then she'd gone on to describe Bubbles, a blue-and-black tetra with a plumy tail. Rob had already been given strict instructions to go to the fish tank and say hi to him tonight at parents' night.

"Okay, how about we make a deal, Hayley? You finish up your milk and that last meatball and I'll let you choose which shirt I should wear to parent–teacher night."

"You've got a deal, mister," she said happily, spearing the last meatball. "Let's go upstairs right away. I don't want you to be late, because I want you to have time to look at what I made for you. I left it on my desk."

"And you won't tell me what it is?"

Hayley shook her head. "No. It's a surprise."

A surprise that had left his daughter near to bursting with excitement for the past two days while she worked on her mystery project at school. That, combined with Hayley's pride at having read aloud a chapter book called *The Animal Rescue Club* to Miss Radcliffe, was enough to make him think that Jade Radcliffe possessed some serious talent in the teaching department.

Hayley drained her milk glass and set it on the table. "There." Wiping her milk mustache with her napkin, she pushed back her chair. "Let's go, Daddy."

"No dessert?"

"I can eat it later when Grammy and Poppy come over. This is too important. Let's go."

"These dishes have to be put away before Grammy comes or I'll never hear the end of it."

"I'll help."

Rob's eyebrows shot up at the offer. Hayley wasn't keen on kitchen duty.

With the dishwasher humming its way through the wash cycle and the counters sponged off by Hayley, Rob folded the damp dish towel over the oven door.

"Come on, Daddy," Hayley urged, tugging his hand. "You're going to be late if you don't hurry."

"After you, princess," he said with a sweep of his arm, grinning as she tore out of the kitchen, up the stairs, and down the hallway, flying past the gallery of framed photos devoted to her, Becky, and him.

Hayley had switched on the light in his bedroom and was already pulling open the closet's accordion doors when he entered.

The closet was spacious, too spacious.

A few months after Becky's death, his mother and Emma had gone through Becky's clothing, saving a few special pieces for Hayley and donating the rest to one of the charities where Becky had volunteered, one for women who were victims of domestic abuse. Since then, his shirts and trousers hung neatly from the dry cleaner's wire hangers. Next to them, his police uniforms formed a block of blue and black, with the department's patches affixed to the sleeves' shoulders gleaming gold and red. Beneath the clothes, his service shoes were lined neatly, regimentally.

Rob tried not to think about how much he missed the old clutter, when Becky's dresses and blouses had been mixed in with his, when her shoes had been strewn haphazardly the length of the closet, when he'd had to get down on his hands and knees to uncover a matching pair of his own. To alleviate the pain, he focused on Hayley.

She was standing in front of his shirts, a finger pressed to her lips as she considered. It didn't take her long to choose. "This one, Daddy. It makes your eyes look nice." She lifted an azure-blue sleeve.

It was the shirt he'd worn in Norfolk, the night of the torrential storm when he'd met the woman in the bar and then had sex that surpassed the elements raging outside. He hadn't worn the shirt since then, as putting it on would only remind him of how she'd taken it off. God, her mouth and the scrape of her nails across his abdomen had driven him wild. The memory alone was enough to make his heart thud heavily against his rib cage. This was *not* the shirt he wanted to wear to parents' night.

Standing on tiptoe, Hayley reached up to slip the hanger off the metal rod.

"Wait a sec, Hayley." He plucked a pale-gray shirt hanging next to it. "How about this one?" he asked, holding it in front of his chest. "I like it better than that one."

"No, Daddy, I want you to look *good*."

He laughed, shaking his head. From the mouths of babes. "Are you sure I have to wear the blue one?"

She nodded energetically. "Definitely."

"All right. Why don't you go and get your reading done while I change?"

"Okay, but remember, don't take too long. And don't spend too much time talking to Grammy and Poppy. And don't forget that you're supposed to ask Miss Radcliffe if I can take riding lessons with her. Jenny's mom has already signed her and Carly up."

Not this again. His daughter was nothing if not tenacious, and since she'd learned that Jade Radcliffe was giving riding lessons at Rosewood, she'd been at him nonstop. For the umpteenth time he wished Maryanne Ferris hadn't enrolled her daughters in Jade Radcliffe's program. It made it all the more difficult to divert Hayley. "Hayley, I don't know if it's a good idea to have your schoolteacher also give you riding—"

"But Jenny's mom signed her up as soon as she heard Miss Radcliffe was teaching. Lessons start next week, Daddy." He couldn't miss the pleading note in her voice.

"Okay, I'll see what I can do."

Although Jade knew it would take only minutes to set up her laptop and open the PowerPoint presentation she'd created for the evening, she arrived at school a full half hour early on Thursday night, the dreaded parents' night.

In the ten days since school had opened, the classroom had already undergone a radical transformation. Colorful drawings decorated the upper registers of the walls. The ones she liked best were the self-portraits. She'd asked the kids to depict themselves engaged in their favorite activity, so there was Kyle with a baseball bat; Alana with her dog; Chris swimming; and Hayley standing next to a dapple gray pony. Hayley had worked so hard to get the pony's face "just right." It was the same with the other portraits; Jade loved how her students' personalities shone in each.

On top of each desk was another project the kids had completed: They'd written letters to their parents describing something they especially liked about their school day and something they wanted the parents to inspect in the classroom. Patrick and Arthur liked learning about how the pyramids were built and wanted their parents to look at the diorama of the Nile the class was building with plasticine, paint, and twigs. Half finished, it covered the length of a long table in the back of the room. Eugene liked the job chart. He was especially pleased that this week he was in charge of feeding the fish.

The fish were a big hit with most of the class. Many of the letters talked about Bubbles, Willie, Flash, Fin, Nemo, and Target. Jade had placed the first packet of marked and graded work sheets next to the students' letters. It would give the parents something to read if their attention started to wander while she went over the list of restricted-foods birthday parties and reminded them to limit the amount of sugar- and fat-laden treats and above all to avoid any nuts in the food they brought to school.

Her eyes swept the room, looking for any stray bits of paper that might have fallen onto the carpeted floor, as mentally she went through her to-do list. What had she forgotten? Then her gaze landed on the table by the window. It was bare.

"Oh my God, the sign-up sheets!" she muttered in a panic.

Hurriedly, she reached into her messenger bag and drew out the sign-up sheets she'd made for parents to volunteer as chaperones, give talks about their jobs, and serve as parent liaisons to the class. The liaisons would help organize the holiday party before school let out for winter break. She was planning to make photo frames for the kids as going-away presents, since Sandy Riley would be returning to the class.

And the name tags and Sharpie pens—she'd forgotten to put those out too. She'd better get her act together before the parents arrived. Her heartbeat picked up at the thought of the parents she had yet to meet. While a number had already ventured into the classroom to introduce themselves, many had not—either because their children rode the school bus or because they'd decided to allow their seven-year-olds the thrilling independence of marching into the school building unaccompanied. Standing by the window to adjust the blinds against the morning sun, she often saw the distinctive blue-and-silver patrol car pull up to the curb and watched Hayley scramble out the passenger door.

It was just as well that it was impossible to view the interior of the police car and catch a glimpse of Hayley's father. Tonight was already too soon. She'd told herself a hundred times that it was ridiculous to be more nervous about meeting Rob Cooper than about meeting any of the other parents—for instance, if Deirdre was anything to go by, Mr. and Mrs. Cerra were going to be quite a challenge. An anxious little girl, Deirdre tended to have frequent meltdowns.

Rob Cooper was just a man. Just a dad. She could deal with him.

"Hi, are we too early? Would you like us to wait outside?" a cheerful voice inquired.

Jade turned to the couple standing by the open door. The woman she already recognized. The athletic, brown-haired man next to her must be Posey's dad; they had the matching looks husbands and wives sometimes shared. "No, please come in. You're Posey's parents, right?"

"Yes, I'm Gail and this is Chip," Gail Hall said, shaking Jade's hand energetically. "Posey is very happy to be in your class, Miss Radcliffe. Such a relief—she had a rocky start last year."

"I'm glad to hear that. She certainly seems comfortable."

"Does that mean she's chattering nonstop?" Chip Hall asked with a wry smile. "She does that. It runs in the family, doesn't it, Gail?"

His wife elbowed him in the ribs. "Chip!"

Jade smiled. "It's nothing I can't handle." Then, gesturing to the table, she said, "There are name tags for you on this table as well as some sign-up sheets for the holiday party and field trips and volunteer opportunities . . ."

At the sound of more voices, Jade glanced over her shoulder. A throng of adults had entered the room, and they were looking about with open curiosity.

Parents' night had started.

She barely budged for fifteen minutes as parents came over to introduce themselves. Though most were cheerful and polite and restrained—Jade was a substitute teacher, after all—the extremes presented themselves too. Mrs. Kemp gushed like a fountain about how wonderful Jade was and how much Victoria adored her. But if Anne Kemp behaved as if Jade and she had been best friends forever, Eugene Harrison's parents didn't hesitate to show their antipathy. Eugene senior—or IV—

could barely work his stiff lips enough to manage a hello before ignoring Jade completely to study the room with an equally dismissive air. Eugene's mother, Christy, all sparkly with her diamond earrings, Tiffany chain necklaces and charm bracelets, and a boulder of an engagement ring, must have decided it was crucial to remind everyone of the Harrisons' net worth by wearing it to parents' night.

The first sentence out of Christy's mouth indicated just how much she cared about her son's new school. "I can't possibly volunteer for anything right now—I have too many important obligations." Her second was no more endearing. "However, I will be meeting with Mr. Guerra next week. Eugene needs a more advanced curriculum than the one you're offering. I can tell he's bored."

Jade's eyebrows shot up. The comment about the curriculum was a bit rich, as the Harrisons hadn't even heard what the year's curriculum encompassed. "Actually, the second-grade curriculum is quite varied. As you will see, we cover a good bit of ground."

"Then maybe Eugene's boredom stems not so much from the curriculum as from *his present teacher,*" she murmured with a superior smirk, before she and her snob of a husband turned away to go park themselves behind Eugene's desk.

Jade had no time to react because yet another mother appeared before her. Easy to guess who it was; Mrs. Cerra was practically vibrating with anxiety, so nervous, one would have thought it was she who was about to speak before the assembled adults. Patiently, Jade listened as she recited Deirdre's allergies, wondering all the while whether Mrs. Cerra thought she couldn't read. Jade had already received—and read—several notes warning her of Deirdre's susceptibility to pollen, dander, and mold.

"I'm just so worried that the upcoming field trip to the apple orchard will be too much for her. Of course, I know how much Deirdre would enjoy the outing," she finished, looking desperately unhappy to be faced with such a dilemma.

"Perhaps you'd like to volunteer as a chaperone on the trip, Mrs. Cerra. That way, if Deirdre does have a problem with her allergies, you'll be on hand. The sign-up sheet is right here." While Mrs. Cerra bent like a human question mark over the table to read the sign-up sheet with a diligence usually reserved for legal documents, Jade glanced at her watch. Four minutes before seven. She was determined to start on the dot—and end just as punctually.

She crossed the classroom to lower the projection screen and then turned to her desk to open the Power-Point program. She heard yet another group of parents entering the room but kept her gaze focused on the screen. They could say their hellos and sign up—or not—for whatever activity piqued their interest after her presentation.

When the first slide appeared on the screen, she drew a breath and straightened, ready to greet the assembled parents.

Her gaze swept the wide semicircle of adult faces. When she got to where Hayley's metal-and-wood desk was positioned and to the lone man sitting behind it, she stalled.

It couldn't be.

It was.

Chapter ❧
ELEVEN

THEIR EYES met and locked in a clash of intense blue and green. For days she had been steeling herself, prepared for his disapproval. But it was her own stark horror as she recognized the strikingly handsome man in the deep-blue shirt—the very shirt she'd stripped off his muscular torso—that left her reeling.

She obviously had the absolute worst luck in the world. Of all the people in Warburg, Rob Cooper was the one she most wanted to convince that she'd become an upstanding, straitlaced, buttoned-up, *respectable* person, a proper elementary-school teacher.

Yet barely a month ago, she'd been writhing and moaning for him—without a stitch or a button on.

How could *he* be the guy she'd slept with in Norfolk, the guy who'd given her an unforgettable night of scorching sex? Giantlike in Hayley's chair, Rob Cooper looked way too stiff to know how to do half the stuff they'd done together. But though she'd have given the last penny she owned to be wrong, she knew that cleft chin; she'd traced the beard-roughened indentation with the tip of her tongue. She knew those blue eyes as well. When he'd pushed himself deep inside her, those same eyes had seared her, electric and sizzling hot.

He was watching her just as intently now. But the effect was quite different: His glare was as cold—and as terrifying—as a nuclear winter.

So he'd recognized her. Great, just great.

The tiny part of her that had been hoping against hope that he would fail to connect her with the woman he'd met in Norfolk withered beneath his icy stare. Of course, with her lousy luck, she should have realized that would have been as likely as winning the Lotto.

He'd obviously identified her and was probably fantasizing about throwing her in jail for the next twenty years.

Life was so unfair. If he'd looked like this in Norfolk, so stern and condemning, she'd never have agreed to dance with him, let alone take him upstairs to her hotel room—God, why hadn't she recognized him? He'd been the bogeyman of her youth.

A dreadful answer sprang to mind. Maybe she *had* recognized him. Maybe she was such a twisted mess of a human being that some part of her had known precisely who he was and opted to spend a night rolling between the sheets with him anyway.

No, she thought with a mental shake. Not even at her most self-destructive would she have gone near Officer Rob Cooper, Warburg's very own RoboCop. He was too darned scary.

Another image of them together—of her body straining against his as he entered her from behind, of his hands fondling and stroking her breasts while he drove deep inside her, touching her core while she shuddered and trembled around him—had her wishing the floor would open up and swallow her whole. But it didn't, and she was left standing there, exposed to the chilling blast of his anger.

The discordant squeak of chairs and the restless stir and shift of bodies abruptly reminded her of the seventeen couples who were also staring at her. How many minutes had elapsed while they'd been waiting for her to start, waiting for her to say something? The smug smile on Christy Harrison's lips answered her: too long.

Damn. She had to pull herself together or she'd compound the disaster by messing up her presentation. She could do this. She simply had to pretend Rob Cooper wasn't there. If she didn't look at him, it would be as if he didn't exist. No biggie. Out of sight, out of mind . . .

Did anyone actually believe in this positive-thinking malarkey? she wondered, fighting a rising panic. How could she possibly ignore him when he sat there, a living, breathing reminder of her latest screwup?

And, man, he really had the whole wrath-of-God act down pat, didn't he?

Just focus on the freakin' screen, she told herself.

The roaring in his ears made it impossible to hear a single detail of Hayley's supposed curriculum. Nor had he been able to focus on the projection screen; his gaze had narrowed to one and only one object: her.

He couldn't believe it, had nearly fallen off his undersize plastic chair when she looked over at him and he saw Jade Radcliffe for the first time in years and, *click,* an image of his sinfully sexy siren—naked and writhing beneath him—was superimposed over demure Miss Radcliffe, his little girl's idol.

Jesus H. Christ, there she was, standing in front of the class in a slim skirt that fell nearly to her ankles, ballet flats, and a simple buttoned top, the very picture of innocence and modesty, gulling everyone as she talked calmly about God only knew what, and all he could think about was what she was hiding beneath that schoolmarm outfit: an impossibly sexy body that was all taut curves and silken flesh.

And he'd touched and tasted every sweet inch of it.

Memories hot and vivid flashed in his mind.

He thought of the blue-violet butterfly that floated just below her hip bone, remembered pressing his mouth against it and feeling her skin quiver beneath his lips, recalled the tangy taste of her when he'd drawn his tongue slowly down her cleft and probed her slick heat. He could hear the exact pitch of her moan as he thrust into her, filling her, driving them both toward the edge, and it was enough to make him want to jump out of his chair and drag her out of the classroom and . . .

Do what exactly? a voice asked.

That was the hell of it. He was damned if he knew what to do in such a situation.

Jade would never say another condescending word about people who read aloud verbatim from their PowerPoint presentations. With Rob Cooper's furious gaze fixed unwaveringly on her, it was a miracle she'd managed that much. Even then she'd been forced to lean against her teacher's desk to support her trembling legs. The edge of it had bitten deep, leaving grooves in her palms.

She tried not to rush through the last slide, which showed the kids working on the diorama of the Nile, and squelched the impulse to sprint out of the room when the screen went blank.

Then she was surrounded by chattering parents and was absurdly grateful to talk at length to them; Rob Cooper wasn't among the group.

"I just wanted to tell you how much Sam is enjoying the year so far. I simply love the picture he drew of himself with our dog, Barney."

"I'm glad to hear that, Mrs. Powell. Sam's a lot of fun. He's got a very developed sense of humor." To the delight of the other boys in the class, Sam had brought a whoopee cushion in for show-and-tell. After the gut-busting laughs—which had Sam, Kyle, Jay, Chris, James, and even Eugene Harrison rolling on the floor—had subsided, Jade steered the discussion to other funny noises: the trumpeting of an elephant, the rumbling of a hungry stomach, the croaking of a bullfrog. Alana had raised her hand and said she thought the funniest sound was her little sister's laugh. The show-and-tell session had led to the prompt for the day's journal entry: writing about the funniest noise ever.

"Older brothers," Mr. Powell explained with an apologetic shrug. "Speaking of which, we better go see what the gang's been up to. We've got our thirteen-year-old twins, Charlie and Derek, babysitting. To avoid any disasters, we took the precaution of telling the three of them that Officer Cooper would be here tonight and that if there was any trouble, he'd be coming by the house later in his patrol car. Good to meet you, Miss Radcliffe. Bye, Rob."

Jade could only nod. The huge lump lodged in her throat made speech impossible. She'd been so busy *not* looking, she hadn't realized Rob was the last parent left in the room. She wished there was somebody else; she'd have been happy to listen to Christy Harrison in all her glittering disdain.

What to say to him? Something along the lines of: *Hiya, stranger. Missed me?* Yeah, right. She'd rather be dragged over burning coals than admit she knew what he looked like beneath that shirt—good God, it really was the one he'd been wearing that night in Norfolk.

He looked at her, his expression as far from friendly as Mars was from Earth. "From cruising bars to teaching seven-year-olds—you do it all, don't you?"

She swallowed, and the lump that had been lodged in her throat sank right down to the pit of her stomach. It didn't make speaking any easier, and she truly had no idea how to deal with the situation. Not that he was giving her a chance to speak. He'd already started again.

"So answer me this: Did you know who I was at the bar?"

Heat stole over her. "I—I—No—" She shook her head violently.

"Yeah, I think you did know," he contradicted forcefully. "I think you wanted to screw me, in every sense of the word."

She stared at him. "Are you nuts? I haven't seen you in *years*. And you didn't look like you."

"Of course I did," he replied. "Which means that you're a liar."

Her hands balled into tight fists at her sides. She could practically feel the steam shooting out of her ears. "No, it means you're totally obtuse. I did *not* recognize you!"

He raised a mocking brow at her outburst. "If what you say is true, then that means you're into random pickups with strangers. I'd say either of those makes you unsuitable to teach Hayley. I'm calling Ted Guerra tomorrow and having her transferred to Mrs. Creighton's class."

The pain of his announcement surprised her. After all, she'd already wondered how he'd react to her—someone he regarded as an ex–juvenile delinquent—teaching his daughter. That he'd had sex with her too clearly disgusted him. Well, in that respect, the feeling was mutual. She wasn't exactly thrilled to discover her mystery lover was a moralistic prig.

And damn her body for reacting so traitorously. She shouldn't be ridiculously aware of his nearness and the heat coming off his body or how infuriatingly sexy he looked even when filled with righteous disapproval. How could she be feeling the electric sizzle between them—the same as she'd felt on that dance floor—when she knew who he was and didn't remotely like him?

But she *did* like Hayley, who was bright and eager to learn, and who was furthermore a deeply sensitive little girl. When Jade had discussed parents' night with the class earlier in the day, she'd seen how hard it was for

Hayley when the other kids talked about their mothers *and* fathers being there. As someone who had lost her own parents, she understood the pain Hayley felt at such moments, how much the little girl must miss her mother. She thought she could help Hayley with some of the things she was going through . . . help her grow.

But it looked like she wasn't going to get the opportunity. Hearing Rob Cooper say he intended to yank Hayley out of her class, away from what he doubtless considered her corrupting presence, hurt her. And it galled that he was behaving as if everything were her fault, as if she'd bewitched him into being her sex slave.

If memory served, it had been he who cupped her ass and pulled her flush against the very solid evidence of his desire. It had been his roughly whispered "Do you have a room?" that had turned her brain to mush. No matter how much he wanted to pretend otherwise, he'd been every inch the eager participant.

Although she was sorely tempted to spit in his perfectly sculpted face, she told herself to behave maturely. Professionally.

She raised her chin and summoned her most even and detached tone. "Hayley's a lovely little girl, and I think that we've already formed a nice bond. I'm sorry to hear that you feel that I can't teach Hayley. But as her father, you have to do what you feel is best."

A clever response, Rob acknowledged. Phrased to maximize his sense of guilt and remind him of what he knew perfectly well: Hayley adored Jade Radcliffe. He'd have a devil of a time explaining to her why she was being switched to Mrs. Creighton's class. Just thinking of how unhappy she'd be made his gut twist.

He felt pretty damned rotten about the flash of hurt he'd seen in Jade's eyes when he announced his intention to pull Hayley from her class. He didn't understand why it should bother him that he'd hurt Jade or why he felt such guilt—where she was concerned, he didn't want to feel anything except anger.

What was it about her? She was unquestionably the wrong type of woman for him, yet he couldn't stop looking at her. Nor could he stop remembering how it had been between them.

Jesus, he thought, struggling to absorb it all. It had been hard enough to come to terms with the fact that his young daughter's teacher was also a former juvie, that the first time he'd run into her she was passed out and reeking to high heaven, the charming aftereffects of a house party he'd helped bust. That she'd also snuck into the Den with a fake ID, been the cause of a fistfight, and was the reason he'd been tied up in the station booking all concerned while Becky lay dying—*No.* He pulled his thoughts up short. He couldn't link those incidents or his mind would friggin' explode.

But if that history was hard enough to accept, what was he supposed to do with the uncomfortable fact that Jade Radcliffe also happened to be the green-eyed wild-cat he'd fucked almost every way he could imagine? And that even now, when he knew who and what she was, she still made his pulse run wild—and his body harden with need?

How could she stand there, only inches away from him, with such self-possession? He wanted to see that cool composure slip and know that she was as off balance as he.

He angled his head and gave her a long hard stare. It was a look that had a proven track record of intimidating the hell out of people. "Yeah, I'd say it's definitely my prerogative to do what I believe is in Hayley's best interest. So, now that I've determined she won't be your pupil, you might as well 'fess up. You *did* recognize me in Norfolk and decided it would be fun to pull the wool over my eyes and sleep with me, didn't you?" Sure, he was harping on the issue, but it was important for him to know Jade had intentionally seduced him that night. For them to have been caught up in some intense mutual attraction was too disturbing a notion.

What a megajerk, Jade thought, as the hold on her temper snapped. For a brief moment she was actually happy Hayley wasn't going to be in her class, because now she was free to tell this oaf exactly what she thought.

"If you had half a brain, you'd realize what a stupid idea that is. You're the last person I'd want to do *anything* with. I'd have beat the world record sprinting out of that bar if I'd known that in addition to being the cop who busted me twice, you're a hypocritical prig—"

"Who are you calling a hypocritical prig?" he snarled softly.

She was too angry to care that his expression had turned thunderous. Shooting him a contemptuous glare, she said, "The truth hurts, doesn't it? Fact check: *You're* the one who asked *me* to dance, the one who asked if I had a room in the hotel, the one who used every condom I had and would have probably gone through more of them if there'd been any. So don't attempt to rewrite history and pretend I lured you to the hotel room to have my wicked way with you. We were two consenting adults. No laws were broken. While I'll certainly miss having Hayley in my class, the upside is that I won't have to deal with you and be reminded of the lousy mistake I made sleeping with you." Her fury growing with each point she made, she began to jab his chest with her index finger for emphasis. But when she finished with a damning "So I'd appreciate it, Officer Cooper, if you'd take a really long hike off a really short pier—" he caught her wrist, holding it between their bodies.

"That night we spent together was a lousy mistake, was it?"

Ignoring the firestorm sweeping through her simply because his hand was encircling her wrist, she thrust her chin out mutinously and glared at him. Her pulse was hammering against the pads of his long fingers. It galled her that he doubtless felt it. "Absolutely. A colossal mistake. One of my worst."

"Liar."

They stared at each other as the whispered word hung in the air between them.

And as the seconds slipped by, she was filled with a rising sense of despair. Because not only was he right—this time she *was* lying—but also because it was happening again. *It* being the strange, electrifying sense of connection between them. Only now it was a thousand times more unsettling. How could she feel this out-of-control attraction to *Rob Cooper*?

"I really don't care what you think," she enunciated through gritted teeth, afraid that if she opened her mouth, her voice would come out all breathy and weak from the need raging inside her.

"Well, I'm going to share anyway. I don't believe you think the night we spent together was a mistake at all. I don't believe you've forgotten the things we did together or how I made you feel. But I *do* believe that you'd like me to do all those things again." His voice was low and rough. It, along with the heated words and the feather-light stroke of his thumb on the inside of her wrist, sent sensual shivers racing through her. Her nipples tightened into aching buds against the fabric of her bra, while heat pooled inside, melting her.

Desperate, determined, she struggled against the want. Blast him for making her feel this way.

"Again, so sorry, but I don't care. Now, you'll forgive me if I refuse to indulge your bloated ego. I need to get home." Intending to usher him out, she turned toward the door, only to let out a growl of frustration when he kept his hold of her wrist. "Mind unshackling me?"

"I'll let you go after you've proved just how indifferent you are."

"What? Are you nuts? I don't have to prove anything to you—though anybody else would recognize that I *am* proving my complete disinterest by asking you to leave my classroom. Do I honestly look like I want to throw myself at you?"

Rob didn't need a second invitation. He let his eyes travel slowly over Jade, taking in her flushed cheeks, her heaving breasts, and the brilliant radiance of her wide green eyes. She was as beautiful as he remembered, and right now just as aroused as he. "Yeah, you do."

Jade managed only a strangled "arggh!" of outrage before Rob, with a tug on her wrist, pulled her off balance. As she teetered, her free hand landed against his chest. He captured it too.

"Looks like I've caught you." Succumbing to the hunger inside him that had been craving a taste of her for the past hour, Rob kissed her.

His kiss was fierce. It took, it plundered, and it demanded she respond in kind.

The touch of his firm lips, the bold sweep of his tongue against hers, rocked her, triggering an explosion of desire within her. Jade succumbed. With a desperate moan, she bit down on his lower lip. Flinging her suddenly liberated arms about his neck, she arched into him.

It shouldn't be like this, this maddened stampede of need tearing through her the moment they embraced. No sexy music was driving their bodies together, no half-lit room with a king-size bed was awaiting them as their tongues dueled and their hands grasped and stroked. Her second-grade classroom was the un-sexiest room imaginable. And now that she and Rob knew each other's identity, they should both be repelled, not fused together by raw passion and sweeping desire.

Unable to resist the aching pleasure his knowing caresses aroused, she pulled his dark head closer, kissing him feverishly.

Jade's kiss, as hungry and carnal as he remembered, pushed him to the brink. Rob no longer cared who she was or wasn't, he only wanted her. Time and place lost meaning. All that mattered was the need to feel her melting around him, to have her shudder and cry out in exquisite pleasure as she climaxed in his arms. Mindless, his hands streaked down, one circling her waist while the other grabbed fistfuls of her skirt, bunching and hiking it up to touch skin as soft as sun-kissed satin.

Her legs were trembling and, as his hand moved toward her panties, she moaned, the sweetest sound. When his fingers slid under the elastic band, her moan turned into a broken, desperate whimper.

She was as close to the edge as he, he thought with fierce satisfaction.

Then he touched her, brushing her curls, then slipping down her cleft and into her slick heat, and she felt as incredibly, mind-blowingly good as he remembered.

Her body was clenching convulsively around his fingers. The sensation drove him wild. He needed to be deeper inside her, replacing his fingers with his cock, thrusting into her and rocketing them both to a shattering climax. His craving for Jade obliterated all else.

"Do you have a condom?" He barely registered his own roughly whispered words. It took Jade's forceful shove, sending him stumbling backward in surprise, to make him fully comprehend what he'd said and for sanity to return.

But it was too late.

"Get out!"

Jade's agonized expression was a swift kick to the gut. "I—Jade—I'm—" he stammered.

Oh, God! she wailed silently. Did he think she was going to talk to him after what he'd just said? She'd never been so mortified in her life, and she'd lived through more than her fair share of embarrassments. Did Rob actually think she went to parents' night with condoms packed in her laptop case? Maybe he believed she stored Trojans in her desk so she could have quickies during snack time?

He thought she was a slut. *Just like your mom was,* a cruel voice taunted her.

Rob still hadn't moved. "I told you to get out, damn it," she said, aware that tears were beginning to fall down her cheeks but unable to stop them. She was equally unable to control the shrill note in her voice as she demanded, "Just leave."

Wordlessly, Rob opened the door, and Jade gave silent thanks to the Powells for having shut it after them. Otherwise, any passerby could have seen Rob and her.

"Jade—" Just over the threshold, Rob had turned back. "I'm really—"

He got no further.

With an anguished snarl, Jade slammed the door in his face, sank to the carpeted floor, and wept.

HE'D GONE and screwed up. Royally.

The thought drummed in his head even as Rob reached his car in the school's lot. His cellphone was in hand, his thumb had already scrolled down to Ted Guerra's number—he'd seen the school principal through the open door of his office talking to the Harrisons, so Rob figured there was a good chance he'd pick up—to make what was fast disintegrating into a halfhearted attempt to switch Hayley into Mrs. Creighton's class. Hayley belonged in Jade Radcliffe's class, no matter what his personal feelings were. No matter how he'd just managed to make Jade loathe him.

But the phone was already ringing and, what the hell, Tricia Creighton was a good teacher. Of course, if Rob's brain had been functioning, he would have guessed what Guerra's response to his request would be.

Ted squashed the idea flatter than a bug. "Sorry, Rob, but I'm unwilling to transfer Hayley to Tricia Creighton's class. Tricia's a veteran teacher, so I've placed a couple of students with her who were disruptive with their first-grade teachers. Even if Tricia didn't have some behavioral problems in her class to contend with, Hayley is a very sensitive little girl. It would be hard for her to switch classes, and switching into a class where some of the kids are acting out would be especially difficult. I don't want to put Hayley in a situation that might have a negative impact on her emotionally and academically.

There's no point. Jade Radcliffe and Hayley are a good match, Rob. I've been dropping in to observe Jade's class and see how things are going. Hayley's flourishing. She participates and she's clearly comfortable with the class dynamics. Moreover, she already has a number of friends in the class. I hope you'll soon come to recognize what a good experience she's having with Jade Radcliffe."

There, of course, was the crux of the problem. Rob had seen ample proof of Jade's qualities as a teacher. The evidence was in the homework packets Hayley was assigned, a fun mix of traditional exercises and more-creative assignments, and in the way Hayley raced up the elementary-school steps each morning. Every parent dreamed of a school year beginning like this for his or her child.

He couldn't bring himself to divulge that there were other aspects that made the classroom situation impossible. Ted wouldn't know about Rob and Jade's ancient history, and it went against Rob's principles to speak of them. She'd been underage, and her case was long since closed. He damned well wasn't going to discuss their all-too-recent history either.

The conversation concluded and Rob hung up, feeling frustrated and increasingly guilty. As much as he wanted to make the messy situation with Jade disappear, wishing wouldn't make it happen. Removing Hayley from Jade's class wasn't going to make him forget the night he and Jade spent together or the way she'd kissed him minutes ago.

He could taste her on his lips.

There was bitter with the sweet, however. He could still see her tormented expression as she ordered him out of the classroom. He could still hear her ragged sobs as she broke down and cried on the other side of the door. He'd stood in the hallway like an impotent clod, wanting to go back into her room and say *something* but knowing his presence would only make things worse.

He had to apologize to her. He'd behaved like an ass. He'd *sounded* like such a dumb fuck. That his brain had been fried by lust was no excuse for his behavior. How could he have ever thought sex with Jade in a classroom a possibility? Asking her for a condom was, without a doubt, the most idiotic question he'd ever uttered.

She must despise him—if not for his ill-timed, moronic question, then for his condemning, holier-than-thou attitude.

She'd called him a prig and a hypocrite. It rankled that he couldn't dismiss her accusations outright. He'd be the first to admit that he was tough; he was a cop. But he also believed he was ultimately fair-minded.

Yet he'd been anything but concerning that night in Norfolk. He realized now that it had been easier to play the blame game and tell himself that he'd been caught in Jade's sexual lure than to admit he'd made plenty of the moves that led them to her hotel room. Because to admit that uncomfortable truth would be to acknowledge that he'd desired a woman who wasn't Becky—and desired her with desperate intensity.

Acknowledging that he *still* wanted Jade was even harder, especially now, knowing who she was and what a mistake it would be to get involved with her.

He drove from the elementary school on autopilot. It being a weeknight, Warburg was quiet. Lights shone over front doors and glimmered softly in upstairs windows, giving the houses a snug, sleepy look. Pulling into his own driveway, he saw that the family room at the end of the house was illuminated. His dad and mom would be in there, watching TV as they awaited his return. His gaze traveled to Hayley's window. It was dark, but he knew she'd still be awake. She'd be too excited, wanting to hear exactly what he thought of Miss Radcliffe.

Unbuckling his seat belt, he remained immobile, staring at the small house he and Becky had bought six

months into their marriage and trying to reconcile what
he felt for Jade Radcliffe with the life he'd made with
Becky in the trim little Colonial, with the love they'd
made in there.

From where he sat, it was an impossible task. Whatever it was he felt for Jade—and damned if he could
identify it yet—he knew it bore no resemblance to what
he'd had with Becky.

But somehow that didn't lessen the fierce hunger that
consumed him whenever Jade entered his thoughts.

Hell. Well, there were a slew of things he craved but
didn't let himself have. Jade Radcliffe was going to enjoy
the number-one spot on that particular list, he thought
as he climbed out of the car.

He'd apologize to Jade for his actions and he'd keep
Hayley in her class, but then he was going to maintain his
distance. After all, Jade would only be teaching through
the fall semester and then she'd be out of their lives.

Walking up to the front door, he spied one of Hayley's
makeshift horse jumps and bit off a curse. Hayley was
going to be disappointed, but there it was. No way was he
signing her up for riding lessons at Rosewood.

Because getting any more involved with Jade could
only spell trouble.

All Jade wanted was to go back to her cottage, crawl
into bed, pull the covers over her, and will the world
away, but she'd promised to drop by the big house after
parents' night. She knew her sisters well. If she didn't
show up, they'd come to her place—and they might not
leave. The sooner she gave them a highly edited version
of the night's events, the sooner she could forget the true
horror of the evening and lock it away with all the other
shitty memories she had of Rob Cooper.

Except that not all of the memories she had of him
were so very lousy. Had he been drunk that night in

Norfolk or had someone slipped him a happy pill? she wondered as she stomped up the front-porch steps, aware that the scowl on her face was probably as heavy as her tread.

Luckily, Rosewood was a huge old house and Georgie and Will's rooms faced the back, so the noise she was making wasn't likely to wake them up. As she passed a carved gilt mirror in the parlor, she smoothed the lines of her face, checking, too, that she'd scrubbed all the traces of her tears in the elementary-school bathroom.

She found Miriam in the library, watching a movie. Grace Kelly was on the screen. It took Jade only a second to identify the film; she loved *To Catch a Thief*.

"Hey, where are the others?"

"Margot ran upstairs to check on the kids, and Jordan's making popcorn. Travis, Andy, and Owen went to do the barn check."

"Owen probably wanted to sneak Cosmo some extra bedtime treats."

Miriam nodded and stretched. "Yeah, Owen's a soft touch when it comes to Cosmo. The guys were also going to drop by Thistle Cottage and look at Ned's bathroom. Owen wants to redo it for him and is recruiting Travis and Andy to convince Ned that an update is essential."

"That'll take some serious convincing."

"Yup. So we get to continue with our Grace Kelly fest. It's in your honor, Jade. Margot told me you brought up *Rear Window* the other night and how since then Jordan and she have been dying to see her in action. You missed *High Society*."

"Bummer."

"So how'd it go tonight?" Miriam asked. She pressed the PAUSE button, freezing the image of a gorgeous Grace Kelly with her arms around Cary Grant's neck, her eyes shining with triumph as she told him she'd figured out he was the infamous cat burglar.

What great stuff, Jade thought. Too bad her life wasn't like that. Instead of Cary Grant, she got a jerk who wanted to know whether she had any spare condoms. What did he think, that she kept them in her teacher's desk, next to the confiscated chewing gum?

Feeling depressed, she dropped down onto the sofa beside Miriam. "Sorry," she apologized, when they bumped shoulders. With a groan, she laid her head against the cushion of the deep-green velvet sofa.

"It was that bad, huh?"

"Pretty darned hellish," Jade admitted with a sigh.

"I'm surprised. You worked so hard putting your presentation together. It was great."

"That wasn't the awful part."

"Oh. Gotcha. It was the doting parents."

Jade lifted her head to stare moodily at the screen, then wished she hadn't as Miriam said, "Hey, have you been crying? Your lids are all red."

Damn. She hadn't thought anyone would notice. Silly of her. Miriam was as perceptive as her sisters. "It's not a big deal."

"What happened tonight? Did Rob Cooper or the Harrisons give you a hard time?"

"Both, but the former took the prize."

"What did Cooper do? Try to arrest you?"

"Ha. Not funny, Mir."

"Sorry."

"Forgiven," Jade replied. Miriam was her closest friend. She'd stuck with her even when Jade had been at her most self-destructive, about as fun to be around as poison ivy.

"So what happened between you and Rob Cooper?"

Though Miriam was a few years older, she wasn't that old—Jade could tell her about the night she'd spent with

Rob Cooper and not have her faint from shock or *completely* freak with worried disapproval, which effectively crossed both Jordan and Margot off her Share Latest Stupidity list. "Mir, do you remember when I came home from Florida, how I told you I met a guy in the hotel?"

"The hottie?"

"Yeah." Jade nodded glumly, remembering how, even hours after rolling between the sheets with Rob, she'd been humming with sexual satisfaction. She'd always thought she had pretty good internal radar when it came to jerks. Clearly it needed a major repair job.

Or maybe the problem was her. She'd known who he was tonight and she'd still let him kiss her. And a lot more besides, her guilty conscience reminded her. Like almost making her come in his arms—in her classroom. *Oh, God.*

"Sure I remember you mentioning him." Miriam laughed. "You were looking like my cat, Lulu, after a saucer of cream. Very happy. What's your Norfolk hottie have to do with how your parents' night went?"

Jade shifted uncomfortably on the soft velvet cushions. "Well, it turns out that the hottie was Rob Cooper."

"What?" Miriam shrieked. "He's—Jade—that's—*oh my God!* It's one thing not to bother getting a guy's number; I didn't realize you couldn't be bothered to find out his *name!*"

Okay, so maybe Miriam was reacting a little more intensely than Jade had anticipated. It must be the fact that she was getting ready to tie the knot with Andy. "I didn't really think knowing his name mattered," she said defensively. "And, FYI, he didn't seem to think knowing *my* name was all that essential either—"

"What's this about not knowing names?" Jordan entered the library, carrying a truly enormous bowl of popcorn. "Did you forget the name tags? How'd it go otherwise, sweetie?"

"Yeah, tell us everything," Margot added, a few steps behind her.

"Yeah, Jade, tell them *everything*," Miriam said, folding her arms across her chest. Her posture reeked of maturity.

Oh, crap. The trouble with Miriam was that she wasn't only Jade's friend, she was Jordan's and Margot's as well. Mir looked up to them, admired them—which wasn't to say that Jade didn't as well, but in addition to worrying just how badly they were going to react to what she told them about Rob, well, it was also kind of weird to be sharing this stuff with her sisters.

But a glance at Miriam's set expression told Jade it was useless to prevaricate. So much for giving Jordan and Margot a neatly edited version in which all the messy and less-than-stellar moments were carefully deleted.

Shooting her best friend a dirty look, she said with a sigh, "You guys better take a seat. And, Jordan, you'll definitely want to put the bowl of popcorn down." No sense in having good popcorn tossed all over the floor when Jordan fainted from shock.

Ten agonizing, embarrassing, heat-crawling-over-her-cheeks minutes passed while she hemmed and hawed her way through her account of meeting a really good-looking sexy guy in Norfolk, spending the night with him, and then discovering to her considerable dismay that the man she'd relegated to a fond (though steamy) memory was very much in her present—because he was none other than Officer Rob Cooper, aka RoboCop, aka Hayley's dad. Deciding she might as well get the worst of it over, she included her and Rob's mutual horror at parents' night when they recognized each other. But she kept to herself the final, truly mortifying bit, when Rob had kissed her and stroked her until she nearly climaxed, and his appalling condom request.

Not only was the story embarrassing as all get-out, but in order to stress that she wasn't a complete idiot, she'd already mentioned the word *condom* a few too many times in front of Jordan.

Jordan had her own unpleasant prophylactics memories. Back when she was pregnant with Olivia and married to her first husband, Richard, she'd happened upon a bunch of them in Richard's suit pocket. Suffice it to say, the condoms weren't being used by Jordan and Richard.

Jade didn't want Jordan to have to relive the anguish of that by uttering the word anymore. And revealing that she'd allowed Rob to kiss her again, or that the moment he'd touched her she'd practically come in his arms, was too upsetting to admit aloud. This was *Robo-Cop*, after all.

So she ended her story with, "Then Cooper told me he was going to have Hayley moved into Tricia Creighton's class, and he left. Good riddance—to him, not to Hayley, who obviously gets her brains from her mother." Just to make sure everyone knew there was nothing left to the story, Jade grabbed a handful of popcorn and shoved it into her mouth.

Unfortunately, Margot wasn't buying it; her older sister knew her too well. She pinned her with a long look. Jade wouldn't have believed the itchy flush covering her throat and cheeks could intensify. It did. She felt like she'd broken out in a full body rash of guilt.

Stuffing her mouth with popcorn hadn't been such a brilliant idea either. When she swallowed, the kernels scratched the inside of her too-tight throat.

A silence descended over the room. While Miriam and her sisters absorbed the story, Jade looked around the library—anything to avoid looking at their expressions—as if she'd never seen the portrait of Tallis,

Rosewood's first stud, or noticed the gold fringe on the lamp shades, or traced the swirling pattern in the Oriental rug with the toe of her shoe.

Jordan spoke first. "Well, I think you handled the situation admirably, Jade. I mean, what an impossible situation. And I must say, Rob Cooper is behaving very badly. I'm surprised. He should know better."

Jade's jaw went slack with astonishment to hear her sister criticize Rob Cooper, who basically epitomized moral rectitude.

"If I didn't think it would only aggravate what's already a difficult situation, I'd be tempted to give him a piece of my mind," Jordan continued, apparently oblivious to her youngest sister's shock.

"You and me both," Margot said. "Good for you for handling parents' night *and* Rob Cooper."

That was the amazing thing about Margot and Jordan: Just when Jade was sure she could predict how they would react to her most recent debacle, they surprised her. She'd been expecting to be ostracized for having indulged in anonymous hotel sex. Instead, she got their love and support.

"And what about the Harrisons? Were they true to form?" Miriam asked.

"You know, I'd forgotten about them," Jade said, almost cheerful to be discussing them. "But, yeah, I'd have to say old witch Nonie Harrison would have been right proud of her daughter-in-law. I have a hunch that Christy will be trying to switch Eugene out of my class too. According to her, I'm not providing a stimulating enough academic environment for Eugene—who's not such a bad kid."

Jordan, who could give Emily Post a run for her money, snorted loudly. Margot, Miriam, and Jade had to stifle their collective giggles at the sound.

"How absolutely typical," Jordan said, with a disgusted shake of her head. "I just bet Nonie put that idea in Christy's head. Well, if I know Ted Guerra, he'll turn the Harrisons down flat, which of course will only enrage Nonie and Christy further and make them even more determined to get their way. Gosh, Jade, I am so sorry you had such a rotten night."

"*Está bien,*" Jade said with a careless shrug. The petty maneuverings of the Harrison clan didn't rank very high on her list of worries. She was far more concerned with what Ted Guerra would say to Rob Cooper and what her principal would think of her if Rob chose to enumerate his reasons for taking Hayley out of her class.

She really wasn't looking forward to being called in to the principal's office to account for herself—it brought back shades of high school.

At least her sisters were there for her, as they'd always been. Truth be told, she was always a little flabbergasted by their unwavering support. Though she knew she was looking a gift horse in the mouth, she couldn't help asking, "So you guys aren't going to tell me how utterly stupid I was down in Norfolk?"

Margot lifted an elegantly arched brow. "I assumed you'd worked that one out for yourself, kiddo."

"And though I don't approve of hookups, at least you were smart enough to use protection," Jordan added, amazing Jade anew. Then again, having Owen as a hubby was about the best antidote one could find for easing painful memories of Richard, Jordan's louse of an ex. Jordan and Owen would have gone through their fair share of prophylactics, of that Jade was sure.

Grinning, she said, "Yes, indeed, we went through my entire supply." Her grin turned to laughter as her sisters and Miriam succumbed to fits of mirth.

"Hey, have I told you guys lately how lucky I am to have you around?" Reaching for the popcorn again, she grabbed a handful and shoved it in her mouth.

Margot leaned over to give her a fierce hug. "The feeling's mutual, kid." Settling back against the sofa's cushions, she cocked her head and studied Jade, a smile playing over her face. "So, that Rob Cooper. He's pretty cute, isn't he?"

The popcorn in Jade's mouth went flying.

The next morning, in search of a mega caffeine fix, Jade stopped at Braverman's Bagels on the way to school. Braverman's not only had the best bagels, muffins, and deli sandwiches in town, but George Rollins, who manned the espresso machine in the morning, made a terrific triple-shot cappuccino. A large cup of that and maybe a pumpkin muffin with a cream-cheese filling—one of Braverman's seasonal specials—and one could face just about anything. Jade figured she needed all the extra help she could get.

While Tricia Creighton had sagely predicted how tough parents' night would be, she hadn't mentioned anything about the morning after or what to say when the principal asked why the parents of her students were determined to pull their kids from her class. Then again, Tricia probably never had that problem.

Entering the deli, Jade inhaled deeply. The scents in Braverman's were always yummy, but especially so in the morning. The bagels were fresh out of the oven and cooling on the racks, the breakfast pastries nestled in a tantalizing row of cloth-lined baskets, and their yeasty, sugary aroma mixed with the scent of roasting coffee beans. Heaven.

Three people stood before her in line, and by the time the first customer was served and paid, she was nearly salivating. She was also a little panicky, because, even at that hour, only three pumpkin cream-cheese muffins remained and the first customer bought one of them. Jade wasn't overly superstitious, but she figured her day would be ruined before it even had a chance to go south if she didn't get a pumpkin muffin. Roger Braverman, the owner, was about the only baker in Warburg who could give Jordan a run for her money.

She fixed her eye on the remaining pair as the second customer, a middle-aged woman who definitely wasn't a regular, dithered over whether she wanted a cinnamon raisin bagel, blueberry peach scone, or a pumpkin muffin. When the woman finally chose the scone, Jade breathed a sigh of relief. Only one person stood between her and the last two pumpkin muffins. And the man in front of her looked more like a bagel kind of guy.

When he ordered an everything bagel with cream cheese from Roger, Jade barely refrained from doing a fist pump. Yes, the morning wasn't a total disaster.

"Please don't tell me you plan to snatch up both of those pumpkin muffins," a voice said.

Startled, Jade whirled around. A woman her age with black hair and blue eyes set in a heart-shaped face was standing behind her. Dressed in black Lycra exercise pants and a form-fitting long-sleeved T-shirt, she looked like she was about to hit the gym.

"Um, no." Jade shook her head as she tried to place the woman. "Two would be greedy."

"That's a relief. I saw you watching them kind of intently, so I started worrying you were going to snag both of them. You're Jade Radcliffe, right?"

Jade nodded, frowning unconsciously because she still hadn't identified her.

"Emma Cooper," the woman said with a smile. "I was a year behind you in high school. I'm Hayley's aunt. She loves your class and is constantly talking about you."

"Oh!" was all Jade could manage. Another Cooper, and she hadn't had that coffee yet. *Of course* this was Rob's younger sister. They had the same eyes and hair. But Jade didn't remember being in high school with her;

she'd been too steeped in the misery that was her teen-age life to notice much.

"Roger's pumpkin and cream-cheese muffins are my absolute favorites, even if eating one means I have to tack on a half an hour extra to my workout. Good thing I'm teaching a strength class today."

"You teach fitness?"

Emma nodded. "At Body Complete."

That explained Emma's taut physique.

"Hey, Jade, top of the morning to you. You want your usual?"

She turned to find that the customer before her had walked away from the cash register, white paper bag and paper coffee cup in hand. "Please, Rog," she said, stepping up to the register, where Roger Braverman stood, looking dapper in a checked shirt and a fire engine–red bowtie.

"A triple-shot cappuccino for your sweetheart, George," Roger called.

Stationed by his enormous gleaming espresso machine, George gave a nod. "You're looking fine this morning, Jade."

"Thanks, George. Back atcha."

"What would you like with that coffee, Jade?" Roger asked.

"I'll take a pumpkin muffin. You might as well bag the other one too. Emma Cooper's also a fan."

"Hey, Emma," Roger said with the same easy familiarity. "You fueling up for your class?"

"That's right. And can you pop a blueberry one in the bag for Rob?"

"Sure. How about one for Scott?" Roger asked after he'd added a fat blueberry muffin to the bag.

Emma shook her head. "He's working a later shift today. He can buy his own." To Jade, she said, "You're lucky you came in before me, because I probably would have snatched up both those pumpkin muffins. Rob loves them too. He'll have to settle for blueberry today. I love my brother, but it's possible I love these muffins even more." Her smile turned sly. "Of course I could tell him *you* bought the last one. He wouldn't begrudge Hayley's favorite teacher a well-deserved muffin, especially when you had to work overtime at parents' night yesterday. How was it, by the way? I hope Rob didn't give you a hard time."

Jade returned the large paper cup Roger had just handed her to the counter, as her suddenly nerveless fingers would have bobbled it otherwise.

"Uh, well, I really couldn't say—" she managed to reply. The most accomplished actress would have had difficulty responding normally to Emma's question; the words *Rob* and *hard* conjured memories hotter than the coffee in Jade's cup. She only hoped that if Emma noticed her embarrassment, she'd chalk it up to a new teacher's self-consciousness.

Then, before Emma could ask any more questions that would doubtless prove acutely mortifying, she grabbed the coffee and muffin. "It was nice running into you, but I've got to head off—lots to prepare for today." If not for the fact that she'd have doubtless ended up with coffee splattered down her skirt, she'd have sprinted out of Braverman's and the company of one more Cooper.

It was the *not* knowing that caused the muscles in the back of Jade's neck to tighten until it felt like a knife had been thrust between her shoulders. Even though Jordan had said Ted Guerra would dismiss both the Harrisons' and Rob's requests to transfer their children, Jade wasn't convinced. She kept expecting Ted to walk into her room or send his assistant to take over for her so he could dispense the bad news in his office.

During recess, while the kids played a quick game of

dodgeball that she and Andrea Hess, the gym teacher, organized, she found out from Andrea that Ted was away for the day, observing another elementary school. Then, at lunch, she took a minute to check her iPhone and saw that she had one message. It was from Ted, asking her to come to school early on Monday morning so that they could discuss the feedback he'd received from the parents after parents' night.

The delay in hearing the bad news only made things worse. It made her heart ache, as if it were being torn into pieces. How could it not when Eugene got every clue right in his crossword puzzle and gave her a huge gap-toothed grin after she stuck a WAY TO GO! sticker on his sheet? Or when Hayley read *Henry and Mudge* aloud to her without faltering over a single word?

Finished with the story, Hayley had closed the book with a happy sigh and traced the picture on the paperback's cover with her index finger. It was of Mudge and Henry sitting side by side, with Henry's arm wrapped around his dog's massive shoulders.

"Someday I want to have a dog like Mudge, and he can play with my uncle Scott's dog, Dexter. I think Mudge is the kind of dog who would like horses too; don't you think so, Miss Radcliffe?"

"I think he's just the sort of dog that would like horses."

"I bet he'd even like goats. Armadillos too," she added with a decisive nod of her head. "Mudge is definitely the kind of dog I'd want."

And Jade thought of how much she would miss hearing Hayley's ideas and her dreams over the next few months. The little girl was so quirky and sweet. Jade would miss having to come up with precise answers for Eugene when he asked about Egyptian pyramids and how they cut and carried and transported all those blocks of stone, because Eugene liked to hoard facts the way a squirrel does nuts. And she'd definitely miss his daily report on Nemo's whereabouts. Eugene had discovered that the tetra the class had named Nemo liked to hide in the sunken pirate ship. He had a personal *Finding Nemo* project going on.

It wasn't even a full two weeks into the school year. How could she have become attached to these kids so very quickly?

When the bell rang for dismissal, the kids all hurried over to their cubbies to shrug into their windbreakers and sweatshirts, and to grab their things. Hayley's cheerful call of "See you Monday morning, Miss Radcliffe!" before she raced out of the classroom, her purple backpack bouncing against her, had Jade blinking back foolishly sentimental tears.

She straightened the desks in the now-empty room and picked up stray odds and ends until the room was neat and orderly, ready to welcome the kids on Monday morning. Her last task was to insert the automatic fish feeder onto the wall of the aquarium, so the fish would have food over the weekend. It was good that the weekend was here, she told herself. She'd have two days of working with the horses and ponies. Two full days to put the disastrous encounter with Rob Cooper behind her and regain some sort of equilibrium.

Perhaps by Monday she'd be able to listen Ted Guerra break the bad news without bursting into tears.

HAYLEY HAD a playdate at Jenny Ferris's, and because it was a Friday, Rob had agreed to let her stay for dinner. Maryanne, Jenny's mom, was making chicken fajitas. According to Hayley, they were the best. After dropping her off, with a reminder to help set and clear the table, Rob went back to the station to swap his patrol car for his Mustang and change into a pair of jeans and a short-sleeved polo shirt. Somehow he knew that being dressed in his police uniform when apologizing to Jade Radcliffe wouldn't go over too well. The sight of his police car might get her back up too.

The mid-September afternoon had turned warm, almost summerlike. Rob drove with the windows down, and although he'd traveled only a few miles from the center of town, the air somehow smelled sweeter here, redolent of meadows and dense canopied trees. It was beautiful countryside and, as he turned into the winding drive that led to Rosewood, he tacked on the adjective *grand* to the description. The driveway to the Radcliffes' historic home was longer than some of Warburg's streets.

The Radcliffes had always been one of Warburg's leading families. With the death of RJ Radcliffe, the patriarch, things had changed a bit—but not much, Rob reflected, as he drove along the long rows of wood fencing that protected the horses grazing in the pastures. Faced with bankruptcy due to the gargantuan debts their father had left behind, Jordan, Margot, and Jade had managed to hang on to the family estate and their horse-breeding business, both of which had been in the family since the nineteenth century. Despite the emotional ties the property held for the daughters, a lot of people in town had expected them to sell. Rosewood would have brought a pretty penny. Instead, they'd defied those expectations, choosing to try and preserve their home and heritage.

While the sisters—even with Margot's success as a fashion model—probably couldn't boast the kind of fortune their father had once enjoyed, they'd managed to keep the horse farm going. Not just going but prospering, if the number of horses he passed in the fields were any indication. Even with Rob's untrained eye, he could see they were beautiful animals, sleek-coated and muscular.

And now Jade had decided to expand Rosewood Farm's business by offering children's riding lessons. Rob figured a fair number of Warburg's equestrian set would want their kids to ride at Rosewood simply because of its exclusivity. The snob factor would count for a lot among some here. But most would choose Jade because of her ability as a riding teacher. Considering her own extensive riding background and the fact that she'd taught her nieces and nephew to ride, that was pretty much a given.

He didn't drive up to the stately house with its imposing columns and wide porches. Instead, he pulled up behind the largest of four barns—which, as barns went, were pretty grand too—and parked next to a late-model SUV he recognized as belonging to Travis Maher.

Rob liked Travis. Though he was a good ten years older than Rob, Travis had never given him a hard time when he was a rookie on the force—probably because Travis was the antithesis of his father, Red Maher, who'd been a mean-tempered drunk and a far-too-frequent guest of the station's jail cell. Rob didn't think Travis had shed many tears when his father's liver gave out. Nor had Red's long-suffering wife, who'd moved away after his death. Rob suspected Travis would have left Warburg too, if not for the fact that he'd found his calling working as Rosewood's trainer and manager. And then there was Margot Radcliffe.

They were married now, and Travis was the envy of most men in Warburg—the holdouts being those who would like to be in Owen Gage's shoes and married to Jordan, the eldest sister. Now that Jade was back in Warburg, he really didn't want to think about how many men would begin lining up for the chance to date her.

Calculating that the largest barn would hold someone who could tell him where Jade was, he entered it, taking his sunglasses off to peer down its wide aisle. A few yards down, he saw a woman brushing a big dark-brown horse.

It was Margot Radcliffe, who, even after two kids, was still landing modeling jobs. It was easy to see why. She might've been dressed in breeches; a plain, long-sleeved T-shirt; and riding boots and have her hair pulled into a careless knot at the back of her head, but, with her face and body, all a photographer would have to do was point his camera and click. The resulting image would be stunning enough to land on the cover of a glossy beauty magazine.

The scrape of his shoes against the cement floor had Margot pausing in her grooming, her brush resting on her horse's dark flank. Turning to see who was approaching, her face registered surprise and then a flash of something that was harder for him to identify.

"Officer Cooper. This is unexpected." Her smile, though polite, was definitely cool.

"It's Rob, Ms. Radcliffe. I'm off duty."

Her expression didn't grow any warmer. "Can I help you?"

Okay, Rob thought. He was fairly certain he could now ID the fleeting emotion he'd seen on her face: It was anger. Margot Radcliffe was pissed off at him, which meant she must know something about what happened last night. Well, she was Jade's older sister and had been her guardian too. The sisters were close. She had a right to feel protective.

"I was wondering whether Jade was around. I'd like to speak to her."

"And as you're off duty, this visit won't be in an official capacity?"

"Thankfully, no."

She cocked her brow. "Are you here as a parent, then? Or as something else altogether?"

The question put him on alert. Exactly how much did she know about Jade and him and their recent activities? Entirely too much for his liking, he decided.

Rob wasn't used to being looked at as if he had six legs and a really ugly pair of antennae.

"As a parent," he replied, pointedly ignoring the other role she'd hinted at. "I have a couple things I need to discuss with her."

"You can always try." Her amused tone made it clear he had a snowball's chance in hell of getting Jade to talk to him. Then Margot looked past him and her smile warmed and spread. "Travis, hon, look who's dropped by. He's here to see Jade. Want to take him down to the ring?"

"Sure." Travis came up to them and folded his arms across his chest. "Rob," he said by way of greeting.

Okay, the count was up to two in terms of frosty family members. "How are you, Travis?"

"Good, thanks. I haven't seen much of you lately. You been busy?"

"Yes, I guess so."

"Traveling?"

"Yeah, I did some traveling. I went down to Norfolk for a conference."

"A real educational experience, no doubt," Travis said.

Shit. Rob had a sudden nasty suspicion that Jade must have told them of their encounter in Norfolk too. If so, it was no wonder that Margot, who in all their previous encounters had been friendly, was generating the warmth of an iceberg. It also explained the steely glint in Travis's eyes.

But if they were aware of even a tenth of what Jade and he had done together, their reaction was fairly restrained. In their place he'd be tempted to wring the neck of any guy who'd spent a stormy night having wild sex with his little sister.

The realization made Rob's gut twist with guilt. Nevertheless, he managed to return Travis's gaze levelly.

Wrapping an arm about Margot's waist, Travis dropped a light kiss on the corner of her mouth. "I'll be back in a few," he told her.

With a nod of his head and a terse, "Come on, Rob," Travis led the way out of the barn and into a courtyard between the horse barns, then down a gravel path that presumably led to wherever Jade was.

They'd marched in silence for about a hundred yards when Travis spoke. "Just so you know, Jade's very important to this family. None of us want to see her get hurt. You'd do well to remember that, Rob."

For Christ's sake, he thought as his hackles rose. On the verge of asking Travis if he thought trying to intimidate an officer of the law was a smart move, he caught sight of her. She was standing in the middle of the exercise ring, her long, sun-streaked hair blowing in the breeze, and suddenly he no longer cared what Travis Maher thought. His only interest was in Jade.

Her attention fixed on the three ponies circling her, she hadn't noticed his and Travis's approach. The kids riding the ponies were trotting, and Jade was them giving instructions in a clear voice.

"Katiebug, I'd like you to do a circle here and bring Maggie up behind Hopscotch. I'm getting the impression that she likes to lead the show. I want her trotting as nicely for you wherever you are in the line. That's right, just trot right between the in-and-out." She pointed, indicating a path between two jumps.

Rob watched Kate—that would be Jordan's eldest child—guide a dark-reddish-brown pony with a black mane and tail in a circle so they ended up at the back of the line. The pony's color was called bay; he remembered the term from one of Hayley's efforts to educate him.

"Nicely done. Just keep Maggie at that pace, and if she starts getting fidgety, circle again."

"Liv, you feel anything wrong?"

There was a shake of a black riding helmet. "No." But the answer ended on a note of uncertainty.

"How about checking your diagonals?"

"Oops. Sorry, Aunt Jade."

"No need to apologize. Sit a beat and tell me whether you can feel the difference."

"Yes," she answered, nodding. "I can tell."

"All righty, then. Now, Max, I can tell you're letting your outside heel come up, because you're starting to tilt in the saddle. Drop it down, kiddo, or you'll tilt right over. And keep your eyes up. There you go, that's much better. You were looking like the Tower of Pisa before."

"That's a building in Italy. Owen showed it to me. It leans but doesn't fall over. It's cool," Max replied.

"Indeed it is. But you don't want to look like it when you're riding, right?"

"Right."

Listening to the exchange, Rob grinned. This must be what Hayley responded to: Jade's ability to mix humor in with her instruction, engaging the kids without dumbing the discussion down.

"Now that we've got you balanced in the saddle, Max, I'd like you to squeeze your lower leg a bit more. Dickens is starting to get a little poky. Can you feel how he's falling behind the bit? See if you can wake him up. Otherwise, Hopscotch is going to trot right up his hindquarters, and Dickens won't like that, will he, Georgie?" she asked the little girl who was standing next to her in the center of the ring, watching the lesson. By the girl's size, Rob realized she couldn't be more than four years old.

The little girl shook her dark-brown hair vigorously. "No," she said emphatically. "Daddy says never to ride too close to another horse's rear end, 'cause you might end up getting hurt."

"That's absolutely correct, and your dad should be bringing Doc down for your lesson in a few minutes."

"Daddy's right over there, Aunt Jade. With that man. Hi, Daddy," she called, waving.

"Hey, there, Georgie. I'm going to get Doc saddled for you now, but how about I give you a riding lesson today? This man's name is Rob Cooper, and he wants to talk to Aunt Jade."

Even from this distance, Rob could tell Jade had gone stock-still. He supposed he was the last person she was expecting to see. Rob raised his hand in a half wave, and at last he had a reaction: Her features tightened in a fierce scowl.

"Fancy that. She doesn't look too thrilled to see you," Travis remarked with more than a hint of laughter. "You're going to have your work cut out for you, Cooper, to even get the time of day from her." Raising his voice, he called, "I'll be back in a minute with Doc,

Georgie. Do you want me to ask Owen to bring down Archer and Ginny, Jade? He just arrived."

"Uh, yeah, that'd be great."

Her voice had sounded like a rusty squeak, but Jade was still recovering from her shock at seeing Rob Cooper standing next to Travis. Shock and dismay.

And, blast it, why was her heart pounding like a jackhammer simply because he was there, just twenty feet away? She didn't even like the man.

And what could he possibly have to talk to her about? Perhaps he wanted to list *more* reasons why she should be barred from teaching Hayley. He'd probably spent last night writing them down.

Well, he was on her turf now, and, by golly, she wasn't going to talk with him until she was good and ready.

She continued with the lesson, telling the kids to pick up the canter, pleased when all three, even Olivia, picked up the correct lead. Still, there was room for fine-tuning.

"Max, keep your inside leg still. It's starting to swing like a metronome. Olivia, your leg is plenty still, but your heel is creeping up. That's right. Good correction. Kate, I want to see you looking all the way around the corner. Remember, you always have to be looking at the next point. Okay, now, before you guys bring your ponies down to a walk, I want you to settle smoothly back into the saddle without losing the canter's momentum. That means you're going to be sitting deeper in the saddle and squeezing your leg while your hands remain quiet and steady on the reins. That's it, very nice. All right, ask them to walk, and, Max, remember to keep your hands low as you tighten them; otherwise, Dickens will stick his nose in the air."

Her attention switched to her nieces again. "That was pretty good, Kate, though I think Maggie took a few more steps in slowing down in this direction than in the other. You'll want to pay attention to that, Katiebug."

"Okay, Aunt Jade."

"Good girl. And, Olivia, I'm super-proud of you. That was excellent. Give your ponies pats, kids, and let them take a lap around the ring at an easy walk. We'll finish up with around-the-world and Simon says."

As focused as she was on her nieces and nephew and on her new schooling ponies, Jade was uncomfortably aware of Rob, who'd now positioned himself by the rail and was apparently hanging on her every word.

As if, she thought with a snort. He couldn't possibly have been interested in hearing her tell Kate to transition smoothly from a canter to a walk and not allow any sloppiness from Maggie simply because she was a new pony, or remind Max to keep his leg steady and in alignment.

She always tried to end the kids' lessons with a couple of games; it was an easy way to make sure a horse was properly cooled down. Cooling off a heated horse was one of the horse-care concepts kids had difficulty grasping. Even kids who knew horses well, like Kate, Max, and Olivia, skimped unless reminded.

Today, Jade extended the game period even longer, half-hoping that, after watching Olivia, Max, and Kate touch their right toes with their left hands and their ponies' tails with their right hands, Rob would grow bored and go away. Never to be seen again.

But when Max crowed with delight because he'd won the day's round of Simon says, Jade glanced over at the rail. And there he was.

He was such a cop, she sighed inwardly. Stubborn and determined. It was a shame she couldn't stop remembering what he'd been like as a lover.

But then Travis arrived, leading her old pony Doc. Owen and Tito followed with Archer and Sweet Virginia. Always super-generous with Jade, Tito volunteered to take the ponies back up to the barn with Olivia while Max and Kate hacked Archer and Ginny. Although she accepted the offer, she wished he hadn't been so thoughtful.

And when she factored in Owen and Travis's presence, there were just a few too many helpful adults around, with everything moving a tad too efficiently. To compensate, she spent several minutes checking Archer and Ginny's girths, fiddling with their throatlatches, and making sure Kate's and Max's stirrups were even.

"I don't think there's anything left to check, Jade. You might as well give Rob a break and listen to what the guy has to say," Travis said.

"Now, here's an instance where you and I disagree, Travis," said Owen, who was busy helping Olivia run the stirrups up on Hopscotch's saddle. "I think Jade should make Cooper wait a good long time."

"That's because you're still steamed over getting a fine from him," Travis replied, lifting Georgiana into the saddle. She looked adorable sitting on Doc.

Owen nodded his dark head. "Absolutely. I consider Jade's giving him a hard time payback. Couldn't happen to a nicer guy."

She wouldn't have thought it possible, but having her brothers-in-law discuss Rob Cooper was actually more unsettling than the prospect of marching over to him and finding out what it was he wanted to say. Once he'd said his piece, she could start to forget his existence.

"Travis is right," she said in a resigned tone. "I better go see what he wants." When they grinned at her, she shook her head in exasperation. "You know, sometimes you guys are such *guys*."

"Even so, we must have some endearing qualities." Owen's grin widened as he added, "I guess even Cooper does."

Just thinking about what endearing qualities Rob possessed caused a very unlike-Jade blush to steal over her cheeks. "Right. I'm outta here," she said, and stomped off before their annoying grins turned to laughter.

It was weird, Rob thought, watching Jade stride across the sandy ring toward him as if she were marching to do battle. On the one hand, he knew a great deal about her. He'd spent an entire night exploring that long-limbed body of hers, discovering what she liked and how she liked it. He knew the sound of her breathless moan when his mouth traveled along her inner thigh, the way her fingers clutched his head to hold him close as his tongue bathed the puckered aureole of her breast before drawing it deep into his mouth and sucking hard.

On the other hand, he didn't know how she took her coffee.

Weird, indeed. At least he knew that she liked pumpkin cream-cheese muffins. Emma had told him about meeting Jade in Braverman's earlier that morning, and, for some reason, knowing that he and Jade shared the same taste in baked goods had made the corners of his mouth curve upward.

Women usually liked his smile. With Jade, it had the opposite effect. As she ducked between the wooden rails, her own mouth flattened in a grim line. Then he recalled what an ass he'd been last night and realized that he'd probably have to do a lot more than smile to get her to not want to spit in his eye. And though he'd told himself he was there at Rosewood primarily for Hayley's sake, he knew he didn't want to be enemies with Jade. Exactly what kind of relationship he was looking to have with her, he couldn't presently define.

Jade stood a good six feet away from him. But that was close enough for him to see the glitter in her leaf-green eyes, the red flags of anger staining her cheeks, and to take an appreciative inspection of her long legs encased in rust-colored breeches and tall brown leather riding boots. She looked as different as day from night in her riding gear rather than in the outfit she'd been wearing in Norfolk, but that didn't make her any less alluring or prevent his pulse from jumping as desire pumped through his veins. Christ, why did she have this effect on him?

She crossed her arms in front of her chest, all crackling defensiveness. "Travis said you wanted to talk. So?"

"I'd like to apologize." If his voice sounded terse, it was because he was more than a little annoyed that his body was reacting to her simply because she was standing there. Unbelievable.

A single eyebrow rose mockingly. "You know, I can think of a whole boatload of things you might want to apologize for. But I'm afraid I don't have that much time. Or interest." She turned on her boot heel.

"I'd like to apologize for what I said about taking Hayley out of your class. It was wrong and uncalled for." Rob felt a surge of satisfaction that his words had her glancing over her shoulder and that the angry glitter in her eyes had been replaced by astonishment.

"The only excuse I can give you is that I wasn't thinking too clearly last night." His mouth lifted in a half smile. "Seeing you was a bit of a surprise."

"Apology accepted."

She'd turned back to face him, but she'd yet to smile, Rob noted. He remembered her smile as being pretty amazing, full of mischief and joy. "Hayley really likes being in your class, and it would be foolish to move her. I was stupid even to consider such a thing."

Jade wasn't often at a loss for words, but her usual gift for snappy comebacks or even diversionary remarks had deserted her. Any clever retort was swept aside by a swell of happiness at hearing that Hayley would remain in her class. Worried that if she opened her mouth, all manner of gushy and effusive stuff might come out of it, she kept it shut. The last thing she wanted was to sound mushy, especially in front of Rob.

That some of the happiness buzzing through her might be due to the fact that Rob had taken the step to apologize to her, she absolutely refused to consider.

Affecting a casual nonchalance wasn't easy, but she attempted it anyway. "I'm glad to hear she'll be staying. Hayley has nice friends in the class. I'll look forward to seeing her on Monday. Um, thanks for coming by to let me know." She spoke through lips that felt simultaneously rubbery and stiff, as if she'd just been treated to massive novocaine injections from a not-so-friendly dentist.

Rob hiked his thumb over his shoulder in the direction of the riding ring. "So, are those ponies you're using for your riding school?"

His question had her brows drawing together in a quick frown of confusion. Was he intentionally trying to throw her off balance with these remarks? She was not going to let this guy unnerve her simply because he'd busted her teenage self twice and made her adult self orgasm she couldn't remember how many times. She wished he didn't look so good in his faded jeans and polo shirt; it would have been easier to remain riled if he'd shown up in his police uniform.

"Yeah. We already had two ponies and I bought four new ones. Um, I have to head up to the barn now. I have some horses to exercise." It wasn't a lie. She was due to ride Valentine and Carmen. But she'd have been tempted to invent just about anything, if it meant getting rid of him. Those blue eyes were too intense. She swore she could feel the heat coming off his body, and she wasn't even standing next to him.

"I'll walk you back up."

What was she to do? Tell him he couldn't? But why in the world was he doing this? She wouldn't have pegged him for an obtuse clod, but he didn't seem to be getting the very clear will-you-*please*-buzz-off signals she was sending.

"They look like nice ponies."

She didn't bother to stifle her snort. "Well, that's generally the goal when you go pony or horse shopping: to not come home with the equine from hell."

"I'd like to sign Hayley up for riding lessons with you."

His words sent her stumbling on a pebble. Righting herself, she glared at him. He was doing it on purpose, this whole let's-say-totally-off-the-wall-things-to-Jade-and-see-whether-she-falls-on-her-face ploy. "This is a joke, right?" she snapped. "Because yesterday you seemed real keen to tar and feather me and run me out of Warburg on a rail."

It wasn't the only thing he'd been real keen to do, Jade thought, but she would rather be devoured by fire ants than go near that topic.

"It's not a joke. Everyone says that your lesson program will be the best in town, and Hayley is desperate to have lessons. I promised them to her for her birthday."

"Nice of you, but you've been misinformed. There are lots of really good riding instructors around Warburg. Go to Steadman's—"

"First place I went," he interrupted calmly. "Adam and Sara Steadman told me you'd be the best teacher, hands down."

She rolled her eyes. "The Steadmans are biased. They sold me my first pair of jodhpurs. Try Steffi Connors at Winsome Farm. She gets lots of kids."

"I'd rather have Hayley ride with you. Do you have an opening for a beginner? She's had some lessons, but I'd like her to start right."

The man must be seriously unhinged. Having her teach Hayley to ride was the worst idea ever, and yet he seemed to think it was just fine and dandy. Being Hayley's teacher at Warburg Elementary would already bring Rob into Jade's life too often. Giving her riding lessons at Rosewood would exacerbate the problem tenfold—the problem being that, whenever Jade saw Rob, she couldn't stop thinking about how he looked naked and how he'd made her feel when he was moving inside her.

A situation like this should be avoided like the plague.

Unfortunately, she couldn't think of a plausible lie when he was looking at her with his electric-blue gaze and determined expression. Why she found that concentrated focus unbearably sexy made her wonder if she was as certifiable as he.

Then Rob said, "So you do have an opening?" And she knew she'd blown her chance by hesitating too long.

She sighed heavily. "Look, it's just not a good idea for me to teach Hayley. I'm her teacher. She should take lessons with someone else."

"And yet you've agreed to let Jenny Ferris sign up and she's in your class too," he pointed out.

Crap. In her distraction, she'd forgotten that Hayley and Jenny were best buddies. Hayley would know where Jenny was riding this fall and would have shared the info with her dad.

"That's different," she muttered.

"The only difference I can see is that I'm Hayley's dad. You're not going to hold what happened between us against her, are you?"

She narrowed her eyes. "No, I'd say that's more your style."

"Ouch." For a second he was silent. "Okay, I deserved that. I admit this thing between us is somewhat awkward. But I want to make Hayley happy, and she's so excited at the prospect of taking lessons from you. I don't like disappointing her if I can help it." As he said this last, he reached up and tugged his earlobe.

It was that simple, unconscious gesture that made Jade relent. Hayley made the very same one—tugging absently on her earlobe—whenever she talked about the things she loved, like going to her grandparents' home for Sunday dinner or playing catch with her dad.

No matter what else was going on between Rob and her, Jade couldn't forget that he was a widower raising his daughter alone and doing whatever he could to make her happy. Refusing to give Hayley lessons would bring Jade on par with the Grinch. But just because she was caving didn't mean she had to be gracious about it. No one had ever accused her of being a saint.

"I have Tuesdays and Thursdays available. Lessons are twenty dollars. Take your pick."

"How about both?" Her slack-jawed stare had him grinning widely. "She really likes ponies."

Jade shut her mouth with a snap. "Fine. Whatever," she ground out. "Make sure she has a hard hat. And since you already haunt Steadman's Saddle Shop, ask Adam next time you're in if they have any secondhand jodhpurs."

She was surprised to see him stiffen.

"I can afford to buy new gear."

Ah, so he was proud, she thought. Well, she could relate to that. "It's your money," she said with a shrug. "But I can guarantee you Hayley will outgrow her riding clothes in three months. Riding's not a cheap sport. If you intend to keep her in the saddle, you should economize where you can. Because once she talks you into buying a pony, you're going to start feeling poor real quick." Irritated by the spurt of pleasure that filled her when her words erased his tension, she said, "Well, this has been fun, but, as I said, I have horses waiting for me." She jerked her thumb in the direction of the main barn.

Rob was surprised by how much he wanted their conversation to continue, but he said, "Oh, sure. I don't want to keep you from your work." He liked talking to her, liked her wit and the offbeat sense of humor she'd displayed. He really liked her decency in agreeing to give Hayley riding lessons. Not everyone would have done so.

He'd surprised himself as much as he'd surprised her when he'd abruptly asked about lessons for Hayley. But suddenly it had seemed ridiculous that he should look anywhere else. Jade was obviously a great teacher, both in the classroom and in the riding ring. And he wanted the best teacher he could find for Hayley.

So what if having her take lessons with Jade contradicted everything he'd told himself last night. Maybe being around Jade wasn't such a bad thing. It certainly felt fine right now, more than fine.

"So, see you." She turned to head into the barn.

"Wait," he said abruptly, though even a blind man could have seen her impatience to be gone and rid of him.

"Yes?"

"I was wondering whether you were free this weekend. Perhaps we could go out tomorrow."

"Like on a *date*?" Astonishment widened her green eyes. Truth be told, Rob was equally taken aback. Where the hell had those words come from?

He certainly hadn't *intended* to ask her out. In the bar in Norfolk, he'd admitted to himself that it was time to consider dating again. But his brain had obviously gone haywire. Jade Radcliffe didn't possess a single one of the criteria he was looking for in a woman. Okay, that wasn't strictly true. . . .

While he was still struggling to unscramble his wits, Jade had already recovered from her surprise. She was smiling at him at last. Smiling with what Rob could only describe as unholy glee.

"Sorry, but I'm afraid I have to decline," she said, and her smile grew even wider, brilliantly showing him just how very un-sorry she was. "I already have a date tomorrow. A very hot date. So long, Officer Cooper."

With that she sauntered off, leaving him scowling in the sunny courtyard long after she'd disappeared into the barn and wondering who in hell she was dating, while at the same time recalling with torturous clarity just how hot a night with Jade Radcliffe could be.

Chapter ✤
FOURTEEN

WARBURG WAS far too snobby to support a bowling alley, but luckily Route 50 offered businesses and entertainment for real people. Jade recognized, however, that if the Reverend Stuart Wilde hadn't come into her life, she might never have discovered this gem of a place. Thanks to Stuart's bringing her here beginning in her miserable sophomore year, Roxie's Bowlarama became a place of sanity and camaraderie. Sanity from the pressure cooker that was Warburg High, with its hostile social cliques, and camaraderie from a man who was forty-five years her senior and who possessed limitless patience and kindness.

She remembered Stuart handing her a bowling ball and telling her he'd found bowling strikes to be the best way to alleviate his frustration with the world and even with the Almighty. Stuart was no slouch on the lane. With him teaching Jade, it hadn't taken her long to begin throwing strikes. He'd also taught her how to forgive her troubled teenage self, those lessons far harder to master than tossing a heavy ball down a narrow lane and knocking over some pins. It had been a slow process, hindered by some serious backsliding.

Yet even when she screwed up, Stuart never gave up on her. His friendship had endured, even after Jade technically no longer needed it, when she began to get her act together. That this funny and wise man should care so much when, unlike her family at Rosewood, he had no obvious reason to, filled her with gratitude to this day.

Not for anything would Jade stand Stuart up on one of their bowling nights. Not even for a date with Rob Cooper. She still couldn't believe that Rob had asked her out. Or maybe she could.

She had a fair idea of what he'd like to do on a date with her. And if he'd been anybody but Officer Rob Cooper, father of Hayley Cooper, she might have been tempted to ask for a rain check. Such was the man's sex appeal. But while she'd succumbed to his attractions once—twice, if she counted their kiss in her classroom, which was pretty difficult to discount—she didn't intend to succumb to temptation again. So no dates with the terrifyingly sexy Rob Cooper on the calendar for her.

Luckily for her, Stuart was great company. He was in rare form tonight, having just thrown a hambone, his fourth strike in a row. After the pins had tumbled with a satisfying clatter, he turned around and beamed, his round face lit with happiness.

"Not bad for an old man," he said, pulling out a pocket handkerchief and mopping his brow with it.

"Not bad at all. Have you been sneaking down here on your own and practicing, Stuart?"

"I've merely been working on the timing of my release, my dear. I can do that anywhere. It's all in the visualization." He tapped the side of his forehead as he took his seat.

Jade knew all about visualization. Her problem was that she kept visualizing Rob Cooper looking as delicious as sin when he'd asked her out yesterday, rather than visualizing the proper hook for her bowling ball's trajectory. The guy wore his blue jeans well. "This might end up being your night, Stuart, but I've got to warn you, I'm not going down without a fight. You know how much I hate to lose."

He nodded with the serenity of a man who had a comfortable point lead. "That I do. So let's see if you've got some magic up that sleeve."

Jade grinned. She loved bowling and especially loved winning at it, but seeing Stuart's plump face glowing with satisfaction was equally fine. "All righty, then. Why don't you take a good look at this release and tell me if the angels aren't weeping with envy?"

His parents had invited Hayley to sleep over, leaving Rob with little to do except perhaps sit and brood about Jade Radcliffe. So when Eric Drogan called to ask whether he felt like tagging along while he did some research for an article, he accepted. Given his mood, Rob would have preferred to go to the gym and lift weights and then toss back some cold beers with Eric, but he supposed checking out a bowling alley wasn't too lousy an alternative.

"We're doing a series of articles on family-oriented businesses and activities in and around Warburg, to encourage people to get outside and explore the county's offerings. I've never been here, but I've heard it's a great place," Eric said as he and Rob crossed the parking lot, which flickered red and gold from the neon lights spelling out ROXIE'S BOWLARAMA.

Rob opened one of the double glass doors and held it for Eric. "Who told you about it?"

"Reverend Wilde."

"Yeah?"

"Yeah," Eric answered with a grin. "I ran into him on the street the other day and began telling him about the series. I asked him whether he had any place to recommend. Apparently he's a regular here."

"Go figure." Perhaps the reverend was on to something, though. From the looks of it, Roxie's Bowlarama was the happening place on a Saturday night, Rob thought, stepping into the brightly lit interior and hearing the sound of balls rolling along the polished wood alleys and clattering into pins and, over that, the rocking strains of the Steve Miller Band's "Jungle Love," which was pumping from the speakers.

Although practically all of the bowling lanes were occupied, a line of customers was waiting to rent bowling shoes and balls. The woman behind the cash register, who was also dispensing advice about what size ball to rent, was in her mid-fifties, had platinum hair piled in a beehive, and rhinestone-encrusted glasses perched on her nose. To complete the retro look, she wore a flaming-pink bowling shirt with *Roxie* stitched on the left breast. Rob decided it was a safe bet that she was the proprietress.

Eric had reached the same conclusion. "I want to ask Roxie a few questions for the article before we scope out the place. Once we've soaked up the atmosphere, we can bowl a few frames if we're feeling inspired. It'd be interesting to find out whether you're as lousy at bowling as you are at b'ball," Eric said.

"Care to lay down some money on that hope?"

Eric grinned. "A sucker I am not."

Roxie Donoghue was delighted that the *Warburg Courier* intended to run an article on her bowling alley. Calling an assistant over to help the other customers, she happily answered Eric's questions about her establishment. "Oh, this is a wonderful destination for a family outing, especially when the weather starts to turn lousy, though as you can see, we get lots of people in on nice evenings too. We have good fun here, from league bowling to friends just coming in for a game."

"How long have you owned Roxie's?"

"Close to ten years now. When I bought the place, it was kind of sad and dreary. I renovated it completely and refurbished the lanes. Now they're the best around.

My husband, Earl, he runs the snack bar. That man makes some mean nachos. Tell him to give you an order on the house."

"Thanks, we'll definitely sample them. Roxie, can you give us an idea what age you think is suitable for kids to start bowling?"

"Gosh, we've had kids in here as young as three years old bumper-bowling with a six-pound ball. They need both hands to roll the ball, of course, but they just love the game. Whether they hit any pins or not hardly matters. We offer lessons starting at age eight, but even before then kids can pick up the essentials of the game and have a grand time here. Scoring's a lot easier, too, now that it's computerized."

She waited while Eric jotted down notes, then asked, "So who told you about us?"

"Reverend Wilde. He says he comes here often."

Eric's answer lit Roxie's face. "That Stuart is such a love!" she exclaimed. "I swear, he is just the kindest, most thoughtful human being I know. Almost makes me want to go to church." Her saucy wink had both Eric and Rob grinning in return. "I'm going to have Earl put an extra scoop of ice cream on Stuart's brownie tonight— Stu's got a serious sweet tooth. He's here, you know."

"Stuart Wilde's here tonight?" Eric asked.

"Uh-huh. With his bowling partner, Jade Radcliffe."

Rob—momentarily diverted by a woman who was seventy if she was a day, who'd decided to rent a glittery purple bowling ball—snapped to attention. "Did you say Jade Radcliffe?"

Roxie nodded. "She and Stuart have been coming here for years. I'm so glad she's back home from college. She keeps Stuart in tip-top bowling shape. They're quite a pair, those two."

"Hey, Eric, maybe we should go pay our respects to Reverend Wilde," Rob said.

"Sounds good." Turning back to Roxie, Eric said, "Thanks for all the information. If I have any more questions, can I call you?"

"Sure thing. Here's our card." She took a business card with red-and-gold lettering from the stack next to the register and handed it to him. "Earl and I are here just about every day. And don't forget to try those nachos. Stuart and Jade are bowling in lane thirteen— Jade's lucky number."

Aware that his mood had improved 100 percent the moment he'd heard that Jade was here and that her companion was an AARP-card-carrying minister, Rob trained his gaze on the distant lanes as he and Eric walked past bowlers taking aim at wooden pins.

"Question for you, buddy. How much does your sudden eagerness to see Reverend Wilde have to do with his partner?"

Eric didn't miss much. It was why he was a good journalist. It was also why Rob didn't bother to deny the obvious. "She's Hayley's teacher. And Hayley adores her. Naturally I want to say hi."

"Naturally. Does she by any chance look like her half sisters?"

Rob would probably have come back with some sort of parry, but his eyes had zeroed in on Jade, metallic-blue bowling ball in hand. She was making her approach, taking four steps and then swinging her right blue-jeaned leg back in a graceful slide as her arm swung and then released the ball. Rob took his eyes off the sweet swell of her butt long enough to watch the ball roll down the alley and hook slightly to the left as it neared the pins. The ball hit them dead center, toppling all ten with a loud clatter.

Her exultant "Yes!" was louder than the noise of the pins being swept back. Hips wiggling, she performed a little dance, and the memory of her body moving in time with his made his heart thump heavily in his chest. But when she spun around with a smile bright enough to light up the entire place, his heart doubled its beat with the urgency of desire.

His involuntary response unnerved him. Okay, she was an undeniably beautiful woman. Yes, they'd had great sex together. And clearly he was still attracted to her, but that she should affect him so, make him want her instantly, absolutely, simply because her smile had enough wattage to light up a bowling alley, was crazy.

"How about that for a release, Stu?" she crowed, her voice ringing with delight.

Observing from where he sat on a molded plastic chair, Stuart Wilde grinned widely. "Very nice, my dear. Perfect timing. But I still won, so prepare to open your wallet. Earl's brownies will be just cool enough to eat."

Jade pursed her lips in a playful moue. "Lucky for you today was payday."

"And thanks to your good deed in recommending Roxie's for our article, Roxie told me that your brownie will be accompanied by an extra scoop of ice cream. On the house," Eric finished as he and Rob walked up to him.

Stuart shifted around in his seat. "Eric! And Rob Cooper!" he exclaimed happily. "Good to see you both! So, Eric, you decided to take my recommendation to heart."

"Of course. Many thanks for the tip, Stuart. Roxie's Bowlarama will be one of the highlights of the article."

"That's splendid news." Stuart smiled. "And Officer Cooper came with you to make the stamp of approval official?"

"Something like that," Rob replied easily. "Good evening, Stuart." He paused. "Hello, Jade."

He decided to interpret the dumbfounded expression on her flushed face and the fact that her feet appeared to be super-glued to the boards as a good thing. It meant she wasn't indifferent. He needed to know that this strange attraction wasn't one-sided. "Jade, have you met my friend Eric Drogan?"

With the alacrity of a man who appreciated beautiful women, Eric closed the distance separating them and stretched out his hand to shake Jade's enthusiastically. "I'm very pleased to meet you, Jade. Rob's been holding out on me."

Rob saw the panic in her wide green eyes at his friend's remark.

"Excuse me?"

"He neglected to mention how lovely you are."

Eric's smooth line caused a spurt of jealousy to flare inside Rob. It was instantly doused by Jade's reaction. The irritation that stole over her face told him she wasn't interested in guys talking about her looks, no matter how dynamite they were. Now that he thought of it, he should have guessed that having men fawn over her beauty wouldn't impress her. The ones who'd drooled over her in Norfolk had been summarily dismissed.

But Eric was a lot smarter than them. He switched tacks as soon as he saw her reaction. "Though Rob did tell me what a wonderful time Hayley is having in school."

His second effort earned Eric a smile. "Hayley's a great girl."

That Jade still hadn't acknowledged him, even though she was talking about his daughter, filled Rob with amusement—and a dash of impatience.

Just how long would she hold out?

A little longer, it seemed.

"So what's this about Roxie offering free ice cream?" she continued. "Tonight's loss to Stuart means I'm buying the brownies. I might as well console myself with a free scoop of coffee ice cream."

"Since I'm feeling so extremely satisfied with my win, it's going to be my treat, Jade."

"But, Stuart—"

"No buts," he said with a shake of his head. "You need to save your paycheck for your new ponies' stomachs. Eric, Rob, can I offer you one of Earl's brownies? They're exceptionally fine."

"No, thanks," Rob replied.

"Not for me either," Eric said. "I may sample the nachos, though—they're on the house too."

"Then come and let me introduce you to Earl and the delicacies of his snack bar." Stuart made a grand sweep of his arm in invitation.

"You all go on ahead. I need to stow my ball in my bag and change my shoes," Jade said.

"We can wait, my dear."

"No, no," she insisted. "Besides, there may be the nine o'clock rush on the brownies."

That set Stuart Wilde's feet in motion. Eric, shooting Rob a knowing glance, obligingly accompanied him.

Jade retrieved her bowling ball from the ball return, only to find Rob sitting in Stuart's seat. Her expression wasn't meant to boost his ego.

He smiled nonetheless. "So, Stuart Wilde. He was your hot date?"

She cast him a haughty look as she marched toward her seat. "One of the hottest." Dropping into it with what he knew was a deliberate lack of grace, she bent forward and pulled a black bowling bag from beneath the seat.

He watched her stow her ball and then pull off her shoe. He remembered nipping the high arch of her foot and feeling her entire body shudder. "Stuart's a good man," he observed.

"The finest."

"You know, some people think I'm not so bad either."

She turned to look at him, her expression one of pure astonishment. "Really? How remarkable."

He fought a grin. "There's my mother. She likes me. And Hayley assures me I'm the world's best dad."

"Well, that's very nice. It's good to have a fan club, but if you're out here recruiting new members, I'm afraid I'm not a big joiner."

"I'd say we both joined—and pretty enthusiastically too—back in Norfolk."

She jammed her feet into a pair of black suede Pumas. "That was so last month, dude."

"And then there was parents' night."

"You're going to make me say it, aren't you?"

"Say what?"

She zipped her bag and stood, then gave him a smile as sweet as a five-pound bag of sugar. "That I wonder what I ever saw in you."

He laughed as he, too, rose, enjoying that she wasn't trying to impress him in the least. "Jade, I think you know the answer to that. So, you feel like getting that brownie now?"

How was she supposed to eat a brownie with Rob watching her? Eating her coffee ice cream was bad enough; his gaze tracked each spoonful she put in her mouth. The snack bar was typically crowded for a Saturday night, and Stuart and Eric were engaged in an animated discussion. About what, she had no idea. She couldn't seem to focus on anyone but Rob.

By the last spoonful, her throat was tight with awareness and her mind full of lascivious thoughts in which melted coffee ice cream and muscled flesh predominated. Poor Stuart would probably have a seizure were he to glimpse the graphic images flashing in her mind.

She glanced at the brownie sitting on the paper plate, afraid to touch it, convinced that even a minuscule crumb of the moist fudgy cake would feel as scratchy as sandpaper going down her esophagus.

Damn it, she loved her *après*-bowling brownie!

Rob showing up here when she was having her night out with Stuart, who was like a great-uncle to her—warm and caring and supportive, and above all *non-sexual*—was a gross injustice. His presence had blown her self-control to smithereens. This was neither the place nor the company in which she should be imagining all the different ways she could be having sex with a man she wasn't sure she even liked and who she was pretty sure didn't particularly like her—how could he, when he didn't know her? The entire situation was enough to make her want to scream, which of course she couldn't, because then Rob would know how much he disturbed her.

And part of her was convinced that was the point behind aiming his laser-beam stare directly at her mouth. To rattle her until she was a quivering mass of nerves. He was such a cop.

It rankled, too, that she'd been doing a pretty good job of being a model Warburg citizen. Since returning, she'd been as boring and straitlaced as anyone could hope for. Then Rob had turned up at parents' night. She'd been prepared for RoboCop but not for the Rob Cooper staring at her now, as if he, too, was thinking about tearing off clothes and dribbling sticky sweet ice cream over hot flesh. The idea that he might be sharing the same graphic fantasies left her feeling as if every nerve ending in her body were short-circuiting. None of her college flings had left her feeling so out of control. How could Rob have this power over her when no one else had?

Rob Cooper might have been an officer of the law, but he was serious trouble.

The solution was to ignore her reaction to him completely, deny it with everything she had. Defiantly, she picked up her brownie and took a huge bite. She probably looked like a gopher with her cheeks bulging out, she thought, but who cared? Chewing vigorously, she fixed her gaze on the red plastic salt-and-pepper shakers and concentrated on not choking and spewing brownie all over the round metal table.

"Jade, my dear, Eric was wondering whether you'd care to bowl a few more frames tonight."

If she were to open her mouth now, the gunk inside would be equal to the grossest of horror films and would have Rob looking away awfully quick, but she couldn't bring herself to do it. So she was stupid enough to be vain around him.

Shaking her head violently, she swallowed hard—and, yes, the damned brownie did feel like sandpaper going down her throat—before croaking, "Sorry. I need to get home. I've got a full day of training tomorrow. Here, Stuart, take the rest of my brownie. I can't finish it." She passed him her plate.

"You don't want to take it with you?" Stuart eyed the three-quarters of brownie that remained.

"Nope. And I wouldn't want it to go to waste."

"Well, then," he said happily.

She smiled at the man who had an even sweeter tooth than she. Bending over, she grabbed her bowling bag and stood, waving brightly at the three men. "See you."

"Good night, my dear. Drive safely."

"Nice meeting you, Jade," Eric said, his expression one of vast amusement. "Hope we'll run into each other again."

Somehow, in the time it took for Eric to finish his sentence, Rob had already circled the table. "I'll walk you to your car."

"No, that's okay, I—"

His look silenced her. When he put his hand around her elbow and all those aforementioned nerve endings began sizzling like there was no tomorrow, she knew she was in trouble.

The parking lot was still full of cars and the illuminated neon shone jewel-like against the blackened sky.

"This is totally unnecessary," she repeated, wishing he would leave her alone so she could regain some semblance of control over her body.

"No. It's not unnecessary. You're a woman. All it would take would be for someone to grab you, shove you into an idling car or van, and head out on Route 50. In less than two minutes, someone could make you vanish."

She glanced about the parking lot, which had abruptly taken on a much more sinister aspect. "You do know how to scare a girl."

"It seems to me you bounce back pretty quickly, and, for the record, I'd bet you'd fight any attacker like a hellcat. Nevertheless, only a fool takes unnecessary risks, and I'd be a lousy cop if I didn't make sure you were aware of them. I'd be an even lousier man if I didn't offer to escort you to your car."

Chivalry from a strong man—there was nothing sexier. But why did it have to be Rob Cooper, Officer Rob Cooper, who was making her weak-kneed with his macho protective impulses? Try as she might, she couldn't ignore the effect he was having on her as they walked side by side, the heat from his body meeting hers, the dark of night a cloak enshrouding them.

The darkness offered a delicious temptation: escape. In this setting she could forget her ambivalence toward him and toy with the delicious idea of abandoning her struggle against the intense physical attraction she felt whenever he was near. She could turn to him as easily as the breeze stirring the September night.

The notion was seductive. Her body responded, her heart thumping rapidly, heavily, making each breath she took an effort. Her senses suddenly extra-acute, she could hear the crunch of the gravel beneath their shoes, the roar of cars speeding past, and even the altered rhythm of Rob's own breathing. As she inhaled, the soapy male scent of him made her head swim, and she remembered when her face had been pressed against his warm, naked flesh and she'd learned all his scents.

Clearly she had three choices. One: stop breathing and pass out. Two: breathe and jump him. Three: get the heck out of there before she succumbed to option two.

Option three it was, because she had no death wish, and she wasn't insane enough to think that jumping Rob—a police officer and the father of one of her students—in a public parking lot was what model citizens practiced.

Still several yards away from her Porsche, her feet ground to a halt. Dragging her keys from the front pocket of her jeans, she jangled them and then, in her most everything-is-just-dandy voice, said, "Here I am, safe and—"

Her words evaporated in the air as he turned to her. Like her other faculties, her night vision had grown as sharp as Superman's. Rob's face was all slashing angles and broad planes. No man should be so ridiculously handsome, she thought.

She looked into his eyes and saw everything she was feeling mirrored there: the feverish desire, the hunger. Helplessly, she licked her upper lip, which was parched for the touch of his mouth.

"Jesus," he whispered roughly. "What is it about you?"

The question must have been rhetorical. Before Jade could get her lust-dazed brain to formulate a reply, his mouth was on hers, ravishing, devouring.

It didn't matter that kissing Rob was wrong for countless reasons. She could no longer resist the power he wielded over her. She needed the taste of him. She needed the feel of his arms pulling her close, of his fingers caressing the sides of her face, tracing the line of her jaw and then the nape of her neck, loving how sure, how knowing his touch was, how it made her nerves dance and her insides melt. Later she'd deal with how utterly duncical being in his arms was; for now, all she wanted was for Rob to keep making love to her mouth like he'd never stop.

She arched against his muscled length and opened her mouth wider, tangling her tongue with his, setting sparks of arousal shooting through her. The memory of how his hands would feel stroking the rest of her had her body growing tight in anticipation. Need had her pressing closer, her hands clenching into fists about his neck.

And suddenly an alarm began blaring loudly enough to wake the dead.

Not just any alarm, but her Porsche's alarm. She'd been gripping the damned remote-thingy so tightly, she'd accidentally pressed the panic button. To make matters worse, she realized what she'd done only after she jumped about a mile, frightened out of her skin.

Feeling like an idiot, she fumbled with the remote and finally the quiet returned. Thankfully, the crazy lust that had seized them did not. Nothing could shatter a mood like having one's eardrums pierced by a 125-decibel screech.

"Sorry about that," Jade muttered. She wasn't sure if she was apologizing for setting off her car alarm or her wild response. God, he was going to start thinking she was a nympho or something, and she really wasn't. It was just him.

"It happens." Rob cocked his head toward her car. "So you still have the Porsche."

"It was my mom's." Only she knew how nonsensical her reply was, since any sentimental affection she'd had for her mother vanished the night Jade discovered her to be a liar and an adulterer. But she'd much rather talk about her mom's car than what had just happened between them. That was truly dangerous territory.

"Yeah, I imagine Hayley would have a hard time giving up something that belonged to Becky."

There was a big difference between her mom and Hayley's, Jade thought. Becky Cooper had doubtless been a kind and considerate human being. In comparison, not only did her mom fall far short of the mark, but Jade did as well. After all, she'd been trying to be wholly good for only a few weeks and, thanks to her inconvenient attraction to Rob Cooper, she was already in danger of messing up.

"Your wife must have been very special."

Rob looked at Jade. Even in this less-than-romantic setting, a half-lit parking lot, she was temptation personified. Her hair, mussed from his fingers delving into its thick mass, tumbled past her shoulders, and her mouth was deliciously swollen from his kisses. And yet instead of desire, he ached with a sense of loss.

He wondered whether he was losing his mind. One minute he'd been kissing Jade as though he couldn't get enough of her, but now all he could think of was how much he missed Becky and what they'd had together. He'd buried Becky five years ago; right now was one of those times when it felt as if the dirt covering her grave were fresh.

Irrational as it was, a part of him still linked Jade with Becky's death. He knew it wasn't fair, his mother's lecture about not blaming Jade for a cruel twist of fate unnecessary. But when missing Becky cut like broken glass, he lost his ability to be fair.

"Yeah, Becky was special. She was incredible."

Jade's ears had recovered from the blare of the car alarm, and it was easy to catch Rob's quiet reply.

More than his words, it was the bleak emotion in them that sent her own spirits plummeting. *Great.* Not only was she attracted to a totally unsuitable man, but said unsuitable man was obviously still in love with his dead wife.

Suddenly all Jade wanted was to crawl into bed—alone—draw the covers up and make the world go away.

For some absurd reason she also wanted to bawl like a baby. Indeed, the tears were welling up in her eyes. "Gosh, it's late," she said, determined to leave before a single tear betrayed her. "Thanks a bunch for the police escort, but I think I can make it safely from here." Careful to press the correct button this time, she unlocked her car. Hurriedly, she opened the door and slipped into the bucket seat.

Only when she was several blocks away did she regain her composure. One thing was abundantly clear. She was going to have to take serious evasive tactics when it came to Rob Cooper. Like his patrol car, the man should come equipped with flashing lights to warn of danger.

Chapter ✣
FIFTEEN

RIDING HELPED restore Jade's equilibrium. There'd been very few times when it hadn't, the exception being the pitch-dark days of her adolescence, days filled with death, betrayal, and self-loathing. Luckily, her world was a lot brighter now, and having four ponies to ready for her lesson program, three horses to train, and the additional tasks she helped with at Rosewood—whether riding or longeing an extra horse or two or helping Ned with one of the yearlings—left her with little downtime to worry about anything else in her life, including Rob Cooper.

She spent Sunday working with the new ponies herself, putting them through their paces to keep them alert and well schooled. Since having them relaxed and mellow was as important as ensuring they were well schooled, she rode them early so they'd have plenty of time to graze, romp, and roll in one of the pastures as well. She wanted happy ponies to greet the kids when lessons began.

Then she moved on to the equines that stood taller than 14.1 hands. Owen and she had devised a schedule for his gelding's training. Jade worked with Cosmo every other day, with Owen taking the remaining days, riding him while Ned, Travis, or she coached him. Cosmo was a great horse, big and playful and athletic. He was smart too. At age five, he already understood that once he'd blown off a little steam, he had to settle down and pay attention.

And when she coached Owen on him, Jade could tell that Ned had pulled off a brilliant match when he'd encouraged Owen to buy him. Owen had made enormous strides as a rider in learning how to ride a green horse. He was already as proud as he could be of Cosmo. Their bond would only strengthen over the years. Considering that before coming to Rosewood, Owen had never even ridden, it was pretty cool that they'd made a convert to their horse-mad equestrian community.

She wasn't a Luddite; she loved her iPod and iPhone and booted up her computer every day. But she'd rather spend her day with her butt in a saddle than splayed in a chair staring at a computer screen. Knowing that at Rosewood she and her sisters were helping to keep the connection between horse and man alive and strong was incredibly rewarding. No modern technological gadget could touch that.

In much the same way that she enjoyed teaching children because they were fun and open to learning, she enjoyed the challenge of training young horses like Valentine and Carmen, the two mares Travis had assigned her along with Cosmo. Like the gelding, they'd just turned five and had an abundance of talent. For this reason, Travis and Margot had decided to bring them along in their training. Selling a horse that had already won in the show ring or had its jumping skills brought to the next level could only boost the farm's reputation as a source for exceptional prospects.

A full Thoroughbred, Carmen had enough rocket fuel to take her rider roaring across the countryside and soaring over every fence they came across. The only hitch was that three-day eventers also had to perform basic dressage maneuvers, movements that involved control and precision.

Jade's job was to fine-tune Carmen's jumping skills and develop her confidence in executing the dressage movements required at the first level in three-day eventing: yielding to the rider's leg (which demonstrated a horse's suppleness), circling, coming to a halt, shortening and lengthening the stride at the trot and canter, and changing the length of the rein at the trot and canter.

Of all the exercises, this last was where Carmen had the most difficulty. Being a "hot" horse who liked speed and lots of it, she viewed a relaxed hold on the reins as license to fly. Getting the mare to maintain the same pace throughout when all she wanted to do was move like a high wind whipping over the plains required all of Jade's skill and patience.

That afternoon when she jumped Carmen, she concentrated on the approaches to fences and keeping her rounded as they galloped between them. In addition, she practiced another exercise that involved pacing: half halts. Half halts were used to collect a horse several strides before the takeoff for a fence and were an essential technique for show jumping, where jump courses often were designed with tight corners and tricky approaches.

Travis, who'd come down to the outdoor ring to watch her jump, had set up a small course of four fences for her: two set at four strides apart and the other pair at a distance of five strides.

The goal of the day was to get Carmen to add or eliminate strides as she negotiated her approach. A big jumper, Carmen had no problem eliminating strides between the fences. She responded beautifully when asked to pick up steam quickly, moving into a full gallop between the sets of jumps. The half halts Jade asked for were more problematic. Carmen initially resisted, straining at the bit.

"Okay, what am I doing wrong?" she asked, bringing Carmen back to a trot.

"You held her back a fraction too long on that last

go-around. It allowed her to think about the bit too much," Travis said.

Jade nodded and, picking up the canter, tried again, concentrating on releasing the reins more quickly after the initial check. The second attempt was markedly better.

She glanced over to the middle of the ring, where Travis was leaning against a wall jump.

He nodded in satisfaction. "That was good. Your hands were clean and fast, and she listened to you. This time around, let's have her put it all together. Take the first fence at a trot again and remember to sit deep in the saddle to maintain the vertical, so she really gets back on her haunches. I'd like to see her take off from right here," he said, and walked over to the fence he'd selected. With the heel of his field boot, he drew a line in the sand about three feet in front of the fence.

"When she lands, bring her up to full speed in as few strides as you can manage. Once she's there, give her a half halt and bring her down a notch to take the last two fences."

Before gathering her reins, Jade took a minute to empty her mind of everything except what she planned to ask Carmen to do and where. This was the last set they'd jump today, and she wanted to end it on a positive note for the young mare.

The reason Travis and Ned had such hopes for Carmen's future as an eventer was that, in addition to her speed, stamina, and huge jumping ability, she was as bright as a newly minted penny.

When they took the small-jump course again, Carmen was ready and willing to give the changes in pace Jade asked for, and she took the jumps with her usual confidence.

As Jade brought Carmen back down to a walk, she patted her sweat-coated black neck enthusiastically and then moved her hand up to scratch the mare just above her withers, a spot Carmen loved to have tickled. Jade was still patting and praising the mare when Ned entered the ring with Valentine.

"You about ready for this sweetheart, Miss Jade?"

"Your timing's perfect, Ned."

"How'd Carmen go?"

"Jade had her going real well," Travis answered for her.

"Tuesday will be a lot tougher, when we start to work on leg yields with her," Jade said. The session would be a short one so Carmen's brain didn't fry from overtraining.

"Nah," Ned replied, shaking his head. "She's starting to get the hang of it. I bet she'll do it just fine at the walk, maybe even at the trot—not that there's any rush. Most important thing is not to get her scared about tripping over herself as she crosses her legs to move sideways. We'll take as long as we need until she figures it out." He pulled out a white fleece saddle pad that he'd carried tucked under his left arm. "Want to hop off her so we can put your saddle on Valentine?"

"Sure thing." Jade dropped her stirrup and let her boots hang, enjoying the stretch to her hamstrings and calves. "Thanks for bringing Valentine down, Ned."

"No problem. Tito's got Night Watch tacked for you, Travis. And Margot said she's going to ride Brown Betty in the indoor ring so Betty doesn't get distracted." Brown Betty, a striking liver chestnut, was one of their best four-year-olds and, as Mystique was her dam, a favorite of Margot's. Jade had a hunch Margot was going to keep the young mare at Rosewood no matter how many offers she received. And that was fine, Jade thought. Once she was sure her dual career as schoolteacher and riding instructor was a reality, she planned to someday fall in love with one of their horses and claim it for her own.

It was far better to fall in love with a horse than with a man, she told herself a tad defiantly, for just then Rob

Cooper appeared in her mind's eye, all lean, muscled body and piercing blue gaze.

For Pete's sake, she thought with a snort. This was ridiculous. Rob did not belong in her brain. She was busy.

"Did you say something, Jade?" Travis asked.

"Nope." She put a fist to her mouth and pretended to cough. "Got a bit of dust in my throat." Bringing Carmen to a halt, she bent at the waist and swung her right leg over the saddle to dismount.

Landing lightly on the ground, she lifted her saddle flap, unbuckled the girth, and pulled the saddle off Carmen's steaming back.

At least Rob hadn't stormed her consciousness while she was negotiating fences astride Carmen, she thought. But that was small comfort. She'd always been so good at ignoring guys before.

The specter of Rob Cooper had always loomed too large in her life. Unfortunately, now she had to deal with the effects of the flesh-and-blood man, a man who knew how to make her own flesh quiver and her blood sing.

Monday morning found her sitting in Ted Guerra's office with a large coffee from Braverman's perched in her lap.

"Sorry I missed talking to you on parents' night, Jade. I was waylaid by several parents. How'd it go?"

She suppressed a shudder at the thought of what would have happened if Ted Guerra had interrupted Rob and her in mid-kiss. "Parents' night? It was kind of daunting, to tell the truth."

He nodded sympathetically. "The first time can be pretty intimidating. And I don't think it ever becomes anything one looks forward to, but a number of parents came up to me and told me how impressed they were by your enthusiasm. So you should be proud of yourself." Reaching for his own cup of coffee, he took a sip, swallowed, and cleared his throat. "Unfortunately, there was some criticism. . . ."

Ted paused before continuing, and in that fraction of time, Jade was abruptly glad she'd had the sense to forgo her favorite pumpkin muffin that morning. The cream cheese would have curdled in her stomach.

"Parents' complaints aren't uncommon, Jade. I usually don't bother to bring them up with my staff, but the Harrisons are a . . . well, a vocal family. I don't want you to be blindsided by anything you hear."

Ted rose several rungs in Jade's estimation. It was a nice feeling to realize that he was the kind of principal who looked out for his teachers—even his lowly substitutes.

"The Harrisons? Did they ask to switch Eugene out of the class?"

"Yes." His face revealed his surprise that she'd guessed what they would do. She decided not to share her old history with other members of the Harrison clan and that she'd already been a target of their very vocal disdain. "So I told Eugene and Christy once again that I have a policy of not moving students—"

"Again?" Wow, they'd certainly been busy, Jade thought.

Ted inclined his head. "It's clear the Harrisons have a bee in their bonnet about you teaching their son, so I'd like you to go the extra mile in providing little Eugene with lots of opportunities beyond the assignments."

"I'd be happy to," Jade said with an easy shrug. "Eugene seems to like school."

"Hope his parents don't ruin the experience for him." Grimacing, Ted picked up his coffee and took a long sip, as if to wash the sour taste from his mouth. "I'm glad to see you're not going to bear a grudge."

The word made her think of Rob. How funny. She'd

been sure he would hold a grudge far longer than he had. "Did any other parents phone in their displeasure?"

He gave a dismissive sweep of his hand. "Things will sort themselves out as the fall progresses. You have the trip to the apple orchard soon, don't you?"

She blinked, somewhat confused by the abrupt switch of topics. "Uh, yes. It's on Wednesday."

"Have you got enough chaperones signed up?"

"Yes. Deirdre Cerra's mom is coming. I thought I might call Posey Hall's mom, Gail, and ask if she wants to as well. She's the class parent."

"How about asking Rob Cooper instead? As an only parent, it would be good for him to have a chance to see Hayley among her peers. This will let him do so in a natural way. Why don't you give him a call?"

That cleared things up in a hurry. Rob had called him—she had expected no less—and this was Ted's way of trying to smooth out a wrinkly situation. While she was grateful that Ted hadn't been willing to move Hayley out of her class, she really didn't want Rob tagging along on a school outing. He'd invaded enough of her life.

Ted must have noted her hesitation. "Both Hayley and the class could benefit from Rob acting as a chaperone. So often it's the moms who accompany a class trip."

He didn't need to say more. A fist squeezed about her heart as she thought of Hayley, who'd been without her mother for years now, and how she must feel on these mom-studded events. She nodded. "Okay."

"Good." He checked his watch. "I'll let you go so you can call him. They won't have left for school yet."

Rob was drinking coffee with one hand and stowing the dirty breakfast dishes in the dishwasher with the other. "'Bout time you went upstairs and washed your face and brushed your teeth, sweetheart."

Hayley lifted her glass and drained it. Noticing that she was about to wipe her mouth with her forearm, Rob cleared his throat and said, "Try a napkin." Sheepishly, she picked it up off her place mat and patted away a thick milk mustache.

She was sliding out from her seat at the breakfast table when the phone rang. "I'll get it," she volunteered.

Rob set the mug down and grabbed the phone from the wall cradle. "Got it. You go on upstairs and get those teeth clean. The clock's ticking. And don't forget to bring down your school bag."

"As if, Dad!" Hayley said with an exaggerated roll of her eyes before racing out of the kitchen.

Rob grinned. If Hayley had had her way, they'd have been at school half an hour ago. She'd been over the moon when he told her that she was going to have lessons twice a week at Rosewood.

"With Miss Radcliffe?" she'd breathed, her eyes round with excitement. For the entirety of the weekend, she'd been all horses, all the time. It was a miracle she hadn't insisted on eating only oats, apples, and carrots.

He answered on the next ring. "Hello?"

"Hi, um, it's me, Jade Rad—"

"Yes, hi. I recognized your voice. Good morning." He waited to hear the reason she was calling, and, in the brief silence, his pulse quickened. Whatever contradictory emotions she inspired in him, he could no longer pretend that he was in any way immune.

"It's about the apple-picking trip to Newton's Orchard. We need another parent to accompany us."

The words sounded as if they were being dragged from her mouth. Ted Guerra must have put her up to this, he decided. He glanced at the wall calendar. "It's on Wednesday, right?"

"That's right. It's fine if you can't get away from work. Really. I can call—"

Her patent reluctance to invite him on the outing brought another grin to his face. "Wednesday's not a problem. I'll trade shifts with my brother, Scott."

"Oh." There was a pause. "I'll put you on the list, then. Bye."

"Bye, Jade. Great talking to you." He laughed softly as he heard an unmistakable growl of frustration just before she hung up.

A picture of a scowling Jade sprang to mind. Inviting him as a chaperone might have soured her mood, but he'd lay odds that by the time Hayley hurried into the classroom to share her excitement at the prospect of taking riding lessons with her, she'd have regrouped. Hayley would never guess that her teacher was anything less than delighted to have her dad come on the class trip.

And that was an excellent reason to like Jade a lot.

Monday and Tuesday were filled with Egyptian pyramids, mummies, and gods, writing prompts for the kids' daily journals, math word problems, and making lists of all the different apples they could name and which apple recipes they liked best. Jade already considered Hayley bright, but the little girl had hurried into the classroom on Monday morning positively glowing from the dual pleasure of taking riding lessons at Rosewood and having her father accompany the class to Newton's Apple Orchard.

"Do you think I could bring one of the apples from the orchard to give to my pony after my lesson, Miss Radcliffe?" she'd asked, her eyes lit with excitement. "My dad said he'd help me pick a special one."

"An apple would be just the thing, Hayley, but I'll want to show you exactly how to feed it to the pony."

If possible, her answer only made Hayley's eyes shine brighter. "Okay."

At circle time at the end of Tuesday, Jade and the kids

sat on the floor and discussed what they'd be doing the next day. It soon became clear that having a Warburg police officer on the trip was pretty darned exciting stuff for the boys in the class too.

"We'll have to be really good tomorrow, won't we, or Officer Cooper will arrest us," Arthur Garner said, with what Jade considered excessive relish.

"I would hope you'd all be on your best behavior in any case, Arthur, which means that Kyle, Sam, and you will need to keep your hands to yourself. And no fake tripping so you can bump into one another either," she said, sidestepping the question of Rob Cooper's arresting anyone, a thought that made her distinctly queasy.

James spoke up. "Will he bring his handcuffs?"

She should have guessed how endlessly fascinating a figure like Rob would be for these boys. At their age, her nephew Max would have peppered his teacher with a thousand and one questions. "I don't think so, James."

"Will he wear his uniform?"

"Highly doubtful. I think you can rule out Officer Cooper picking apples in his police uniform."

The answer left several of them looking vastly disappointed.

Eugene raised his hand. "If he doesn't bring his handcuffs, then how will he catch the bad guys?"

"Apple orchards aren't where bad guys usually spend their time, so I'm pretty sure it will be all right if Officer Cooper leaves his handcuffs at home." She cleared her throat. "Now that we've settled that question, let's decide what recipes we might want to make from the apples we pick. . . ."

After the kids voted for candied apples and fritters— and maybe muffins if there were enough apples left over—the bell rang and it was time to gather their belongings and pack up. As the kids dashed to their cubbies to collect their things, Eugene approached her.

"Miss Radcliffe?"

"Yes, Eugene?"

"Can I ask my parents to come on the apple-picking trip too?"

Oh, joy. "Of course. Your parents would be more than welcome."

Eugene beamed. "My daddy probably won't be able to, because he has to work, but my mommy might."

"Well, you ask her when you get home, and she can call me tonight or simply show up tomorrow in time to leave with us on the bus, okay?"

With a quick, happy nod that contained the same bubbling excitement Hayley had displayed, Eugene ran off to grab his backpack. Recalling Christy Harrison's mention of her jam-packed schedule of very important responsibilities, Jade hoped Eugene wouldn't be too disappointed if his mother declined his invitation.

One thing was certain: This apple-picking trip was going to be loads of fun.

Chapter ✤
SIXTEEN

JADE WOULD never have anticipated that teaching at Warburg Elementary, starting a riding program, and helping train Rosewood's horses would consume so much of her energy that she was actually surprised to receive a call from Greg Hammond. The private investigator gave her the news that he had a preliminary list of men—or bastards, as Jade thought of them—who might have been involved with her mother. Of course, as soon as she heard that, her former urge to discover the identity of her mother's lover returned full force.

They'd arranged to meet on Tuesday evening, after she'd finished exercising the horses and ponies. Their rendezvous would be at a Chinese restaurant in Leesburg where, Jade was confident, they wouldn't run into anyone she knew.

As she watered and then fed the ponies, she couldn't help wondering who'd made it onto the list. Reaching Sweet Virginia's stall, she dropped three sections of hay onto the bedding and offered Ginny a *"buen provecho"* before shutting and bolting the stall door and brushing her hands on her breeches.

That was it. The ponies were set for the night. She'd have just enough time to shower and change before she had to meet Greg—Jade's internal monologue was interrupted by Margot, who'd wandered into the barn.

"Hey, Jade. Need a hand with these cuties?"

"Thanks, but it's a wrap. Ginny and her pals are happily munching away. Then it's sweet dreams for the lot of them."

"Wow, you got your chores done fast," Margot said as they stepped outside and together pulled the barn's sliding double doors shut. "Which is good. We're having dinner on the early side as it's a school night. Come on up to the house and join us. Ellie made three turkey pot-pies. Jordan's bringing a huge salad and I think I heard her say something about a peach crumble for dessert. There's ice cream in the fridge. The gang's gathering in a half hour."

Jade's stomach rumbled, her exemplary lunch of a pb&j sandwich, carrot and celery slices, and a pear a distant memory. "That sounds great, but I'm going to have to take a pass. I've got plans for dinner tonight."

"Oh, that's nice. Who are you having dinner with?"

Drat, she should have said she had a meeting at school. "Uh, I don't think you know him."

Her answer must have set off Margot's internal radar, since between Margot, Jordan, Travis, and Ned, they knew an awful lot of people in Loudoun County. Even Owen, a relative newcomer to Warburg, was accumulating acquaintances fast, thanks to his architectural restoration-and-design firm.

"Jade, is something going on?" Margot asked in a voice tinged with concern.

Sometimes her older half sister forgot that she didn't have to act as Jade's guardian anymore.

"It's nothing. Really."

"Then why am I getting a bad feeling in the pit of my stomach?" Margot folded her hands across her chest and waited, feet planted on the gravel of the barns' courtyard, looking like she'd be willing to stand there for hours until Jade gave her the full story. Hours that Jade didn't have to spare if she wanted to arrive on time to her meeting with Greg and finally read the names on that list.

Sighing, she realized she had to tell the truth. She didn't want to lie in any case: She'd told Margot enough lies and half-truths as a teen.

"The person I'm meeting is named Greg Hammond. He's a private investigator I've hired to find out who TM was." She kept talking even when Margot's mouth fell open in astonishment. "And don't say I shouldn't try to find out who the scumbag sleeping with Mom was, because you'll be wasting your breath. If you were in my shoes, you'd do the same. You know you would, Margot. You can tell Jordan it's no use trying to dissuade me either, since I'm sure this will be topic number one at dinner tonight."

"Jade, listen, I—"

She shook her head. "Sorry, but there's no changing my mind. I've got to go or I'll be late."

She hurried off toward her cottage, miserable at the thought that she was again causing Margot distress.

Although she'd rushed through her shower and dragged on a pair of cords and a sweater, she hadn't dared speed on her way to the Moon Palace. She was convinced that if she did, Rob Cooper would be there to intercept her with flashing lights and a blaring siren, and she really and truly had no desire to explain to him where she was going in such a hurry or why.

She spotted Greg seated at a corner table. He was sipping tea from a blue-and-white porcelain cup. The bowl of crispy fried noodles in front of his plate looked untouched. The man was clearly disciplined. She loved dipping those noodles in sweet-and-sour sauce. She could empty a bowl of them awfully fast.

He rose from his chair as she approached, but she waved him back down. "Have you been waiting long?"

"The tea hasn't even cooled yet."

This evening he was wearing a suit and tie. She wondered whether he'd needed the suit for one of his investigations. She couldn't help but be fascinated by his line of work.

"So what names have you come up with?" she asked as she sat down next to him.

He passed her one of the menus. "Let's order first, so the waiter doesn't hover. He must be new. He's extremely eager."

Indeed he was. All it took was Jade turning her head in his direction for the young man to hurry over to their table.

"May I take your order? Some tea?" he added hopefully.

"I can vouch for it." Greg lifted his cup.

Jade saw a glass-and-metal sugar dispenser next to a bottle of soy sauce. Unsweetened Chinese tea was too bitter for her taste buds. "Sure, that'd be nice. And some ice water, please."

The waiter nodded. "Do you know what you'd like to order, or would you like more time?"

Having been to the Moon Palace before, she didn't bother to consult the menu. "I'll have the steamed dumplings and the sesame noodles." If her stomach became cramped with nerves again, she could have them boxed to eat later.

"And I'll take an egg roll and the double-cooked pork with eggplant." Greg handed back his menu.

After the waiter had poured her tea and hurried into the kitchen to relay their orders, Jade looked at Greg expectantly. "So?"

He didn't make a move toward the briefcase that she'd spied resting by his leg. Instead, he asked, "How are things going at home and your new job?"

"Good. The kids I'm teaching are great. We're going

on an apple-picking trip tomorrow, our first field trip. Classes in my new riding program start the day after that."

"And things are good between you and your sisters?"

Her brows drew together as she recalled the stricken look on Margot's face. "Yeah, things are good."

He cocked his head inquiringly. "Things are good, but . . ."

She picked up her chopsticks, pulled them out of their paper wrapper, and separated them with a snap of her wrists. "Margot knows I'm meeting you here."

"Ah. I was wondering how you'd keep the fact that you'd hired me a secret from them. It'd be difficult, especially since you and your sisters seem very close." He took a slow sip of the hot tea. "So Margot's upset."

"You could say that."

"And you are too, because worrying her makes you feel lousy. Which brings me to my next question. Knowing the way you're feeling already, are you absolutely sure you want to take this next step? You don't have to look at the names on my list, Jade. You can just walk away and let it go. Enjoy your students, your horses, and your relationship with your family. Live your life—it sounds like it's a fine one. Discovering the identity of TM might shoot it all to hell."

He was making a valid point, she conceded with an inward sigh. Things were basically going well for her. Why stir things up?

Tracing a random pattern on the black tablecloth, she said, "I'm not sure I can explain why this means so much to me. All I can say is that since I read my mom's diary, she's been a stranger to me. If I know who TM is, perhaps I'll be able to understand her. I'm willing to deal with whatever happens as a result." Raising her gaze, she met his squarely. "Could I please see the list?"

Greg gave no clue to his thoughts as he stared her

down for seconds more. Then, bending over, he rummaged in his briefcase and, when he straightened, a file was in his hand. Setting it on the tablecloth, he opened it and said, "Remember, this is just a preliminary list that I've drawn up. Since you're determined to see this thing through, I thought we could go over names tonight. As my investigation continues, it's possible other names may surface."

Opening the file, he picked up the top sheet of paper and handed it to her.

Her heart changed its tempo, thudding heavily in her ears as she took the list and read five typed names: *Tom Medina; Taft Miner; Tony Myers; Timothy Marquand; Christopher McCallister.*

Frowning, she looked up. "Christopher McCallister?"

Greg nodded. "You probably know him as Topher—"

"Oh! Of course. *Topher* McCallister. I saw the C and blanked."

"I gather he's been called Topher since day one. He's the oldest son of Eleanor and George McCallister. You were in high school with his younger brother, Dean."

"Yes," she answered, fighting a blush. She suspected that Greg knew about the spectacularly stupid make-out session she'd engaged in with Dean McCallister at a house party. She'd necked with Dean to wreak vengeance on Blair Hood, who'd been spreading vicious stories about Jade's mom. Blair had had the major hots for Dean. Jade had succeeded in exacting her adolescent revenge against Blair but hadn't escaped the evening unscathed. Feeling rotten about herself for having used Dean, she drank way too much. When, after receiving a call from the neighbors about the noise, the police arrived to bust up the party, she'd been passed out. That was the night Rob Cooper entered her life. He'd driven her home in his police car, and at some point during the trip she'd puked all over the backseat.

God, what a mess of a kid she'd been, she thought, with a familiar shiver of self-disgust.

Pushing the loathsome memories aside, she focused her attention on the list, concentrating on the name she knew best. "How old is Topher again? I think he used to come to the Radcliffe Roast, Mom and Dad's big annual bash, but I don't remember much more about him than that."

"He's a year younger than your sister Jordan. After graduating from college, he came back to Warburg to work in his father's insurance company. He's now its VP."

"I guess he wouldn't have been too young for Mom," she said in a voice tinged with doubt.

"He's the youngest of the group, but I put him down as a possible candidate based on the fact that he considers himself quite the Lothario."

She definitely wasn't going to be able to eat her order of dumplings and sesame noodles. Her stomach was already in knots and she had yet to discuss the four other names Greg had supplied.

"And the others? I don't recognize them. Oh, wait— Tom Medina. He used to come to the Roast too."

Greg nodded. "Tom Medina was a business associate of your father's. Unfortunately, some of his hot investing tips didn't pan out, although he personally didn't suffer financially."

"And you think Tom Medina might have been the type who would sleep with Mom? What a charmer."

"Medina's second marriage was already on the rocks. And your mother was a beautiful woman."

"What about these guys?" she asked, tapping the paper with her index finger. "I definitely don't recognize their names."

"Taft Miner owned a restaurant in Leesburg your parents liked, Miner's Mill. He sold it shortly after their deaths and moved to Charleston, South Carolina. Timothy Marquand owns Beresford Jewelers. He'd joined the Warburg Hunt Club about four months before your mother's diary started."

"So there would have been time for them to get acquainted. And how about Tony Myers?"

"He works as a stylist at True Beauty, the salon in town."

"A stylist?"

"A stylist who looks like an Argentine polo player."

Jade shook her head. "You can scratch him, Latin-lover looks notwithstanding. Mom wouldn't have been willing to risk someone guessing about her affair. Too many women who loved to hate her patronized True Beauty."

"Women like Nonie Harrison and Pamela Hood?"

She didn't ask how he knew about her mother's social rivalry with Nonie and her sister, Pamela. Greg was obviously very thorough at his job.

"What if your mother knew that they'd had affairs with Tony too?"

She blinked in surprise and then wondered at her reaction. Why should she be shocked that these other women were having affairs? Then another thought occurred to her, and this time she couldn't hide her shock. "Wait a sec—Nonie Harrison and Pamela Hood are sisters. Do you mean they were sleeping with the *same* guy?"

He smiled. "Too kinky for Warburg?"

"Well, yeah!" Flabbergasted, she sank back against her chair. "How wild. I admit to being completely blown away by that piece of info. And it's quite effectively killed my appetite—a tragedy, since I love sesame noodles. But back to Mom. So what you're saying is that she might have risked an affair with this Tony guy because whatever ammunition Nonie, Pamela, and their friends had would have been rendered useless since they were sleeping with him too?"

He shrugged. "It's possible. I've encountered stranger things. It could also be the reason tongues started to wag so viciously when your mom and dad died. This would have been a good way for Mrs. Harrison and Mrs. Hood to cover up their own actions."

Well, Greg had warned her of the pitfalls lying in wait if she chose to pursue the investigation. Just going down the list had made her head pound, and now she was feeling positively ill.

She rubbed her forehead to soothe the tension there. "Crikey. I guess you should investigate all of them, then."

"All right," he said with a nod. "I'll get on it and see if any other names come up."

He plucked the file in front of her and closed it, and she realized that the waiter was bringing metal-dome-topped dishes toward to the table. She liked that Greg was so careful.

"Are you really not going to be able to eat any of this?"

With a rueful smile, she shook her head. "Nope. Sorry, I guess I'm not much in the way of a restaurant date."

"You're just fine." Addressing the waiter, who'd begun placing the dishes in the middle of the table, he said, "We've decided we'd like to have these boxed to go. Could you do that for us?"

"Of course. No problem, mister."

Alone again, Greg said, "I'll get back to you with what I've learned. In the meantime, enjoy those students of yours."

"Thanks."

"I hear Nonie Harrison's grandson is in your class." At her raised brows, he grinned. "Oh, yes, most of Warburg has been made aware of that fact, as well as Nonie's strong feelings about a Radcliffe—and Jade Radcliffe in particular—teaching her grandson."

"It must be galling for the poor thing."

"Pretty much," he agreed cheerfully.

"Well, I'm sure I'll lose a lot of sleep worrying over that."

"Don't bother. Seems to me you'll need every minute of sleep if you've got a class field trip tomorrow. Dinner's on me," he said as the waiter returned with two paper bags.

"But—"

"No buts. I'll call as soon as I have something to tell you."

"Okay. And thanks."

Jade walked into her cottage to find Margot and Jordan sitting on her living-room sofa. "Being energy conscious, I was sure I hadn't left the overhead light on," she remarked, dropping her bag by the sofa. "Glad to see you guys made yourselves at home." Without sparing them another word, she went into the kitchen, took a fork from the silverware drawer, and pulled out the carton of dumplings from the paper bag, stowing the sesame noodles in the fridge. She turned to find Jordan standing on the threshold.

"Jade, we'd like to talk to you."

"Natch." Walking past her, she returned to the living room and dropped into the wide chair that faced the sofa at an angle. Propping her feet on the ottoman, she opened the cardboard box and speared a dumpling. "Okay, have at it. Tell me how stupid I was to have hired a detective." She shoved the entire dumpling in her mouth, chewing busily as she prepared for her sisters' lecture.

"You're not stupid in the least. Margot and I would have done precisely the same thing."

She barely managed to keep the half-chewed blob of

pork in her mouth. Swallowing hastily, she managed, "What?"

"We understand why you need to do this—"

"It doesn't mean that we're not worried about how it might end up hurting you even more, though," Margot added.

Jade swallowed again, this time against the emotion that was causing her throat to tighten. How had she managed to luck out and have such great sisters? "I'm sorry I didn't tell you about Greg Hammond sooner. I was sure you guys would be really upset with me."

"If anything we're upset *for* you," Jordan said.

"But if it's what you need to do, then just know we're here for you, sweetie."

"Thanks. Have I told you that you two are amazing?"

"Don't you forget it," Margot said with a grin.

Jordan leaned forward to squeeze Jade's leg. "You're mighty fine too, you know."

"Don't you forget it," she said.

"So tell us about your detective," Margot said. "Has he got any leads?"

Suddenly ravenous, Jade began polishing off the dumplings as she filled them in. "He's got a list of names he's looking into for me." She decided not to name any names until she'd heard more from Greg. Four of those five men—perhaps all of them—were innocent until proven guilty.

"And this detective, are you sure he's good?" Jordan asked.

"Oh, yeah," she said with a nod. "He's sharp. He's already found out stuff about Warburg's citizens that I would never in a million years have suspected." Her mouth stretched into a wide smile. "For instance, he discovered who Nonie Harrison and Pamela Hood were burning up the sheets with back when Mom was having her own affair." This piece of information was priceless;

she couldn't resist sharing it with the two women she loved best.

Margot's crow of delight filled the room. "Oh, do tell!"

"You wouldn't know him, Margot, since you prefer Serenity Spa's salon treatments."

"Wait, you mean Nonie and Pamela were both cheating with staff from True Beauty? I hadn't realized they had so much eye candy in the salon."

"Oh, no, Jordan, Nonie and Pamela are really special sisters. Apparently all they needed was one prime specimen."

"One?" Margot's jaw dropped. "Oh. My. God!" Dropping back against the sofa, she kicked up her heels in delight. "Do you think they did threesomes? Jordan, I love you, but no way am I ever sharing. Same goes for you, Jade."

"There goes my secret fantasy," Jordan replied dolefully, before succumbing to a fit of giggles. "Oh, Lord," she said, wiping tears from the corners of her eyes. "You've got to hand it to Nonie: Her hypocrisy is unparalleled."

"True," Jade said. "The woman is a champion."

Margot was still shaking her head in amazement. "It's a real shame we didn't have this nifty nugget of information when Nonie was busy with her smear campaign against you and your mom, Jade."

"I don't know. I'm not convinced it would have prevented much that happened, especially since I was hellbent on making dumb decisions at every opportunity." Dismissing the subject with a shrug, she summoned a grin. "Thank God I'm so mature and responsible now. Not even Rob Cooper's presence or, for that matter, Christy Harrison's is going to faze me on tomorrow's outing."

"What! Jade Radcliffe, how dare you hold out on us

like this? Why is this the first we've heard of Rob and Christy accompanying the class?" Margot cried.

"I've been trying really hard not to think about it, that's why. Denial is a river in Egypt. I also get to have Deirdre Cerra's mom—do you know her?"

Jordan gave her a sympathetic look. "You poor thing. Just remember to bring a paper bag."

"A paper bag? What for?"

"In case Helen Cerra starts to hyperventilate."

"Oh, great."

Chapter %
SEVENTEEN

THE NEXT morning was sunny, with just the right amount of nip in the air to know that summer was finally over and that the days of thick knit wool sweaters and crackling fires on the weekends were fast approaching. A perfect morning for apple picking.

Jade dressed casually, choosing navy corduroys, a gray ribbed henley, and a pair of old paddock boots. She twisted her hair into a knot at the nape of her neck and chose her favorite silver chandelier earrings, because they made her feel good. She figured that might come in handy, what with Christy Harrison's critical eye fixed on her every move, Helen Cerra's thousand and one anxieties, and, most worrisome of all, Rob Cooper's distracting presence. Shepherding her eighteen second-graders around the apple orchard would be much easier if she didn't have to contend with the three adults.

At school, she picked up the lunches the cafeteria was providing for the trip, packed them into two large cardboard boxes, and carried them back to the classroom. Hayley and Rob had already arrived, Hayley talking animatedly to her dad as she showed him the fish in the tank, introducing him to Bubbles, Nemo, and company.

"Hi, Miss Radcliffe!" Hayley hurried over as Jade entered the classroom.

"Hi, Hayley. Showing your dad the fish?" she replied with what she thought was a commendable degree of composure, since the last time she'd seen Rob she'd been in his arms. To prove to herself that she could continue in this calm and collected vein, she added, "Good morning, Officer Cooper."

"Good morning, Miss Radcliffe," he replied just as formally. "Can I help you with those boxes?"

She stepped backward hastily. "That's all right. I was just going to set them here." While she might be able to pull off talking to him, letting him touch her in even a casual graze of the fingers was a big no-no.

The sound of children's voices coming down the hall reached her. Jade straightened from where she'd set the boxes with an easy smile, sure she'd heard Victoria Kemp and Lucy Richter's voices among them. Victoria and Lucy would need to be greeted, then she could drift over to her desk and do her best to forget about Rob Cooper looking very fine in wheat-colored jeans and a brown flannel shirt. The fabric would probably feel incredibly soft beneath her fingers.

"Hi, Miss Radcliffe," a chorus of voices rang out. Victoria, Lucy, Jay Blount, and Chris Alden swept into the room with all the energy of seven-year-olds about to go on an adventure—sneakers pounding, book bags bouncing, jackets and sweatshirts flapping.

"Hi, guys, you all ready for our trip?"

Heads bobbed in affirmation. "Are we going to be in your group, Miss Radcliffe?"

"I'm going to read out which parent will be in charge of which group of kids once I've called attendance and we've made sure everyone is here." She'd drawn up two separate lists last night, one with four groups, another one with three, in case Christy Harrison couldn't come on the outing. Jade still had no idea, since Christy hadn't bothered to leave a message or email Jade the night before. "For now I need you all to put your things away in the cubbies, take out last night's homework and put it in the tray on my desk, and then take your seats."

Over the next few minutes, the rest of the class rushed into the room. All the kids were bursting with excitement at the first field trip of the year. All except Eugene. Among the last to arrive, he entered holding his mother's hand, but one look at his tearstained face and Jade knew Christy wouldn't be joining them.

"Hi, Eugene; hello, Mrs. Harrison. We're just getting ready to divide the class into their groups so everyone will know who's going to be with which parent. I'm so glad you could come with us this morning," she said politely to Christy, in case she'd guessed incorrectly and Eugene's tears were about something else entirely.

"No, I won't be coming this morning. I thought I could—for goodness' sake, will you stop crying, Eugene? The way you're carrying on is ridiculous."

"You said you'd *come*."

"And then I remembered I had a commitment I couldn't miss," his mother enunciated through her clenched teeth. "I've already explained this to you several times."

"You never come." Eugene's voice was small, plaintive, and if it didn't pierce his mother's heart, it did Jade's. By no stretch of the imagination had she been pleased at the prospect of Christy Harrison accompanying them, but she'd have dealt with her presence—no matter how insufferable she might prove to be—to have Eugene as excited and happy as his classmates.

Jade cleared her throat, drawing the little boy's eyes to her. "Eugene, I'm sure your mother will be able to come on our next field trip, because she'll have a lot more time to arrange her schedule."

A smart child, he didn't look convinced. Jade respected him too much to continue feeding him lines. "I'd like for you to put today's homework in the tray on my desk and go sit at your desk so that we can go over the rules for the trip and all that important stuff, okay?"

"Okay." The word came out reluctantly.

"Goodbye, Eugene." His mother bent down stiffly and kissed his cheek.

"Bye," he mumbled, before turning away to stomp toward the back of the classroom. His shoulders were slumped, and Jade saw him rub a forearm across his eyes and knew he was wiping away fresh tears. The poor kid was the picture of dejection.

"I'm sure he'll be feel better once we're at the orchard. There'll be so much to see and do."

Christy coldly dismissed her concern. "Of course he will." Then, with a glance at her gold wristwatch, she said, "I must go." But suddenly she caught sight of Rob standing by the bookshelves, flipping through David Macaulay's book on pyramids, and said, "Officer Cooper's going on the field trip? I would think he'd have more pressing things to do than spend an entire morning at an apple orchard." She paused to rake Jade with a condescending look. "Then again, maybe he wants to ensure his daughter is adequately supervised."

A veil of red descended before Jade's eyes. "Gosh, I would think Officer Cooper's decision to come today had more to do with wanting to be an involved parent and making Hayley happy. But I can see why that idea wouldn't occur to you."

Christy Harrison's face tightened into a hard mask, but Jade was herself too angry to care that she'd offended her. "If you'll excuse me, I have to get the class ready so we can board the bus on time."

His station by the bookshelves was close enough for Rob to overhear Jade and Christy Harrison's exchange. He hadn't even attempted to play deaf. It would have been impossible. Just as his eyes kept straying from the book's incredible drawings of pyramids to steal a glance at Jade, so, too, his ears had been tuned to catch every remark she made to the kids as they came into the class-room. He liked listening to her exchanges with the kids. She had a nice rapport with them, one that combined an easy authority and genuine affection.

Christy could take a few lessons from her, he thought. But it was unlikely Mrs. Eugene Harrison IV would ever acknowledge she had anything to learn from Jade. It seemed the long-standing rivalry between the Harrisons and the Radcliffes was alive and well.

He watched Jade stride across the room to her desk. She always carried herself well, but he could detect the tension stiffening her spine to ramrod-straight.

He didn't blame her for being furious at Christy's comment. If he hadn't been 100 percent sure that she would very much resent his interference, he'd have defended her as readily as she'd defended him.

That she'd praised him as a parent surprised the hell out of him. Surprised and pleased him. It was one thing for his family to say what a good job he was doing with his daughter. To have Jade recognize how hard he was trying to be the dad—and mom—Hayley needed meant an enormous amount.

It was funny how much his opinion of her had changed since he first read the letter from Ted Guerra and learned that Jade would be Hayley's substitute teacher until Sandy Riley returned. His feelings for Jade might still be confused and conflicted, but one thing he did know: She was a good teacher.

It was time he acknowledged a second thing about her: Jade Radcliffe was one of the sexiest women he'd ever met. At eight forty-seven in the morning, he shouldn't be thinking about loosening the knot at the nape of her neck so her thick, sun-streaked hair would fall over the backs of his hands or how he might then wrap the silky strands in his fists and draw her close for a kiss, letting himself have a long, slow taste of her.

Would one taste be enough? He refused to answer the sudden thought. Remembering that he was in the company of eighteen hyper-observant second-graders, he tamped down his imagination, lest it run rampant with scenarios of what it might take to satisfy his hunger for their teacher. But when Hayley, who'd been assigned to Rob's group—along with Rosie Baxter, Colleen Griffin, James Wessel, Kyle Parsons, and Chris Alden—tugged on his sleeve and then pulled his head down so that she could whisper in his ear, "Isn't Miss Radcliffe pretty, Daddy?" he smiled and said, "Yeah," unperturbed at Hayley's beaming delight.

They arrived at Newton's Orchard without mishap. Jade hadn't had to whip out the paper bag she'd brought along with the first-aid kit to minister to an agitated Mrs. Cerra, and no one complained of motion sickness when the bus left the town limits and hit the small, winding roads that led through gold-leafed woods and past fenced pale-green pastures to the two-hundred-acre apple farm.

She hadn't had to worry about Rob Cooper either or pretend to ignore his piercing blue gaze. He'd been too busy answering the boys' endless questions. It had started with Arthur and Patrick asking him about the neat stuff police officers got to do, the others joining in as their initial awe and shyness at having a real live police officer in their midst wore off.

It was easy to watch him surreptitiously. She often had to turn around in her seat to make sure everyone in the rear of the bus was behaving. Since previously she had been the one subjected to Rob's close-eyed scrutiny, the switch was a nice change.

He handled being the star of the bus ride with ease, answering the boys' questions but bringing them back down to earth whenever their excitement over the topic of bad guys and car chases and guns threatened to get out of control. She was also fair-minded enough to admit that no matter how much she personally would have preferred him to skip the outing, he was not only making Hayley's but the boys' day. And he was awfully cute when he blushed beet red after James Wessel loudly informed Chris Alden that Rob was almost as awesome as Superman.

Upon their arrival at Newton's Orchard, they clambered off the bus. Before they headed into the faded red barn that served as the orchard's store and greeting center, Jade called out for them to stop, so she could perform a quick head count. As she did, she noticed that all the boys were gathered around Rob, like electrons to a nucleus.

"Arthur, Sam, and Patrick, I need you to remember that when we go into the orchard, you're to stay with Mrs. Cerra and the rest of your group. And Eugene, Paul, and Jay? That goes for you as well. You're in my group, not Officer Cooper's. This orchard is big and I don't want anyone getting lost. So, just to avoid confusion, let's get in our groups now, please. That's it, thank you," she said as the six boys shuffled over to her and Helen Cerra. "Now, are you ready to go inside and meet Mr. Newton so he can talk to us about the apples he grows on his farm?"

A hay-wagon ride along a rutted track dividing the rows of old dwarf apple trees, with eighteen kids bouncing energetically upon the bales and singing "I like to eat, eat, eat apples and bananas" at the top of their lungs and off-key to boot, was not normally conducive to romantic thoughts. Something in the air, which was warmed by crystal-clear autumn sunshine and perfumed with ripe apples and sweet hay, must be causing it, Rob decided. To him, Jade had never looked lovelier than now, with the sunshine playing over her relaxed smile and her lightly tanned features. Her green eyes shone as vivid as gemstones when she laughed as the wagon lurched over a rut and the singing fell apart as the kids squealed in ecstatic excitement. The fresh autumn morning had him appreciating something new about her. She was far more than simply sexy. She was truly desirable.

Jade had her arms draped along the wagon's wooden sides so as not to jounce against Eugene and Lucy, who were sitting on either side of her. Now that the singing was over, she was talking to Eugene, asking him if he could recall the different types of apples that Mr. Newton cultivated. Lucy joined in and then Sam Powell did too, but Eugene beat them hands down. The little boy's smile, which had been absent for most of the morning, was now wide on his face.

A shame Christy Harrison couldn't see what Jade had accomplished or share in her son's pride in his knowledge.

The tractor rumbled to a stop and the farmhand jumped down, jogging around to the back of the wagon to help everyone out.

"All right, kids, get with your groups," Jade instructed.

Obediently, they scampered over to their designated adult, the half-peck bags emblazoned with *Newton's Apples* flapping against their pant legs.

"Thank you. We're going to be picking apples along this row here." Jade pointed down a long stretch of gnarled dwarf trees, heavy with red York Imperials. "Mrs. Cerra, why don't you take your group down toward the end? My group will follow, and, Officer Cooper, if your group could pick from the trees closest to the lane?"

"Sure." He nodded, and when she flashed him a quick smile, it was as if he'd just earned a commendation.

"Then let's get picking. And remember what Mr.

Newton said: Don't climb the trees, because that can hurt their limbs and perhaps yours as well, and watch out for bees. They like apples as much as we do."

"I don't like bees," Victoria Kemp offered.

"Bees are important 'cause they help make the apples grow. That's why it's important not to kill them with sprays. 'Cause that hurts them and the environment too," Hayley said.

"Good for you, Hayley. You were listening carefully to Mr. Newton. Victoria, I'm sure Deirdre's mom will help you watch out for bees."

Mrs. Cerra nodded bravely. "And Miss Radcliffe has the first-aid kit with her."

"Which I would rather not have to use, so everyone please be careful," Jade said. "So, are we all set to fill these bags with delicious apples?"

Jade listened to the chatter and exclamations on either side of her with a smile. Every York apple picked seemed to be bigger and shinier than the one before. The bags had grown super-heavy from all the gigantic apples they'd picked. Boasts of who had the heaviest bag were followed by loud groans and grunts and the rustle of paper as the bags were hefted then plunked onto the dried grass.

She'd give them five to ten more minutes. That would be enough time to fill the remaining bags and call a halt to the morning's activity before the kids grew tired and restless. The orchard had a picnic area with a nice grassy spot where the kids could run around after they'd eaten lunch. Then it would be time for a bathroom stop at the welcome center before they boarded the bus to return to Warburg. And wouldn't it be lovely if some of them fell asleep on the way back.

A bee buzzed near her hair. Waving it away, her eyes locked with Rob's. She'd done a good job of not looking at him during the past forty minutes, but that didn't mean she hadn't been paying attention to his conversation with Hayley and the rest of his group. Her initial reluctance to have him on the apple-picking trip had stemmed from the conviction that his presence would distract her. She'd been wrong. Her focus was just fine. The real problem in having him at the orchard was that she was once again seeing a side of Rob she'd rather not have seen. He was a good guy. At least her instincts hadn't steered her wrong in Norfolk. But now, seeing how great he could be and knowing how thrilling it was to have his mouth moving over hers and his clever hands caressing her, it made remembering that she should keep her distance that much more difficult.

Rob's gaze continued to hold hers, as if he were relaying a message. An unaccustomed shyness swept over her, making her feel like a very different person from the one who had spent a stormy night wrapped in his arms.

Before she could berate herself for her ridiculous reaction, Lucy Richter ran up, eager to show her the best apple she'd picked yet.

"You're right, Lucy. That's a really beautiful apple, and the little green stripes on the bottom are super-cool. You have just enough time to pick a couple more—and maybe they'll be as fine as this one—before we climb onto the wagon and ride back to the picnic area."

"Okay." Lucy spun around and raced back to where her apple bag was propped against the base of the tree.

Jade clapped her hands. "Five-minute warning, kids," she called. But with all the chatter and activity, only half the group appeared to hear. Shaking her head, she opened her mouth to shout again, when a piercing whistle came from behind her. She and the children froze, and even the birds seemed to stop singing in order to pay attention.

She didn't need to glance over her shoulder to verify

who'd whistled. Didn't it figure that Rob Cooper would be able to whistle loudly enough to hail a cab a city block away? She sighed with a mixture of frustration and admiration.

"All right, listen up, kids. The wagon's going to be coming to collect us and bring us to the picnic area where we'll be eating lunch, so you have five minutes to pick a few more apples and then you need to line up with your bags of apples. Everybody understand?"

A chorus of "Yes, Miss Radcliffe," answered her.

The tempo to their movements changed. The kids now scurried like squirrels desperate to get their hoard of acorns in their burrows before winter's onslaught.

Jade dropped a final few apples into her own bags. Picking them up, she carried them over to where she'd set the first-aid kit down earlier. As she passed Rob, she said, "That's some whistle."

"It comes in handy."

"That it does." She paused a beat. "Thanks."

"You're welcome." His smile warmed her right down to her toes and caused her breathing to go a little funny. Two and a half hours in his company and Jade recognized the signs. She was in real danger of getting seriously hung up on Rob. Especially as, for the first time since discovering that Rob Cooper, aka RoboCop, and her mystery lover were one and the same, she was starting to imagine what it might be like to be with him, not just for sex but for—

Jade gave herself a mental shake. Here was proof of how dangerous a man like Rob could be. She didn't do relationships.

She recognized enough of her mother's character inside herself to know that she would screw one up royally.

But the thought persisted, teasing and oh-so-tempting.

Determined not to show how vulnerable the idea made her, how much a part of her longed to be in such a relationship with a man like Rob, she gave him her cockiest, most carefree smile.

"Care to give us a repeat performance so we can get these champion apple pickers lined up?" she asked.

"A repeat performance, huh? Nothing I'd like better." Luckily for Jade, he didn't push the suggestion deeper into inappropriate territory. Watching him insert his index finger and thumb in his mouth and sound a second blast wreaked quite enough havoc on her. Kooky but true, she was a sucker for seriously loud, even ear-piercing whistles.

If he were hers, she could get him to give her lessons in how to whistle like a pro. There would be things she could teach him too.

Only a pack of seven-year-olds rushing toward her with bulging bags of apples could have dislodged this last treacherous thought.

She smiled in gratitude at her small saviors. "Line up alphabetically, guys, so I can make sure you're all here."

There was a scramble and even a little jostling as they sorted themselves. The new line formed, Jade began calling out names as she patted sweaty heads. "Chris Alden, Rosie Baxter, Jay Blount, Deirdre Cerra, Hayley Cooper . . ." and down the line she went, all the way to Posey Hall. There she stopped.

"Eugene?" She looked about. "Where's Eugene?"

Her worried gaze traveled the long row of trees before she spotted him. On tiptoe, he was attempting to grab an apple that was partially hidden by a cluster of leaves. "Eugene! You need to come and join the line right now!"

"There's a really good apple here that I'm getting for my mommy." He jumped, waving his hand for the apple just out of reach, and missed.

Jade frowned. "Time's up, Eugene. There are lots of

apples in your bag that will be perfect for her. Please come over here."

"This one's special. I need to get it." He began jumping again, with both arms raised overhead. He gave a triumphant cry as his hands closed about the leafy mass. Then his cry became a startled shriek of pain.

Jade was already sprinting. She reached him by the second shriek, this one even more panic-stricken and agonized.

She grabbed his flailing form and spun around, using her body to shield him from the angry cloud of bees that had descended. She held his quaking body until she could no longer hear the angry buzzing around them.

Raising her head carefully, she said, "It's okay, Eugene. The bees are gone."

Wrapped in her protective embrace, Eugene continued to tremble in fear and pain. "Mommy! I want my mommy!" he wailed, his voice choked with tears.

A mere glance confirmed her fears. Angry red circles dotted the tender flesh of his hands and arms. The swelling was starting already.

"We'll call your mom, I promise, Eugene. But right now you have to hold very still. I've got to get these stingers out. Then I'll put an ointment that I've got in my first-aid kit on the bites. The ointment and cold compresses will help make the pain go away. There, see? I've already gotten one out. Hang on, tough guy, we're going to get every last one of them. That's the way, you're being super-brave. . . ."

Christy Harrison was waiting beside her Mercedes station wagon when the bus rolled in to the school parking lot. Arms crossed, her mouth a flat line beneath her oversize sunglasses, she radiated anger.

Jade couldn't blame her. She'd be scared too if her child was stung by five bees. Jade had monitored Eugene closely, in case he displayed any signs of anaphylaxis. Fortunately, his breathing remained fine, and though there was a fair amount of swelling, it was no more than one might expect from that many stings. And as it was still possible for Eugene to develop an allergic reaction, Jade was actually happy to see Christy.

A visit to the pediatrician would reassure them all.

"Look, I see your mom," she said, pointing out the bus's window.

Seated beside Jade, Eugene craned his neck to catch a glimpse of his mother, and his face, pale from tears and pain, brightened. "Yeah." Abruptly, his expression grew apprehensive. "Do you think she's going to be mad at me?"

She squeezed his shoulder, where he'd received no bites. "No. Absolutely not. Sometimes parents seem angry when they're simply scared. Hearing that you got stung by bees would have definitely been scary for your mom. It'll be a big relief to see you're okay."

"The stings still hurt." He lifted his arms to inspect the red welts.

"They probably will for a while yet. But you're a tough guy, aren't you, Eugene?"

He gave a crooked smile. "Yeah."

Seated two rows behind them, Rob smiled too. Jade had been terrific with the boy. She'd handled the emergency with speed and calm, keeping Eugene's, as well as the other children's, fear at bay. She'd even managed to calm down Helen Cerra—who'd immediately begun carrying on about paramedics and hospitals—by saying, "Mrs. Cerra, I don't think an EMS team is necessary at this point, and it will only make the event scarier for Eugene if you keep talking about it. What would be helpful is if you and Officer Cooper could look after the kids in my group while I tend to Eugene and then call his mother."

An excellent tactic to keep the woman busy and pull her back from the brink of hysteria.

Taking on half of Jade's group posed no problem. The kids were tired from the morning's activities, hungry for their lunches, and subdued from having witnessed Eugene's encounter with the bees. They sank down on the grass and dove into their packed lunches. Rob was able to keep an eye on the group and also watch over Jade and Eugene, in case they needed him.

Because beneath her calm control he could see how distraught she was, her lower lip held tightly between her teeth as she applied the ointment to Eugene's stings. Once finished, she wrapped two instant compresses against the swollen areas, rubbing her face with trembling hands. Then, drawing a deep breath, she'd pulled out her cellphone to call Eugene's mother. But wherever Christy Harrison was, she wasn't picking up. Forced to leave a message, Jade had to soothe the frightened and hurting boy all over again.

Taking in her tense form and pale face, Rob would have liked nothing better than to wrap his arms around her and offer her some comfort, but with nineteen witnesses, there'd been nothing he could do but sit and wish they were alone.

The bus driver cut the engine, and Jade stood and turned around to address the class. "Okay, kids, we're going to head back to the classroom and get ready for art with Mrs. Natick. But first I'd like everyone to thank Mrs. Cerra and Officer Cooper for coming with us today."

"Thank you"s mingled with the slap of sneakers on the floor of the bus as the kids filed out.

Rob was the last to step out of the bus, his gaze immediately seeking Jade and Eugene. The boy was at his mother's side. Jade, carrying both her and Eugene's bags of apples, stood a little off to the side. The children stood in a line in front of her, and Jade was checking that they were all accounted for when Tricia Creighton came out of the building and approached them.

"I have a free period now. Why don't I take the class inside and get them ready for art class?" she suggested, and Rob decided that she must have heard about Eugene's bee stings from Ted Guerra. After leaving a message with Christy, Jade had then called Ted to let him know what had happened.

The look of gratitude was plain on Jade's face. "That'd be really great. I'd planned to have the kids put their apple bags along the wall beneath the chalkboard. Their names are on their bags."

"Okay." Tricia Creighton nodded. "I'll see you in a few minutes." Then, casting a quick sidelong glance at Christy Harrison, she mouthed, "Good luck," to Jade before clapping and calling the class to attention.

Rob bent down and gave Hayley a kiss. "You be good, sweetheart. And help Grammy and Poppy tonight. I'll see you in the morning." He'd be on duty until nine o'clock that evening, so Hayley would be sleeping at his parents', something she did whenever he had an evening shift.

"I will. Bye, Daddy."

As Rob straightened to watch Hayley go, he heard Christy Harrison loudly tell Eugene to go and sit in the car. She was going to drive him to the hospital, but she had something to say to his teacher first.

"Is Eugene's pediatrician unable to see him?" Jade asked.

Christy's voice dripped with scorn as she whipped off her glasses to stare contemptuously at Jade. "My son needs to go to the emergency room. He should have been taken there directly. This is yet another area where you have clearly been negligent. When I talk to Ted Guerra, I intend to see that he does something about it. This time it won't be a question of removing Eugene from your class but of your being dismissed—"

"Just a second." Rob wasn't going to remain silent while Christy Harrison lashed out at Jade. "Jade was terrific when Eugene got stung and did everything that was required for the stings. Moreover, she stayed by his side throughout, right up until the bus pulled into the parking lot. If he'd shown the slightest indication that he was having a reaction, she'd have seen it. By the way, you're probably unaware of this, but the reason Eugene was stung in the first place is because he disobeyed Jade. Instead of lining up with the rest of the class, he remained by one of the apple trees. You see, he'd spotted a special apple in one of its upper branches and wanted to pick it for you."

As he'd offered his defense of Jade, Christy's face paled. By the time he'd finished, it had gone bright red. If possible, her eyes narrowed further, to a knife's edge, and when she replied, it was in a tone that was equally cutting.

"I must say I'm surprised to hear you of all people stand up for her. Especially considering what my mother-in-law told me about the night of your wife's death. Is it true? Were you really arresting Jade at the Den while your wife lay dying?" Her cold, mean eyes flicked from him to Jade, and she smiled. "The ER doctors at the hospital will be very interested to hear about the so-called care my son received from you. So will my lawyer. You can tell Ted Guerra that he'll be hearing from him."

The silence was shattered by the slamming of Christy Harrison's car door. The engine came to life with a roar and then the car was peeling out of the parking lot.

And still Rob could feel the fury pouring out of him. The meddlesome bitches, he thought, seething. Damn

Nonie Harrison and her daughter-in-law for gossiping about Becky's death.

"Is it true?"

He turned at Jade's question, only belatedly realizing that, while Christy's comment might have infuriated him, its effect on Jade would be as destructive as a bomb blast.

When he hesitated, she asked again, and this time her voice shook.

"Yes, it's true." If he'd ever wondered if Jade had somehow been aware of the circumstances surrounding Becky's death, he had his answer in the anguished stammer of her reply.

"Oh God, I'm so sorry. I knew she'd died a while back, but . . . I had no idea. . . ." Her words faded away as their gazes met.

Jade stared into the pain-filled depth of Rob's blue eyes and saw in them something she'd seen time and time again—each time she looked in a mirror. The horror of what she'd just learned increased a hundredfold. "You blame me for her death," she whispered.

"No—"

But Rob's denial took a fraction of a second too long. And it took only that infinitesimal amount of time for Stygian darkness to invade her soul.

"Yes, you do. And all I can say is how sorry I am to have played any role in your and Hayley's loss. But you know what? You're just going to have to find someone else to blame. I'm full up with the guilt I'm already hauling around."

There were days, particularly during October, when the anniversary of her parents' deaths neared, when Jade was haunted by the memory of her dad lying critically injured in the hospital after the plane he'd been flying crashed, his body badly broken, inside and out.

Even though years had passed, Jade still wondered if

her dad might have survived his injuries if only she'd been able to swallow her cry of pain and loss when she heard him whisper her mom's name. It had been her cry that told him his wife had not survived the plane crash.

If not for her, Dad might be alive today. And she wouldn't have to live with the thought that she had triggered the embolism that killed him.

It was no easier living with the knowledge that her mom had died thinking of her as a disappointment. No matter how much Jade tried to be a decent person, she'd never be able to change her mother's opinion of her.

So, no, she couldn't bear the impossibly heavy guilt of thinking that she was the reason why Hayley was without her mother's love . . .

Or that, because of her, Rob had lost the woman he adored.

Oh God, she thought, shuddering, no longer able to contemplate the horrible role assigned to her. With lips that felt oddly frozen, she addressed him, careful not to meet his gaze. "I've got to go inside and talk with Ted Guerra."

As she fled into the school building, she wondered how long it would take before she could handle this new pain.

She feared it might be forever.

Chapter ❧
EIGHTEEN

IT HAD been a quiet night in Warburg. The calls that had come via dispatch were all routine: An elderly man had slipped while stepping into the bath, and his wife was terrified he'd broken his back; a family had mistakenly set off their security system and no one could remember the code or password; a couple had left their garage open and had returned from work to find their top-of-the-line Italian racing bikes gone.

The only incident that even ranked as serious involved the elderly man, but the EMS arrived at the couple's home within seconds of Rob, and the paramedics immediately set to work, lifting the man out of the tub while Rob calmed his distraught wife. Not even that kept him from thinking about Jade for very long.

His shift over, Rob found himself heading toward Piper Road rather than in the direction of his own place.

Even as he turned into the drive for Rosewood Farm, he knew there were a half dozen good reasons not to seek Jade out. The reasons could have numbered into the hundreds, every one of them excellent, and he would have ignored them too.

He needed to see her, couldn't stop picturing her horrified expression or the raw pain that dulled the brilliance of her eyes. Jade was so adept at presenting a carefree attitude, and there was such a remarkable energy and vitality about her, that one forgot she'd suffered a great deal in her life. As he'd learned today,

hidden behind her freewheeling demeanor were un-
healed wounds.

His car's headlights picked up a flash of red, and he
made out the shape of Jade's Porsche. He slowed and
then stopped in front of a cottage with a columned
porch. Lights shone through the curtained windows.

He got out of his car and rapped on the door.

Footsteps sounded and the door swung open with
Jade already speaking, her speech obviously prepared.
"Will you quit it? I'm fine, really. You don't have to—"
Seeing him on her porch stopped the sentence mid-
stream. "Oh," she finished hollowly.

"You open your front door like that? You didn't even
look to see who it was." Even if he hadn't just come off
duty, he'd have been appalled at the lack of caution she
displayed.

"Of course not." She folded her arms around her middle, as if hugging herself. "I thought you were Margot.
What are you doing here?"

"I came to see you. You should take a minute to see
who's on the other side of the door before opening it.
Warburg's not without crime."

"Right," she snapped. "Next time I'll look and definitely *not* open the door." She eyed him suspiciously.
"How did you know this was where I live?"

He raised a brow. "I used observational skills honed
from years on the force. Your Porsche is parked outside.
Are you going to let me come in?"

"Why don't you use your excellent observational
skills to figure that one out too?" She paused and then
said, "In case you're unsure, I'll give you a hint. The
word starts with an *N* and ends with an *O*."

He bit back a smile, vastly relieved that she was acting
all piss and vinegar toward him. He wanted her to be
the strong, dynamic woman he was coming to admire.

"Too bad, because we need to talk." He stepped over

the threshold and brushed past her, ignoring her growl of frustration. A quick glance was sufficient for him to take in the funky charm of the interior. Its playfulness and airiness suited Jade's character. The light colors and clean lines of the furniture did too. "You have a nice house."

"Owen and Jordan did the renovation. It's a great place to hang out and be alone," she said, stressing the last.

She might be acting all defiant, but her expression was shadowed. He didn't like the idea of her here, forlorn. In that, he apparently wasn't alone. If Jade had gone so far as to prepare speeches when she opened the front door, her sisters must have waged quite a campaign.

"Are you okay?"

"Sure." Her chin rose a notch, but the show of bravado failed. It only made it easier for him to see her drawn features and red-rimmed eyes.

As if she guessed that he wasn't falling for it, she redoubled her attempt. "Of course I'm fine. Why shouldn't I be? It's been a *great* day. And now that we've got that straightened out, will you please go on your merry way—"

"What Christy Harrison said today was way out of line. Moreover, it wasn't true."

"Funny, I distinctly remember you confirming what she said. Your wife died the night you were arresting me at the Den."

"Yes, but I don't blame you for it. Not anymore."

A slow shake of her head was all she needed to express her disbelief.

How to get her to understand what he'd never consciously acknowledged but now knew to be true? Impulsively, he grabbed her hand and pulled her over to the long off-white sofa. He sat down, bringing her with him.

"Hey, buster, who do you think you are? I specifically *didn't* invite you to sit down—"

"A gross breach of politeness, but I'm willing to overlook it. I need you to listen, and I'm hoping to have better luck if you're sitting. You certainly didn't seem inclined to when you were standing and glaring at me."

"I can sit and glare. And I can ignore too."

"I've already noticed you're multitalented," he replied, unfazed by her dirty look. Jade could give as good as she got. But so could he.

"Listen to me, damn it. Yes, there was a time, whenever I thought of how Becky died, that I couldn't help remembering you and that if you hadn't been stupid enough to step your underage foot inside the Den, I wouldn't have had to drag you down to the station and waste my evening dealing with you. I blamed you for a good long time, Jade. It was wrong of me, and stupid too. Because if I were to hold you responsible, then I would also have to blame my father, my uncle, and even my brother Scott for having influenced me in deciding to become a cop. Because if I hadn't been a cop, I wouldn't have been anywhere near that goddamned bar on the night Becky died.

"But when I was grieving for Becky, you were an easy target to rail against: a smart-ass adolescent. The thing is, I probably wouldn't have needed you as a scapegoat if I wasn't feeling so incredibly guilty myself. I never suspected that Becky was suffering from something more serious than a nasty stomach flu. I should have made her go see a doctor, but it never occurred to me that her body was fighting for its life."

Rob was sitting close enough to Jade to feel her recoil, then begin to shake as she listened to his explanation. But he was convinced it was better to state things baldly if they were to have any hope of settling the question between them. If they were to have any hope of a future together. And suddenly he knew that he very much wanted Jade Radcliffe in his life.

He reached out and cupped her chin with his hand, drawing her head around so that he could look at her, impossibly moved when he saw the tears filling her eyes. "Don't cry," he said softly.

"I can't help it," she replied in a raw voice. "Your wife, Hayley's *mom,* is gone because of—"

"A cruel turn of events. A twist of fate. Becky's death was meaningless and senseless. It shouldn't have happened. But holding you responsible doesn't change any of that. And now that I know you, there's no way I could ever blame you for it."

"What?" she said, clearly startled.

"It's true. For the first time in a long time, I feel something—something good. I'd forgotten how much I love life. And the reason I'm remembering is you, Jade."

Awe made her heart strangely heavy. Her gaze locked with Rob's. He'd lost so much, yet instead of despising her for the inadvertent role she'd played in his loss, he was saying that she'd given him something. The notion boggled the mind, yet the light in his brilliant eyes never wavered.

"Jade." Her roughly whispered name was a seductive command. Irresistible.

It was impossible to know where this thing between them might lead. But for now, for the present, for tonight, she knew all that mattered. She longed to feel Rob's arms around her again, to be swept away by the promise of his kisses, to fall under the spell of his mouth and hands caressing her, to answer the pounding rhythm of his body moving deep inside her.

And to offer him the same fierce, glorious pleasure.

The desire she'd battled since parents' night broke free. She accepted its superior strength, understood that

this man meant too much for her to walk away. What
would happen would happen. Her lips brushed his,
featherlight. Her hand slipped into his.

"Come with me."

The hushed, deliberate mood that pervaded was no less
potent for its quietness, no less thrilling for its purposeful-
ness. Clothes were shed slowly, to sighs and husky murmurs voicing their appreciation, their pleasure. Naked,
they faced each other, their bodies mere inches apart
while their hands touched and mouths drank, relearning
and exploring anew.

"You're trembling," he whispered, trailing his mouth
down the slope of her shoulder, breathing in the warm
scent of her, as his hands cupped her breasts, kneading
gently.

"I know. I can't stop."

"Are you nervous?"

"No—yes, I guess I am. This feels different somehow." How much different, how *important,* she couldn't
admit to him—or herself.

"Yeah. It does."

It helped to know that he recognized it too; it made her
feel less vulnerable emotionally. The physical responses
he aroused were overwhelming enough. Like now, she
thought, as his tongue dipped into the hollow of her
collarbone while his thumbs stroked her nipples in ach-
ingly slow sweeps. He remembered just how much pressure she liked. She arched in silent supplication, letting
loose a moan of gratitude when his mouth replaced his
thumbs, latching on to one breast, then the other, and
drawing her nipples deep into his mouth as he suckled.

Liquid heat pooled deep inside her as streaks of pleasure lashed her. The dual onslaught made her knees
buckle. Luckily, the bed was within reach. She fell back

upon the blue-and-white-patterned comforter, exulting in the weight of his body as he followed her down. Wrapping her legs about his hips, she rubbed the steel silk of his shaft and felt herself grow slick with desire.

"Please, I need you."

His smile was fierce, beautiful. "You have me, sweetheart. Take me any way you want."

The room might have spun a little just then, whirling with all of the ways she'd like to make love with him. A kaleidoscope of delight. The best part was that she could pick one and know she'd enjoy his choice equally. A win–win situation. She pushed Rob over onto his back and climbed over him, pulling her nightstand drawer open and retrieving a handful of condoms, then letting them fall within easy reach.

At his raised brow, she said, "Every modern woman should be thusly equipped."

He squeezed her butt. "I am in total agreement."

"Good." She gave him an impish wink. "Now, I seem to recall this as being very nice." Balancing with her knees on either side of him, she positioned herself over his hips, letting her short curls brush the tip of his cock. When it lengthened, straining, when his hips bucked in instinctive response, she smiled, awash with feminine power. "Does it meet with your approval?"

"It does." His voice lowered to a rough whisper. "I've dreamed of you like this, Jade."

"Me too," she said, and, with the beat of his heart hammering against her flattened palm, she sank down his rigid length, letting him fill her, inch by dizzying inch. To the sound of his soft groans of pleasure, she began to ride.

Rob's eyes held hers as he answered her every descent with a powerful thrust, watching her graceful body undulate as his hands covered her breasts and fondled them boldly. He kept pace as her rhythm quickened, as her core tightened, milking him, as she quivered from the sensations racking her.

She was beautiful as she neared her climax, her slender body tensing as she reached for it, her hair flowing wildly about her shoulders, the image of a wanton goddess—*his* wanton goddess, a voice inside him decided possessively. Knowing what would bring her to her peak, and desperate to give her that pleasure, his hands moved. One clasped her hip, urging her to take him even deeper, while the other hand moved between her legs to brush her swollen clit. With a shattering cry, her body bucked and her passion broke over him like a tempest unleashed. The force of it triggered his own climax. With a hoarse groan, he surged into her, coming in a flood that left him shaken and dazed.

Spent and seemingly boneless, she collapsed on him. The slap of their slick bodies made him smile as he lazily wrapped his arms about her damp back. Nuzzling the crook of her neck, he inhaled the floral scent that clung to her hair and realized he felt better than he had in weeks. It wasn't just the sexual release, powerful though it had been, but the sense of rightness as he held this armful of warm girl close. It felt almost as if he was absorbing her into himself. She might wreak havoc in his life, but she also was a perfect fit.

And she was funny, smart, sensitive, gorgeous, and sexy as hell, and his body was already responding to the sweet curves draped over him. Shifting his head against the pillow, he found her lips and kissed her deeply, savoring her. Languidly, their tongues dueled, and with each thrust, parry, and slow suck, heat built between them.

A roll of their bodies put Rob on top. Dragging Jade's arms overhead, he gave rein to his hunger, trailing his mouth along the insides of her arms and circling the sensitive underside of her breasts as she writhed and whispered her need. Her words inflamed him until his own body shook with need.

"My turn. Open for me, sweetheart." He rocked his hips, pressing his cock against her cleft.

Her breath caught on a soft moan as she met his thrust. Then, drawing her instep up his calf, she teased huskily, "Missionary pose, huh? Kinda dull."

"Brat." He laughed and nipped her earlobe. "I promise I'll do my best to keep your attention from wandering."

Much later, a sleepy-eyed and sated Jade watched Rob pull on his clothes. She felt too good to move. Sitting up was a definite impossibility. Besides, if she sat up, the graze of the soft cotton sheet against her naked skin would remind her of how his hands had caressed her while they made love, and she would start to want him again.

His lovemaking had been exquisite. Sometimes teasing, other times demanding, he'd wrung responses from her that made her feel as if she'd never really been touched before. At another time it might have worried her that Rob seemed to know her body better than she, but right now all she could think was that she was one incredibly lucky girl. She stretched and smiled, contented as a cat.

"Want to tell me what that smile is about?"

"I've decided that maybe the missionary position isn't so dull after all."

A grin spread across his face. "Only 'maybe'? I thought I had you converted." He gave an easy shrug. "That's all right, I'll be happy to continue doing the good work." Buttoning the top metal button of his jeans, he crossed over to the bed and sat down, his weight causing her to roll into him. She put her hand on his blue-jeaned thigh and felt his quadriceps harden beneath it.

In response, he laid his hand on her naked shoulder, then slowly trailed his fingers over its rounded contours.

"So about this thing between us: Are you okay with it? Because I want to keep seeing you and spending time with you."

She tamped down the panic that threatened. "Let's just take it one day at a time. I don't want Hayley to figure out what's going on and begin to form expectations. I don't want her to get hurt."

Clearly pleased that she wanted to protect Hayley, Rob nodded. "Fair enough. But, Jade, you should know I believe in commitment. If we're together, then it's only you and me. I don't share."

Before she could retort that she wasn't the kind of person who slept around when dating—easy to say, as she'd always avoided relationships—his lips were over hers and he was kissing her with a thoroughness that had her toes curling and her fingers clutching at his back. Then he was gone, the front door shut firmly behind him, and Jade was still trying to catch her breath and calm her pounding heart.

How had this happened? she wondered as her panic returned. How, after going out of her way to avoid emotional entanglements, had she managed to not only find herself in a relationship but in one where the stakes were so high?

Because she was very much afraid that, after tonight, she was already half in love with Rob Cooper.

Chapter ❧
NINETEEN

THE PONY barn was full of little people diligently at work yielding currycombs and bristle and soft brushes. After demonstrating how to use each brush, Jade had divided the group into pairs to work on three ponies first. Walking up and down the aisle, she'd observed them, making sure they were moving safely around the ponies attached to the cross ties. Then at each station she gave a demonstration on how to pick the ponies' hooves, the most essential grooming lesson of the afternoon.

Once she was satisfied that they'd gotten the hang of manipulating each of the grooming tools, she—along with Tito and Ned, who'd volunteered to help out until the kids reached the stage where they could groom and tack on their own—returned the ponies to their stalls so the other three could be readied.

Next came a lesson in how to tack. Using Doc Holliday because he was an old pro, Jade showed them how to insert the bit of the bridle into his mouth. Something of a show-off, Doc curled back his muzzle as if to show the kids exactly where they should exert pressure against his yellowed teeth. Adjusting the noseband and the throatlatch was more straightforward, involving only a discussion of how snug the noseband should be and how much give the throatlatch should have.

As the ponies all used snaffles and none wore a martingale, she postponed any further discussion of the parts of a bridle for the next lesson. It was pointless to overload the kids with information they wouldn't be able to retain, and, besides, she could tell how keen they were to get in the saddle.

Nevertheless, she did take the time to stress the importance of proper saddle placement. A saddle placed too low or high could hurt a pony's back, causing it to go lame. "And we don't want that, do we?"

Six heads shook in solemn reply.

She smiled as she ducked down to grab Doc's girth and buckle it.

This was going to be a really good group. All the kids in it were happy to be there—not a one pushed into taking lessons by an overambitious parent. But even in this eager lot, Hayley stood out. Since walking into the pony barn with Jenny Ferris, the two of them looking adorable in their jodhpurs and paddock boots and with their riding helmets tucked under their sweatered arms, Hayley had been following Jade's instructions to a T.

It was pretty neat—in fact, what she'd dreamed of when opening the riding program—to spot the passion of a horse lover in a little girl and to know that Jade would be fostering it. Though this was her goal for all the kids in the program, Jade admitted that seeing the telltale spark in Hayley's eyes was extra-special after sharing the previous night with Rob.

The prospect of being in a relationship continued to unnerve and unsettle her. But this, nurturing a love for these special animals, was something she could offer Hayley. In doing so, she would be giving something to Rob, his only daughter's happiness inextricably linked to his own.

The weather was cool, but Jade far preferred to teach outdoors. They'd be riding inside and under banks of artificial lights soon enough. Once all six ponies and kids were down at the ring, she instructed them on the proper mounting technique (allowing for a little boost to the fanny to help the smaller kids pull themselves into the saddle). Stirrups were adjusted so the bottoms of the irons hit at the anklebone. Next she discussed the reins, so that everyone understood how long they should be. Yanking on ponies' delicate mouths was not allowed. With their eyes up, heels down, backs straight, and knees tucked into the saddle roll, the kids nudged their ponies onto the rail.

With greater and lesser degrees of success.

Little Samantha Nicholls, astride Hopscotch, was going nowhere fast. Poor Hopscotch probably couldn't even feel the six-year-old's legs urging him forward.

Jade pressed her lips together to keep her laughter inside. Samantha was too cute.

"Remember how I showed you to soften your hands on the reins, Sam? That's what you need to do here when you ask Hopscotch to move forward. Give him a little harder of a kick with the heel of your boot—it won't hurt him, I promise—and a loud *cluck* too." She made the sound out of the side of her mouth to encourage the chestnut gelding, and fortunately their combined efforts did the trick. Hopscotch obligingly ambled over to the rail to walk behind Archer, who was being ridden by Mack Reynolds. "There you go, Sam. Good job."

Tucking her hands into the pockets of her vest, Jade leaned against the wooden painted wall jump and scanned the six ponies. "Now, all of you need to remember to keep a safe distance between your ponies. No horse or pony likes to have a nose stuck in its tail. Hayley, as you and Sweet Virginia are leading right now, you don't have to worry about that, but you should know that she sometimes likes to get a bit too close, especially if she's behind Dickens. They're sweethearts."

Before the kids began peppering her with questions about whether Ginny and Dickens would marry, she said, "You all are sitting pretty well in the saddle. Let's see how you do dropping your stirrups while your ponies are walking. You're going to have to keep your legs squeezing the saddle while you do this. All right, ease your toes out of the irons and let your legs drop. No need to tighten your hands on the reins, Jenny. Did you see how Maggie tossed her head? It's because you were pulling on the bit. We want to have gentle hands. That's right, now she's happy again. Her ears are pricked forward. Okay, kids, now comes the hard part. You're going to slide your legs up and put your feet back in the stirrups just by feel. No looking down and no bending over to adjust them. And you want to position the bottom of the stirrup just under the balls of your feet. It takes a lot of concentration, so I want all of you to take a minute and think about how your legs are going to move up the saddle a couple of inches and how your feet are going to find the stirrups, all without moving your hands or wiggling your bodies. Riding is about doing things very smoothly. That's what we're practicing here." She paused, giving them time to prepare. "Ready? Okay, then, let's see what you've got. . . . "

Rob arrived at Rosewood and made his way to the outdoor ring, where, one of the stable hands had told him, Jade was teaching her lesson. A couple of parents were already standing by the rail and, spotting him, waved a hand in welcome. He cut across the cropped grass to join them.

"Hayley's doing really well, Rob," Maryanne Ferris whispered.

Rob's gaze swept over the line of ponies and stopped at Hayley's fuchsia sweater. She was leaning over the reddish-gold pony's neck, her left arm stretched out, trying to touch its ear. He had no idea why Jade was having Hayley and the other kids do that, but since all he cared about was that Hayley wasn't lying in the dirt with a broken neck, he figured he might as well accept Maryanne's assessment.

"And how about Jenny?"

"She'll be in bed by eight," she predicted happily. "Jade's doing a great job. They're working so hard."

Again, Rob had to take Maryanne's word for it. Then Hayley was rounding the corner and he saw the fierce concentration stamped on her face.

"Hi," he mouthed.

Her brown eyes connected with his and she flashed an ear-to-ear smile. Then her gaze snapped back to stare between the pony's ears. Whether his daughter was riding well or not might be debatable. That she was having the time of her life was not.

The lesson lasted another ten minutes, and by the end Rob thought that Hayley, too, would probably be in bed by eight o'clock. He hadn't realized how many things a rider had to pay attention to at the walk and trot. Riding involved some serious multitasking.

Jade called the kids into the middle of the ring so that they could line up in front of her and dismount. Not even now, with the lesson nearly over, did she glance over to where the parents were grouped. Her focus was complete.

In the quiet of the afternoon, it was easy to hear her calm instructions. "Before you drop your stirrups, I'd like you all to sit tall in the saddle with your tummies in, eyes up, heels down, and your hands quiet over the pommel of the saddle. Very good. This is how you want to present yourself and your pony when you are called into the middle of the show ring, and some of you may want to enter a horse show one day."

Easy to predict what one of tonight's topics of conversations at the dinner table would be. Rob already knew he wouldn't offer a token resistance when Hayley announced her latest ambition of entering a horse show. With another kid he might worry about the potential for spoiling, but Hayley would work her fanny off to achieve her goal and would learn a lot in the process.

Jade had gone over to adjust the angle of Samantha Nicholls's lower leg—he guessed the little girl must be Samantha, because Joy Nicholls was watching them fixedly. Just then one of the grooms and Ned Connelly, silver-haired but moving with the vitality of a man twenty-five years younger, ducked between the wooden rails and stepped into the ring. They walked up to stand in front of the line of ponies. When Jade stepped back, she said something and the two men fanned out so that they all were within easy reach of the bridles.

Jade spoke again and loudly enough for him to hear. "In a dismount, you need to move as smoothly as possible so your pony doesn't get nudged and think it's being told to walk. Hayley, can you bring Sweet Virginia forward? I'm going to have you demonstrate for the others so they can see what they need to do. Is that okay with you?"

Hayley's black riding helmet seesawed as she nodded.

"Good. Now, a dismount is basically the opposite of how you mount a horse. You all are smart, so you'll get the hang of it quick as a wink, but, just as with mounting a horse, it's important to dismount correctly.

"Hayley, first you need to drop your stirrups and let your feet simply dangle. Next, you're going to take the reins in your left hand and place them near the pommel as you swing your right leg over the cantle. As your right leg reaches the left, you need to shift your right hand to the cantle—the back of the saddle. Terrific. Did you see how Hayley did that, guys, and how now she's sort of lying with her tummy on the saddle? All she has left to do is slide gently to the ground. Go ahead, Hayley."

When Hayley nailed her landing like a gymnast coming off the apparatus, Rob grinned. It was all he could do not to shout, "Way to go!"

But if he had, he might have drowned out Jade's words, which right now carried so much weight for his daughter.

"Well done, kiddo. A top-notch demonstration. Now, can you slip the reins over Sweet Virginia's head while Ned, Tito, and I watch the others take their turns?" As she passed Hayley, Jade gave her a pat on the helmet.

The warmth that unfurled in Rob's chest as he watched Jade with his daughter ought to have surprised him. A mere month ago he'd scoffed at the notion that he might ever feel this way for a woman again. That the woman in question would be Jade Radcliffe was even more inconceivable.

He'd obviously gotten a lot smarter since school had opened.

And a hell of a lot luckier.

The ponies had been untacked and gone over with a soft brush before being led back into their stalls, the tack had been neatly stowed away on the saddle trees and bridle hooks (a lesson in tack cleaning would come next week), and parents and kids were reunited with lots of excited exclamations and quizzing regarding the whereabouts of backpacks and sweaters and jackets.

Listening, Jade made a mental note to install a lost-and-found box in the club room for kids prone to having their belongings go missing.

She was pleased with the afternoon's lesson. The ponies had performed impeccably; the kids' behavior was downright sterling. And she hadn't even gotten frazzled when Rob had showed up. She knew the riding lessons wouldn't always go this smoothly, but starting off on the right foot *and* hoof made Jade hopeful.

Waiting beside the pony barn's wide doors as parents

herded their kids in the direction of the parking lot, she stretched surreptitiously. Exhilarated as she was by the adrenaline high of having taught a good class, she was also a little tired and a great deal hungry. Once she finished riding Cosmo, Carmen, and Valentine, she was going to raid her freezer. She seemed to remember that Jordan had stashed a frozen mac and cheese in there.

"Thank you for the lesson, Miss Radcliffe."

Hayley looked pretty adorable standing in front of her. She'd taken her helmet off and was swinging it by the chin strap so that it knocked against her jodhpur-clad legs. Her black hair, the exact same shade as Rob's, was matted against her head.

"You're welcome, Hayley. So where's your dad?" She hoped the question came out casually enough. She didn't want Hayley to suspect that she'd been keeping an eye out for Rob. He'd been considerate to keep his distance, but then he'd disappeared.

"He'll be right back. He said he had to get something from the car."

"Oh." It alarmed her how her stomach fluttered in anticipation at the thought of him standing close to her again. Much better not to think of it, then. "You did a really nice job on Ginny, Hayley."

"She was *so* great. She's the nicest pony I've ever ridden. And I like Hopscotch too. I gave him part of my apple, 'cause my dad sliced it into pieces for me."

"I'm sure Hopscotch loved his treat. I'm glad you like him. You know my niece Olivia? She picked him out for me."

Her eyes widened. "You mean she got to ride him and help you decide whether to buy him?"

"Yup. I had her, Kate, and Max try out Hopscotch, Sweet Virginia, Maggie, and Dickens. They were pretty good judges, don't you think?"

Hayley nodded in wide-eyed wonder. "That must have been so much fun."

"Since you'll be taking lessons twice a week, you'll get to try the other ponies out too. You'll have to tell me if Hopscotch is as great as Ginny."

"He will be."

Jade already knew Hayley well enough to sense that would be the case. Hayley was fiercely loyal once she made an attachment.

The sound of crunching gravel had Jade turning her head. She blinked at the approaching vision. With the sun angled low behind him, Rob's tall, strong body was outlined in fiery gold. He looked . . . well, godlike. Of course, it was merely an optical trick, making the fact that Jade's heart had begun bumping madly against her chest all the more embarrassing.

Was this how Margot and Jordan saw Travis and Owen—awash in gold and disturbingly special—when the men were doing nothing more than walking in the afternoon sunlight? Was this why her sisters sometimes seemed so loopy, because they were battling hallucinations?

A smile was playing over the lips that she'd kissed last night. "Hi."

If possible, her heart bumped and thumped even more erratically. There was no reason to behave as if that two-letter word had never been addressed to her, or as if she'd never been spoken to in a deep, smiling voice. That way led to madness. Or love. And then perhaps to a mad love. And that she could link Rob Cooper with those words was enough to freak her out. Jade gave a quick hard shake of her head to empty it of any further treacherous and downright crazy ideas.

"No? You don't want this?" Rob asked. Jade belatedly registered the paper bag he was holding out to her. "I kinda thought you would. It's a pumpkin cream-cheese muffin from Braverman's. My sister, Emma, told me it's your favorite." He jiggled the bag.

"You got a muffin for me?" It didn't even bother her that her voice came out as an astonished squeak. Or that she was easy, won over by a melt-in-your-mouth muffin. At the moment, not even a box in Tiffany's distinctive shade of robin's-egg blue could have competed with the unadulterated delight the Braverman's logo printed on the white paper bag produced.

"A token of our appreciation," he said, passing the bag to her.

Maybe it hadn't been an illusion; maybe Rob *was* kind of a god if he knew enough to bring her a pumpkin cream-cheese muffin after a long day.

"Thank you, Hayley, thank you . . ."

"Rob," he supplied, laughter threading his voice at her obvious reluctance to address him by his first name in front of Hayley. "Hayley, you must have worked up an appetite with that terrific riding. I bought you a muffin too. It's in the backseat, kiddo, along with a carton of milk."

She was off like a shot, calling, "Bye, Miss Radcliffe. See ya tomorrow at school," as she flew around the barn in the direction of the parking lot.

He stepped closer. "Hey, I thought of you today. A lot."

Her heart would not quit slamming against her chest. How could it, when he said things like that so simply and straightforwardly?

"I guess you crossed my mind a couple of times too. Of course, my day was probably quite a bit busier than yours, as I was helping the kitchen staff cook apple fritters, making apple graphs, and reading and correcting journal entries about the trip to the orchard. Eugene was the star of many stories, but you came in a close second."

She'd spent a fair amount of her day worrying about

how Eugene was faring. Ted Guerra hadn't heard anything from the Harrisons or their lawyer, which meant that Christy had probably struck out in getting the ER doctors to say Jade had failed to treat Eugene properly for his bee stings. But Eugene's absence from school bothered Jade. He'd have really liked working on the apple graphs. She would call the Harrisons again later to see how he was doing, not that she expected them to pick up if they had caller ID.

"A busy day indeed. I'm glad I warranted even a passing thought." When Rob smiled crookedly like that, he had the cutest dimple. "Am I going to see you this weekend? Hayley's been invited to Posey's house for a sleepover Saturday."

"To Posey's? That's nice." She was having trouble concentrating.

The dimple deepened. Were dimples supposed to be sexy? "Say you'll see me Saturday night, Jade."

"I—yes."

"Good." He exhaled a pent-up breath and laughed. "You had me in a state of suspense there." Then his hand was cupping the back of her neck and he was kissing her with enough heat to make her head spin like a top. Drawing back, he gazed at her as if he liked what he saw, which only made her dizzier.

"Gotta go. It's a school night, you know. I'll be thinking of you." He kissed her again. Quickly, fiercely, and when their lips parted, she could only be grateful she was leaning against the barn door's frame. Her knees had turned to jelly. The rest of her was equally useless; the bag with the muffin nearly dropped to the gravel from her fingers. And for the life of her she couldn't stop staring up at Rob's handsome face.

"I assume this means you and Jade have patched things up," Margot said. Her sister's amused tone performed a miracle. Jade regained her senses. She straightened as if her back had suddenly been fused with an iron rod.

Rob's reaction was far more relaxed. He stepped back, letting his hand slip from Jade's neck. "Yeah, she's decided to forgive me."

Margot offered him a wide smile, one of the ones she reserved for people she liked. "I'm so glad to hear that."

He nodded easily in reply before shifting his attention back to her. He didn't seem fazed by Margot, which Jade found kind of remarkable. Her sister's stunning beauty and confidence generally transformed men into babbling idiots or mute lumps.

"See you, Jade."

"See you. And thanks for the muffin." Considering that her heart was still playing leapfrog in her chest, she was pleased at how normal she sounded.

"Anytime. I figure I owe you after all those donuts you sent me."

She smiled weakly, while beside her Margot whispered a shade too loudly, "Busted."

Trying not to squirm when one was definitely in the hot seat wasn't easy. "Oh, yeah. I'd almost forgotten about those donuts."

The mirth in his eyes told her he wasn't buying her line. "I was a real hit with the guys in the department for a while there. Bye, ladies."

Margot managed to keep quiet for about three seconds after he'd walked away. "Way to go, sweetie. Rob not only is a hunk with brains, but he's also got a sense of humor. And let's not overlook the fact that he knows how to kiss. I approve of a man who kisses like he means it."

Jade did too. "Margot, you are so superficial."

"Too true." She sighed heavily. "It's a lucky thing that in addition to being a seriously fine-looking, intelligent male—which often sadly seems to be an oxymoron—who knows how to use his lips, he's also a protector of law and order and a loving dad. Wow, you really have hit the jackpot."

"Will you stop?" she grumbled, feeling her cheeks grow hot. "Some of us have work to do. I've got to get Carmen groomed and tacked—right after I eat this muffin." She opened the bag and, pulling it out, gave a sigh of bliss. Rob had picked one with a generous cream-cheese center. The first huge bite had her thinking of the ways she might thank him on Saturday night, and she smiled as lust mixed with cinnamon, pumpkin, nutmeg, and sweetened cream cheese. Delicious and possibly addictive. She took another bite and let her imagination run rampant.

"Actually, that's why I came to find you. You don't have to inhale that muffin at warp speed. Carmen's already groomed for you."

Jade paused and swallowed. "She's groomed?"

"And looking like a million bucks—not to sound too superficial. Topher McCallister called while you were teaching. He's heard we have a promising eventing prospect and wants to see her in action." She glanced at her watch. "He should be here in about twenty minutes. Sorry to throw this at you, but Travis thought you'd be the best person to put Carmen through her paces. You've been doing so well with her. Andy put your saddle out along with Carmen's bridle, but I imagine Topher will bring his own saddle."

Topher McCallister. It was a shock hearing his name. She hadn't thought of him since she'd read his name on Greg Hammond's list of possible candidates who might have been involved with her mother.

Greg was busy making his inquiries, but that shouldn't prevent her from doing a little investigating too. This was a golden opportunity to ask Topher a few subtle questions.

"It's no biggie, Margot. Today's Carmen day for

jumping anyway, so we're not messing up her workout schedule. What's Topher up to these days?" Then, so Margot wouldn't suspect she had anything but the most casual interest in him, she took a humongous bite of her muffin and chewed busily.

"I've heard he's very active in the Warburg Hunt Club. He's also big into cross-country events and point-to-point races. Personality-wise he hasn't changed much. He still has an ego the size of the Goodyear Blimp."

Would it have floated his blimp-size ego to sleep with her mom? It was possible, she decided. Her mother had been beautiful; fooling around with her behind RJ Radcliffe's back would have been a major notch in a lot of guys' bedposts.

"Well, Carmen's like a Ferrari. She's got enough flash and power to satisfy the most narcissistic and overcompensating of dudes. He'll probably love her."

"Luckily he's an excellent rider, and Kevin Donnelly, his trainer, is a good guy, so we don't have to worry about whether Carmen would be in good hands. From what Travis says, Topher seems pretty eager to buy."

Jade popped the last of her muffin into her mouth. "Well, then. Time for me to show him what Carmen's got." But if she discovered that Topher had been sleeping with her mother, it would be kingdom come before he ever owned one of Rosewood's horses.

In the main barn's office, she grabbed a quick cup of coffee and thanked Andy and Travis for making Carmen's coat and white blaze shine with horse-show-ready luster, the way all of Rosewood's horses were presented when potential buyers came a-calling.

Like most females who'd just been treated to a deluxe spa treatment—complete with mane pulling, ear, muzzle, and fetlock clipping, and a pedi, her four hooves gleaming with hoof dressing—the mare knew she looked good. When she saw Jade walking toward her, she tossed her black head proudly, making the cross ties dance, and gave a snort of welcome.

"Hey, you sexy thing," Jade murmured as she reached out to scratch Carmen beneath her jaw, another of her favorite tickle spots. "Going to strut your stuff today for the man who's got an eye for mighty fine equines?"

"Be fair, that's not all I have an eye for," a male voice joked. "It's Jade, isn't it? It's been too long. May I say that you are looking mighty fine as well?"

Topher McCallister was like many men who thought that, because they were good-looking, they only had to toss off a compliment with a flash of a practiced smile to have a woman's brain go as soft as an underboiled egg.

He must be nine years older than she—Jade recalled Greg telling her that Topher was a year younger than Jordan. He had the blond, muscled equestrian look down pat, dressed in a blue-check button-down shirt, a navy cable sweater, and fawn-colored breeches with brown field boots. Margot would have said that he looked like a Ralph Lauren wannabe.

Even if Jade didn't have Rob to hold up as the gold standard in terms of sexy, charismatic guys, she'd have found Topher sadly lacking. On another day she might have been tempted to let him know it.

Instead, she gave him an easy smile. "Hey, Topher. How are things?"

"Good. Really good. So, you're home from college. The grapevine has it that for the past four years you put all the other collegiate riders to shame. Way to go. You doing any competitive riding now?"

"I'll probably enter some shows next summer. For now I'm busy teaching and helping train our prospects."

He nodded and his gaze shifted to the mare before him. "This is Carmen, huh? Nice-looking."

What a load of bull. They both knew Carmen was a

hell of a lot more than "nice-looking." But she stifled the spurt of annoyance his comment caused. "Carmen's got it all. Looks, brains, heart, and speed. In addition, she's a blast and a half to ride. Always keeps you on your toes."

"Yeah? I like a female who presents a challenge." Unfortunately, Topher was looking at her—her mouth specifically—rather than at Carmen when he spoke.

Ugh. The longer she spoke to him, the higher the "ick" factor climbed. But just because she didn't like him, that didn't mean he'd gone and slept with her mom. Steering the conversation in a direction that might yield an answer was proving trickier than she'd supposed, though. Now that she was face-to-face with him, she couldn't think of anything to ask except, "Hey, Topher, are you into sleeping with other men's wives? Like my mom, for example?"

Luckily, if the afternoon turned out to be a bust in terms of figuring out whether Topher McCallister was TM, the hero of her mom's diary, she could always cede the field to Greg Hammond. He had to have more-sophisticated ways of ferreting out information.

Travis, Margot, and Ned came out of the office, where they must have been having a last-minute huddle, discussing what price to negotiate if Topher made an offer for Carmen.

Better horse dealers than these three a person couldn't find. It was time to concentrate and do what she could to help the sale: ride Carmen and show him just what a special mare she was.

After shaking hands with Topher, her family set to work. Ned gave a rundown of Carmen's bloodlines; Travis talked about how much he liked their stallion Nocturne's get (a topic near and dear to his heart since it was Travis who'd bought Nocturne, introducing a new bloodline to Rosewood's stock), and Margot com-

mented on the progress Carmen was making in dressage.

The sell wasn't heavy-handed, though. Every nugget
of information came with a question about Topher's
family, who'd known theirs for years, or about his job in
insurance and his activities at the Warburg Hunt Club,
Warburg's most important—and exclusive—social and
equestrian institution.

And while they shot the breeze, Topher got to see that
Carmen had lovely manners. No fuss was made when
Jade bridled her. A swish of the tail was her only reaction to having the girth tightened about her belly. She
walked out of the barn alert, her ears cocked forward,
and her carriage confident.

There was still enough light to ride outdoors, which
was great, as it offered better viewing than in the indoor
ring, where Carmen's black body would get lost in the
shadowed corners. And jumping outside would show
how she behaved in an environment where there were
far more distractions.

Jade warmed up the mare, letting her work off some
of her friskiness. An experienced rider, Topher wouldn't
be surprised to see how hot to trot Carmen was; a potential eventer had to be full of rocket fuel. What a buyer
wouldn't want to see was a horse that was completely
loco, too revved up to respond to its rider's aids. Although Carmen loved speed, she knew when it was time
to settle down and work. Topher would be impressed by
that, as well as by the fact that the mare, young as she
was, *liked* to work.

Warm-up complete, Jade began to show Carmen off.
It was fun. Illuminating too, as it made her realize how
far the mare had come in terms of the fluidity of her
gaits, the suppleness of her body. The dressage work
they'd been doing was really paying off. Once Carmen
was nice and limber from the flatwork, Jade took her

over a combination of fences: a wall, a chicken coop, a brush jump, and then a triple combination—a line of three brightly painted rail jumps, spaced at different distances—to demonstrate the mare's agility and scope.

As she cantered over the course, feeling the mare beneath her eat up the ground with her powerful strides and then soar over the fences, Jade knew Carmen was being scrutinized intensely, her every movement analyzed and judged. She got the distinct impression Topher was looking at her just as intently.

His interest was probably in part professional—he wanted to see whether she was struggling to control Carmen—but she suspected there was another motive for his unwavering attention.

He was checking her out from head to toe and, she sensed, paying particular attention to her ass.

His interest didn't faze her in the least; the only thing that mattered was that her mom had had a pretty good butt too. Maybe Topher was an ass man.

If it had been Rob standing where Topher was now, the story would be entirely different. She wouldn't be feeling completely cool and detached, not when a single glance from Rob could melt her insides, send her brain spinning, and cause her heart to gallop faster than even Carmen going full throttle.

It was time she faced the facts. She had it pretty bad for Officer Rob Cooper.

And wasn't this the perfect moment to nail the last fence that Travis had suggested she take, a big brush jump that had Carmen picking up and folding her knees as nice as you please. They landed smooth as butter, Jade settling her rear back into the saddle while Carmen cantered on, snorting a little as she shook her black head, her way of saying, "Wasn't that fun? Let's do it again."

With a bittersweet smile, Jade reached out and scratched

Carmen's black mane as she brought her down to an easy trot. If Topher was seriously considering buying a three-day-event horse, he'd have to be a dunce not to invest in Carmen. She was strong, fast, 100 percent sound, and she loved challenges. Although there were other young horses that Travis would assign her, Jade would miss the mare.

At least she'd had the opportunity to help in her training. That was something to be proud of.

She trotted Carmen over to the center of the ring and then halted. "So, Topher, is your appetite whetted? Feel like trying her out?"

"Most definitely."

"Can't say I'm surprised," Jade said with a smile before swinging her leg over the saddle and dismounting lightly. Looping an arm inside the reins, she gave Carmen a fond pat and made quick work of running up her stirrups and loosening her girth. She slipped her saddle off the mare's back so he could replace it with his own, larger one. Within minutes, Topher was guiding Carmen back out onto the rail.

Jade went to stand by Ned, Travis, and Margot, who'd stayed put by the wall jump while the saddles were exchanged and Topher mounted Carmen. A lifelong rider, Topher didn't need a gang of people helping out. The commotion wouldn't serve Carmen either. "Nice work, Miss Jade. The two of you looked real good."

"Thanks, Ned. It'll be interesting to watch Topher and see how he clicks with Carmen."

"He's a good rider. They'll get along just fine. It'll be a shame to say goodbye to Carmen," Ned said.

"Exactly what I was thinking. She's a fun horse."

Travis wrapped an arm about Jade's shoulder and squeezed it briefly. "You've done a great job with her. I could see Topher's eyes light up when you took that combination as easy as one, two, three."

"Thanks. You know, this weird thing happened when

I finished jumping her. All of a sudden I knew that I'd be saying goodbye to Carmen soon, whether it's Topher or someone else who buys her. And I actually felt tears come to my eyes. I must be getting sentimental in my advanced age. Pretty soon I'm going to be as bad as you, sis, wandering off to bawl my eyes out every time we make a sale."

"I'll start buying more packs of Kleenex."

Jade hid a grin at Margot's dry tone. Her sister didn't like being teased about the crying jags she succumbed to whenever they said goodbye to one of their horses.

"On the plus side, if Topher buys her, at least Carmen will still be in the area. That's something," Jade mused. "And will you look at how sweetly she's going for him? Should we up her price?"

A laugh burst out of Travis. "You are such a shark."

"Hmm," Jade said with an answering grin. "Maybe I am. Maybe I'm just a Radcliffe. What do you think, Margot?"

"I think that as usual you are scarily brilliant. Dad would be proud of you." While Jade savored the notion that their father would have been pleased with her suggestion, Margot continued, "We should definitely up our asking price. From what I know of Topher, he's the kind of guy who enjoys spending a lot simply because he can."

"So we'll be adding to his happiness quotient by having him spend an extra ten thousand on Carmen," Jade said, getting into the spirit of the thing.

"Whoa, easy there, you two," Travis cautioned. "Let's wait and see how happy he is after jumping Carmen before we start boosting her price."

It didn't come as any surprise to Jade that Topher loved Carmen's big, bold jumping style as well as the amount of ground she covered in a gallop.

He had a grin on his face as he dismounted. "She's a real sweet ride."

"That she is." Jade kept her reply casual. There was no need for a hard sell. "I just wanted to say bye. I've got another mare to exercise." She stuck out her hand, a habit she'd picked up from Travis and Ned, who always shook hands with the people who came to look at Rosewood horses.

Topher took her outstretched hand, then must have decided to keep it. "You know, now I realize why you look different from Margot and Jordan. You've got quite a bit of your mom in you, don't you? I always considered her one of the sexiest women in Loudoun County. And because I appreciate beautiful, sexy women who can also ride like nobody's business, how about coming out for a drink with me?"

Oh, God. Just when she'd gone and resigned herself to the idea that it was too difficult to determine if he'd been involved with her mother, Topher had to toss out a statement like that, muddying the waters once again.

But would he really be interested in her if he'd had an affair with her mom? Personally she thought that was too creepy for words, but obviously it happened and not only in *The Graduate*. If she went out and had a drink with him, maybe the atmosphere—heck, maybe the alcohol—would loosen his tongue and she'd know for sure. "I might be free to have a drink."

"How about Saturday?"

Topher moved fast, that was for sure.

"No, not Saturday." Saturday she'd be seeing Rob. Recalling their first meeting, she knew Rob could move plenty fast too, but he'd never given her the impression that he was a slick operator. Nope, Rob was just hot. Very hot.

"Then let's get together tomorrow. We'll go to the Brass Horn," he said in a decisive tone that told her he was used to having his suggestions become reality. "I'll pick you up—"

"No—no." She didn't relish having to fend him off if he wanted to make out in his car. Somehow she thought he might go for that sort of thing. "I'll meet you there," she said. It would help her avoid any attempt on his part to come inside the cottage.

"Okay. I have some afternoon meetings, so let's meet at six."

Jade nearly rolled her eyes. Why did it never occur to some guys to ask their date whether a certain hour would be convenient for them?

Tito had entered the ring to take Carmen back up to the barn. Topher handed him the reins, then said with a nod to Margot and Travis, who'd also approached, "Travis, Margot, as I was just telling Jade, Carmen's a real treat to ride."

"Well, come on up to the office and we can talk a bit," Travis suggested.

"Be happy to. See you at six tomorrow, Jade."

"See you," she replied with a bland smile. Aware that Margot was giving her a hard look, she hurried out of the ring ahead of them.

She should have known that Margot would come and find her as soon as she could. "Jade, are you seriously going out with Topher tomorrow?"

She paused in the midst of centering Valentine's martingale to shrug. "Yeah. He asked me to have a drink. I didn't see why I shouldn't say yes—"

"And what about that truly major kiss I saw Rob and you share? That wasn't reason enough to say 'thanks but no thanks'?"

Jade tried to ignore the niggling feeling in the pit of her stomach. "It's no biggie, Margot. I'm just having a drink with him."

"But why? You can't be interested in him—oh, my God! Jade, no, this is a really bad idea."

"What?"

"Don't feign ignorance. I've spent longer than you playing the nasty TM guessing game." She crossed her arms in front of her. "Topher's on your detective's list, isn't he?"

She shrugged. "And what if he is?"

"Then you should let this detective you hired do his job."

Dropping to one knee to check the fastenings on Valentine's jumping boots, she muttered, "I am," before scooting around to Valentine's other hind leg, avoiding Margot's skeptical gaze.

"Bull. Jade, this has all the makings of a disaster. And what about Rob?"

Jade straightened. "What about him?" she asked guardedly.

"What are you going to say if Rob finds out you're going out with Topher—a guy who has *on the prowl* written all over him? I can't imagine he'd be too happy about that."

She couldn't either, and it made the niggling worry in the pit of her stomach tighten into a hard lump of anxiety. "I'll deal with it."

Margot gave her a long look and then sighed. "I wish you'd reconsider."

"I can't, Margot."

"Oh, sweetie," Margot said sadly.

With its leather-covered stools, dark-wood tables, polished-brass bar fixtures, and ceiling beams, the Brass Horn Pub had the sort of "olde English" feel to it that made it popular with tourists. The locals liked it too, because it had an excellent selection of beers and ales on tap and a decent-size parking lot—a bonus in a town where parking was limited.

It appealed too because of its proximity to the Coach House. One could meet for drinks at the Horn and then mosey on next door and finish the evening at the more sophisticated Coach House—whose cuisine made it a destination restaurant. But a growing number of the pub's customers were choosing to stay and dig in to the menu's offerings of shepherd's pie, fish and chips, or burgers and, on weekend nights, to listen to the live bands the owners hired.

Luckily, the live music didn't start until after 8:00 P.M. All to the good, since Jade wanted to be able to hear what Topher had to say. The sooner she could decide whether he really might have been her mother's adored TM, the sooner she could split.

She was running late for her so-called date with him, despite having given the minimum attention to her appearance. After showering off the sweat from her workout with Cosmo and Griffin—a two-year-old dark-gray gelding that Ned had suggested she might like to begin training—she'd pulled on a pair of pencil-leg black jeans and a multicolored knit wraparound sweater that she'd snatched up on sale at Anthropologie.

Fussing with her hair had been out of the question; the day had been too long, the entire week too long, to exert that kind of energy. And why bother anyway? Impressing Topher wasn't her aim. After blow-drying her hair, she let it hang down her back. Lip gloss was applied not out of vanity but to soothe her bottom lip. She'd unconsciously been gnawing all day, the result of second-guessing the wisdom of meeting Topher for a drink but also of fretting over Eugene Harrison's continued absence from school. This last had worried her enough to ask Ted Guerra for advice. Far more sanguine about Eugene's absence, Ted had nonetheless promised to call the Harrisons himself if Eugene didn't return to class on Monday.

Preoccupied with figuring out how to resolve what was clearly becoming an increasingly uncomfortable situation with the Harrisons—the elder Harrisons, that is—Jade could only muster faint amusement at the fact that she'd sought an authority figure's help to handle a problem.

Not so long ago, her rebellious self would never have dreamed of consulting her principal for anything. And as for that other authority figure who'd played such a huge role in her defiant youth, never in her wildest imaginings would she have predicted she'd find herself half in love with Rob Cooper.

Her feelings for Rob were a topic she was trying not to think about. They were too big, too scary. Contemplating them was like jumping off a cliff into the waves of a dazzling azure ocean and then hitting the water and feeling its vastness close over her head.

No matter how good a swimmer she might be, there was no stopping the panicky sensation that she might not be strong enough to navigate this new element or ever reach the surface.

Fridays were Fridays; even the Brass Horn's large parking lot was full. Jade was forced to circle the lot a couple of times before hitting the jackpot and spotting a car that was leaving. After pulling into the empty space, she got out and slammed the Porsche's door, glanced at her watch, and frowned. She hadn't been able to call to tell Topher she was late, since by asking Travis for his cell number she would have risked running into Margot and seeing the disappointment on her face.

Her family had done so much for her, and once again she was letting them down. Better to get the evening over and done without involving them. She'd caused them enough distress.

It would be a typical twist of fate if it were all for nothing and Topher, deciding he'd waited long enough, had left the pub, she thought, as she hurried to the entrance and pulled open the carved oak door.

Rob loved his hometown, with its beautiful location among Virginia's rolling hills. As a cop, he appreciated the fact that the crime that existed in Warburg was, for the most part, mainly property crime. As in most towns in America, drugs were to be found, but substances like methamphetamines and heroin hadn't made any real inroads.

Cocaine and prescription-drug abuse were a different story. The town's profile—moneyed and sophisticated, with a sizable number of residents considering themselves quite the jet-setters, who liked to vacation in Palm Beach or Aspen in the winter and Cabo or Mallorca in the spring—created far too welcoming an environment for dealers. The drugs' presence and the chilling potential for serious crime that accompanied them enraged him. Each time he was able to bust a dealer or nail a user was a sweet victory.

Today was no exception. The bust had been especially fine—neat and serendipitous. Rob had pulled over an electric-blue souped-up Subaru Impreza that blew past his speed trap. The driver was a Caucasian homeboy who luckily wasn't so stupid as to try to outrace him or use the heat he was packing when Rob asked for his license and registration.

The license and registration both came up clean. But the kid was nineteen years old and living in a D.C. area that was seeing a spike in crime. What was he doing tearing through Warburg at 3:00 P.M.? Then there were his eyes. They held more fear than even a pricey speeding ticket should warrant.

Heeding a gut instinct, Rob called for backup, and his brother Scott was there in two minutes. Seeing the flashing lights of Scott's patrol car in his rearview mirror, Rob approached the Subaru and asked Jimmy Winn to step out of his car.

The kid complied readily enough.

But then Scott pulled up in front of the Subaru, effectively blocking it. Climbing out of his cruiser, Scott began to walk toward them.

Having a second uniformed cop approach must have triggered the kid's panic, sending it into the red zone. Abruptly, he tried to dive back into the car. Rob, already on high alert, was faster. Hauling him back, he pinned Jimmy against the side of the car.

A pat-down that wasn't nearly as invasive as a TSA search produced the Glock 19 the kid was packing. Sending a prayer of gratitude that the kid hadn't been stupid or scared enough to fire it, Rob read Jimmy his Miranda rights.

Jimmy chose to remain silent while Scott proceeded to search the Subaru's interior. He changed tactics when

Scott came upon the plastic-wrapped stash of coke tucked away in the spare-tire well, promising to tell them whatever they wanted to know. So while Scott stayed behind to have the Subaru impounded, Rob and a handcuffed Jimmy took a quick trip to the station, where they had a very successful chat.

It turned out Jimmy Winn was a runner but still fairly new at the game of shuttling back and forth between the dealer and the users, who put in orders for their coke to be delivered to them like pizza or Chinese food. Caught red-handed and with the charges piling up fast against him, Jimmy had the wits to cooperate, understanding it might help him down the road in a plea bargain.

Within an hour, he'd given them the name of the dealer in D.C. and the address in Warburg where he'd made a drop-off to a couple of high school kids. He'd also provided their first names (not even these kids were stupid enough to have given him their surnames) and detailed physical descriptions. To demonstrate his good-will, he told them where in Leesburg he'd been heading to drop off the rest of the coke, information the Lees-burg police would be extremely grateful to receive.

Later, while Jimmy sat with a DEA agent and a law-yer, Rob's uncle Joe sent Rob and Scott, along with Phil Grimaldi and Tory Bryant, two other officers on the force, to pay a visit to the address Jimmy had supplied. Their luck held. With the parents God-knows-where, the kids were starting their Friday partying early. The cops busted the lot of them.

With the station populated by scared-stiff adolescents, Rob found himself comparing this bunch to the teenage Jade of years ago.

She'd been just as scared and defiant as these kids. The difference was that underneath that defiance there'd been a deep unhappiness, an unhappiness caused by the tragic loss of her parents. These kids, slouched sullenly on the plastic chairs, exuded boredom and a gross sense of entitlement.

Rob had enough experience dealing with teen delinquency to recognize that if Jade hadn't been so mired in misery, she probably wouldn't have gotten into the trouble she had. This wasn't to say she wasn't a real spitfire, however, he thought with an inner smile. She was that and more, and he was pretty stuck on her.

If these kids were smart, they'd figure out a way to turn their lives around, as Jade had. He hoped for their sake they were.

Pleased with the afternoon's busts, Uncle Joe told Rob to head on home. "Phil, Tory, and I will talk to the kids' parents when they get here. A talk I hope they never forget. You did good work today." With a pat to Rob's shoulder, Uncle Joe rounded his desk and sank into his creaky chair.

Since Rob's uncle was not a man prone to praise or favoritism, those words meant a lot. "Thanks."

Scott stuck his head through the open doorway. "My shift's ending, Uncle Joe, but if you need me to stay—"

"You're on duty tomorrow, right?" At Scott's nod, Joe said, "No, you go on. You'll be back here soon enough."

"So how about celebrating with a brew at the Horn, since today you proved once and for all that you are a master of the speed trap?" Scott asked Rob as he stepped into their uncle's office. "The beer's on me," he added with a grin.

"I'd take him up on that, Rob. Offers like that come once in a blue moon from Scott."

Scott clutched his breast. "Uncle Joe, you wound me."

"Not funny, Scott," Uncle Joe returned with a scowl. "Not when that punk was packing a Glock. We're damned lucky he didn't lose his head and start shooting. Christ. Cocaine and Glocks in Warburg. I hate it."

"Why don't you show those parents just what the delivery boy who dropped off their darlings' blow had stuck inside the waistband of his jeans? It might scare some sense into them," Rob suggested.

"Not a bad idea. I just might do that. Well, you two go enjoy that beer. You've earned it. And, Rob, hug Hayley for me. You both having dinner with Megan and Jim?"

"Yeah. Hayley and Mom have been cooking. Dinner is Mom's special meatballs and an apple cake. We've got more apples at home than we know what to do with."

Uncle Joe rubbed his belly. "Meatballs, huh?"

Rob hid a grin. "You should drop by later. You know Mom always makes enough to feed an army."

"Might do that—if my appetite isn't soured by these outraged, whining parents."

"You ready for that beer, Rob?"

Rob checked his watch. He didn't want to be late for dinner at his parents'. Hayley would be eager to have him taste the meatballs she'd helped make. "Yeah, but I can only stay for one."

"Hell, I wasn't inviting you for two. You did good today, little brother, but not that good."

The after-work crowd filled the Brass Horn. As she entered the bustling pub, Jade scanned the patrons standing by the bar. Relief filled her when she didn't see a single blond-headed man there. The relief was odd, since she was still consumed with the need to discover the identity of TM. So why was she just as happy that Topher wasn't standing there, drink in hand?

The question remained unanswered until she looked across the crowded barroom and saw him at a table next to the paneled wall. He must have been on the lookout for her. The second their eyes connected, a smug smile of satisfaction spread over his face. Half rising, he summoned her with a wave that was a tad too imperious. There was the answer to why she'd been happy not to spot him. Now there was no way to avoid his pompous attitude for the next hour.

Threading her way past occupied tables, she was halfway to Topher's when she abruptly realized he wasn't alone. A woman was sitting at the table, her back to Jade. All Jade had time to note was a magenta blouse and long dark-brown hair secured in a high ponytail, and then the woman was rising and turning.

The smile pasted on Blair Hood's face was pure poison.

"Hi, Jade. Long time no see."

"Hello, Blair. Yeah, it's been quite a while." She could have added that never would have been too soon, but that would have been catty. She didn't intend to stoop to Blair's level.

"Hey there, Jade. Take a seat," Topher said, and he gestured to the chair next to him and opposite Blair. "Blair and I have been catching up. You guys were in the same grade in high school, right? You two keep in touch much since graduation?"

"No, not really," Jade said. A glance at his frat-boy grin told her he was totally clueless. He had no idea that she and Blair had been mortal enemies in high school. His satisfied expression spoke only of a male ego deeply gratified at having two good-looking females at his side. There'd have been something else there, a sly smirk, if he was aware that Blair had been the architect of Jade's most miserable moments in high school.

And there were plenty to choose from. Blair and her friends had circulated rumors about Jade's mom cheating on her dad; they'd amused themselves and all their Facebook friends by Photoshopping Jade's face onto a naked porn star's body. And though Jade had never gotten solid proof, she was pretty sure it had been Blair who placed the anonymous tip to the cops informing them of minors drinking at the Den, a call Blair would have placed after ditching Jade at the bar and only when she herself was at a safe remove.

Jade was the first to admit that she'd been an idiot to believe, even for a millisecond, that Blair, after about twenty months of hating her, would suddenly perform an about-face and decide she wanted to be Jade's BFF and hang with her at the Den. In her own defense, Jade had been pretty messed up, having just discovered her mom's diary and all the ugly secrets inside those pages. Otherwise she might have recognized Blair's offer of an olive branch as yet another of her nasty games, a setup. Blair had been so eager to get her into a place where she could get busted, she'd even given Jade a fake ID.

Jade had never been a saint, not now and not in high school. Early on in their guerrilla war, she'd retaliated against Blair by making out with Dean McCallister. A football jock and pretty cute, he'd been extremely popular. Blair had been dying to go out with him and thought the house party would be the night it became "official"; Jade made sure it didn't happen.

The moment had not been Jade's finest; she loathed having used Dean to get back at Blair (though at least Dean had enjoyed a serious snogging session before passing out from the shots and beer chasers he'd done).

The memory made her pause.

Blair, Dean, Topher, and her. The connections were a little too cozy. It would be too weird for words if, on top of everything else, Topher and her mother had been involved. But she wasn't likely to find out about what he'd been up to seven years ago if Blair was with them.

Jade had ignored Topher's suggestion that she take a seat. "I can see you and Blair are enjoying the chance to reconnect, so I'll just head off. You and I can have that drink another day, Topher." *Or not,* she added silently. She'd suddenly decided that Greg Hammond could deal with ferreting out TM's identity without any amateurish help from her.

At her offer to leave, a gleam lit Blair's chocolate-brown eyes. It was quickly extinguished by Topher's immediate protest.

"No—no, stay! Among other things, I want to pick your brain about Carmen. I'm seriously considering buying her. Your older sister and brother-in-law gave a pretty good sales pitch yesterday, but, well, let's say I have a feeling you could close the deal." He grinned. "And Blair has a dinner date at the Coach, so she can't stay much longer. You don't mind if we talk horses a bit, Blair?"

"Oh, no, not at all," Blair breathed, doing a good job of acting all wide-eyed and bedazzled with him. Did Blair's performance mean she had him in her sights? Probably. He was good-looking. He had a decent job with initials attached to it. He was rich. And he came from one of Warburg's prominent families.

And Blair was too stupid to recognize what a bore he was. She was also too stupid to realize that, while Topher would happily sleep with her, he'd never enter a serious relationship with her, for the simple reason that Blair didn't ride. Jade suspected that Blair was scared of horses. A blessing, as Blair was the type of person who'd blame the horse she was riding rather than herself for anything that went wrong.

Unfortunately, no matter how little Jade wanted to have a drink with Blair and Topher, she wasn't going to pass up the chance to sell one of Rosewood's horses. Although everyone in her family loved working with the horses—breeding, raising, and training them—selling was a crucial part of what the business was all about. She wouldn't forgive herself if she blew off the chance to convince Topher to buy the mare. By selling Topher one of their horses, Rosewood Farm would receive lots of great exposure.

So she sat and pasted a smile on her face. "Dinner at the Coach House. That's nice," she said to Blair as Topher hailed the waiter.

"Yes. I'm meeting my mother, my aunt Nonie, and Christy."

Egad, the witches of Warburg gathered together around one table. Jade pitied the poor waiter assigned to their table.

"Oh," she replied, absolutely unable to tack on "how nice" to complete the sentence.

"And you're Eugene's second-grade teacher, aren't you? Oh, wait, Christy told me you were just the substitute. Still, how sweet."

"I enjoy it," she replied coolly. "And what do you do, Blair? Have you got a job?"

She gave an insouciant shrug. "I'm waiting until I find something that really appeals to me."

"Well, if you want a job in insurance, Blair, let me know. I can introduce you to some people."

"That'd be great, Topher."

He nodded easily. "Happy to. Wouldn't want you to wander off to big, bad D.C. We need to keep the beautiful girls in Warburg."

Blair shot Jade a triumphant look. Then, as if sensing that Jade couldn't care less about the conversation, she frowned. "I'm still adjusting to being out of college. It was kind of my whole world for four years. Did you feel that way?" she asked Topher.

"Yeah, from what I can remember of it. It was basically one long kegger." When he laughed, Blair joined in, and Jade wished the beer she'd ordered would hurry up.

"I bet you miss school too, Jade," Blair said.

Jade shrugged. "I guess. I'm pretty busy right now living my life—"

"—as a substitute teacher for second grade," Blair finished for her with another laugh. "Which is, like, so ironic."

Jade was going to ignore her, but of course Topher took the bait. "Why would that be ironic?"

"I have friends who were in the same dorm as Jade in college—Adrienne Waltham and Reese Little—so I heard quite a bit about Jade's doings," she told him. "She had quite the reputation. There was even talk about a certain 'advice' column, a very particular kind of advice column, if you know what I mean. *Definitely* not G-rated. The column was written not anonymously but under . . . what's it called again? Oh, yeah, a pen name, but most everyone on campus figured out who was writing it." Blair paused to take a sip of her drink, and when she smiled, she looked like a shark scenting blood. "So, Jade, did you put *sex columnist* on your résumé when you applied for your job at the elementary school?"

It was as if time had collapsed and she was back in the hell of high school, with Blair doing her best to destroy her.

Of course, with Blair being as dumb as she was mean, she hadn't thought through exactly what effect her bringing up Jade's college stint as a sexpert columnist would have. She'd hoped to embarrass Jade in front of Topher, but instead he was looking at her as if he wanted to sign up for a private tutorial on the *Kama Sutra* or maybe invite her back to his place to view his porn collection.

Once Blair realized her miscalculation, it would infuriate her, making her even more determined to try to wound Jade. God, why did some things never seem to change?

"Hey, Blair, didn't you say you were meeting your

family at six-thirty?" Topher made a production of checking his watch. "It's past that now."

Like a contestant in a reality TV show who's just been voted off, Blair barely managed a strained smile for Topher. "So should I call you? I think I might be really interested in insurance."

He gave her a blank look—he'd obviously forgotten his offer to help her find a position the second he'd uttered it—then recovered. "Sure. Definitely. Call me."

"Thanks," she breathed. Leaning in, she kissed him lingeringly on the lips.

A little overdone for a goodbye kiss, Jade thought, and she bit the inside of her cheek as she watched the show, to prevent a snort of laughter from escaping. If Blair weren't such a witch, Jade might've had a soft spot for her; she was so entertaining.

But now she had to deal with Topher, who was looking like he'd hit the Friday sex jackpot. She'd let him down easy by talking up Carmen for fifteen minutes, then nothing was going to stop her from blowing this joint and going home. She could nuke a frozen burrito, kick off her boots, put her feet up on her still-unblemished sofa, and zone out in front of the TV. It would be sheer zombie bliss. Or she could drop by Hawk Hill and raid Jordan and Owen's fridge, which would be stocked with even yummier things than a burrito. And Neddy would be about ready for bed, freshly bathed, dressed in his footed pj's and smelling of baby powder, as cute as anything on Earth.

Yeah, it was definitely time to wrap up this total flop of an evening.

"So, Topher," she said brightly. "Have I told you about the last time I took Carmen out for a cross-country jaunt? There's nothing she likes better than to tear across fields and soar over embankments. Carmen's got some outrageous speed in her. . . ."

* * *

Scott and Rob found seats at the bar not far from the beer-tap handles, a prime spot where they were able to order a Flying Dog porter for Scott and a Dogfish Head brown ale for Rob. Their pints filled, Scott clinked his glass against Rob's.

"Here's to pulling off some seriously good shit today, Rob." His voice held a note of rare solemnity.

"Glad you had my back. Uncle Joe was right. Warburg's no place for coke and Glocks."

"We'll have to make sure that dealer and all his scum associates get the message."

"Let's drink to them getting it loud and clear," Rob agreed, clinking their glasses together a second time.

"Must be a good band tonight," Scott mused, glancing about. "It looks like half of Warburg's here. Hey, that's Randy over there with her cousin Liz. Mind if I go say hi?"

"Be my guest." As Scott made his way over to Randy, his latest in a never-ending slew of lady friends, Rob turned in the direction he'd taken, intending to wave hi to Randy from his place at the bar.

He never got that far, never got past the couple seated at a table by the wall.

Jade had her back to him, but Rob knew it was her. He recognized the thick, gold-streaked tumble of hair, the slim hand that raised the beer glass to her lips— hell, he even recognized the small, bony point of her wrist. He'd kissed and stroked every one of those parts of her—and hundreds of others. They were burned into his memory.

She was with a guy who looked familiar, so he was most likely a local. Rob put him at around thirty. He sported a preppy look, complete with an expensive haircut and a big, fat stainless-steel watch. His black sweater was probably cashmere. Rob didn't give a shit about his moneyed looks. He didn't even mind the fact that he was hanging on Jade's every word. She could make a grocery-shopping list sound fascinating.

No, what bugged him was the expression on the guy's face as he leaned close to her—he looked like he wanted to eat her up.

Rob wasn't accustomed to jealousy. He and Becky had been high school sweethearts. And even though Becky had been extremely popular, with her doe-brown eyes and wavy brown hair, everyone had accepted without question that she was his.

What was going on here? Rob wondered, his eyes boring holes in Jade's back. He thought he'd made it clear how serious he was about her. Was she just using him?

Jade picked up her beer glass and took a sip. Setting it down, she angled her head to say something to her date. Something that had him placing a hand on her forearm and moving in to kiss her on the lips.

The damned kiss seemed to last for an eternity. Seconds into it, Rob's gut was already twisted into a tight knot of pain. The pain didn't lessen when she pulled back and rose to her feet, because he saw that her beer glass was still sitting on the table and was more than half full. The Jade Radcliffe he knew would have pitched it in the guy's face without hesitation if she hadn't wanted his kiss.

When she'd stood and shouldered her handbag, the guy with her got up too and tossed some bills onto the table. Clearly he intended to accompany her out of the Brass Horn. To do what? Continue where he'd left off?

"So who are you planning to arrest now?" Scott joked. Fixated on Jade and her date, Rob hadn't even noticed his brother's return.

That's exactly what he would like to do: drag that guy

off in handcuffs to the station, toss him behind bars, and throw away the key. Perhaps a little dramatic, but at least it would ensure his hands and mouth stayed the hell off Jade.

As for Jade, he wanted to kiss her until she trembled with passion, kiss her until she whispered his name in breathless wonder, kiss her until she knew he was the only one for her.

Instead, he got an elbow in his ribs from his brother. "Seriously, Rob. Who's got you so hot under the collar?"

Rob jerked his attention away and turned back to the bar. "No one," he answered, lifting his pint glass. "I was just wondering if you were going to stick me with the tab." He drank deeply, wishing he could erase from his mind the image of Jade kissing another man.

"Oh, good. Because for a second there I thought you were planning to go and throttle Topher McCallister for having his hand on Jade Radcliffe's lower back. Not sure Uncle Joe would be too happy about that. And would I ever stick you with the tab?"

Topher McCallister? Rob refused to glance over his shoulder to take another look. If memory served, Topher had been a year or two ahead of him in school. "Is that who that was?" He thought he sounded convincingly indifferent.

"Yup, and from the looks of it, Topher's still a hit with the ladies. At least he has taste. That *was* Jade Radcliffe with him, right? Eric's right. He told me she has to be the prettiest second-grade teacher Warburg's ever seen. Interesting. That thundercloud expression has settled over your face again."

"Fuck off, Scott."

Scott gave a bark of laughter. "Well, that answers all the questions I had for you tonight." Patting Rob on the shoulder, he said, "Want me to go distract Topher? I'm sure there's something we can talk about."

"No, thanks."

"Just as well," he said with a shrug as he turned back to the bar and picked up his beer. "They've left."

Damn. Now he'd be left to suffer the torment of wondering exactly where they'd gone.

Chapter ❧
TWENTY-ONE

JADE'S SATURDAY seemed like a vacation, the day filled only with riding, so easy-paced that she found her thoughts circling back to the evening ahead, wondering when Rob would drop by.

She couldn't call him, of course. To do so would smack of neediness. While she might be all aflutter at the prospect of seeing him, she didn't want him to know how deeply nutty she was about him.

Her sisters figured it out soon enough, though at first Jordan and Margot thought the drink she'd shared with Topher the night before was the reason for her preoccupation. Naturally, Margot had felt compelled to tell Jordan about Jade's date with Topher, and the two of them had gone into mother-hen mode the second they discovered Blair had been there too.

That was Jade's fault. She'd let slip that Blair had been at the pub and was as witchy as ever. Her only excuse for such a basic mistake was that she'd been distracted, simultaneously fielding their questions about Topher while listening to Georgiana recite the parts of the horse. Her little niece was using Maggie as a model because Kate was grooming her out on the cross ties. Georgiana was doing amazingly well for a four-year-old, so far needing help only when she got below the cannon bone on the bay pony's slender leg.

Luckily, both Olivia and Kate were there to help their cousin with patient prompts of "fetlock," "pastern," "coronet," and "hoof," because Jade had an additional distraction to deal with.

It had occurred to her that maybe she should cook something for Rob. Had he said he'd be over in time for dinner? God, what could she possibly make? Between Ellie and Jordan's cooking and the frozen wonders she constantly pilfered from Margot and Jordan's freezers, she hadn't put in a lot of practice. Or any practice.

So when Jordan stuck in a sneak question, asking whether Topher was TM while Jade was busy watching Kate position herself so she could brush the bay mare's long black tail, she first looked at her sister blankly and then shook her head.

"No—at least I don't think so. I didn't really get a chance to steer the conversation in that direction. I arrived at the Horn late. Blair was already there, and after she left I didn't want to stick around. In addition to being a miserable example of humanity, Blair wears way too much perfume. Reminds me of a poison cloud. I swear the pub reeked—"

"Blair's back in Warburg?" Jordan asked just as Margot voiced her own question. "Whatever was she doing with Topher?"

"Yeah, she seems to be back, and as far as I can tell, her primary interest is to audition for the role of Topher's one and only," Jade said, answering them both. "She was none too happy to see me. But that's hardly news."

"So she's still in high school mode. What a shame," Jordan said.

"And so predictable. Those Harrisons are so freakin' immature. It drives me nuts."

Jade cleared her throat loudly, nodding at Georgiana, Olivia, and Kate. "Careful there, sis."

Margot looked abashed. "Sorry," she mouthed. Then, louder, "Does she intend to stay in Warburg?"

Jade nodded. "Yup. She wants Topher to find her a job in his insurance company or something like that." Then, seeing that Georgiana was struggling to remember a vocabulary word, she said, "That part of the hind leg has a different name from the forearm. It starts with a *ga*. Can you remember it?"

"Gaskin," Georgiana cried, giving a little hop for emphasis.

"That's right."

"And then comes the hock," Georgiana continued.

"You're on a roll, kiddo," Jade said, with a smile that faded when she returned to the previous topic. "Of course, even though Blair is unemployed, she doesn't think much of my job. It was kind of funny—she not only derided my being a lowly substitute teacher, she also implied that I wasn't good enough to do that."

"What bull—" Margot began, quickly tacking on "—oney. You're a terrific teacher. What could she possibly know about your qualifications?"

Jade shrugged. "My guess is that she's gotten an earful from Christy. And apparently Blair had friends in my college dorm. She probably asked them for whatever gossip they knew." She decided not to mention that Blair had brought up her advice column, not with Kate, Olivia, and Georgiana present. Even though they were now busily occupied grooming Dickens, those little pitchers had mighty big ears.

And if she told them about the sexpert business, her sisters would inevitably want to hear how Topher had reacted to the news, and then she'd have to tell them that he tried to come home with her last night.

Having him kiss her had been bad enough. She'd let him only because he'd informed her he was going to buy Carmen and wanted to seal the deal with something "friendlier" than a handshake. In the parking lot he'd tried to get a whole lot friendlier, but she'd nipped that particular male fantasy in the bud.

The only guy whose sexual fantasies she wanted to indulge was Rob. Should she cook something for him tonight? she wondered again. Then she realized she had the equivalent of a culinary expert on hand. "Hey, Jordan, is there something foolproof I can cook that a man would appreciate?"

Margot and Jordan were helping currycomb Dickens, because he'd rolled in the pasture and looked more like a pinto than an all-white pony. Jade saw them exchange a look.

"You're planning to cook?" Jordan asked.

"Yeah, I thought as it's the weekend I'd christen the stove. No big deal."

"Of course not."

Jade thought she heard Margot snort with laughter, but when she glanced over at her, her sister had ducked behind Dickens's neck.

"What? Is there anything wrong with deciding to cook a homemade meal?" she demanded. "I wouldn't want to hurt Owen's feelings and never use the kitchen he built."

"You can make a cold pasta sauce. It's super-easy. All you need is basil, chopped tomatoes, olive oil, and lots of garlic. You have a food processor in the cabinet above your fridge. The recipe takes about five minutes and it's absolutely delish. All you actually have to cook is the spaghetti."

"I can do that." Even she could dump spaghetti in boiling water and stir.

"Certainly you can. And I'm sure Rob will love it," Jordan said with a smile.

Jade shot Margot a disgusted look. "Do you ever keep anything to yourself?"

"Nope. We're your sisters. That means we get to share everything, not just clothes—and this is a pretty major moment, cooking for your guy. I almost had a meltdown when I cooked Travis his first meal. I made scrambled eggs. I was so worried I was going to screw up." She gave a wide smile. "He loved them."

Of course Travis had loved every bite of Margot's eggs. How could he not, when he was crazy for her and had been for as long as Jade could figure such things out? She wasn't sure Rob would be so forgiving of her nonexistent culinary skills.

By six o'clock, Jade had a bowl full of chopped canned tomatoes, a mound of chopped basil, and a slightly smaller one of garlic. She'd even pinched a loaf of Italian bread from Jordan, who always seemed to have stuff like that in her kitchen, and had asked how to make garlic bread.

Who would've guessed it was so easy, a mere question of slicing the bread and then slathering it with melted butter, olive oil, chopped garlic, and some chopped parsley? If she hadn't been so nervous, wondering when and then *if*—as the clock ticked with unnerving loudness—Rob was going to show, she might have even enjoyed the whole adventure in cooking.

At the moment it felt too much like she was waiting for a guy, and not just any guy but one that she desperately wanted to please. And when the knock came on the front door, a part of her was alarmed at how everything inside her went a little loopy, in tight circles of joy, at the prospect of seeing him. Of spending an entire night with him. How had this happened to her?

Perhaps that was why she was so determined to play it cool when she opened the door. "Oh, hey," she said as her heart cartwheeled against her ribs.

"Hey."

She stepped back to let him enter. She was glad he was wearing a thick charcoal-gray sweater that zippered at the collar with his jeans. If she'd had to raise her hands to take his jacket, he'd have seen she was trembling.

"Have you eaten? I was just fixing something," she said ultra-casually.

"No, I haven't. I came straight here after dropping Hayley off at Posey's."

Was it because she was trying to play it cool that he seemed reserved in return? Stranger still, even though she could sense his aloofness, she was equally aware of the weight of his gaze as she led him past the living room and dining room into the kitchen.

As she'd never really tried to do more in her kitchen than grab something from the fridge or cupboard and go, she hadn't realized how small the space was. Or maybe it had shrunk. Somehow she couldn't avoid brushing against Rob as she rummaged in the cabinets, looking for a pot in which to cook the pasta. Every time she brushed him, her pulse leaped. Lord, she was supposed to cook in this state?

Normal, act normal, she coached herself as she filled the pot with water.

"So how was your night yesterday? Do anything special with Topher McCallister?"

She sloshed water onto the floor, narrowly missing her shoes. With a muttered curse, she set the pot on the stove, grabbed a dish towel, and swabbed the floor—extra-thoroughly to give her time to think. Straightening, she tossed the damp towel onto the counter. "How'd you know I was with Topher last night?"

"Because I saw you. I was having a beer at the bar with my brother Scott. You were sitting at a table with Topher. Obviously you didn't notice me." He folded his arms across his chest and gazed at her levelly. "That was quite the kiss."

Damn. She could only imagine what he was thinking. "Would you believe it was supposed to be an alternative to a friendly handshake? You see, Topher had just decided to buy Carmen, one of the horses I've been working with. Unfortunately, Topher went a tad overboard in the PDA department."

Rob still wore that closed expression on his face.

"Wait. You're not jealous, are you?"

She'd posed the question teasingly and was instantly appalled at herself. But she wasn't in the habit of having to account for her actions to a man, of having what she did be important. It occurred to her, too, that perhaps she wanted to rile Rob a little and put a crack in the reserve she sensed in him.

But she didn't really want to make Rob jealous, did she? Because that would be bent. Was she that much like her mother that she needed to be given proof that she was special? Was this why her mother had been seeing another man? To make Dad jealous?

And if she was anything like her mother, what was to prevent Jade from behaving with the same foolish cruelty? Her doubts made her feel as fragile and shallow as spun glass, brittle and too easily broken.

As the silence stretched between them, she wondered what else she might destroy.

Rob's sigh broke the silence. He dragged a heavy hand through his dark hair. "Jealous? Yeah, I was. Still am, I guess. Tell me, Jade. Did you and he continue the kiss in private?"

At least she had the answer to one of her troubling questions. Rob's admission hadn't given her any twisted pleasure or triumph.

Shoving aside the rest of her worries, she shook her head emphatically. "No. I left the Horn and went over to Hawk Hill, Jordan and Owen's place, and read *Duck on a Bike* to my nephew Neddy. He's got the barnyard sounds down pat, which makes him far more entertaining to hang out with than Topher. And despite what you think you saw, Topher's a lousy kisser. Truly."

A smile had appeared on Rob's face, and it lifted the corners of his mouth. It lifted her heart as well. He closed the distance between them and pinned her against the edge of the counter. She felt the tantalizing heat of him through the denim of their jeans.

"Nothing's worse than a lousy kisser," he observed.

"You can say that again. Of course, I've been terribly spoiled of late," she said, her body tightening in anticipation of Rob's certifiably excellent kisses.

His grin erased any remaining traces of tension in his expression. "Topher's all wrong for you, anyway." He lowered his head slowly, until all she could see was the electric blue of his eyes.

"And you're so right?" she whispered.

"Yeah, I am."

His kiss proved it beyond a doubt.

His lips teased with a few fleeting brushes, letting the taste and whisper-light pressure beguile her before they settled over her mouth to claim her wholly. With a mew of pleasure, she invited him to enter, and his tongue swept inside as his arms tightened around her, fingers slipping under her green cardigan to stroke the curve of her waist.

Like a match to kindling, his touch set flames of need dancing over her. She trembled, greedy for more. Molding herself against him, she nibbled and licked the underside of his freshly shaven jaw, the corded column of his neck, the shell of his ear. She smiled as his breathing changed, becoming heavy and labored. Her hands swept over his frame, setting his muscles aquiver, and her hunger grew.

She hadn't realized that knowing Rob as a lover, knowing his body, its pleasure points, and what aroused him to a fever pitch, would increase her desire so. Even in her mindless state of need, she recognized that this was special, that what they had was extraordinary.

It wasn't simply that Rob had all the right parts and moves. It was some deeper connection between them that took their lovemaking to a new and different plane of experience.

Her hands moved to his waistband to tug open his belt, pop the metal button of his jeans, and then hold her breath, the better to hear the quiet rasp of his zipper as she drew it down. It was almost as thrilling and sexy as the low rumble of laughter emanating from his chest.

"In a hurry?" he whispered as his mouth traveled to the hollow behind her ear, alternately tonguing it and then letting his teeth nibble on her lobe. Her cardigan open now, his fingers stroked the sensitive flesh of her abdomen in long, leisurely sweeps.

"Yes." The single word was all she could manage, for as she spoke, her hand found him. Rock hard and yet wondrously alive, he throbbed heavily in her grip, the promise of sensual bliss. Closing her fingers around his shaft, she felt him shudder, and his breath came out in a long hiss. "And I'm hungry."

"Hungry?"

She smiled. "Ravenous. For you." Continuing in the spirit of complete openness, she confessed, "My dinner will be a poor second. I can hardly cook."

"Ah, sweetheart, then I am definitely the man for you. In all ways," he added, with what could only be called a cocksure grin.

"So it's all right if I sample the goods?" She let her fingertips circle the head of his cock, grinning as he growled low in his throat.

"Be my guest."

* * *

He'd made her scream with pleasure when he was deep inside her. Later, he made her moan in delight when he slipped a forkful of tomato-garlic-coated spaghetti into her open mouth. He'd not only cooked, but he'd sponged and wiped the counters while she put the dishes away (the least she could do after he'd provided such a delicious meal) and then led her back to bed to spend the rest of the night making love.

In between, they dozed, his forearm wrapped about her, his breathing steady against the shell of her ear, his muscled body curled about hers, his solid presence protecting, comforting.

They talked too. Holding hands in the dark, they talked about Hayley and how funny and clever she was. Then Jade spoke about her family and how good it felt to be contributing to Rosewood Farm's success through her riding program and the training she did with Rosewood's young horses. But it was when Rob told her about the arrests he'd made the day before that she knew beyond a doubt: She'd fallen totally and completely in love with him. And the feeling was as scary as she'd thought it would be.

At the words *drug runner* and *Glock,* cold fear gripped her. She turned in his arms, desperate to see his face. "You arrested a drug runner? And he had a gun? You could have been killed."

"I can handle myself."

"But . . ." The fear was attacking her brain, making her thoughts sluggish.

"I'm a cop, Jade. My job has its dangers. For the most part they're few and far between, but I'm never careless. You and I both know from experience that a life can end at any time."

He was right. A life could end at any time, whether from a terrible, tragic accident or simply from doing the job one loved. Just as being a police officer held risks, so, too, did the kind of riding Jade did. He wouldn't ask her to stop riding—the sport was in her blood and marrow; being a cop was an equally integral part of who Rob was.

"I'm glad you're safe," she said quietly, determinedly beating back the fear.

"I do have at least a couple of reasons to live." Taking her hand, he'd pressed his mouth to her knuckles, and her heart squeezed at the gentle gesture.

This was it, she thought. She should tell Rob how she felt, let him know that she'd fallen for him. Openness in a relationship, along with safe sex, was what she'd always advised to the readers in her column.

But dispensing words of wisdom was a lot easier than putting them into practice. Being upfront about Topher's kiss had been easy. He meant nothing to her. Revealing that Rob held her heart terrified her.

Keeping the words locked inside, she gazed at him, searching out his features in the shadows of the darkened room.

"Just stay safe, okay?" she said, pressing her mouth to the base of his throat and feeling a sweet piercing pleasure as he pulled her closer still, settling her against the muscled wall of his chest.

"Always," he promised.

Cocooned in his embrace, she listened to the rhythm of his breathing deepen and slow, only then whispering the words she'd been too scared to utter before.

"I love you."

Chapter ❧
TWENTY-TWO

HE COULD get used to waking up with Jade. It wasn't even dawn when her alarm clock buzzed, but Rob found himself smiling anyway. An armful of warm Jade was a great reason to smile.

Remembering their lovemaking from the night before made his smile grow. Then, when she rolled over to sprawl on him, her breasts pressing against his chest, her hair a mad tangle teasing his skin, and her eyes glowing with a happy mischief, another part of him grew too.

Jade was nothing if not observant. Brushing her thigh against his erection, she said with a playful grin, "Top of the morning to you too. Feel like taking a shower with me, big guy, before I go take care of my ponies?"

"I'm pretty sure that answer is what's termed a no-brainer." He laughed.

"Well, I didn't know how quick on the draw you might be in the morning," she teased. "Though parts of you seem pretty alert."

He swatted her lightly on the butt. "Let's get wet."

Yeah, she was fun and energetic and game, and he loved having her long legs wrapped around his hips, meeting him thrust for grinding thrust while hot jets sprayed down upon them. She came in a shuddering climax, triggering his own near-violent release. The kisses she rained over his face as they both regained their senses were hotter than the shower.

She was also surprisingly sweet. He loved her shy smile of unexpected pleasure when, after dressing—he in his jeans and she in a pair of breeches and a cable-knit sweater that looked about as old as she—he offered to help her with the ponies.

"You sure you don't need to leave?"

"I've got some time. I'd like to spend it with you."

"Well, all right, then."

And his heart swelled when she slipped her hand in his. As slim and strong as the rest of her, it felt good—and right—in his grasp.

"I'll make you breakfast afterward," she continued as they headed out into the crisp morning air. "I do an outstanding bowl of cereal."

Feeding and watering the ponies was unlike anything he'd ever experienced. He found himself chuckling at the ponies' excited whinnies when he and Jade, arms loaded with hay, approached the stalls. The sounds the animals made changed then, and the air filled with grinding and munching and slower contented snorts. Jade made quick work of watering, dragging a hose from stall to stall and replenishing the buckets. Though it was fun, he also appreciated the dedication and time it took to care for the horses at Rosewood, day in and day out, in good weather and bad. Jade was probably so used to this life, she wouldn't see it as the huge responsibility it was.

By the time they'd finished giving the ponies their breakfast and were making their way back to Jade's cottage, the sun had risen. The dewy grass glistened and the leaves on the trees sparkled bright red and gold.

"It's beautiful here," he said as they paused before the cottage's front step.

"Yeah, it is." She opened the door and stepped inside, shucking her sweater. "We're lucky. Even with Margot taking on fewer modeling jobs, we've managed to keep Rosewood Farm operating in the black. Jordan's design company, Rosewood Designs, is doing well, so she's able to put some of the money she makes back into the farm. If I can build up my lesson program, then I'll be able to do the same."

Walking as she talked, she led him back toward the kitchen, making a beeline for the coffeemaker. Grabbing two cups, she filled them with steaming coffee, handed him one, and smiled. "I should give you fair warning that the real goal of the children's riding program is to make lifelong horse nuts out of each and every one of my students. It's a sport that comes with a pretty steep price tag. But because you seem like a nice guy, I'll give you a really good deal on that first Rosewood horse you buy for Hayley."

He opened the fridge and took out a container of milk. At her nod, he poured some into her cup and then into his own. Leaning against the counter, he took a sip. His eyebrows rose in surprise.

"This is great coffee."

"Thanks." She seemed ridiculously pleased at the compliment. "Owen taught me how. He takes things like good coffee very seriously. We've turned him on to horses too."

"In Hayley's case, I think it's safe to say she's already a horse nut. But at least now I've been warned. I'll open a horse fund to go with the college fund I started when she was a newborn."

"You opened a college fund for her? Good for you."

The wistful note in her voice had him remembering that her father left his three daughters with what rumor had was a prodigious pile of debt. He was suddenly glad that she had such a close bond with her sisters. "So how about that cereal you promised to wow me with?"

"Coming right up." She, too, seemed to want to avoid

any melancholy memories. "I can also do toast. Ellie Banner, Rosewood's housekeeper, gave me some strawberry jam she made."

He grinned. "Cereal and toast with strawberry jam. I'm overwhelmed. Can I help?"

"No, it's totally under control. You can keep the coffee coming, though."

He sat at the small kitchen table while she set about preparing their breakfast. Once she'd placed the cereal and the toast on the table and brought over the butter and jam, she sank into the chair beside him and launched into a lively commentary on the art of buttering toast.

The performance, a riff on a TV cooking show, was damned entertaining. The joy she got out of explaining how to spread sliver-thin slices of butter over warm toast and exactly how much jam should be allotted for each slice was infectious—the joy she got out of *life* was infectious.

She was good for him.

He wanted more. Much more, he decided. He wanted days with Jade and her quick intelligence and offbeat humor. He wanted nights with her generosity and passion.

She'd finished her first slice of toast. No time like the present, he decided. "I was wondering if you might be free to—" he began, only to have his sentence interrupted by the peal of her cell.

She picked it up off the table where she'd deposited it when they came into the kitchen. Her lips pursed as she read the display. "It's Topher." She sighed. "I should see what he wants."

Rob could have told her what he wanted, but he didn't want to spoil the morning. Furthermore, he didn't believe in wasting his breath. She'd already thumbed the button and said, "Hello?"

She was silent while Topher made what was evidently a long-winded pitch.

"Sorry, Topher. I can't tonight. I have to prepare for school tomorrow." She paused to listen to his reply, and Rob saw her green eyes flash with annoyance. "Yeah, well, you'd be surprised how much time goes into preparing for a full day of school. On top of that, the class is starting a new social-studies unit."

She fell silent again. "Okay, I guess I have time for that. I'll see you later."

She ended the call and caught his look. "What?"

"Are you going out with him again?"

"No—not really." She opened the box of cereal she'd selected from the cupboard and poured it into two large ceramic bowls that were white with multicolored dots. She passed him one bowl and the carton of milk. "I'll let you pour. How much milk to use on cereal is such an individual decision."

He waited several beats, and when it was clear she wasn't going to pick up the dangling thread of her earlier comment, he said, "So, 'not really'—what does that mean?"

She gave him a long look. "It means that I refused to go out to dinner but said I'd be willing to be around the barn at four this afternoon when he comes to sign the papers for Carmen. Why he needs me around is a deep mystery, since Margot and Travis are the deal makers and Ned and Felix know Carmen better than anyone. But, as I told you before, we're keeping our horse farm afloat financially—not an easy thing to do in this economic climate—and we wouldn't be even glimpsing a profit if we went around alienating our clients. Does that answer your question?"

"Yeah." He sloshed some milk over the cereal, dug up a spoonful, and shoved it in his mouth, chewing vigorously.

Okay, he had to stop overreacting.

He could handle the idea of her seeing Topher at Rosewood. After all, Topher wouldn't be so stupid as to try to stick his tongue down Jade's throat with Travis Maher nearby. Swallowing, he gave her a teasing grin. "This is exceptionally tasty cereal."

"I know," she said, beaming. "Cap'n Crunch is the best."

"The toast is delicious too." He took another bite of jam-slathered toast.

"Well, I can't take the credit for that. It's Ellie's jam."

"No need for modesty," he said. "You spread the butter."

She nodded happily, clearly relieved that they'd overcome the hurdle of Topher's all-too-obvious interest. "I did, didn't I?"

For his part, Rob was pleased that he hadn't ruined the goofy silliness of their breakfast. He hadn't felt this lighthearted in many a morning.

He leaned over and kissed her, savoring the taste of her, more delicious than any jam ever created. As their tongues mated, the heat between them flared. He smiled as she raised her arms to loop them about his neck and parted her lips wider, deepening their kiss.

With a low growl of approval, he wrapped his arms about her waist and shifted back in his chair, lifting her onto his lap. The move allowed him full access to her neck, and as he dragged his mouth down its length, he breathed in her warm soap-scented skin. His head spun with memories of her in the shower, wielding the bar of soap all over their entwined bodies.

Free to rove, his hands cupped her breasts, and a savage pleasure flooded him as her nipples grew pebble-hard against his palms. He knew if he opened the closure of her breeches and slid his hand inside her panties and touched her, she'd be hot and wet for him, as intensely aroused as he—and he wanted her with a force that left him shaking.

"Jade," he whispered as his hand closed about her breast, fondling it. "Let me take you back to bed."

Her eyes fluttered shut as she arched her supple body against his hand. "Mmm-mmm," she moaned. Disappointment flooded him as she straightened. "I'd love to, but unfortunately even a quickie would take too long," she said, regret in her voice. "I'm teaching the whole nepotic gang in a half hour, Neddy and Will included. They'll be rolling in any minute."

How many women would give up their precious Sunday morning to teach their nephews and nieces? he wondered, floored anew by her energy and generosity.

"Okay." He gave her a final kiss, knowing he'd be remembering the sweetly wild taste of her for the rest of the day.

His need unabated, he lowered his hands from the soft globes of her breasts and brought them to the relatively safer region of her back, stroking its silken length. Yet even there her response, a supple arch against the flat of his hand, like a sleek cat demanding to be stroked, had him wishing he could strip off her top and rain kisses down her spine to the sweet curve of her buttocks, while his fingers roamed and dipped—God, what had made him think touching her back would be "safe"? He could graze her pinkie, and desire would explode inside him.

With an effort, he reined in his hunger. "I was thinking earlier, I'd like to reciprocate for this fine breakfast you served. Come to dinner tomorrow."

"Dinner?" Again, he glimpsed in Jade's shy surprise a side of her she rarely revealed.

"Yeah, with Hayley and me. We make a mean pizza."

"Do you think it's a good idea? Will Hayley—"

"She'll love it. She's nuts about you, Jade. I want you to be with us."

"Well, okay, I—" Her answer was cut off by the peal of her phone. With an apologetic look, she leaned forward and grabbed it, glancing down at the screen.

With the phone cradled in Jade's hands, Rob could see the words PRIVATE CALLER displayed. At least it wasn't Topher calling again, he thought. But when she pressed the ON button and brought the phone to her ear, he was close enough to hear a man's voice say, "Jade, it's me, Greg." He felt the instant stiffening of her body and saw the telling look of horror that crossed her face just before she slid off his lap to carry the phone out of earshot.

The conversation lasted less than twenty seconds, but the obvious tension in Jade told Rob plenty. Greg was somebody important and Jade didn't want Rob to know about him. He'd never seen her look so guilt-stricken—except perhaps the night he'd busted her at the Den with a fake ID.

She'd been silent, listening intently. Then he heard her say, "Yes. I can do that." Her gaze swung to his face, then skittered away. "Listen, I'll call you back."

She hung up but remained standing by the entrance to the kitchen, staring into middle space.

"Everything okay?"

She started. "Yes. Of course. Why wouldn't it be?" Her voice was too casual.

"Who's Greg?"

She looked at him. No, she looked *through* him. He might have been holding her in his arms minutes ago; right now it was as if she were a million miles away.

"Greg? He's a"—she hesitated, as if searching for some acceptable description—"a friend."

He told himself to ignore the jealousy that, like a snake, had uncoiled to slither cold and lethal through his insides. "I see. So about dinner Monday—"

"I'm sorry, I can't. I'm busy tomorrow."

He knew, as the snake struck and sank its fangs deep,

that the reason she'd be busy was Greg. "What's going on, Jade? A second ago we were discussing dinner with you, me, and Hayley, and from the sound of it you wanted to come."

Oh, God. Jade cast a desperate glance in the direction of the front door. Would that she had special powers; she'd will it to burst open and have Olivia and Max tear inside with their usual high spirits. Quick on their heels would be Georgiana and then Kate, who, like Jordan, was always so self-possessed. Only the kids' chattering presence filling her small cottage would distract Rob and his too-perceptive gaze from uncovering her secrets.

She struggled to maintain a calm façade, which Greg Hammond had blown to bits with these few words: *I think I've found your TM, Jade. Are you free to meet me tomorrow?*

She didn't know how successfully she'd hidden her reaction from Rob; she was still reeling from the aftershocks of Greg's announcement.

After all these years, the idea that she might learn the identity of her mother's lover was nearly impossible to grasp. The news made her heart pound, less from excitement than from a strange sort of dread. The reaction was unexpected, and all she wanted right now was to have a moment alone to sort out her feelings, at the very least to pull herself together. Instead, she had to pretend that her world hadn't altered dramatically because of Greg's call.

"Jade?" She heard the trace of impatience in his voice and realized she hadn't answered his question.

"What?" she asked, stalling. The kids really should be coming any second. . . . *Please be on time.*

He crossed the kitchen to where she stood, though *stalked* might have been the better verb to describe the predatory grace with which Rob moved in his hunt for the truth.

"Why am I getting the feeling that this guy Greg is someone I should know about? Exactly how close is your 'friendship'?"

His hands had settled over her elbows as she'd crossed her arms over her middle. She shook him off as sudden aggravation filled her. She didn't like feeling cornered, didn't like feeling guilty. Most of all, she didn't like knowing that she was damaging her relationship with Rob—even though she wasn't going make any attempt to fix it by explaining.

Because what would he say if she revealed that Greg Hammond was a PI she'd hired? What would he say if she told him that once Greg gave her TM's name, she had every intention of confronting the man?

He'd try to stop her. Of course he would. Rob might be her lover, but he'd been a cop for a lot longer. There was no way he'd approve of her actions.

Freed from his grasp, she stepped back, refusing to waver when his expression turned bleak. "What makes you think that just because we're sleeping together you have the right to know everything that goes on in my life?"

Her comment had his mouth flattening in a grim line. "We're not just sleeping together, Jade."

No, when he held her last night she'd felt cherished and protected. But he didn't really know her. She wasn't perfect or kind or sweet. In time he'd see that all too clearly. Would he want her in his and Hayley's lives when he found how very unlike his wife, Becky, she was? She doubted it.

"At this point that's all we're doing, and maybe I don't want to go where you're trying to push me. I don't like feeling boxed in, and I *really* don't like being interrogated about my every move. In fact, I hate it." Even as she spoke, she knew she was hitting below the belt. Yet another reason she wasn't good for him: She didn't fight fair.

The situation overwhelmed her. Too much was happening to her, and she couldn't figure out how to handle it all. Yes, she'd fallen in love with Rob, but she was a rookie at being in love. In contrast, her need to discover the identity of TM was familiar. It had taken up residence in her heart the night she found her mom's diary in the closet where Jordan had hidden it. She couldn't abandon that need, not when she was on the verge of learning the truth.

Yet if she told Rob what was going on and how Greg Hammond fit into her life and that she'd hired him to track down TM, she was convinced that was exactly what he'd ask of her. How would he feel when she refused, when she told him that she had every intention of confronting this TM?

From where she stood, there didn't seem to be any way she could avoid hurting Rob. And that reinforced her most fundamental fear: She might love Rob, but that didn't necessarily mean she was a good enough person for him.

And right now she doubted whether she ever could be. Her attempts at self-improvement, her hope to emulate Margot and Jordan, would end in failure. Deep down, she was too much like her mom. The proof was the pain in Rob's eyes. She'd put it there.

"Damn it, Jade!" His voice was a combination of frustration and hurt. "I'm not trying to box you in and I don't want to interrogate you. What I want is for you to be a part of my life, but I need to be able to trust you if this relationship is going to have any chance."

Closing the distance between them, he clasped her shoulders. Though she could feel the tension in him, his hands were gentle. "Talk to me, Jade. Tell me what the deal is with this guy."

She looked up at him and then just as quickly looked away. "I can't tell you."

"You can't?" he asked in disbelief.

"I can't," she repeated through clenched teeth.

"You can't or you won't?" His voice had a sharp edge now.

God, this was awful. As the tears welled up in her eyes, she fastened her gaze on the distant sofa in the living room. The sight of it had her recalling the night Rob told her that, for the first time in a long time, he felt something good and that she was the reason.

And now she'd ruined things between them. Her throat tightened convulsively. She swallowed, then forced herself to say the words. "The answer is, I won't tell you. So I don't think we should see each other anymore."

"You want to call it quits now? Over this? Jade, what the hell is going on?"

She gave a tight shake of her head, remaining obstinately silent.

His hands dropped away. "My mistake. I thought you recognized how special what we have between us is. That you wanted to see where it could go. I guess I was wrong about that. I guess I was wrong about you." The words were like a cold blast, leaving her chilled and shaken. "Right. Well, since neither of us has anything left to say, there's no point in my sticking around."

She forced herself to remain rooted as he walked away, his steps ringing on the wooden floor. But at the sharp slam of the front door, sobs overtook her. Raising her hands to her face, she wept.

AT SCHOOL on Monday, she fought the pounding headache that had plagued her since Rob walked out her front door. The temptation to call in and request a substitute had been great. It had been years since she'd felt so sick at heart, so rotten to the depths of her soul.

But getting a substitute for the substitute teacher would only make her feel more like a pathetic loser. Besides, missing school was the easy way out. In her state of self-loathing, she wasn't going to permit anything to be easy. And she was supposed to be starting a new unit in social studies on the first Americans. Being absent for that introductory lesson would put the rest of the week in disarray.

She hid her misery behind as carefree a demeanor as possible. For the most part she succeeded—except when Hayley raised her hand. Her usual cheerful self, Hayley and her intuitive comments widened the crack in Jade's heart. More painful still was that Jade could now perceive so much of Rob in the little girl.

How was she to survive seeing Hayley every day and knowing that she'd destroyed the chance to be with both father and daughter?

Only the thought that at 3:15 P.M. she had a rendezvous with Greg Hammond kept her from picking up her cellphone during her free period to call Rob. But a tiny part of her held out the hope that maybe, just maybe, after she'd met TM face-to-face, she'd find a way to explain herself to Rob.

And maybe he'd be able to forgive her.

Eugene Harrison's seat remained empty, but when she went to the office to inform Ted Guerra of his continued absence, Ted's assistant, Dolores, told her that he was in a meeting. Jade wrote a note for him instead and dropped off a homework packet she'd put together for Eugene, so that he wouldn't fall too far behind.

When at last the bell rang for dismissal, she concentrated on saying goodbye to the students and reminding the boys to bring home the various jackets, baseball hats, and sweatshirts that had collected in their cubbies. Only after James Wessel left the classroom, trailing a plastic bag bulging with an assortment of clothes, did she let her gaze go to the window.

She'd thought it would hurt too much if she caught a glimpse of Rob waiting outside to pick up Hayley. She hadn't expected that not seeing him would be equally painful.

The clock on the wall read five minutes past three. She moved quickly about the empty room, straightening chairs, checking that things were neatly stowed away. Grabbing her bag, she flicked off the classroom lights, shut the door, and hurried to her car.

Greg had asked her to meet him in the parking lot of a coffee shop in Upperville. The drive took longer than usual because she ended up behind a school bus. Oddly, she welcomed the delay caused by the frequent stops; the eagerness she'd thought would seize her at being so close to learning TM's identity was overshadowed by a heavy sense of loss.

The breakup with Rob was the immediate cause, but there was an additional reason. This week would mark the anniversary of her parents' deaths. Contemplating their last moments as her father's Cessna lost

altitude and plummeted toward the waters of the Chesapeake never got easier, and ever since finding her mother's journal, other thoughts had plagued her. Had her
dad been able to forgive her mother's betrayal? In turn,
had her mom regretted her actions or had she been
thinking only of TM as she met her death? And had she
even spared a thought for the teenage daughter she'd
come to despise?

For so long, Jade had told herself that discovering the
identity of TM would offer her some sort of emotional
closure. Now, however, she wondered whether it wouldn't
merely open the door to more anguish.

Greg was waiting by his car. Standing with one leg
crossed in front of the other, he was sipping coffee from
a paper cup and had his cellphone pressed to his ear.
Normally Jade would have been amused by how clev-
erly he managed to be invisible in plain sight. As it was,
she was simply relieved she didn't have to search for
him. The two aspirin she'd swallowed to combat her
headache were fighting a losing battle.

Before climbing out of the Porsche, she slipped her
sunglasses on. She needed protection—not so much from
the weak afternoon sun as from Greg's scrutiny.

Unfortunately, they weren't enough, for the first thing
Greg said was, "Are you all right?"

"Why shouldn't I be?" Ever so casually, she adjusted
the glasses a fraction higher on the bridge of her nose.
With a nod at his paper cup, she said, "So I take it we're
not meeting TM in the coffee shop?"

"No need to. We're going to meet him at his office. It's
right over there." He pointed across the parking lot to a
nondescript, low-slung building made of concrete, with
large windows that were tinted brown.

As they walked toward the office complex, Jade tried
to picture her beautiful and somewhat silly mother, a

woman who'd been entranced by finery and everything deluxe, in such a banal setting. Impossible.

She frowned. "Are you certain that this is the TM we're looking for? Obviously they wouldn't have met here, but I can't imagine Mom even wanting to be with a person who worked in such a drab place."

"Yeah, he's the one. I lucked out and managed to speak with him on the phone—his receptionist was out with the flu."

"How'd you find him? He's not one of the TMs on the list, is he?" No one from the list worked in Upperville, she recalled.

"No. When the list of possibles I gave you didn't pan out, I decided that my previous thinking was taking me down the wrong path and that the person we were looking for didn't necessarily come from your parents' social set or—in the case of Tony Myers, the stylist at True Beauty—that he was someone who provided the more obvious services for your mother. I also read your mother's journal again."

As always, the thought of the diary made Jade's insides clench as if she'd ingested Drano.

"But this time when I studied the entries, I made myself forget everything you'd told me, about how your father found the journal and your and your sisters' reactions to it. That allowed me to consider other ideas about who TM might have been to your mother."

They'd reached a short concrete walkway that was edged with rhododendrons. Suddenly unsure whether she truly wanted to go through with this, Jade came to a stop. Greg would understand. Hadn't he himself warned her against pursuing the search?

No, she'd come too far.

Spotting a large wooden sign positioned to the left of the walkway with a long row of names posted on it, she walked up to it. "I guess this is the moment I've been waiting for. What's his name anyway?"

"Tomasz Myszkiewicz."

The name eluded her after the first unexpected *sh* sound. "Excuse me?"

"He's right there. The third one down."

Jade looked where Greg was pointing and read *Dr. Tomasz Myszkiewicz*. Next to his name were some initials she couldn't identify and then the word *Psychologist*.

Such was Jade's continued state of shock that the details of the waiting room were reduced to a blur. She wasn't even sure if the buzzing noise she thought she heard was coming from a white-noise machine or from inside her head; her mind was spinning like a top.

They didn't wait long. Greg gave the receptionist their names, she picked up the phone, and within seconds they were ushered inside Dr. Myszkiewicz's office. Directly in front of Jade was a framed poster of a painting by Magritte: a man in a bowler hat and a red tie with a green apple floating in front of his face. Well, that was suitable, she thought. This situation was entirely surreal.

Ever since reading Tomasz Myszkiewicz's name, Jade's every expectation had been upended. Now, as she looked at the man who'd gotten up from a corner desk to greet them, hysterical laughter bubbled up inside her.

She couldn't believe she'd hired Greg Hammond. What a colossal failure he'd turned out to be. This man, this supposed TM, with his untrimmed gray beard and wire-rimmed glasses and a tan corduroy jacket, could never in a million years have been her mother's lover.

But just as she was about to drag Greg out of the office, with its two reclining leather chairs and matching ottomans, and tell him that he'd bungled the job big time, Dr. Myszkiewicz spoke.

"Miss Radcliffe? I'm Dr. Myszkiewicz." His voice held a trace of an accent, lending his baritone an element of the exotic. "This is far too late in coming, but I am terribly sorry for your loss. Your mother was an extraordinarily dynamic woman." He was studying her closely. "The resemblance is striking."

"So you actually knew my mother?" She sounded stiff and oddly defensive, but she was unable to make herself relax. "May I ask how?"

"Why, she was my patient, of course."

The buzzing inside Jade's head stopped, replaced by an utter blankness, like a heavy snowfall coating the world with inches of white. She couldn't think, could only hear the word *patient* echoing again and again.

"Why don't you sit down, Miss Radcliffe, Mr. Hammond?" he said, gesturing to a sofa. Tan colored, it matched his jacket. She chose the side where a large ficus tree stood. Greg took the other end. As Greg settled against the cushions, Jade felt his eyes on her, but for some reason she couldn't bring herself to meet his gaze, no matter how much silent support she might find there.

Dr. Myszkiewicz pulled a chair away from his desk and swiveled it to face them. "Mr. Hammond indicated that you had some questions about your mother for me."

Yes, and upon hearing that she had been his patient, the questions haunting Jade had grown exponentially. Where to begin? She hardly knew.

The hell with it, she thought. A psychologist—he was probably used to people blurting out stuff. "My mother kept a diary. In it she talked about a man called TM. He was her lover. Are you the TM she wrote about?"

He didn't appear shocked by the question. "Yes and no."

Like a volcano, sudden fury erupted inside her. She glared at him. "What in freakin' hell is that supposed to mean? My father found that diary. It tore him apart. So you damned well better be straight with me."

"Jade." Greg reached out and touched her arm—either to steady her or to warn her, she didn't know which. Didn't care either. Impatiently, she shook it off.

"Perhaps I should explain why your mother was seeing me."

"What an excellent idea. Though if you could avoid the wishy-washy double-talk, I'd be super-grateful."

He seemed unaffected by her sarcasm. "Your mother came to me for help with a number of issues that were causing her deep unhappiness."

Like how much she disliked her only child. Jade hated the idea of her mother ever thinking of her as an *issue*. But obviously in a masochistic mood, Jade needed to hear Dr. Myszkiewicz confirm it. "And I was one of them."

He inclined his head, his brown gaze regarding her steadily through the lenses of his glasses. "That's true in a sense, though I'd say her problems with you were just the most recent in a long succession of difficulties she had with women, in particular those she perceived as the sexual competition."

"I was only a kid—"

"No, Miss Radcliffe, you were not," he corrected. "You were an adolescent, and thus to your mother you changed from a sweet angel to a threat to her supremacy. If you think back, I believe you'll remember her behaving with much the same irrational aggression toward your half sisters. Of course, with Margot and Jordan—I do have their names right?"

At her mute nod, he continued. "The tensions in their relationships began much earlier, I suspect, because from the day she and your father wed, she viewed them as rivals for his love. In addition, there was no previous bond with either girl. There would have been a fair amount of hostility on their part too. After all, she was the stepmother, the interloper. With you, however, the anger and hostility, the constant warring, really began to dominate your relationship only when you reached your teenage years."

It was possible he was right. Although Jade remembered her mother's attitude as born overnight, with her suddenly exhibiting the full-fledged hostility of an archenemy, perhaps the antagonism had developed more slowly and she, wrapped in pubescent self-absorption, simply hadn't noticed.

"One of the reasons your mother came to me was to try to understand the feelings that were driving her anger toward you as well as toward other women—particularly young, attractive women. She wanted to learn how to control her aggression. As you might imagine, much of your mother's problem stemmed from her insecurities about her own appeal—"

"Mom insecure? No way. She was dazzling; she could wrap any male, aged thirteen to eighty-five, around her finger."

"Agreed. But that didn't prevent her insecurities from affecting her behavior. Her self-doubts had begun to have an impact on her marriage too. As she neared the age of forty, she began to obsess that she wouldn't be beautiful enough to keep your father's love and that, if she lost her looks, she would lose him. This only exacerbated the threat she perceived in you, Miss Radcliffe. She came to see you as a symbol of what she was terrified of losing—youth, beauty, and sexual promise."

"I . . ." Jade began, only to fall silent, too saddened by the portrait he'd painted to continue.

"This is difficult to absorb, I know," he said gently. "What you should remember, though, is that your mother came to me because she recognized the depth and severity of her problems and needed help. She saw that she was destroying her relationship with you and understood that if she continued to treat you as an enemy, she would lose not only you but possibly your father as well. She admitted that he didn't like the fights that had grown increasingly frequent between you and her. Her decision to seek professional help showed how much she loved both you and your father—not the reverse."

Overcome, Jade slumped forward on the sofa, covering her face with her hands as she wept for all the long years she'd been wrong about her mother. All that anger, all that misery, had been without cause.

At last she straightened, and Dr. Myszkiewicz passed her a box of Kleenex. Dabbing her eyes, she blew her nose and drew a shaky breath. "Here's what I don't understand. The diary Mom wrote. In it she seemed even more filled with hate for me than she was during the worst of our fights. And you were in the entries too. But you didn't come off as a shrink—a doctor," she corrected hurriedly. "She wrote as if you and she were lovers. And why did she call you TM and make it sound like you were some mysterious man, not a doctor?"

He sighed heavily. "Let me start with the easy question. From the start of our sessions, your mother decided that she would address me as TM because Myszkiewicz gave her quite a bit of difficulty."

For the first time since entering the office, Jade smiled.

"Calling me 'Doctor' was equally hard but for a different reason. Even though your mother sought me out, she felt deeply ambivalent—embarrassed, even—at consulting a psychologist. Linked to that was the firm belief that your father would be aghast to learn that she was seeing me. It's why she kept our sessions a secret, so your father would never know his wife was 'so screwed up.' Those were her words, not mine," he finished ruefully.

"Yeah, that sounds like something she'd have said."

They exchanged a slight smile.

"With respect to the diary, I'm afraid you have me to blame. I encouraged your mother to write down her feelings."

"But why would she need to do that when she was seeing you?" she asked, perplexed.

"Soon after we began treatment, your mother told me that when she was away from here she felt as if she couldn't control the emotions inside her, that they were causing her to lash out. I should tell you, Miss Radcliffe, that your mother's sense of being at the mercy of her feelings and impulses is a common reaction. Once a patient undergoing therapy begins to voice long-suppressed feelings, it can be incredibly difficult to then keep them in check.

"Thinking it might be beneficial, I suggested a journal or notebook where she could express her feelings and get them out of her system in a safe way. Unfortunately, I made the mistake of not anticipating that your mother would choose a diary in an eye-catching hue and that your father might read its contents."

"Mom liked flash."

His smile widened briefly. "Yes. As I'm sure you can imagine, she was quite the most exotic creature ever to grace this office complex. Now, as to what she wrote in the journal and the tone in which she wrote it, this is trickier for me to answer. Obviously I never read it. But from your and Mr. Hammond's remarks and what your father apparently concluded when he found it, it sounds as if your mother was undergoing a classic case of transference."

At her puzzled look, he explained, "By transference I mean that she was transferring some of her feelings about men onto me. She was probably feeling an immense gratitude that she had someone who was listening to her and understanding what she was going through and not judging her. That sense of euphoria could have caused her to write wildly exaggerated descriptions of me. I'm sure you recall that your mother had a flair for the dramatic. As for our having any kind of relationship other than a doctor-patient one, that is simply not the case. Even if I had been a very different, not to mention unethical, man, I don't believe I could have seduced her away from your father, no matter how deep her gratitude for me ran. She loved him."

"Do you think my dad died—" Jade had to take a deep breath to steady her voice, for the pain of her parents' deaths was now suddenly as fresh as if they had died that very day. "Do you think he died believing Mom was unfaithful? He and my brother-in-law Travis Maher fought over Mom a couple of weeks before the crash. Dad accused him of being her lover, so clearly he was haunted by the idea that there was another man." She made herself take another deep breath, but her voice trembled nonetheless when she asked, "What if, when their plane went down, he didn't know the truth?"

Dr. Myszkiewicz reached forward and squeezed her hand. "Here I can put your mind at ease. That positively was not the case."

Jade was somewhat taken aback by the unequivocal response. She'd been expecting a soothing but ultimately vague reply. "How can you be sure?"

"Because in the two sessions prior to their trip to interview a prospective trainer for Rosewood Farm, I'd made considerable progress in persuading your mother to tell your father about our work here. She'd sensed a distance in him—caused no doubt by his discovery of her journal. As she'd stopped writing regularly in it, she probably hadn't noticed its absence. I managed to convince her that opening up to your father about her problems and explaining that she was trying to solve them would help their relationship. She promised me she was going to talk to him while they were in New Jersey and away from Rosewood. I received a telephone call from her while they were on their way to the airport. She was crying—crying with happiness. She'd told your father everything. He was going to accompany her to our next scheduled session."

"Oh God!" Wrapping her arms about her middle, she rocked on the sofa. "Couldn't you have contacted me about her years ago? Do you know what I would have given to know any of this?" she cried.

"Actually, no, I couldn't have contacted you," he replied, his voice heavy with regret. "First of all, patient confidentiality would have prevented me. Then, too, even though you were your mother's next of kin, you were a minor when she and your father died. I very much wish, however, that I had been aware of your father's discovery of the journal. I might have found a way to contact your sisters and thus been able to clear up the misunderstanding. Unfortunately, that wasn't the case."

Jade thought she understood his position, but at the moment she was remembering the years spent struggling with her bitterness, confusion, and resentment. To learn that all the horrible things she'd come to believe about her mother were based on a gross mistake was as disorienting as what she'd felt that long-ago evening when she first opened the diary.

What alleviated her sorrow was the realization that, far from being hateful and faithless, her mother had been brave. She'd been trying to be a better person. She'd cared enough about being a mother and wife to confront what were evidently long-standing and deep-seated emotional problems. To take that difficult step required courage.

And thank God Mom had chosen to tell Dad about Dr. Tomasz Myszkiewicz. All her mom would have had to do was describe her therapist's somewhat fuddy-duddy appearance for her dad to understand that the doctor would be the last person her mother would choose as a lover. Having just experienced it herself, Jade knew the piercing relief her father would have felt at learning that his suspicions were false and his wife truly loved him.

At least when he died Dad had known the truth.

A memory, fresh and vivid, flashed in her mind. It was of Rob holding her after they'd made love and telling her of having arrested the drug runner. She remembered her fear at the thought of what might have happened to him had the runner drawn his gun, and she remembered his response. *You and I both know from experience that a life can end at any time.*

Gripped by urgency, Jade sprang from the sofa. "Excuse me, but I need to leave right now. There's someone I have to call."

JADE'S CELLPHONE was in her hand by the time she rushed out of Dr. Myszkiewicz's office and into the late-afternoon sun. She pressed the ON button, having turned the phone off earlier to avoid any interruption during her meeting with TM.

The phone came on with a message on the screen. Ted Guerra had called—twice—and he'd also left a voice mail.

When she listened to it, the principal's tone was brusque. "Jade, I need to speak with you. It's about an important matter. Please come to my office. I'll be here until five-thirty."

She glanced at the iPhone's clock. It was just twenty minutes past four now. She was amazed to realize she'd been talking to Dr. Myszkiewicz for only an hour. She scrolled through her address book until she reached Rob's home number and selected it.

Please answer, she thought, listening to the rings. Instead, the machine switched on, with Hayley's voice instructing her to speak after the beep.

Closing her eyes as a wave of disappointment washed over her, she hung up. She couldn't leave a message. Hayley would recognize her voice, and that would lead to awkward questions for Rob. She didn't have Rob's cell number in her contacts and there was no way she could bring herself to call the police station, not with the way things stood between Rob and her.

God, she'd been such an idiot to freeze him out. She'd try him again later. Hopefully she'd be able to fix things between them, repair the hurt she'd caused. She might as well drive back to school and deal with whatever Ted Guerra needed to see her about. Perhaps by then Rob would be home and picking up.

Jade's steps echoed in the now-deserted elementary school. But as she neared Ted Guerra's office, she saw that the door was open and a rectangle of light spilled onto the buffed linoleum floor. Knocking on the glass inset of the door, she called, "Hello? Ted, it's me, Jade. I got your message."

"Jade. Come in," came the reply.

Ted was behind his desk. He rose when she entered but didn't come around to greet her, and his expression lacked its customary friendliness. "Please take a seat."

"What's wrong, has something happened? Is it something to do with Eugene?" She tried to think of anything else that might be amiss but came up blank. Granted, she wasn't firing on all cylinders. It had been a hell of an afternoon, and she was exhausted.

He didn't answer her question, saying instead, "I had a visitor to my office this afternoon, Jade, who brought to my attention one of your activities in college, of which I had been previously unaware. I was told that you wrote a column for your school newspaper. After the meeting I checked the résumé you submitted to us. It says that you were on the school newspaper's staff, but there's no mention of your having penned a column. Is that because your column was devoted to the topic of sex?"

She'd guessed what was coming the second Ted pronounced the words *activities in college,* but still, when he finally asked about the specific nature of the column she'd written for two years, it felt like a brick had been slammed into her chest.

She was left stunned, unable to draw a breath.

It was happening again. Blair Hood was setting out to annihilate her, but this time with a single, lethal blow. She was going to be sacked from a job she loved and was pretty good at. Once this was in her personal file, it would be highly unlikely another school would ever hire her; she'd be lucky to get an interview.

That wasn't the only repercussion. As the scandal got out and word spread, and gossip distorted, there'd be parents who would rather see hell freeze over than enroll their children in her riding program.

But worst of all was what Rob would think of her. If he hadn't started to have doubts about whether there could be a future for them, this scandal would clinch it. Jade knew she wasn't exaggerating in dubbing it a scandal. She'd starred in enough of them in Warburg. Moreover, she knew exactly how fast word would spread in this small town. Her past sins would be resurrected and made even more lurid with each retelling. . . .

"Jade? I'd like an answer."

"Yes." Her voice came out a hoarse whisper. "I wrote a biweekly column. To label it a sex column, though, is a gross exaggeration. It was more an advice column—"

"An advice column pertaining to sex—"

"Sexual *relationships*," she retorted. "Sexual relationships between two individuals of the age of consent."

"Which by many would be considered an inappropriate topic for an elementary-school teacher to address."

"Only if they were uptight idiots," she said defensively. "Moreover, I adopted a pseudonym in order to keep my identity private. What I wrote for the college paper was intended for my peers and separate from my actions as Jade Radcliffe. You've yet to read a single piece I wrote and already you're condemning me, Ted."

"Believe me, I will read them." He rubbed the side of his face tiredly. "Listen, Jade. I'm not one of those uptight idiots, but I am this school's principal. I don't want to be having this fight with you. I like you, and you've been doing a fantastic job in the classroom, and I think you could have a great future as a teacher. But in my official capacity I have no choice but to report your college activities to the school board. They'll decide whether to allow you to continue to work in the classroom. If, after reading your articles, I can support you in good conscience, I'll do so fully. I promise you. Given the personalities involved, I believe there'll be a push to meet on the issue quickly. But until the board makes its decision, I'd like you to take a leave of absence. I've already arranged for a new substitute. Sue Wilson will contact you about your lesson plans."

As they had throughout Jade's past crises, her sisters gathered around her, offering their unwavering support. Jade hated that once again she had to watch Margot pace with the protective energy of a lioness and witness Jordan's quiet distress as she worked her rings around and around her slender fingers.

The weather reflected the gloomy mood inside the cottage. The temperature had plummeted and the wind howled angrily outside the windows. When she'd started shivering, Jordan had found an extra blanket for her in the linen closet, wrapped it around her, and then gone off to the kitchen to make some hot chocolate. Jade couldn't drink it, her stomach going queasy at the thought, but at least holding the cup warmed her hands.

"I was stupid," she said dully, so tired of repeating a worn truth. Even with her hands wrapped around the mug and her body enshrouded in sky-blue wool, she continued to shiver. "I should have known that the column made me ineligible to teach."

"Don't say that, Jade. You're a wonderful teacher. Everyone's been coming up to me and telling me so."

Too exhausted to hold it upright, she rested her head against the back of the sofa. "Jordan, that's because people *like* you. Of course they're going to say nice things to you—though you should prepare yourself for a long, dry spell in that regard. We're back to being Warburg's principal source for scuttlebutt. You know, one of the things that was going through my head when I drove to school was how wonderful it was that Mom was trying to fix her problems, because, after finding her diary, I'd felt a fair amount of contempt for her as a human being. Now I guess I'm the sole screwup of the family. Sorry." She closed her eyes.

Ugh. She was indulging in a major self-pity fest, but losing a job and a future with a great, upstanding, non-screwup of a guy could do that to a girl.

Margot's voice had her opening her eyes.

"There's nothing to apologize for, but I can tell you who's gonna be super-sorry: the Harrisons, the Hoods, and all their kin." Margot was still in full storm mode, taking yet another lap around the living room. Jade closed her eyes again so she wouldn't have to look; she was growing dizzy.

"Don't, Margot. I'm sick of trying to get back at them. Besides, it doesn't work; it only makes them more vicious. I'll be fine working at the farm as a full-time rider—if you'll put me on the payroll. It's too bad about the ponies, though."

She heard Margot stop in her tracks. "What do you mean, it's too bad about the ponies? And don't be silly, of course you can train and ride full-time—though that's not going to happen, because you are *not* going to be fired."

"Jade, you don't really intend to give up the ponies," Jordan said.

With a sigh, she opened her eyes and pulled the blanket around her tighter. "I'll have to if parents don't sign their kids up for lessons." At their blank looks, she shook her head. "You guys don't think that this latest mess of mine won't spill over into the riding program like so much toxic sludge? It will, and I can't shoulder the expense of maintaining four ponies."

"We'll help you—"

"No, you won't, Margot. The ponies are my responsibility and thus something I have to deal with."

"Some of your students will remain loyal, Jade. The Donovans, the Ferrises, and then there's Hayley. Rob—"

"I'm not seeing Rob anymore, so that's the only silver lining in this freakin' massive dark cloud right now. At least there won't be the awkwardness of having to interact with him."

"You broke up?" Margot asked, astonishment causing her jaw to go slack.

"Yeah."

"Oh, no, Jade. When did this happen?" Jordan sank down onto the sofa next to her.

"Yesterday. We had a fight." The room suddenly seemed even colder. Jade huddled miserably under the blanket. "I got a call from Greg Hammond, and when Rob asked me about him, I got defensive and angry. I knew if I told Rob that Greg was a PI I'd hired and what he was doing for me, he'd try to stop me. So I told Rob I didn't want to see him anymore, that we were finished. Who'd have known it was for the best?"

"Oh, Jade, I am so sorry." Jordan wrapped her arm about Jade's blanketed shoulder, squeezing it tight.

Margot came over and sat down on Jade's other side, making of their little group a sandwich of sisterly concern. "Call him and explain everything, sweetie."

"I can't do that."

"Jade, are you in love with him?" Jordan asked.

A big clump of pain abruptly took up residence in Jade's throat. "Yeah, I pretty much am, which is why

I'm *not* going to ruin his life by trying to get back into it. I don't want him or Hayley to be a part of the three-ring circus that's about to open in Warburg. Don't worry, I'll get over it."

Even with the comforting support of her sisters beside her, all Jade wanted was to pull the blanket over her head and cry until her tears were spent.

Not even Miriam's calling out as she opened the front door with a ringing "Hey, I've come to lend moral support" buoyed her spirits. Heading straight for her favorite armchair, Miriam dropped into it and propped her feet on the ottoman. "Okay, here's the plan. I say we storm the elementary school and stage a protest. This is a major attack on freedom of speech."

When Jade only managed a weak smile in response, Miriam said sadly, "This is so effin' unbelievably lousy, Jade. You've been working so hard with these kids. Since my first idea was a bust, how about I pull out the Whirley Popper and pop us some popcorn and we have a movie fest? We could start with *Titanic* and then move on to *Armageddon*. But maybe you're more in the mood for *Contagion*?"

"A movie fest. What a great idea!" Jordan exclaimed, jumping up from the sofa so quickly, she batted Jade on the head. "Oh, sorry, Jade! But, really, a night of movies and popcorn is just the thing to take your mind off your troubles. That, and some girlfriend talk. I'd stay, but I have to run in to town to pick up some groceries—"

"Gosh, I have to go too." Margot sprang to her feet as well. "Ellie needs rescuing from Georgiana and Will. I'll be back in a little while, though—maybe in time for the second movie?"

Jade had no idea why they were making such a production about leaving. They'd been with her from the moment she walked into the main barn, shell-shocked by the events of the day. They hadn't even had a chance to absorb everything she'd discovered about her mom and Dr. Myszkiewicz, because then she'd told them about Ted Guerra and started shaking and crying.

"Yeah, sure. Okay." She made an effort to inject some energy into her voice but from Margot's worried expression figured she'd failed.

"It'll be all right, Jade, I promise."

Where Margot got her fierce optimism, Jade hadn't a clue.

"Yeah, I know." That was a real whopper. Unlike Margot, Jade was a realist. She knew better than to think anything would be all right for a very long time.

At Emma's call of "All right, last set of clap push-ups in three, two, one—go!" Rob grunted and lowered himself from his plank position until his nose was an inch away from the gym's black rubber matting. Then he pushed himself off the ground as rapidly and high as possible, clapped his hands and put them back down, and lowered his body again. By the eighth rep of this final set, his muscles were straining, screaming, and sweat poured in rivulets from his shoulders and face. He continued, welcoming the fatigue, driving himself past the pain even when Scott, working out beside him, collapsed to the ground.

"Son of a bitch, Em, you're a sadist," Scott panted.

"Damn straight. Come on, you wuss, you have five more seconds. Go!"

With another curse, his brother heaved himself back into position and pulled off a few more push-ups while Emma counted down the seconds. "Okay, time's up."

Both Rob and Scott shifted back onto their hands and knees, gasping for breath. From above came Emma's evil chortle. "This is such a satisfying sight. I only wish Aaron were here to make the picture complete. The Cooper boys laid low." She snickered again.

Scott lifted his head. "You're skating on real thin ice, kid," he warned.

"Yeah, yeah." Their baby sister was unfazed. "So, you guys ready to call it quits and crawl on home? Or should we end the workout on a high note and finish with some burpees and then some Russian twists?"

"No way!" Scott exclaimed as Rob said, "Yeah, let's do it."

Scott frowned at him. "You're in a hell of a masochistic mood. What's up?"

He'd blown it with Jade, that's what.

Out loud he answered, "Nothing. Are we going to do these or what? I don't have time to waste. Hayley's gymnastics class ends in forty minutes."

Burpees were a vicious form of torture, an exercise that began with a squat, then a back thrust into a plank, followed by a push-up, a quick jump into a squat, and then a vertical jump before landing in the squat again—in order to start all over. The goal was to jump as high as possible and maintain a fast pace even as one's muscles began to feel as if they were filled with battery acid.

Driven by thoughts of Jade, Rob hardly felt them. Christ, what had happened in her cottage? Things had been going so well between them. Then that phone call had changed everything.

Had he really been too pushy in asking Jade who Greg was? He knew he'd been spurred by jealousy, but there was more to it than that. The shuttered look on Jade's face as she'd spoken to Greg, the way she'd shut Rob out completely when he'd asked her about the telephone call, had troubled Rob and made him press the issue.

Then suddenly she was telling him that they were over, as if the connection between them, the feelings he *knew* she had for him, were nothing.

Only a day had passed since she'd told him she didn't

want to see him anymore, but he missed her so damned much. A pain far greater than the one the burpees were causing sliced through him.

"Time's up," Emma said. "Nice job, Rob. Scott, take my advice and cut back on the stout at the Brass Horn."

"Shut up, Em. I think I'm gonna puke." Scott was bent over, his hands propped above his knees as he struggled to catch his breath.

"Save it for later. We still have the Russian twists," Rob said, before grabbing the bottom of his T-shirt to wipe the sweat off his face.

Scott raised his head and cast him a baleful glare. "Jesus, Rob, whatever's bugging you must be pretty major if it ain't out of your system—" He broke off as his gaze shifted. "Hallelujah," he said, straightening. "Much though it breaks my heart, my dearest siblings, I believe we've come to the end of our workout. Rob has visitors."

Rob dropped the hem of his damp shirt and looked where Scott's attention was focused, stiffening in surprise to see Margot and Jordan Radcliffe threading their way past the elliptical machines. They were definitely heading toward them.

"Well, that clears up today's mystery." Suddenly Scott sounded annoyingly happy.

"It certainly does," Emma agreed, and Rob would have been deaf not to catch the amusement in her voice too. "But it doesn't change the fact that you need to cut back on the stout, Scott, unless you want your butt kicked on a regular basis. And, Rob, you need to work on sharing. I had to hear it from Hayley about the recent pumpkin cream-cheese muffin purchase you made."

"Get lost, both of you," he replied absently. As Margot and Jordan crossed the expanse of the gym to where Emma had been training them, his mind was awhirl at their unexpected presence. Was it possible something had happened to Jade? The thought turned the sweat on his body to ice. Then he calmed, realizing that if Jade were injured, her sisters would be running, not striding, toward him.

It was far more likely they'd heard that Jade and he had fought and they were coming to skin him alive. Protective as they were, the Radcliffes might overlook the fact that *he* was the injured party.

"Hey, Rob, you ever heard the term *killjoy*?" Scott asked. "Come on, Em, let's go pick up Hayley. I've got a feeling Rob's going to need some emergency babysitting."

He looked at them. "Thanks, guys."

Emma smiled. "You're welcome. It's pizza night, right? We'll save you a couple of slices."

"You're the best, Em. You're okay too, Scott." He switched his focus back to Margot and Jordan, now within earshot.

"Ladies," he said neutrally.

"Rob," Margot returned, while Jordan said, "Hello, Scott; hello, Emma. We've come to speak to Rob about an important matter."

"Your uncle told us where to find you."

They'd already been to the police station. It must be serious.

"If you need privacy, you can go into the staff lounge," Emma offered. "Nobody uses it at this hour. I'll tell Mike at the desk so he knows."

Margot nodded. "Thank you. That might be best."

Rob scooped his sweatshirt off the mat flooring and tugged it over his head. He figured if they'd tracked him here, they'd prefer to talk to him now, sweat notwithstanding, rather than wait for him to shower and change. Besides, like a starving man, he hungered for word of Jade.

As Emma had predicted, the lounge was empty. Neither Rob nor Jade's sisters bothered to sit on the black upholstered sofa or the metal folding chairs positioned around the small circular table. Instead, Jordan said without preamble, "We wanted to talk to you before you heard the rumors that will soon be making the rounds, if they haven't started already. Jade may be fired from Warburg Elementary."

Nothing could have astounded him more. The notion was preposterous and miles from anything he expected to hear. "Are you kidding me? Why would she lose her job?"

"Because the Harrisons and the Hoods like nothing better than to drag the Radcliffe name through the mud, and Blair Hood in particular despises Jade. But, believe me, that's going to stop," Margot answered fiercely.

"What do the Harrisons or the Hoods have to do with her being fired? I know Christy Harrison was upset about Eugene getting stung at the orchard, but Jade did everything and more to ensure Eugene was all right. I don't think she left his side for a minute. They have absolutely no ground to stand on if they try to fire her."

Margot and Jordan exchanged a look.

"They now have more potentially explosive ammunition," Jordan said.

For a second Rob wondered whether they were referring to Jade and him. But to *fire* Jade because she and Rob had slept together would be completely over the top. He was a widower and she a single woman. So what if she happened to be his daughter's second-grade teacher—correction, Hayley's *substitute* teacher, hired only through Christmas.

He was damned if they were going to fire the woman he loved, just because the *timing* of his falling in love was awkward.

And, yeah, he'd fallen in love with Jade. Completely and absolutely. He knew the signs; the sick fear he'd experienced minutes ago at the thought that she might be injured was only one of many revealing beyond a doubt that Jade Radcliffe was in his heart, now and forever.

"What kind of ammunition do they have?" he asked.

"Jade wrote a column in college. It was an advice column, a sex-advice column."

Floored, he gaped at Margot. "Excuse me?"

Margot frowned at him. "It's not nearly as exotic as you think. More and more college papers have them. In my opinion they serve an important function in allowing the students to talk openly and responsibly with their peers about sex and relationships. But someone—and I'd bet every acre of Rosewood that it was Christy Harrison or Nonie—went to Ted Guerra and told him about Jade's column."

It was Rob's turn to frown. "Because he didn't know about it?"

"Right. Jade put down on her CV that she'd worked on the school paper but didn't specify that she'd written her own column." Margot broke off to drag her fingers through her hair in a gesture of frustration.

With a sigh, she continued, "Okay. *Maybe* Jade should have informed Ted Guerra about her advice column, but I can see how she would have thought that what she wrote was strictly part of her college experience and it was the fact that she carved out the time for a demanding extracurricular activity in her already loaded schedule that was significant. It's not as if she's teaching sex education to her class, for God's sake."

"What burns me is that Nonie and Christy and Pamela and Blair will make this into a referendum on Jade's morals," Jordan said.

"A real case of the pot calling the kettle black," Margot said scornfully.

"We brought this for you." Jordan slid her bag off her shoulder and opened it, then withdrew a manila envelope. "Inside are some of Jade's old articles. It's not everything she wrote, but it gives a good idea of the subjects she was addressing and how she handled them."

Handing him the packet, she said, "Rob, you're a parent in Jade's class and an important figure in our community. Could you please read these and, if you don't find them offensive or alarming, could we count on you to do what you can to help her?"

"To say she's devastated by this would be putting it mildly," Margot said. "You've seen firsthand how much she loves teaching, how good she is at it. Now not only is her future as a teacher in jeopardy, but so is her riding program. She can, of course, ride for Rosewood and show our horses in the ring and compete with them in cross-country events, but it would be such a terrible shame—a waste of her talents and a huge loss for the kids she could teach. It infuriates me that Nonie and Christy are willing to be so vindictive."

"So you really think the Harrisons are involved in this business?"

"Definitely," Margot said. "Jade saw Blair Hood—Nonie Harrison's niece—at the Brass Horn last weekend. Blair hasn't gotten past her high school hatred of Jade. And Nonie was livid at not being able to prevent Jade from being hired, and Christy has obviously decided to emulate her in-laws in all things bitchy."

"But Margot and I intend to make it very clear to the Harrisons as well as the Hoods that we've had enough. Their spiteful vendetta against Jade ends now." Jordan's usually serene face was a study in cold determination.

If half of what she and Margot were saying was correct, he could understand their attitude. He'd never been impressed by the Harrisons. Nevertheless, he was a cop.

"Whatever it is you're going to say—or do—to the Harrisons, should I be concerned as a keeper of the peace? Are we talking violence or anything illegal?"

"Rob, anyone who knows me will tell you that I am not an aggressive person," Jordan said. "But our next stop is Overlea, the Harrisons' house, where Nonie, Pamela, Christy, and Blair are doubtless gathered with their cells and phonebooks. And right now I'll admit to wanting desperately to charge in there and begin bloodying their noses. Hanks of hair might start flying too—"

Margot cut Jordan off before she could continue describing her bloodlust. "But luckily we won't have to go against Jordan's peaceful nature. We're simply going to drop by and share some key information that we've recently learned. We think Nonie and her sister, Pamela, will be quite interested to hear it. I have every confidence that once we've had our nice, friendly chat, they're going to reconsider pursuing their campaign to fire Jade."

"Yes," Jordan said. "We're expecting a major attitude adjustment. But if our friendly chat doesn't produce the desired effect, then you should prepare for Warburg to become a very exciting place, scandal-wise. And there may be bloodied noses too."

"Jade's been hurt too many times by these people."

"Okay." Rob gripped the manila envelope containing Jade's articles. A part of him wanted to tear it open and start reading. Another part was filled with trepidation. What if she'd gone too far and been outrageous? She'd been a college student, after all. If the material was inflammatory, would he be able to help her and convince other parents to support her?

"Thanks, Rob. We were hoping we could count on you. We'll be in touch after our visit to Overlea. And, to make your job easier, if we find ourselves forced to inflict bodily damage, we promise to turn ourselves in." Jordan smiled sweetly.

He couldn't help but laugh. "Thanks." But as the sisters turned to leave, Rob said, "Wait. Before you go, do you mind telling me who someone named Greg is and what's his relationship to Jade?"

Margot gave him a considering look. "If we don't, will you still help Jade?"

Rob was all too aware of how quick he'd been to judge and condemn Jade in the past and was determined not to repeat the mistake. Yes, he and Jade needed to repair the rift between them. But that would have to wait until he'd read her articles and figured out a way to help her. As far as he knew, none of the college-newspaper business had anything to do with this man named Greg.

It was time to follow his heart and trust his love for Jade.

"Of course I will," he said.

"Good answer." Margot smiled warmly. "And just so you know, Rob, I think you're a great man for her. But, for both your sakes, it'll be better if Jade explains about Greg Hammond herself."

Alone in the lounge, Rob sat down on the sofa. Flipping the envelope over, he fingered the flap and the metal clasp, hesitating. He was nervous, unsure of what he'd find inside.

Why? he asked himself. He already knew Jade. She was passionate and, yes, at times wild and reckless. But she was also incredibly smart and sensitive. He simply could not imagine her being less than forthright and honest when writing a column about sex.

He hoped that the Jade he knew—the Jade he'd fallen in love with—was going to shine through in the articles she'd penned.

Twenty-five minutes later, he sank back against the sofa. A broad smile lit his face. "Sweetheart," he whispered, "you are a miracle."

*   *   *

Rob knocked on Eric Drogan's door. Expecting him, his friend opened it immediately.

"Glad you got here so quickly. They'll be putting the paper to bed in an hour, so I'll have to write this editorial damned fast."

Following Eric past the living room and into his study, Rob handed him the envelope with Jade's articles. "After reading a couple of these, I think you'll have plenty to say."

Eric merely grunted, sank into an overstuffed chair in need of reupholstering, and picked up the first of the articles.

Leaving Eric to his reading, Rob wandered into the kitchen, where he called Emma to let her know he'd be home in time to tuck Hayley into bed. Then, grabbing two beers from the refrigerator, he opened them and headed back into the study.

Silently, he passed one to Eric, who took a slug, set the bottle by his sneakered foot, and resumed reading. Rob pushed aside an already messy pile of papers and books covering the sofa and sat down to wait.

His beer was only three-quarters finished when Eric looked up.

"Quite an interesting woman you've gotten involved with."

"Yeah. I think she may be one of a kind. So, can you do anything to help me sway public opinion in her favor?"

"I'll certainly do my best. Is she as good a teacher as she is a columnist?"

"She's fantastic. The kids in her class love her."

"Oh, well." Eric gave a philosophical shrug. "I was going to suggest that if the board votes against her, she can come work for me at the *Courier*. It would do Warburg a world of good to have a column like this. And it would definitely boost readership among our younger demographic." He drummed his fingers on the arm of the chair. "I suppose I can't deprive Hayley of her beloved teacher, but perhaps I can convince Jade to write a guest column? A monthly spot in the health-and-fitness section perhaps," he said, as much to himself as to Rob.

Rob grinned. "Give it a shot."

"I think I will. But first things first." Eric stood up, suddenly all business. "I have an editorial to write, so finish your beer and get the hell outta here."

Rob didn't need to be told twice. He wanted to get home and tuck Hayley into bed. If he hurried, he might even be able to read her a few pages from *Misty of Chincoteague,* then he had a long list of parents to call. The more people he reached tonight, the better chance he had of countering the effects of the Warburg gossip mill.

"I owe you, buddy," he said, shaking Eric's hand.

"Nope. This is a good cause. I'm glad to join the fight. Makes me remember what small-town newspapers are supposed to be about: informing and rallying the citizens. Let's talk tomorrow, after people have had a chance to digest my editorial."

Chapter ✣
TWENTY-FIVE

FOR JADE, the next day had a strangely off-kilter sense to it. Her weekday schedule was already ingrained, her alarm clock ringing early so she could tend to the ponies and then set out for school, always factoring in enough time for a quick dash into Braverman's to grab a coffee and muffin.

The first segment of the morning began as usual. She fed and watered the ponies at their normal hour, and when they'd finished their breakfast, she turned them out in the pasture so they could nibble on the short, dry grass and stretch their muscles and she could muck out their stalls with maximum efficiency.

Once the chores were completed, however, the morning loomed like a big empty desert she had to cross. It would, she knew, have been the perfect opportunity to hop into her Porsche and make a Braverman's run. But going into town would entail interacting with any number of people, something she couldn't face. In a place like Warburg, word spread fast. Some people—friends like Roger Braverman and George Rollins and the Steadmans and Stuart Wilde—would stick by her when they learned of her latest fiasco, but she didn't want to witness their consternation that once more she'd become the talk of the town.

Better to hunker down and cut off all ties to the outside world.

Needing something to occupy her so she wouldn't obsess about what was happening in her classroom, she crossed the courtyard and entered the main barn.

Thankfully, Andy and the guys were busy mucking out the stalls in the stallions' and broodmares' barns, so she had to muster fake good cheer only with Ned and Travis.

"Hi, guys, reporting for duty and raring to go," she said when she walked into what had been her father's office. It had changed remarkably little since his death, the notable exception being a second desk, where Margot had installed a Mac and a printer. While Dad had liked his cars and airplanes to be the very latest models, he would have fought tooth and nail over the invasion of a computer in his office when paper, pencil stubs, and ballpoint pens served well enough. "Morning, Miss Jade. Travis and I were just talking about you."

"All good, naturally." A lame joke, but at least she was trying.

Such was the pity level that both men ignored it. "Topher's vet should be emailing us the results of Carmen's exam, which means Topher will probably want to pick her up this afternoon. We thought you might like to give her a farewell workout so she's nice and mellow when we load her into the van," Travis said.

Ned had poured a cup of coffee for her. Passing it to her, he said, "Owen's real busy this week. He, Jesse, and Doug are starting work on that house in Upperville. He was wondering whether you could ride Cosmo for him today. And Valentine could use a good cross-country gallop. I don't want her getting stale in the ring."

At Ned's suggestion that she go out for a gallop, Jade felt some of her world return to order. She folded her arms across her chest and nodded agreeably.

"Brown Betty needs a workout too. Margot and Jordan are tied up with some lunch thing with a couple of other mothers. If you've got time before your lesson kids arrive, we thought that you might also hop on Griffin. If you want, Griffin could be your new project now that Carmen's going to a new barn," Travis added.

"I'm sure Andy would be happy to have you lend a hand exercising the stallions. But I'm guessing that list there will take you right through the early afternoon," Ned said.

Jade would bet that Ned wasn't simply guessing. He and Travis had probably devised a schedule that would allow her fifteen minutes between horses and end just in time to bring the ponies in from the pasture for lessons.

One reason why Travis and Ned were so close was that Travis, too, shared the belief that horses were the best cure for whatever ailed a person. As philosophies went, it was a pretty sound one, and she was grateful to them for compiling a list of horses for her to train.

She was also grateful and profoundly relieved that they weren't hovering anxiously over her. A single grandfatherly cluck of sympathy from Ned or a pat on the back from Travis and she'd have broken down and begun sobbing like a baby.

"That all sounds dandy." Going over to the coffee-maker, she poured herself a cup and tried not to think of the latte she wasn't drinking or the fact that this was first period and the kids would be sitting at their desks, writing in their journals. Had Sue Wilson, the substitute Ted Guerra had arranged to take Jade's place, given them a good prompt? Was Eugene back at school now that she'd been banned? She hoped so, for his sake. Eugene liked school. Determined not to think of Hayley or Rob, she chugged her coffee and set her empty mug by the machine.

"I'll ride Carmen first and then take Valentine out while the morning's fine."

* * *

Testing Ned and Travis's philosophy to the limits, Jade did find a certain peace in the day's riding, but it was hard won. Whenever she forgot to consciously block him from her mind, Rob suddenly appeared. A police officer in touch with the town's goings-on, he would have heard the news by now.

Was he disgusted with her, back to regarding her as some sort of Jezebel who would taint the morals of innocents? Would he cancel Hayley's riding lessons until he could arrange for her to enroll in a program with another instructor?

As the day wore on, her anxiety mounted. She began to wonder who in addition to Hayley might not show up for the afternoon lesson. Though her cell claimed its battery was fully charged, it was as silent as a tomb. No texts, no voice mails, nothing. Surely the fact that her cellphone hadn't rung once since she'd slipped it in her vest pocket was a sign she'd become an outcast.

Luckily, she wasn't in the saddle when the phone did finally ring. The sound of it had her jumping like a marionette in one of Olivia and Georgiana's theatricals. She'd have spooked her mount for sure. As the phone pealed, her usual coordination abandoned her. She fumbled the soft brush she'd been using on Brown Betty; it fell, bouncing on the concrete floor beside the mare's hoof. She made an equal hash of digging the phone from her pocket. When her fingers finally pressed the ANSWER key, she was breathless. How much more pathetic could she get?

"Hello?"

"Jade? Ted Guerra here."

"Oh, hi, Ted." She felt so awkward.

"I'm calling to bring you up to speed on the events that, as I predicted, have moved . . . well, er, speedily. . . ."

Okay, she thought, she wasn't the only one feeling awkward. The knowledge didn't make her any happier.

Ted's awkwardness was because of the difficult position she'd put him in.

"After you and I met yesterday, one of the more active board members contacted me, insisting that I call an emergency meeting to decide whether you'll be able to retain your position at Warburg Elementary."

"An emergency session?" Surely that boded ill for her prospects. There was no need for him to identify the "active" school-board member. Witch Harrison flew mighty fast on her broomstick.

"We'll be meeting tomorrow afternoon at three-thirty P.M. It will be a closed session, meaning that only board members are permitted to attend. But of course you can come—"

"No—no. I'd just as soon not attend." She wasn't a chicken; she'd simply rather face a firing squad and be riddled with bullets and die than face one where she had to live with the wounds and remember the faces of her attackers.

"Yes, well, the discussion at the meeting is bound to be rather heated, especially now that the *Warburg Courier* has jumped into the fray. I certainly would love to know how they got a hold of the story so fast," he added.

The *Courier* had written about her?

Oh God, she thought. Had the Harrisons not trusted in their own power to spread the scuttlebutt and decided to up the destruction quotient tenfold by calling the town newspaper and tipping them off about her own journalistic efforts? Funny, but she'd have thought that Nonie and Christy would prefer knowing they'd *personally* caused her ruin.

Ted Guerra cleared his throat. "But, Jade, I read some of your pieces, and I plan to fight for you. I've forwarded copies to the board members in the hope that others will see what I have—there is nothing objectionable in the things you wrote. Indeed, they're commendable. Your only mistake was in not alerting us about your advice column so that we could deal with any ramifications."

"I—" Emotion choked her. "I'm so sorry, Ted. I didn't think."

"Let's hope I can sway the other board members. I've got to go. There's a lot to be done before tomorrow's meeting."

Disconnecting, Jade glanced at the clock on her phone. By her estimate, in roughly twenty-eight hours she'd know just how much of her life lay in ruins.

It turned out her estimate was wrong.

She learned exactly how great a loss she'd suffered a mere two hours later, when Hayley didn't appear for her lesson. With each minute that ticked by without a brown-eyed, pigtailed girl with a smile like her dad's, Jade's heart constricted. Not even the chatter of Jenny Ferris, Samantha Nicholls, Mack Reynolds, and Callie and Jane Donovan as they groomed the dusty ponies could ease it.

So now she knew beyond a doubt. Mechanically, she helped adjust saddle pads and saddles and eased bits and bridles onto ponies' heads for bodies too short to reach.

She'd broken things off with Rob, and now he had made it clear that the split was permanent. Though she should have guessed it, at the very least anticipated it, *knowing* that Rob wished to end the affair was devastating. It made her realize how much she'd been hoping that things weren't truly over between them, that she'd be able to get him back.

But her foolish mistakes had cost her what mattered most.

Rob was on duty when the school nurse contacted him. Hayley had a sore throat and wished to come home. He swung by the school in his patrol car, collected a wan Hayley, and drove to his parents' house. Luckily, his mother was free to look after her. While she prepared a small bowl of vanilla ice cream to soothe Hayley's throat, he carried his little girl upstairs to what had been his old bedroom but was now hers whenever she visited. A large herd of plastic ponies and horses had edged out the baseball figurines that stood on the built-in shelves.

After checking that she was comfortably settled in the twin bed with daisy-print sheets and that she had a book and some pens and drawing paper to occupy her, he brushed his lips over her forehead and got her to promise that she'd let Grammy know immediately if she started to feel worse.

Just as he was bestowing a second kiss, a call came through on his radio for all available units to proceed to a crash site at the edge of town.

He was the first to arrive at a scene marked by shattered glass, twisted and crumpled metal, and death. The horrific accident had been caused by an elderly driver who, perhaps through inattention or perhaps temporarily blinded by the angle of the afternoon sun, hadn't seen the red light at the intersection he was crossing.

He had run through the light at full speed, straight into the path of an eighteen-wheeler that was cruising through its green light at fifty miles an hour.

Even had the truck driver been able to react, physics was against him. The sheer weight of the truck and its speed made the collision unavoidable. The truck had slammed into the passenger side of the car, killing both passengers: the elderly man's wife of fifty-five years and his sister-in-law, who'd been seated in the back but was wearing no safety belt. The force of the impact had sent her flying out of the car to land twenty feet away. Her broken body lay in a pool of blood.

The elderly driver, though critically injured, had been conscious but unable to answer basic questions. Given the man's age and the severity of his injuries, Rob wasn't sure the driver would survive the ambulance trip. Had the man known about the deaths he'd caused, he probably wouldn't wish to.

The scene would have been gruesome enough if those were the only casualties. They weren't. The ambulances had three others to transport to the hospital: the truck driver, and the drivers of two other vehicles that couldn't avoid colliding with the wreck. At least these others would live to see another day.

The wreckage took hours to clear, by which time rush hour had begun, turning the highway into a massive traffic jam.

As the first officer on the scene, it fell to Rob to file the accident report. Providing as full and detailed a description as possible was laborious but essential, as insurance companies and possibly law courts would be involved.

When at last Rob returned to his parents', it was past seven. To Rob, it seemed as if days rather than hours had passed since he'd seen his daughter. Exhausted as he was, his spirits lifted when Hayley rushed to greet him with a smile. "Hi, Daddy!"

"Hi, sweetheart." He hugged her tight. "How's the throat? Better?"

Hayley nodded.

"Hayley's definitely feeling perkier, though her throat still looks a little too red for my liking," his mother told him when he and Hayley went into the kitchen. "We had a nice, quiet afternoon. She read some of her book and drew some pictures for me and a fine one of Dexter that she's going to give to Scott. Your father played go fish with her. Then we had chicken soup with noodles for dinner."

"Do you want some, Rob?" his father asked, coming

into the kitchen from the den, where Rob could hear the sound of the TV.

"No, I'm good, thanks. We should head home."

"Saw the accident on the news. Tragic sight."

Rob nodded. "Yeah. The husband's still alive though."

"You look beat, son."

At his father's comment his mother's gaze sharpened with concern. "Hayley, you run upstairs now and put your things in your school bag. And don't forget the card you made for Miss Radcliffe. I think you left it on the desk."

Oh, Jesus, Rob thought, only then realizing he'd neglected to contact Jade about Hayley missing her riding lesson. The wreck had demanded all his attention.

His first thought was to call her. Just as quickly, he rejected the idea. He didn't want to talk to her on the phone. He wanted to see her face and those remarkable green eyes that shone with such intelligence. He wanted to see her mouth curve into a smile and feel its warmth penetrate him, banishing the stark horror of the day.

He ached to hold her again.

But his father was right: He was beat, emotionally drained from witnessing such a grisly crash scene and being unable to do more than help load bodies into ambulances and clear the wreckage. He'd wait to see Jade until tomorrow, when the waste and the senselessness of those deaths weren't weighing him down.

The sound of footsteps rushing about overhead reminded him of yet another reason why he couldn't see Jade tonight. He wasn't going to risk Hayley's throat taking a turn for the worse. She needed a good night's sleep so her body could fight this thing.

"Rob, I want to tell you something before Hayley comes down. I don't know whether you heard, but an emergency school-board meeting has been scheduled for tomorrow afternoon."

He looked at his mother in surprise. "That soon?" The second after he put Hayley to bed, he'd go through the school directory and see who else he could call to get their names onto the petition Maryanne Ferris had drawn up.

"Yes. Word has it Nonie Harrison put the thumb-screws on Ted Guerra. Ellen Petras overheard her crowing about it late this afternoon to one of her friends at Anderson's Gourmet Shop. Nonie was buying celebratory caviar. Silly, spiteful woman. She could do so much good, and instead this is where she puts her energy."

His mother would likely have continued in that vein, but Hayley cantered into the kitchen, a folded drawing in her outstretched hand. "Want to see the card I made for Miss Radcliffe, Daddy?"

"You bet." The folded cover showed brightly colored green grass and horses of all different colors and sizes grazing on it. He smiled. "She'll like this drawing a lot."

"And I wrote inside it, telling her that I missed her today. Do you think she'll be back at school tomorrow, Daddy?"

"Not sure about that, but if she isn't, do you want to go by Rosewood and give this card to her?"

Hayley's eyes widened. "Can we?" Her voice was a mix of astonishment and eagerness.

"Yeah, I think we ought to, because it will make her happy."

"What a lovely idea, Rob," his mother said, beaming.

Jade had succeeded in keeping it together during the riding lesson. She might not have managed the same feat when the kids were picked up by their parents were it not for Margot and Jordan.

With their usual unerring instinct, her sisters drew the parents' attention away from Jade by chatting them up. Margot even went the extra mile by talking about her next modeling gig, a subject of irresistible fascination for many of them. They left with their budding equestrians in tow without Jade having had to answer a single embarrassing question.

Once the ponies were fed and watered, however, whatever can-do spirit she'd mustered during the day evaporated into thin air.

She declined Miriam's invitation to go to a yoga class. Then Stuart called to invite her to Roxie's to bowl until her mind was clear. Knowing that might mean she would be bowling until the end of time, Jade gave Stuart a "thanks but no" too.

With his seemingly endless goodwill, Stuart said he understood. Maybe later in the week she'd be feeling up to a match. Before hanging up, he told her that he would be at the big house early in the morning to accompany her, Jordan, and Margot to the family's cemetery, and she had cringed with self-loathing. She'd managed to forget the anniversary of her parents' death.

"I can't believe I forgot the date. Some daughter I am."

"Jade, stop being so hard on yourself. You didn't actually forget it," Margot said.

"It's not as if you don't have a lot on your mind right now," Jordan added. She and Margot had invited themselves for a sisters' night at the cottage, acting as if this was some long-standing tradition of theirs.

Jade couldn't exactly kick them out. First, she knew they would simply ignore her, and second, Jordan had brought over a roast chicken and a huge bowlful of mashed potatoes—the ultimate in comfort food. Even Margot was eating—with far more relish than Jade was.

They'd opted to sit in the living room around the coffee table because, as Margot pointed out, it was easier for Jade to curl up in a ball of misery on the sofa than at the table. A comment that had Jade glaring at her. So much for sisterly compassion.

Watching Margot gobble her mashed potatoes with the enthusiasm of a lumberjack was darned irritating too. Jade put her own plate down on the coffee table and barely resisted curling up in a ball of misery.

With a baleful glance at her sisters, she said, as if apropos of nothing, "I'm thinking of asking Travis for Steve Sheppard's number in Long Island, so I can call him and find out if he knows of anyone up there who's looking for a professional rider."

Margot took her time drawing her fork from her mouth. "Interesting," she said mildly. "Why would you want to find that out from Steve? These potatoes are unbelievable, Jordan."

"It's the butter. She uses sticks and sticks of it," Jade said sadistically. "And I'd like to know because I've decided I'd enjoy working up there. Long Island's cool." And no one knew her there.

Margot's eyes had narrowed at her crack about the butter, but surprisingly her tone remained mild. "I suppose you could ask, but it'd be kind of sad to go away precisely when so much is coming up with Miriam's wedding."

"Jade, how will you organize her bridal shower? As her maid of honor you have a key role that will only grow as the big day approaches," Jordan pointed out.

"Fine, forget it," she muttered. Of course she couldn't abandon her best friend at this crucial time. She'd leave after Miriam and Andy's wedding. "I'd simply like to be someplace where the name Jade Radcliffe means absolutely nothing."

Because she might start crying, she didn't add that even more she longed to be miles away from the man with whom she'd fallen in love and who didn't love her back. She drew her knees up and hugged them to her chest—a defiant ball of misery.

"How about you wait until after tomorrow's meeting before you start gassing up the car, sweetie?"

"Easy for you to say, Margot. Your name's not being dragged through the mud." Being the bitch of the century was a great way to keep the tears at bay, she decided.

Her sisters exchanged a quick glance—probably one of silent commiseration at having opted to spend an evening with their dismal shrew of a sister.

"Things might turn out better than you think." At Jade's raised brows, Margot shrugged. "Just saying."

"Yes, you never know how these school-board meetings will go," Jordan said. "I would stop worrying so much."

How could they be so incredibly casual about this? she thought, glowering at them. "I can't help thinking that you two aren't nearly as concerned as you might be about this situation. When both of you were having major life crises, I was a whole lot nicer to you—"

Margot snorted. Loudly and inelegantly. "Oh, please!"

"Well, maybe not to *you,* but I was really nice to Jordan!"

She didn't know what triggered it—Margot's amused look, Jordan's raised brows, or the outraged pitch of her own voice—but all of a sudden the three of them were laughing. Great whooping guffaws of laughter. Then, as if a switch had been flicked, her laughter turned to wrenching sobs. Just as quickly, Margot and Jordan were there, wrapping their arms about her.

"God, how could I have screwed things up with Rob so badly?"

"Jade, honey, you have to have faith. Faith in yourself and faith in Rob."

"Did you, Jordan? Did you believe things would work out between you and Owen?" she asked.

"Well, not always," Jordan admitted.

"Everyone has doubts at times," Margot said.

"But that's where the all-important faith comes into play," Jordan continued. "You have to believe in the goodness and authenticity of the person you love. I've never regretted putting my trust in Owen."

She'd blown it already, Jade realized. Instead of relying on faith and trust and telling Rob about having hired Greg Hammond to find TM, she'd made him think she didn't care about their relationship, that she was a quitter, crying off at the first obstacle they encountered.

And she was different from her sisters. With Rob and her, it wasn't so much a question of whether she possessed that precious faith in him but whether he could see any good in her.

"No," she said, answering the question out loud. "I've missed my chance with him. It's over."

Jordan shook her head. "No, it's not. Rob's a good man. He's—"

Jade couldn't bear to hear anymore. "Thanks, Jordan, but I already know how great he is, and, frankly, it only serves to reinforce my argument," she said wearily. "I'm going to bed. I'll see you tomorrow."

Rob left Hayley snug in her bed upstairs, her arm curled about a plush teddy bear and her lids already heavy with sleep, and went downstairs to the kitchen. The red light on the answering machine was flashing. Pressing the PLAY button, he grabbed a beer and the two remaining slices of pizza from the fridge and, placing the pizza in the microwave to zap it, listened as the first message came on.

"Rob? Maryanne here. I've got fifty signatures so far from parents. I'm going to the bookstore and the supermarket tomorrow and should be able to round up quite a few more. Call me so we can figure out who else we should approach."

Fifty wasn't bad, he thought, taking a long pull of his Stella. Though twice that number would be even better. They didn't have a lot of time before tomorrow afternoon. He could definitely get everyone at Steadman's Saddle Shop to put their names on the petition for Jade. Then there was Braverman's. Both did a lot of business. . . .

A second voice sounded, cutting into his thoughts. "Good news, buddy. We're getting a flood of emails in to the *Courier* about my editorial. Damned if this isn't turning out to be fun. Call me back."

Another voice filled the kitchen. "Hi, it's Jordan Radcliffe Gage. I'm pleased to report that Margot and I had a very civilized conversation with our good friends yesterday. Noses remain intact."

He grinned. This was definitely good news. He hoped that, between Eric's editorial piece, Margot and Jordan's "friendly" chat with Nonie Harrison and Pamela Hood, and his and Maryanne's growing petition, Jade would be back teaching at Warburg Elementary this very week.

And tomorrow, after he handed the petition to Ted Guerra to present to the school-board members, he and Hayley would drive over to Rosewood. And Rob was going to do whatever it took to get Jade back in his life forever.

Chapter ✗
TWENTY-SIX

GARBED IN heavy sweaters, jackets, and shawls, they walked in silence up the hill; overhead, gray clouds chased one another, urged on by capricious gusts of wind.

The climbing roses that grew along the fence were still in bloom. The pale-pink blooms against the weathered gray of the wood railings and the moss creeping over the aged headstones gave the family plot a haunting, romantic beauty. With Ned leading the group, they passed single file through the rickety wooden gate.

Jade looked at the faces of her family, blood-born and extended—from Margot and Jordan, to Travis and Owen and Ned, to Tito, Felix, Andy, Miriam, and Patrick and Ellie Banner, and finally to Stuart Wilde—who had formed a quiet circle around the three most recent graves, and she thought about how much she loved them.

Lowering her gaze to the headstone before her, she read the inscription: *Nicole Warren Radcliffe, Beloved Wife and Mother.*

Too often when she'd come to this spot, the carved words on her mother's headstone had struck her as a travesty. No longer.

On this bleak, blustery morning, with Jordan and Margot flanking her and Stuart Wilde's strong voice offering comfort from the Gospel of John, a new sensation filled her, one of simple and profound loss.

Gone was the bitterness that had festered inside her for so long.

The reading drew to a close and they bowed their heads in either prayer or remembrance, and Jade found herself filling the emptiness in her heart with a silent whisper. *I love you, Mom, and I'm so sorry I didn't believe in you. Please, wherever you are, know how much I admire what you were trying to do for yourself, me, and Dad.*

There really wasn't anything more important to say than that, she decided. The lesson she'd learned from her mother's attempt to address her problems was one that she needed to apply to the living.

With the workday ahead, none of them could linger in the cemetery. The circle broke, but everyone paused to say a word of thanks to Stuart Wilde. Jade was the last. "That was lovely, Stuart."

"It was a pleasure, my dear. Your family means a great deal to me."

"Well, you are one of us."

"An honor that leaves me humbled." He fell into step beside her, the two of them bringing up the rear of the snaking line as everyone made their way back down the hill to the glorious old house and barns below.

"I'd have thought you realized that we consider you part of the family, Stuart. Jordan doesn't bake her lemon cake for just anybody, you know."

Stuart turned pink as he smiled. "Now I'm not simply honored but gratified." Turning serious, he continued, "So, Jade, may I speak not only as an old friend but as a great-uncle too? Are you all right? Are you holding up?"

"Yes—at least with regard to Mom. I never realized how much anger and resentment was still inside me, even after all these years. It's a relief to miss her again, the way I did in those early days before I found the diary. Actually, and you probably understand this better than anybody, Stuart, I want to say my grief is purer somehow. It's no longer mixed with confusion or hurt, because I finally understand the roots of her behavior."

"And the other?" he asked gently.

They knew each other well. Stuart didn't need to spell out the entire question for her to identify what he was alluding to.

A gust of cold wind sliced at the layers of wool she wore. Shoving her hands deep in her jacket pockets, she smiled sadly. "Ah, well, all will be revealed in a matter of hours, right? High drama in Warburg. It might get ugly," she admitted. "But at least I've grown up enough to avoid the typical self-destructive behavior I resorted to in the past. Rest assured, I will *not* be calling my best frenemy Blair to suggest we go barhopping. In fact, I will avoid any activity that might land me in the Warburg police station, which would result in my not being able to pass go and collect my two hundred dollars. More than that I cannot promise."

"These are all admirable goals. Would you like some company this afternoon while they're voting on your fate?"

She hooked an arm about his, squeezing the sleeve of his green herringbone jacket. This man had kept her company through some of her worst moments, sometimes talking but more often enduring her stubborn adolescent silences with unwavering patience and kindness.

"Thank you for the offer, Stuart. But as I don't have a riding lesson to teach today and Margot and Jordan kept me company yesterday evening, I'm dragooning Ned into taking the littlest clan members to the Shake Shack with me. The goal is to see how much ice cream we can consume in one sitting. I imagine by the time we're finished, Georgie, Will, and Neddy will be so buzzed on sugar, I'll be forced to run laps with them around the property. Then I plan to collapse on my sofa and reflect on my sins until my cellphone rings with news of my fate. I'd invite you along to the Shack, but I think Ned is looking forward to some quality time with the little ones. He's especially proud that he and Neddy share a favorite flavor—strawberry."

"I quite understand. They're fine children and lucky to have such a terrific aunt. Everyone at Rosewood is so happy to have you back where you belong," he said, smiling.

Jade, however, was familiar with her canny friend's ways. He'd guessed that she was thinking of leaving Warburg.

Best to distract him before he broached the topic openly. "Did I tell you that Jordan's been experimenting with a chocolate, walnut, and pear crostata? It's a pretty scrumptious combination. You might even call it divine. I think she mentioned baking one so that you could taste test the latest version."

There were perks to living in a small town. Rob didn't even have to make the rounds of the station to find someone to fill in for him so he could meet with Mary-anne Ferris and take their petition to Ted Guerra before the school-board meeting convened. One of his fellow officers, Tory Bryant, approached him.

"I read in the *Courier* about the flak Hayley's teacher's been getting," she said. "A shame. We need young people to be informed and responsible, not ignorant. If she got kids to remember to put on a condom before having sex, we should be giving her an award, not firing her. Anyway, I told the chief I'd be happy to take the last hour of your shift this afternoon."

When he arrived at the school, Maryanne Ferris was waiting in the school lobby. "Hi, Rob. I've got the peti-tion here." She handed him a stapled sheaf of papers filled with names, addresses, and signatures. "One hundred and eighteen names!" Maryanne said triumphantly. "Ted's in his office."

As the school-board meeting was set for 3:30 P.M., Rob knew he and Maryanne had only a few minutes to make a pitch for Jade.

Handing Ted the petition, Rob said, "Ted, you know I had certain reservations about Jade Radcliffe when the school year started. They were completely misguided. I've seen firsthand what a wonderful teacher she is. You don't want to lose someone this good who obviously loves what she's doing."

"I agree and, as I've told Jade, I intend to fight for her." He paused to flip through the petition. "You've gathered an impressive number of signatures here. This may help convince any board members still sitting on the fence. Thank you, Maryanne, Rob, for making this effort on her behalf."

"We want to do everything we can to keep her as our children's teacher. Do you think the board will actually vote against her when it's clear so many parents and people in the community support her? Has anyone on the board even considered how disruptive and stressful it will be for the children? They've grown so attached to her," Maryanne said.

"That's definitely an argument I'm going to make. Judy Altmann, the school-board president, will be stressing what a superb job Jade has done and that her abilities as a teacher are unquestioned. The challenge will be to convince certain board members that what Jade wrote in college has no relevance in determining her fitness as a second-grade teacher. It helps that people have been talking nonstop about Eric Drogan's editorial supporting Jade. His was truly the voice of reason. Do we want young people to be informed about sex and sexuality through the intelligent writing of their peers, or do we want them turning to the distorted world of reality TV or Internet sites for their information? It's an important question, and I'm glad people in our community are discussing it." Ted picked up the folder on his desk and slipped the petition inside it. "But, unfortunately, there are some who are simply going to focus on the fact that Jade wrote about *sex* and consider it grounds for immediate dismissal." He checked his watch. "Well, our conversation has served as an excellent warm-up. I feel more than ready for the next hour or so of head-butting. I'll put the petition in Judy's hands as soon as I see her."

Rob extended his hand. "Good luck, Ted."

"Thanks," Ted said, shaking it. "I'll need it. Certain of our school-board members' heads are awfully thick."

Rob hoped that Jordan and Margot's conversation with Nonie Harrison had packed enough dynamite to make a lasting impression.

Hayley's first words when he picked her up in the classroom were, "Can we go see Miss Radcliffe, Daddy?"

"Absolutely. You hungry, sweetheart?"

"Yeah. Maybe we could stop at Braverman's on the way. We could pick something up for Miss Radcliffe too. She really liked that pumpkin muffin. You could give her that and I could give her the card I made."

"An excellent idea, Hayley." He ruffled her hair. "So, you have all your stuff? How was school?"

She hefted her book bag and let it drop against the beige-flecked linoleum floor, its thud proof that she did indeed have all her stuff. "It was okay."

"*Okay*"? This from a child who bubbled with enthusiasm when she described the projects Jade had devised for the class or repeated the funny things Jade had said? Nothing would be sadder than if the remainder of Hayley's fall became a string of "okay" days.

Pushing open the school door, he paused, his eyes widening in surprise. A crowd had gathered on the front steps, a crowd composed of many of the parents whom Rob had contacted about signing the petition. He spotted Eric Drogan too. Next to him stood a young woman wielding a camera with a telephoto lens, obviously one of Eric's staff photographers.

Eric must have decided the afternoon's school-board meeting warranted full coverage in the *Warburg Courier*.

Busy scanning the crowd himself, Eric saw Rob and Hayley. He flashed Rob a happy grin as he gave a thumbs-up sign.

Rob waved back. Just then there was a shift in the crowd, and two figures stepped into his line of vision. Jordan and Margot Radcliffe were waiting with other parents from the elementary school, but instead of exchanging idle chitchat, their attention was fixed on the board members who'd begun to arrive and who were climbing the stone steps to the school entrance.

"Daddy?" Hayley tugged his hand. "Why are all these people here?"

"There's an important meeting today and they want to know what's going to happen. Hey, do you see Mrs. Gage and Ms. Radcliffe, Miss Radcliffe's sisters, standing over there? Let's go say hi to them."

"Okay."

Margot was the one who noticed their approach. "Hi, Hayley, Rob."

Jordan turned. "Hello, Hayley."

"Hayley, we missed you yesterday," Margot said pointedly. She'd gone back to watching the board members' progress on the steps, but Rob had no need to see her expression to know her protective instincts were in the red zone.

Understandable, he thought. Nevertheless, Margot

Radcliffe needed to recognize a few facts, the first being that he was no pushover.

"Hayley had to leave school in the middle of the day with a bad sore throat, and I spent the remainder of it helping clear the car crash at the intersection of Routes 50 and 626."

At his explanation Margot turned back, remorse in her expression. "I'm so sorry. The photos in the paper were terrible. It's only that Jade's especially vulnerable right now."

"Hayley and I are going to see her, right after we pick up a snack for Hayley and a muffin for Jade at Braverman's."

Jordan nodded her approval. "She'll like that—"

"Very much." Margot's smile made it clear he was back in favor.

"I made Miss Radcliffe a card yesterday," Hayley offered shyly.

"That she will absolutely love, Hayley," Margot said.

Then Jordan spoke, her voice low and urgent. "She's here, Margot."

Rob looked. There, coming up the sidewalk, was Nonie Harrison, dressed in a gray skirt that screamed *power suit* and thus was a little over the top for an elementary-school-board meeting. Fascinated as he was by the sight of the woman determined to destroy Jade's reputation, Rob's attention abruptly shifted back to Margot. He blinked in awe.

Without a wardrobe change or the help of some makeup professional, Margot had suddenly morphed from a concerned sister into the supermodel whose face and body had earned millions in front of the camera and on the catwalk. All it seemed to involve was a straightening of the shoulders, an angling of the head, and a smile that was as powerful as the sun. She stood out among the sea of faces.

Nonie wouldn't be able to miss her. And he bet that, for all her beauty, Margot would cast cold fear into Nonie Harrison's heart.

Rob noticed that the photographer, probably following Eric's instructions, had moved closer to where they stood. He could hear the whir of the camera's shutter capturing the other school-board members as they mounted the steps of the building. Most nodded pleasantly at the crowd of parents; some exchanged a few words with friends. All tried for an attractive smile for the camera.

Except for Nonie Harrison. Her demeanor as she marched up the steps was more like that of a soldier marching off to certain death. Grim and tight-lipped. Tight-lipped was fine with him. He hoped she intended to keep those lips buttoned when the school board began to deliberate.

But then Nonie saw Margot, and Rob had a moment's worry that she wouldn't make it into the building. She looked ready to faint, her face leeched of color. She faltered and stumbled on the shallow steps, and somehow Margot closed the distance, there to steady her with a hand to her elbow.

Jade's sister had some seriously quick reflexes, he thought, amused.

"Careful, Nonie. You wouldn't want to fall and mess your lovely hairdo. I do so admire the work of your stylist. Eugene's a lucky man to have a wife who takes such good care of herself. I'm always tempted to tell him what an example you are to us all. Do you make weekly appointments, or do you find you need to see your stylist more frequently? Maybe I'll make an appointment with . . . what's his name again? It starts with a *T*, doesn't it? Oh, never mind, I'm sure I'll remember it. Give Eugene my very best, won't you?" With a smile that left Nonie looking almost as gray as her suit, Margot stepped back to let Nonie continue her wobbly way up to the school's double doors.

"Oh, well done, Margot," Jordan said, with deep satisfaction in her voice. "I believe I just saw the picture of a vanquished enemy. And it was beautiful."

"Yes, it was, wasn't it?" Margot sounded equally pleased with herself. "I do think Nonie needed that little reminder of the consequences of her actions. Well, I'd say our work is done."

Jordan nodded serenely. "Yes, it is—unless Nonie has developed a sudden social-suicidal streak. In which case it'll be my turn to have fun."

A bouquet of flowers was propped against the door of her cottage when Jade returned from her expedition to the Shake Shack with Ned, Georgie, Will, and Neddy. She hurried toward the spray of pink and white flowers wrapped in clear cellophane, and her heart thudded in her chest as she took in the pretty arrangement: roses and a white-and-yellow flower with a sweet yet peppery scent that she didn't recognize but knew Jordan would.

It was a lovely bouquet. Hope flared and was extinguished as quickly when she tore open the card and read the words: *Jade, Dr. Myszkiewicz and I wanted you to know that our thoughts are with you on this difficult day. I hope that your meeting with Dr. Myszkiewicz resolved many of the questions surrounding your parents. If I can be of any further assistance, please don't hesitate to contact me. With best regards, GH.*

The flowers were beautiful and incredibly thoughtful. She only wished they were from Rob.

He really had no intention of getting back together with her. The tears that she believed she'd exhausted welled, blurring the edges of her vision as she carried the flowers into the kitchen and located a glass pitcher for them.

Placing the arrangement on the center of the coffee table, she picked up her iPod and scrolled down the list of artists she'd downloaded. Lucinda Williams suited her mood perfectly. Few other singer/songwriters expressed the agony of a shattered heart as well. Within seconds, Lucinda's passion-rough voice filled the cottage. Jade sank onto the sofa and let the tears fall.

"Do you want to knock or shall I?" Rob asked.

"You knock, Daddy," Hayley decided. "And you give her the muffins and I'll give her my card."

"Okay. That sounds like a plan. I better knock loudly, because I can hear music inside." He rapped hard and then stepped back to stand beside his daughter.

The door opened, and the sight that greeted him wrenched his heart: a forlorn and woebegone Jade, her green eyes awash in tears. Hurriedly, she dashed them away with the back of her hand. "Rob? Hayley?"

"Hi, Miss Radcliffe," Hayley said shyly.

"I—I can't believe—" Whatever she was going to say was left unfinished and changed to, "Please come in."

They followed her into the living room, where she hurried over to the docking system and turned off her iPod. Turning around, she exclaimed when she saw them standing, "Oh! Won't you sit down?"

Still beset by shyness, Hayley squeezed in beside Rob on the large chair. However, her timidity didn't prevent her from asking, "Have you been crying, Miss Radcliffe?"

Jade's smile was wobbly. "Yeah, I have been. I've been feeling pretty sad about things lately. Do you ever feel sad, Hayley?"

Hayley took a moment to consider, then she nodded. "Uh-huh. I feel sad sometimes when I think about my mom."

"Me too. My mom's one of the reasons I feel sad. Today is the day she and my dad died. She's been gone for a number of years, and there are so many things I wish I could say to her and I can't."

Oh, God, no wonder she looked so distraught. Rob felt a stab of sympathy. What a hell of a double whammy she had to endure on the same day: the anniversary of her parents' death and the school board's vote on the future of her career. Yet even in the face of her sorrows, Jade had spoken to Hayley with a simple directness. It was exactly how he would hope an adult would talk to a child about such a difficult, wrenching subject.

He shouldn't be surprised. She'd demonstrated that she could tackle difficult topics in the articles she'd written for her college newspaper. Her pieces had been honest and candid and funny, yet they'd also been full of sensitivity.

Jade's explanation had driven away any lingering reserve on Hayley's part. She unwedged herself to go sit beside Jade on the sofa. "I made you this when I was at my grandma's house yesterday. I went there from school 'cause my throat was hurting a lot, but I'm all better now." She offered the card to Jade.

"You made this for me? Oh, Hayley, thank you. I think I recognize the ponies in this paddock. That's Dickens, isn't it?"

"Yeah, and that's Hopscotch and Maggie and Archer, Doc, and Sweet Virginia, and I wrote you a letter too. It's inside."

Slowly, Jade opened it. "*Dear Miss Radcliffe, I missed you at school today. I hope you come back soon. You're fun. From Hayley Cooper.* Oh, Hayley," she whispered. "I'm going to start crying again. Thank you very much. This is the nicest card." She wrapped an arm around Hayley's shoulders and hugged her.

"You're welcome. And Daddy brought you two muffins. He got two because he said you liked them so much."

Her eyes met his and her mouth curved in a small smile. "Thank you."

A knock sounded on the door. It was followed by a call of "Jade?" and then the sound of footsteps—lots of them—and new voices joining in. The living room was soon filled to overflowing with Margot and Jordan and Jordan's older children, Kate, Olivia, and Max, who offered cheerful hi's to Hayley.

"You came promptly," Margot said to Rob, grinning.

"Of course."

Jade glanced at Rob, but when she asked her question, she directed it to Margot. "Where were you?"

"At school. Jordan and I thought it would be wise to remind Nonie Harrison of the consequences of speaking out against you, sweetie." Her grin widened. "I think she got the message."

"It's too bad you weren't there, Jade. Nonie's expression was a sight to behold."

"What?" Surprise laced Jade's voice. "Do you mean she knows that *we* know about—"

"Oh, does she ever."

Rob never would have thought he'd see a smile of such evil glee on Jordan Gage's face, but there it was.

"And we had such a lovely talk with Pamela Hood," Jordan continued. "I think both Nonie and Pamela are going to behave very differently around Warburg from now on."

Jade was shaking her head. "I can't believe you guys did that."

"It was time, Jade," Margot said.

"Past time," Jordan agreed. "According to Maryanne Ferris, Rob's been pretty busy too. Did you know he and Maryanne managed to get more than a hundred signatures on a petition on your behalf? That's a lot of people supporting you."

"So we thought we'd come by and see whether we couldn't do something nice for Rob and Hayley. We were wondering if Hayley might like a riding lesson with these guys and Georgiana. I'll be teaching, Hayley. I'm not quite as good as Jade, but I'll try my best," Margot said.

"We've got a hard hat and everything else Hayley needs," Jordan told Rob. "Also, these guys have been clamoring for me to make some fried chicken. We'd love it if Hayley could come to Hawk Hill for an early dinner."

"Can I, Daddy?" Hayley pleaded, her eyes shining with excitement.

"Yes, but you have to do everything you're told in the barns and around the ponies, okay?"

"I will." Hayley turned back to Jade. "Will you be at school tomorrow?"

"I'm not sure yet, Hayley."

"I hope so. I like you better than Mrs. Wilson."

"That's a very nice thing to hear, though I'm sure that if you were to get to know Mrs. Wilson, you'd like her a lot. Have a great riding lesson."

"Okay, let's go, gang. Those ponies are waiting," Margot said, ushering the children out.

"They'll be finished eating by six-thirty," Jordan said to Rob.

"Thanks for thinking of this for Hayley. I really appreciate it."

A smile lifted Jordan's lips. "You are very welcome. Jade, you call us as soon as you hear from Ted Guerra. Unless you're too busy."

Jade jumped up to kiss Jordan on the cheek. "Have I told you how lucky I am to have you and Margot for sisters?"

"I heard that," Margot called from the entryway. "And indeed you are."

"About as lucky as we are to have you," Jordan said, giving her a quick, fierce hug. "I have a feeling this day is going to end much more happily than it began for you. See you later."

Chapter
TWENTY-EIGHT

THEY WERE silent as they listened to Hayley, Margot, and Jordan's family depart and the slam of the front door closing behind them. Then, as if at the signal of a starting gun, both Rob and she spoke at once.

"I really needed to see you—"

"I can't believe you're here. I thought—"

They broke off to exchange awkward smiles. "Sorry," Rob said.

"No, *I'm* sorry." She shifted on the sofa to give him room. "Can we talk? I need to explain why I behaved like such an idiot last weekend."

As Rob lowered his lean frame onto the twill cushion beside her, Jade drew a breath to calm her heartbeat, which, from the second she found Rob and Hayley on her doorstep, had been pounding madly.

Her attempt failed, for just then Rob reached for her, his fingers cupping her chin. "We'll talk, but first I need to do this," he murmured, and lowered his mouth to hers.

His kiss was gentle and so very sweet. Jade felt those absurd tears well in her eyes again. Slowly, Rob raised his head and smiled with a tenderness that was as moving as his kiss. "I missed you, Jade."

"Me too," she whispered as happiness flooded her. She had a second chance; she couldn't blow it. Taking his hand, she linked her fingers through his. "Rob, I have so much to tell you. But first: the petition you presented to the school board—thank you. I can't believe you did that for me." She swallowed. "I was so scared that you'd never want to see me again after hearing about my column—"

"Shh." He placed a finger to her lips. "I've already read a lot of your pieces. They're great."

"You read my articles? How did you get hold of them?"

He shrugged. "I guess I could have found them in your college paper's archives, but your sisters saved me the trouble."

"Jordan and Margot gave them to you?" The question came out a squeak of surprise. "When?"

"Monday evening. They tracked me down to the gym where I was working out with Scott and Emma and told me what was going on. Jordan gave me a whole packet of your articles she'd printed out. Jade, those pieces you wrote were damned good. You addressed a lot of serious topics that young people need to know when they start exploring their sexuality. And you did a great job answering readers' questions. The tone was all you, sweetheart, a perfect combination of openness, humor, and understanding. You should be proud of yourself."

If Jade hadn't already been in love with Rob, hearing the clear admiration in his voice for her college-newspaper writing would have likely served as the tipping point. She leaned forward to nuzzle the warm column of his neck and breathe in his familiar scent.

"Yeah, but you may be biased."

She felt the rumble of laughter against her lips and opened her mouth against his neck as if she might drink the joyful sound in.

"Guilty as charged. I'm utterly crazy about you." He raised her chin to bring her mouth to his, kissing her more thoroughly this time, his tongue sweeping past her lips to dance with hers. She returned the kiss with a

matching fervor, glorying in the passion that rose effort-
lessly between them.

A part of her wanted nothing more than to continue
kissing Rob until they were naked and rolling across her
bed and he was entering her body in strong, powerful
thrusts, each stroke bringing her closer to a shattering
climax. And as she felt his pace quicken to reach his
own release, as he drove as deep into her body as possible, she would clench him tightly, so tightly that it
would feel as though they were one.

But for that union to be real, she had to give him more
than her body.

Placing her hands on either side of his face, she ended
the kiss with a caress to the five-o'clock shadow darken-
ing the lean planes of his cheeks.

Lowering her hands, she said, "Rob, I need to tell you
about Greg Hammond."

She felt the shift in him, the wary tension that invaded.
This is what her mother must have experienced tenfold,
Jade realized, when she'd explained to Jade's father
about Dr. Myszkiewicz.

"Do you mean the guy who called you on Sunday?"

"Yes. The reason I got so uptight about him—so uptight that I decided it would be better to break up with
you rather than reveal who he was—well, it's that Greg
Hammond is a private investigator. I hired him to discover the identity of the man I thought had been having
an affair with my mom before she and my dad died."

"Jesus, Jade." There was no missing the shock in his
voice.

She sighed. "Yeah. It's a long, crazy story. Basically it's
this: Dad found a journal in which Mom wrote about a
guy she called TM. He mistakenly assumed Mom's lover
was Travis Maher, so he fired Travis from Rosewood
Farm. Then Mom and Dad died in the plane crash, and
Margot came home. She rehired Travis because she

needed him to help run the farm or there would have
been no way to save Rosewood from bankruptcy. Then
she came across the diary in Dad's office desk, and of
course she reached the same conclusion that Dad had.
Luckily, Travis didn't have much trouble setting her
straight, telling her what he couldn't say to Dad. He'd
have never fooled around with Mom for a zillion reasons, the first being that he'd been in love with Margot
for years.

"Unfortunately, neither Margot nor Travis had any
idea who this TM could be. So Margot showed the diary
to Jordan, and that's how I came upon it. I was in her
closet looking for a ratcatcher—that's a riding shirt we
wear to horse shows," she explained when he frowned
at the term. "And I found it under a pile of clothes. Immediately recognizing Mom's handwriting, I read it."

"When was that?"

"About a week before you busted me at the Den.
Reading my mom's journal made me go a little off the
deep end. The journal had other stuff in it besides what
she wrote about TM, quite a few angry rants against
me. It was all pretty upsetting, and when I'm upset I
tend to get a bit self-destructive." The corner of her
mouth hitched upward at her massive understatement.

Before she knew what he was doing, Rob had lifted
her across his lap. Wrapping his arms about her waist,
he pressed a kiss to the crown of her head. "You might
have had just cause. Jesus, this is an incredible story. Go
on, sweetheart."

For a moment she remained silent and simply savored
the care he was showing her. It felt so wonderful to be in
the shelter of his embrace. She understood that the only
way to earn the right to remain there was through hon-
esty.

"I don't know whether you knew my dad, but I guess
I'm a lot like him. I couldn't let go of what I read in

Mom's diary. So after graduation, when I knew I was coming back to Rosewood, I decided to hire an investigator to find out once and for all who TM was. Enter Greg Hammond."

"How'd you find this Greg Hammond?"

"Um, on the Internet."

"What?" Every muscle in his body tightened in outrage. "Jesus Christ, Jade, you know what kind of predators are out there—"

"Greg was legit. I checked him out. And he's a good guy, Rob, not creepy at all—I actually have an extremely reliable creep monitor. But the important thing here is, Greg *found* TM for me. That's what the call on Sunday was about. He'd located him and wanted to know whether I wanted to arrange a meeting with him. Of course, the timing of Greg's call couldn't have been worse. I guess you overheard enough of it to get suspicious—"

"I was jealous."

She leaned over to give him a quick hard kiss. "I forgive you. But I couldn't tell you about Greg, because I knew you'd be upset and go all RoboCop on me. You've got to understand, confronting TM was, well, it was something I had to do. Too many questions had been eating at me for years. But, Rob, there's another reason I balked at telling you."

"And what reason was that, Jade?" he asked.

This close, she couldn't evade the laserlike intensity of his gaze or brush off what she'd just said with some meaningless, witty remark. *Courage,* she reminded herself.

"Do you remember when I told you that I felt like you were boxing me in?"

At his slow nod, she felt her insides knot with the fear that, in spite of everything, she was going to screw this up with the next words she uttered.

"Well, in part I said that in order to push you away so you'd stop asking about Greg, but there was also some truth in it. Rob, this is the first serious, the first *real,* relationship I've had. Things between us became so intense so quickly, I panicked. Can you understand that?"

She waited for his response and, as the silence lengthened, her heart seemed to stop beating.

"Yes, I can understand. And you're right, Jade," he said quietly.

"What?" She shifted in his lap to stare at him. "I mean—"

"You're right about how I would've reacted when you told me about Greg Hammond. I would have done everything I could to convince you not to go with him and meet TM. It's possible I'd have been so bound and determined to prevent you that I'd have overlooked an obvious solution—that I accompany you both." His mouth lifted in a half smile. "But even if I'd had the wits to suggest it, I'd have probably tried to browbeat you into agreeing. Stubborn as you are, you'd have refused."

Jade smiled. "That sounds kind of like me."

"And kind of like me." His lips brushed her hair. "I'm sorry I was pressuring you. I haven't had that many relationships either. But I do know what I feel for you and that it's real—because I've been lucky to feel this once before."

He brought his hands to her face and gazed deeply into her eyes. "I'm in love with you, Jade. I can't help but want you in my life—and Hayley's. Just tell me when I'm going too fast for you or crowding you. Hearing it may hurt, but I'll try to understand."

"Oh, Rob, I love you too." Flinging her arms about his neck, she brought her mouth to his and poured all her joy and relief into her kiss.

His deep groan answered her. Then he was devouring

her lips with a passion that set her head spinning, whirling with happiness and desire.

At last they surfaced for air, both of them panting. Jade knew that her eyes must be shining as brightly as Rob's.

His hand stroked her hair, toying with its ends. With a playful tug he asked, "So while I'm digesting all this, mind explaining what you meant by my 'going all Robo-Cop'?"

She felt a blush cover her face, right to the roots of the hair he'd tugged. "RoboCop was my nickname for you. You may not realize it, but you're a pretty terrifying figure decked out in your uniform, police cap, and aviators. But—and you're the first person I've ever admitted this to—because of you I've harbored a secret crush on Peter Weller for years."

He grinned and settled her back against the hard wall of his chest. "Remind me to come by in my uniform tomorrow. So tell me about this TM. Who is he? Did he admit to being your mother's lover?"

"You won't believe it. I didn't. It turned out that the man Greg tracked down was Mom's psychologist. His name is Tomasz Myszkiewicz. He'd been helping Mom deal with some of her problems—one of them being yours truly," she added with a sad smile.

"You and your mom didn't get along?"

"We did for a long time, but then things changed. She began acting as if overnight I'd turned into a scheming, vicious brat. What haunted me about her diary, besides the fact that she made it sound as if she'd found the love of her life in this TM guy, was the sort of things she wrote about me. I wanted to know what could have possibly made this man so special that he became the center of her life at Dad's and my expense." Her voice dropped. "My mom's attitude before she died hurt a lot, but after finding her diary and reading and rereading those entries, I came to loathe her. In my mind she was weak and careless with love. On Monday, everything changed. I learned how brave she actually was. The reason she wrote about Dr. Myszkiewicz as if she adored him was because he was helping her deal with the problems she'd come to recognize were destroying the most important relationships in her life. Rob, I bolted out of Dr. Myszkiewicz's office intending to find you and tell you everything. I wanted to show the same courage it must have taken my mom to confess to my dad that she'd been seeing a psychologist."

"You think he had no idea she'd been consulting a therapist?"

"No." She shook her head. "It would never have occurred to him. They simply weren't the sort of people to admit to having problems of any sort. For instance, my dad never faced the fact that they were living way beyond their means after he'd lost a ton of money in bad investments."

"I didn't hear from you on Monday."

Jade shook her head. "No. Because I got a call from Ted Guerra, asking me to come to his office. When he informed me that I might be fired because of the articles I wrote, I didn't want you and Hayley mixed up in the ugliness of the town's latest scandal, one where I again had a starring role. And I was sure that after our fight you wouldn't want to be involved with me. When Hayley didn't show up to her lesson on Tuesday, my worst fear was confirmed—that you'd decided I wasn't worth the trouble. Being fired from my job at school was nothing compared to losing you."

"Oh, sweetheart." His fingers slipped under her sweater to caress her bare skin, traveling up and down her spine, soothing the tension in her muscles until she felt like putty beneath his hands. "I should have come by last night. I wanted to. I wanted nothing more than to see you and hold you in my arms like this, but I'd spent all afternoon at a multi-vehicle crash site, helping to pull out bodies—some injured and too many dead—from the wreckage. When I picked up Hayley at my parents' place, her throat was still red and I knew I had to take her home and get her into bed or I'd risk her getting even sicker."

She ran her lips along the length of his jaw. "You did the right thing. You're a great dad."

The corners of his mouth creased in a smile at her compliment. "Thanks. Hayley's been everything to me. It's amazing to have someone else to care about as much again, which is why it was a good thing I went home instead of coming here last night. It gave me a chance to telephone more parents about signing the petition we presented to the board, though it wasn't hard convincing people to sign it. By then most everyone had read Eric Drogan's editorial."

"Eric Drogan? He was the man you were with at Roxie's, right? He wrote something about me?"

"Yeah. You mean you didn't read his editorial?"

She shook her head. "No. When Ted mentioned that there'd been something about me in the paper, I assumed it was negative. I couldn't bring myself to read it."

"It's up on the paper's website. I'll show it to you later. By the way, Eric told me that he'd like you to do some articles for the *Courier*. And you'll definitely want to look at the paper tomorrow. He was at the school this afternoon with a photographer to cover the board meeting. Should be quite a story. And if the photographer caught the expression on Nonie Harrison's face when your sister Margot was talking to her, the picture should be priceless."

"I'll think about all that later. Right now I have something far more important to do." Without warning, Jade slid off his lap to kneel before him, her hands positioned lightly on his thighs. Looking up, she caught his wide grin and gave him a mock scowl.

"Officer Cooper, you have a one-track mind. This is me at my most serious."

"Sweetheart, I take you on your knees before me very seriously." But he dutifully schooled his features into one of grave expectancy.

"Okay. Here goes," she said, adding, "Jeez, this is kind of nerve-racking. I don't know how you men do it. Rob Cooper, I love you. Will you marry me?"

His face went momentarily blank with astonishment. Then, with a loud burst of joyful laughter, he drew her up by the elbows and kissed her hard.

"Jade, honey," he said, laughter still threading his voice, "that was supposed to be my line. I've been rehearsing my proposal, trying to get it just right."

"No." She shook her head. "I needed to be the one to ask. You've already proved how important I am to you, even after I was stupid enough to try to push you away. I want you to know how committed I am to you, how very much I love you, Rob. And, by the way, you still haven't given me an answer."

His every word was punctuated with a kiss. "I would be honored to marry you, Miss Radcliffe. Anytime. Anywhere."

With lips that tingled deliciously, she smiled widely and looped her arms about his neck. "You, sir, have made me the happiest of women. But, Rob, I do need some time before we take that step—do you mind waiting a bit before we marry? You and Hayley are so important to me. I want to be a really good mother to her. I don't want to confuse her by rushing things before she's ready to accept me in her life."

"You'll be fantastic with her. You already are. But we can take as long as you need."

She'd never believed a heart could soar, yet hers did as

she kissed him with all the joy she'd ever felt. In response, he laid her down on the sofa, following until their bodies were in perfect alignment.

Her body fell under the magic spell of Rob's touch, his hands seemingly everywhere at once as he stroked and caressed her. Arching and quivering beneath him, nearly mindless with pleasure, she floated ever higher.

His voice was a husky growl in her ear. "Jade, honey? You're ringing."

"Mmm-hmm." Ringing? Well, perhaps, she thought hazily. Though her body felt more like it was singing for him.

He nipped her earlobe. "Don't you want to answer your cell? It might be Ted Guerra."

She blinked while his words slowly registered. "Oh!" She really was ringing—and from an area very close to Rob's fingers. Hurriedly, she dug her cellphone out of her jeans' front pocket and pressed the CONNECT button.

"Hello?" She hoped whoever was on the other end would assume her breathlessness was caused by a mad dash to her phone rather than the fact that Rob had again lifted her to settle her across the muscled length of his thighs. Or that his hands were splayed along her abdomen, his fingertips idly tracing the curves of her breasts.

"Jade, it's Ted. I have some very good news. I'm pleased to report that the board has decided that you are too valuable a teacher to dismiss over the issue of your college writings. I had been anticipating vigorous opposition from a certain quarter, but, interestingly, it never materialized. The vote was unanimous. You have your job back, effective immediately."

"I'm so happy to hear that." She met Rob's gaze and grinned.

"I am too," Ted replied. "As I said before, you're a fine teacher and doing an excellent job. As a matter of fact, if you're interested in teaching next semester, I may be able to offer you another substitute position, but one with the potential to become a full-time job. Carole Fletcher, one of the third-grade teachers, has just notified me that her husband's company is relocating him. They'll be moving to Texas in December. Do you think you'd be interested in taking over her class? I think it would be a perfect fit, considering that was the grade you student-taught last year."

"I—I—" Dazed by the offer, Jade could hardly form a sentence. "Yes! Yes, very much. Thank you, Ted."

"I do have one piece of bad news for you, however. I received a call from Christy Harrison. She and her husband have decided that Eugene would be happier in a private-school setting. He won't be returning."

"Oh." She was silent, coming to terms with her sense of loss. "I'm sorry. He's such a bright boy, and the other kids learned a lot from his questions and comments. Do you think it would be appropriate for me to write Eugene a note, saying how much the class will miss him?"

"I can't see why not. Come by the office tomorrow and we'll give you some school stationery so that everything will be official and by the book."

"Okay."

Saying that he'd see her tomorrow, Ted rang off.

Rob was beaming with pride. "So, you got your job back."

"Yeah, and I may get hired to substitute-teach next semester for Carole Fletcher, a third-grade teacher. She's moving from the area." For fear of jinxing her chances, she didn't add that Ted had mentioned the job might become a permanent one.

Rob dropped a kiss on her nose. "Congratulations, sweetheart. Not everyone gets a job offer on the day they thought they were going to get sacked."

"Pretty cool, huh? Of course, none of this would have happened if not for you and my sisters." Her tone grew more serious. "Did you hear what Ted said about Eugene?"

"That his parents are putting him in another school? Yeah. It's too bad. He's a nice little boy. But, Jade, maybe it's for the best. Christy would have continued to cause problems for you."

She nodded. "Probably. Rob, I have to warn you, this most likely won't be the last time I get into trouble. I seem to have a penchant for it."

"Sweetheart, I've known you were trouble for quite a while. What I realize now is that you're exactly the right kind of trouble. I love you," he whispered. "Trouble me for the rest of our days."

She smiled. "I think that can be arranged."

Epilogue ✁

Nineteen months later

"LOOK WHAT Aunt Ellie, Emma, and I have brought," Miriam said, entering Jade's old bedroom in the big house where Jordan and Margot were tending to Jade. With all due pomp and circumstance, Miriam balanced a tray laden with crystal flutes. Ellie followed with a magnum of very fine champagne, compliments of Margot's agent, Damien Barnes. Emma, Jade's soon-to-be (as in less than forty minutes away) sister-in-law, carried an equally delicious offering: a small mountain of glistening plump strawberries and a cut-glass bowl filled with whipped cream.

And because this was Jade's big day, she thought with the happiness that seemed to be a constant in her life now, Margot would have let Ellie add an extra spoonful of sugar to the cream.

So much had changed in her life; her sweet tooth remained.

"Your timing's perfect," Jordan said. "Palin and Kristin finished Jade's hair and makeup. We have a few minutes before she needs to put on her dress—"

"Quick, Emma, give the girl her strawberries before she gets anywhere near that wedding dress," Ellie advised.

"Ellie, you don't think I'd dribble strawberry juice on my wedding dress, do you?" Jade asked, grinning.

"Uh-huh." Ellie nodded.

"Oh, ye of little faith. Me staining my clothes is so last decade," she teased. "I'm a new woman now. Still . . ." With a surreptitious wink at Emma, who'd brought the tray over, she daintily plucked a strawberry, dunked it carefully in the bowl of whipped cream, and with a flourish promptly inserted the entirety into her mouth, as the other women burst out laughing.

Miriam popped the champagne cork, and glasses were quickly filled. Margot carried Jade's to her; she sat on an upholstered bench in front of a vanity that Owen and Travis had carried in from Jordan's former bedroom so Kristin and Palin could work their magic.

Laying a hand on Jade's shoulder and giving it a squeeze, Margot cleared her throat. "Ladies, I'd like to propose a toast before the ones that will follow the much-anticipated event downstairs. Let's raise our glasses to our beloved Jade. You're an amazing sister, friend, and teacher. Thank you for being in my life, and thank you for everything you've added to it. Because of you, we have new people to love and call family: Rob, Hayley, Emma, and all the Coopers. Because of you, I have a new personal trainer, who regularly kicks my butt and has me in the best shape of my life. Because of you, I can go to sleep at night knowing that we have Warburg's finest providing on-site protection against any and all bad guys. Because of you, we have a growing riding program that's producing some very fine young riders—with Hayley leading the pack. Today marks the next chapter in the wonderful story of you and your hunky RoboCop. We can't wait to see what comes next. Here's to you, kiddo."

Jade wasn't the only one who sniffed loudly. As she stood to embrace Margot, she said shakily, "You know Kristin will have a conniption fit if I smear this makeup. So no more speeches until Stuart's pronounced the blessed words and I've made an honest man of Rob."

"There's no time, anyway," Jordan said. "We have to get you into your finery so that Palin and Kristin can do their touch-ups and the girls can have their sneak peek. And Charlie will want to take a few photos of us together, and I need to run down and make sure Owen and Scott have got things under control seating the guests . . ."

Putting down her untouched champagne glass, Jade crossed the room to kiss her oldest sister. "Jordan, take a deep breath. There," she said, when her sister complied. "Now, have I told you that I'm pretty sure this will be the most beautiful wedding ever? So relax and finish your champagne, and, Miriam, be ready to pour Jordan another glass. But two is the max for all of you. Tipsy bridesmaids only work in movies."

"Jade, you astonish me," Jordan said. "Aren't you just a little nervous?"

"Nope. Too happy. Now, shall we see if the dress still fits after last night's dinner?" She smiled, thinking that if the wedding date was a month later, she might have had real reason to worry. Only able to confirm her suspicions last week, she didn't want anyone to guess before she surprised Rob with the news that one of their spontaneous bouts of aquatic lovemaking had produced an unanticipated but wondrous result.

She couldn't wait to see his expression when she told him tonight that a little bundle of trouble—joyous trouble—was on the way.

The bedroom had grown more crowded, with the addition of Palin and Kristin spritzing and daubing and glossing and Charlie Ayer aiming his Nikon, the camera's shutter whirring away. "Jade, really, think it over. Ditch that guy at the altar and run away with me."

"I'm tempted, Charlie. But now that I'm a reformed citizen, I tend to worry about things like bigamy. And I can't imagine Anika would be too happy about sharing you either. Shall we ask her, 'cause I think I hear the pounding of flower girls' feet." Anika, Margot's former roommate and Charlie's wife of three years, had volunteered to keep all four girls entertained and their dusky-pink dresses and ivory sashes stain and wrinkle free.

Charlie lowered his camera to shoot Jade a wounded look. "You Radcliffe women have a cruel streak." Then the door opened and his exotically beautiful and adored wife walked in, followed by four of the cutest-looking flower girls she'd ever seen. Anika and Rob's mom, Megan, had already attached their headpieces, composed of miniature pink roses and baby's breath, and the effect was angelic. Charlie must have been of the same opinion, because his face split in a wide grin. "But I forgive you, because you've also provided me with some of the finest material ever. Smile, girls." And the motor of his camera resumed its whirring.

The girls' smiles were sweet to behold, but it was Hayley's expression that pierced Jade's heart. She looked awed, as if she couldn't believe it was Jade inside that dress.

"You look like a princess," she whispered breathlessly. "You're so beautiful."

"Thank you. I hope your dad thinks so too. Do you like the dress? It was my mom's."

"I want to wear my mom's dress when I get married too."

Jade took her hand and squeezed it. "I think that's a lovely idea. I know your dad would agree. We'll remind you when the big day comes. But, right now, are you ready to lead the way and perform your duties as head flower girl?"

"Yeah. I'm going to be watching Daddy's face the whole time. He's going to be so happy."

"No happier than me, kiddo. I'm really glad we're going to be a family."

Hayley nodded, but then a rare shyness stole over her, and she gazed up at Jade through a veil of thick brown lashes. "After the wedding, once we're all living here at Rosewood in the house Kate and Olivia's daddy built for us, will it be okay if I call you Mom?"

Pristine dress be damned. Jade dropped to her knees and hugged Hayley fiercely. "Absolutely. I'd love nothing more, Hayley."

With the flower girls leading, the descent down the sweeping circular staircase was fairly orderly, though perhaps Georgiana's decision to hop down the steps wasn't exactly in the flower-girl handbook. Since Jade's only guideline on this day was to share her and Rob's happiness with the people they loved, Georgie could not only hop down the stairs but then do cartwheels the entire length of the double parlor where the wedding ceremony would be held.

Jade was next, with Emma and Miriam, her bridesmaids, following with her train held carefully aloft. The train wasn't a long one, but Jordan wasn't one to take chances.

Ned was waiting at the base of the stairs. He looked exceptionally dashing in his black cutaway coat and gray pinstriped trousers. But it was the pocket square and the rose tucked into his lapel that for some reason caused an ache in Jade's heart. Perhaps it was remembering the number of times in her life he'd offered his handkerchief when she was bawling in misery. Perhaps it was recognizing anew how vital a part of Rosewood he was, how many seasons he'd watched its roses come into bloom.

He must have been as moved as she, for even as he smiled proudly at her, she saw his throat working, no doubt swallowing a sentimental lump that had formed there. Lord knows she'd fought a number of the same over the past few days.

Wordlessly, she reached out and squeezed Ned's hands.

"You're as pretty as a picture, Miss Jade," he said gruffly.

"Thank you, Ned, you're looking quite dapper yourself."

As they approached the double parlor, Jade could already hear the rustling of the occupants within, feel the hushed expectancy. Jordan, who'd dashed inside to check that everything was in place and at the ready, reappeared.

"All set," she said brightly. "Jade, you've never looked more beautiful. I know you and Rob will be very happy, sweetie."

Jade had no chance to thank her or reply that she and Margot made the most gorgeous matrons of honor a sister could want, because suddenly everything was happening at once. Yet for the moment she was left a spectator.

Her flower girls stopped their twirling on the inlaid-marble floor and came to a standstill. Baskets filled with white rose petals were produced and placed in their hands. The opening strains of Bach's *Jesu, Joy of Man's Desiring* reached them, and Emma, Miriam, Jordan, and Margot blew her a flurry of kisses and then stepped inside.

It had begun, and her heartbeat kicked up a notch.

Ellie, now in charge of the girls, whispered to Hayley and Kate, "Are you ready?" and Hayley, with a backward glance at Jade, grinned and nodded. "Okay, then. Remember, don't walk too fast. Off you go."

Ellie turned to Jade with a tremulous smile. "It's your moment now, my dear," she said, and handed Jade a glorious bouquet of gardenias, calla lilies, and roses in the same pale ivory as her wedding gown.

"I guess it is. Thank you for everything, Ellie. You're the best."

Standing beside her, Ned offered his arm with a grave courtliness. "May I?"

"You may. Thank you for doing this, Ned," she said as she placed her hand on the fine wool of his morning coat.

"Miss Jade, nothing could be more important or give me more pleasure than escorting you down the aisle. I'm as proud as can be of the fine woman you've become. Now, are you ready to take that walk? There's a mighty eager man waiting at the other end."

She kissed his lined cheek. "I am."

Stepping inside, Jade drank in the sight of those assembled, friends old and new. Her world had grown so much in the past year and a half and she was infinitely the richer for it. Rich in happiness, connections, and accomplishments. Then her gaze shifted, traveled down the aisle, and connected with the blue eyes of the man she loved and appreciated more every day.

Rob was there, her very own hero, waiting for her with all the love he felt shining in his smile.

Her own smile parted as her heart skipped with joy.

"Ned, I do believe I've kept this man waiting long enough. Mind if we run?"

ACKNOWLEDGMENTS

My thanks go to Elaine Markson, my agent, for her expert guidance and advice these many years. To Linda Marrow, Kate Collins, and Gina Wachtel at Random House, I owe my heartfelt gratitude for their support and enthusiasm. I couldn't ask for better editors or friends. I cannot thank enough my fellow writer and critique partner, Marilyn Brant, who has read so many drafts of this trilogy that I have lost count. I marvel at being blessed with such a loyal friend.

Without my family, I would not be the person or writer I am today. I love you.

*Read on for an excerpt from
Book One in Laura Moore's
exciting new Silver Creek series.*

Coming soon from Ballantine Books.

"ANNA, IT'S me. David's dead. He passed two days ago."

"Oh, Tess! I'm sorry. Where are you?"

"At my parents. I needed to see them to break the news, and there was stuff I had to arrange—"

"Can you come over? Giorgio is covering tonight's event—a birthday party for a ninety-year-old stockbroker who still plays ice hockey with his great-grandchildren and takes them out on his yacht every summer in Newport. It's only thirty people, so he told me to take the night off." Giorgio Bissi was the manager of La Dolce Vita, the events-planning company where both Anna and Tess worked—rather, where Tess had worked until two months ago.

"Thanks. I'd love to. It's been rough."

"I can't even imagine." Anna's voice was a well of sympathy. "Come as quickly as you can. There haven't been too many delays on the lines lately."

Having grown up in the same neighborhood in Astoria as Tess, Anna knew to the minute how long the subway ride and then quick walk would take to the brownstone apartment on 74th between Second and Third Avenues, where Anna lived with her boyfriend, Lucas, an associate at a law firm who logged insanely long hours.

Forty-five minutes later, Tess was outside Anna's building, shivering slightly in the chilly early November evening. Distracted as she was, she'd left her parents' house without thinking to take her coat or gloves. She pressed number three and Anna's voice came over the intercom.

Tess said, "It's me," and was buzzed inside the small entry hall illuminated by a shiny brass chandelier and matching wall sconces. A large rust-colored floral arrangement set on a long side table marked the arrival of autumn. Tess climbed the winding staircase, her steps ringing hollowly on the marble stairs and, reaching the third floor, found Anna standing in the open doorway to her apartment. Anna enfolded Tess in a fierce hug.

"God, Tess, I've missed you. I'm really sorry about David's death. But to be honest, I'm even sorrier about the hell you've been through. Here." Anna took her hand as though Tess were her baby sister. "Come into the living room. I've opened a bottle of wine and made us something to nibble on. You've lost so much weight."

Anna Greco, Italian American like Tess (though her family came from Naples, whereas the Casaris hailed from the Trentino), was in charge of menu planning at La Dolce Vita and was attending cooking school, pursuing her dream of one day opening her own restaurant. When it came to obsessing about food, Anna was without rival.

For the past two months, food had been the last thing on Tess's mind. And though she'd noticed that her clothes were starting to feel loose, she couldn't actually remember the last time she'd bothered to look in a mirror.

Tess let herself be led into the living room, with its vintage Kilim rug and burnt-gold-velvet sofa and the pièce de résistance, an ornate Murano chandelier that Anna had inherited from her grandmother.

Anna released her hand. "Sit. Eat. I'll just get the glasses and wine." A platter, artfully arranged with paper-thin slices of salami, prosciutto-wrapped asparagus, and mushroom-and-goat cheese tarts, was centered on the mirrored coffee table. Each bite would be delicious; Anna was constitutionally incapable of preparing bad food. For her friend's peace of mind, Tess hoped she'd be able to swallow a mouthful.

She sank down on the sofa in the room she knew so well and felt a wave of disorientation wash over her. It was so strange to be here, to be back in New York. Since receiving the phone call from her estranged husband, David Bradford, two months ago—the first she'd heard from him in twice that long—telling her that he was in Boston, in the hospital, and that the doctors wanted to operate on his brain, Tess's world had narrowed to the confines of Boston's Massachusetts General Hospital. She'd arrived just as the nurses were preparing to bring David to pre-op so the doctors could remove the meningioma the MRI had revealed. Only later did Tess learn that the tumor was recurrent, and that David had first undergone treatment a decade earlier.

Lying in the hospital bed, David had raised his light gaze to meet hers and uttered a single word: "Sorry." Before she'd even digested that that was all David was going to say, he'd closed his eyes, shutting her out and once again leaving her with no answers. Then the nurses had transferred him to the gurney and had wheeled him away.

Confused and sick at heart, Tess had hoped that after his operation she'd be able to question David and perhaps learn something that would allow her to make sense of the man who'd so briefly been her husband.

But when she next saw him, David lay in a coma, unresponsive to any stimuli.

The sound of Anna's heels clicking on the parquet

floor brought Tess back to the present. She straightened and relaxed her hands, which she'd unconsciously been wringing.

Carrying two wineglasses and an open bottle of Sangiovese, Anna sat down next to Tess, poured the deep red wine into the glasses and passed her one.

"Here," she said.

Tess accepted the wine gratefully. At least now she had something to fill her hands; she wouldn't be able to glance down at the faint mark encircling the ring finger of her left hand. For some reason, most likely her eternal, naïve optimism, Tess had continued to wear her wedding band, even after David had walked away from their marriage six months earlier without a backward glance. She'd removed it yesterday for good. How soon would it be until the mark, too, was gone?

"Do you want to talk about it?" Mixed with Anna's concern was a hint of eagerness.

Tess didn't blame her. Her curiosity was natural. Were they to switch places, she'd have had just as much trouble resisting the urge to hear all the horrific but no less juicy details. And as Tess's co-worker, Anna had been given a front row seat from the very beginning of Tess and David's whirlwind romance, the setting a swank cocktail party at a Fifth Avenue duplex with windows on Central Park, which La Dolce Vita had been hired to cater.

The party was intended to launch the political career of some mucky-muck, and the first floor of the apartment had been crammed with lavishly dressed socialites and Armani-suited powerbrokers. Tess had been passing hors d'oeuvres among the guests when David had stepped in front of her silver tray. David Bradford had been as impeccably attired as the other men. With his thick, sandy-blond hair and laughing eyes, he was far better looking than many of them. Tess, however, would never have gone beyond the instant acknowledgment that he was a very attractive man. It was David who'd appeared smitten, struck by the proverbial lightning bolt. After being offered a lobster puff by Tess, he'd ignored the other guests in order to speak with her, stationing himself at strategic points throughout the vast apartment to intercept her as she passed. Later he'd teased that it was her bow tie that had made him fall in love with her on the spot. Looking at it, he'd imagined himself in ten years regaling their children with the tale of how he'd fallen in love with their mother because of her pink-and-purple-polka-dotted bow tie. That was David through and through: outrageous yet sweet.

But now he was gone and Tess remained bewildered, unable to sort truth from fiction, unable to comprehend why he'd bothered to pursue her in the first place. Why he'd bothered to tell her he loved her. Why the need for so very many lies.

"The most important thing is that the doctors assured us that David didn't suffer," she said quietly. She was repeating herself, she knew. She'd probably resort to that stock phrase for a long time to come.

"So did he just . . . *die*?" Anna said awkwardly. "I mean, I know you told me when you first called from the hospital that he'd had an aneurysm during the operation and had gone into a coma. Is that what killed him?"

"No. He contracted pneumonia."

"Oh." Anna paused. "Gosh."

Tess nodded. "Apparently pneumonia is a common illness in coma patients and very hard to prevent. The doctors did what they could, but the pneumonia took hold so quickly. While I sat beside him day after day, watching as the doctors and nurses came in to check his vitals and perform their tests to detect any sign of responsiveness, I don't think I fully understood that the coma hadn't simply robbed David of consciousness. It had stolen his strength, his ability to fight."

Anna knew just how good a fighter David had been. Once the marriage had started to deteriorate with the same dizzying speed with which it had been born, Tess would come over here to Anna's—she couldn't burden her parents with the news that her very short marriage was already on the rocks, not when they'd suffered so much. She'd spent hours on this very sofa, crying from the latest spite David had unleashed while Anna paced the room and cursed him with an eloquence that would have made a marine blush.

"It seemed like they'd only just confirmed the pneumonia and then he was gone," Tess continued. "Passed. I don't think there's any other way to describe it."

"It's all so hard to believe. David was so active. All that running he did. And those weights." Anna was of the philosophy that there was one and only one reason to run and that was to catch a cab. Gyms were also to be avoided like the plague. That she could also eat with the appetite of a truck driver and still look like Monica Bellucci was grossly unfair. Tess forgave her because Anna was the most loyal friend in the world. "At least he didn't suffer at the end," Anna finished.

Again that worn, empty phrase. But what else was there that anyone could say?

"No, he didn't. And honestly, Anna, by that point it was a relief to let him go and not to have to watch him lie in that dreadful nondeath." Raising her glass, she drank deeply to banish the vision of the tubes inserted into his body and the wires attached elsewhere that had served to keep David in that terrible state for far too long. Although now painfully aware of how little she'd known or understood her husband, Tess was certain of one thing: David would have hated being dependent on those machines to keep his heart beating—no matter what his parents wished to believe.

Though she managed to push aside the image of her husband lying unmoving and unresponsive in his hospital bed, it was replaced by another one almost equally distressing, that of Edward Bradford, turning to her minutes after the hospital staff had confirmed David's death. His patrician face had been pale with grief, but his blue eyes had blazed, lit with pain and rage. Withdrawing a white envelope from the inside pocket of his gray wool suit, he'd thrust it like a weapon at her.

Uncomprehending, she'd stared at the envelope and then up at his angular face. "What's this?" she'd asked.

She'd witnessed Edward Bradford's disdain before, but now it seemed etched into his skin. His thin lips vanished in a sneer. "This is yours—the money I promised you. You've fulfilled the bargain. You stayed by my son's side. Take it and go."

The money. The absurd offer David's father had made to give her a million dollars if she stayed by David's side until he had recovered sufficiently to leave the hospital. Edward Bradford had insisted she agree to his insane idea even after she'd made it clear that David had had every intention of divorcing her, that he had told her he'd contacted his lawyer with instructions to begin the proceedings before he'd walked out of her life four months earlier. As calmly as she could, she'd explained to Edward Bradford that she had to get back to New York and her job at la Dolce Vita.

But then the surgeon had come into the waiting room with the news. The operation to remove the meningioma had not been successful. During the operation, David had suffered an aneurysm. He was in a coma. The doctor's prognosis was bleak. With such a severe hemorrhaging of the brain, he had about a 25 percent chance of survival. But from the doctor's tone Tess had understood that he didn't expect David to beat those odds. As the surgeon had spoken, she'd looked over at Madeline Bradford and seen something she recognized. Her expression held the same desperation, echoed the same mute pain, that Tess had seen in her own mother's face when they visited Christopher at the private facility where the Casaris had been forced to place him when they could no longer care for him at home.

Then and there, Tess abandoned any plan to return to New York. Even with the hurt David had inflicted during their short marriage, she couldn't leave him when his life hung in a balance weighted toward death.

Though the Bradfords had made their dislike of her abundantly clear, they obviously believed her presence might help David. They were wrong, but she couldn't bring herself to add to their anguish by leaving. She had enough savings to live on for a while, and she had only to ask and Anna would arrange to have her stuff moved out of the shoe-size apartment she'd rented after David had hied off for parts unknown and stow it in her old bedroom in her parents' brick row house on 46th Street.

Edward Bradford's absurd and insulting offer of money hadn't entered her thoughts.

And yet she'd taken the check, not tearing it into so much confetti as she'd longed to do—if only to erase the contemptuous look stamped on his face. The man had judged and condemned her the second he'd learned that his son had married her—a nobody from Astoria. In his mind, her job as a waitress was barely a step above that of a stripper or pole dancer.

She'd taken the check Edward Bradford had all but thrown at her. But as soon as she returned to New York, she'd gone to her parents' neighborhood bank and arranged to have the money put into a special account to help pay for her brother Christopher's care. The million dollars meant nothing to Christopher, yet he needed it more than anyone she knew.

Edward and Madeline Bradford would never know what she'd done with their money, and Tess was glad. Their knowing wouldn't change their opinion of her or their belief that somehow she'd tricked their son into marrying her.

Perhaps with David's funeral, Madeline and Edward Bradford had found peace. And if their hatred of her provided some release from the grief of losing their only child, well, so be it. Tess would never see them again. Tonight at Anna's, she'd be taking the next step in her plan to get as far away from everything that had happened in the last year as she could.

Anna picked up the tray and offered the assorted appetizers to Tess, then put it back down on the coffee table with a sad sigh when Tess gave a shake of her head.

"I'm glad that David died without pain," Anna continued. "I only wish he hadn't inflicted so much on *you*. I know it's terrible to speak ill of the dead, but I don't know whether I can forgive what he did to you. How could he have *not* told you about the tumor? I still can't believe he married you without ever uttering a word about it."

If only that had been the *only* secret David kept to himself, Tess thought. As it was, everything about their marriage had been based on a lie. The biggest one being that David had never loved her.

That's what she got for believing in fairy tales, for believing for even a minute that a dashing, cosmopolitan journalist would fall in love at first sight with a working girl from Queens, sweep her off her feet, and propose marriage weeks later. How could she have thought that she and David would make it, that they would enjoy a happily ever after?

Most likely it was because the David Bradford she'd

known during those first months had been the most charming man she'd ever encountered. The most determinedly persuasive too. It was only later, after she'd agreed to elope with him and they'd settled into his SoHo loft that, with the suddenness of a light being switched off, his charm had been replaced by a cutting cruelty. Both extremes, his charm and his hostility, had been equally devastating.

She took a sip of wine to wash away the bitterness. "I've gotten to the point where I've stopped asking myself why he did the things he did or what he said and left unsaid about his life. I might go crazy otherwise. But at the hospital in Boston, his mother told me that David's first brain tumor had been benign and that the treatment for it had been successful. He'd only been nineteen at the time, Anna. My guess is that when he started experiencing symptoms again, he simply refused to consider the possibility that the cancer had returned. And not being aware of his history, I didn't think to suspect his headaches of being a sign of something far more serious."

During the weeks she spent by David's hospital bed, Tess had talked to the nurses and doctors, receiving a crash course in malignant brain tumors. Now she recognized how deeply David had been in denial about his condition. The symptoms had been there even during the few months they'd been married. When the headaches he suffered became more frequent and intense, he'd refused to make an appointment with a doctor, blaming her instead and saying that living with Tess was enough to give anyone a migraine. When his mood swings led to vicious outbursts, he'd claimed that the stress of looming deadlines for the articles he was writing was the cause, that and the fact that the woman whom he'd married had turned into an uptight nagging bitch. That would be his cue to storm out of the loft, sometimes not to return until the next day. When he did finally return, his clothes would reek of alcohol and perfume.

"And so what were his parents like?" Anna asked.

She shrugged uncomfortably. "Okay, I guess, considering that I represented an unpleasant surprise. I thought his mother was beginning to soften toward me somewhat near the end." Though not enough to persuade her husband that Tess should be allowed to attend David's funeral, she added silently. The hurt of being barred from the ceremony was still fresh.

"What was David thinking, not telling his parents that he'd married you? What a creep. Absolutely incredible." Anna's tone was scathing.

"David told me he hadn't talked to them in years, so he didn't see why they should come. It was one of the reasons he gave for our eloping, saying that since he'd cut ties with his family, there was no reason to go to the trouble of a wedding ceremony. And by eloping, we'd save my parents the cost of a church ceremony and reception." She'd been so touched by his concern for his parents' finances. And the passionate urgency, the bold recklessness of David's suggestion that they elope, had struck her as deeply romantic. Love had rendered her blind as well as stupid. Her mother would have loved to see her walk down the aisle. On the other hand, as the marriage had ended almost as soon as it began, she couldn't help but be glad that her parents hadn't wasted a penny on it. With the economy in the tank, her father's construction company wasn't making the profits it had.

"Damn, but he was clever at pushing people's emotional buttons." Anna's words came out in an angry huff. "Sure, it saved your parents money, but he wanted to elope so he wouldn't have to deal with anything as complicated as a wedding. He knew that money was tight for your parents with having to pay for Christopher's care, so he used that line to get what he wanted and made you think he was Mr. Generosity for thinking of them." Anna picked up the wine bottle and refilled their glasses. "Tess, I wasn't a good friend. I should have talked you out of marrying that bastardo."

"No, Anna. You've been a great friend. I'm not sure anything or anyone could have persuaded me that David wasn't exactly what he seemed at first."

"Yeah, I know." Anna nodded glumly. "He seemed like such a Prince Charming. Even I was fooled. So, back to the parents. When did you finally meet them?"

"David must have contacted them when he was admitted into the hospital. They were there in his hospital room when I arrived."

"Great place to meet the in-laws. How did they act when they met you?"

"That's an easy one: glacially displeased. After meeting them, I understood why David didn't want them at a wedding ceremony. If they'd had even an inkling that David planned to marry me, Mr. and Mrs. Bradford would have done everything in their power to stop us. Given how super-wealthy they are, they probably would have succeeded. I definitely wasn't what they'd envisioned as wife material for their son. I don't think I'd have even made the cut as one of David's hookups."

"You were too good for him, were too good for the entire family. And that's just your character. Surely the Bradfords weren't blind as well as snotty."

"I'm not sure my looks appealed to them either."

"Prissy puritans," Anna pronounced.

Tess smiled sadly. It would have been nice to have Anna beside her when Mr. Bradford had all but stuffed the envelope containing the check into her hand. She would have told him where to go. Tess had been tempted to. Tempted to rip up the check under his nose and then spit in his eye for good measure. But she hadn't. And so now Edward Bradford had incontrovertible proof that Tess Casari was no better than the money-grubbing fortune huntress he'd chosen to label her as.

"So David's parents were real rich stuck-ups," Anna continued.

"Yeah, pretty much. If the Mayflower had been equipped with first-class cabins, they'd have been reserved for the Bradfords. I've learned that Boston bluebloods elevate the snobbery thing to a whole new level, Anna. But all their wealth and perfect pedigrees meant nothing when David slipped into a coma. Edward and Madeline Bradford could have been my dad and mom when they're with Chris at the facility. Desperate. Powerless. And so sad. It's why I had to stay when they demanded it."

"But why did they insist you stay in the hospital? How weird was that?"

"They had some idea it would make a difference if I was close to David."

"Did they really think you could do something for him that the doctors couldn't?"

"I think they were desperate, clutching at straws. You see, just before David was taken away to be operated on, they overheard him say 'Sorry' to me. They must have believed it meant more than it did. I tried to explain to them that they were placing way too much significance on that one word, and that David and I were as over as a couple could get, that I hadn't seen or even spoken to him for four months. But they were insistent. Modern science was failing them so they clung to a scrap of magical thinking, hoping that my presence could somehow draw him out of the coma. They were willing to believe in anything, even put their faith in someone they despised."

Anna shook her dark head in bemusement. "God, Tess. David's parents probably didn't even realize that you're one of the few people who would immediately understand what they were going through."

She shrugged. "I don't know about that. I only wish my presence could have actually helped David and them. Of course, it didn't, and I left you guys in the lurch. You all must have had to work like mad." The economic downturn hadn't touched La Dolce Vita. Even in the summer when wealthy New Yorkers decamped to the Hamptons or the Vineyard, Giorgio had to turn away clients.

"You didn't. It was only crazy for about ten days. Then Giorgio hired a kid who just graduated from NYU and wants to break into acting. Giorgio'll hire you back in a flash, Tess. We can call him. The birthday bash for the ninety-year-old will be over by now."

This was it. Slowly Tess shook her head. "Thanks for the offer, but no. Anna, I'm leaving New York."

"Leaving? For where?"

"I've decided to try out California." California was as far away from Boston and the Bradfords as she could get without leaving the continent.

"California." From the way Anna pronounced it, Tess could have announced she was planning to move to Mars. Anna fell silent for a moment, her expression solemn. "It's so far. But I understand why you're doing it. I'd want to start afresh, too, if I'd been through what you have. So, where in California?"

Tess leaned over and picked up her handbag, which had been resting next to the leg of the coffee table, and set it on her lap. Opening it, she pulled out a folded map. "I picked this up. It shows the entire state." Moving the untouched platter aside, she opened the map and laid it on the coffee table. "I thought you could help me choose my destination."

"I know!" Anna's dark eyes lit with excitement. "We'll leave it to fate. Wait here. I'm going to get my nonna's favorite scarf. We'll use it as a blindfold. I'll spin the map, and then you'll place your finger down to stop it. Wherever your finger lands, that's where you'll go."